The ForEver Project

The ForEver Project

D. B. Martin

Published by IM Books

THE FOREVER PROJECT

ISBN 978-1-9160886-6-5

"Because I could not stop for death, He kindly stopped for me;
The carriage held but just ourselves and immortality."

Emily Dickinson

Chapter 1

4th July 2029: Jason

Have you ever thought of time as a river, flowing on to… who knows where? And we the flotsam and jetsam floating in it, sometimes damming up, bundles of debris nudging up against each other until a lone piece breaks free. A single piece of driftwood bobbing along on the current, making its way uncertainly through the eddies and undercurrents until finally it reaches the river's end and is pitched, river-bed rubbed and bone smooth, into the great mass of the ocean, the river's end. The sea of forever. Then what does it do – that freed piece of driftwood? Forever…

'We're ready? Are you?'

I break off from my fanciful imaginings and study my potential saviours. Am I ready? I've been preparing for this moment for the last four months – maybe for the whole of my life. We are all preparing for this moment for the whole of our lives; this one moment when the driftwood breaks free… Am I ready?

'Ready,' I say – even though I'm not – and not that they can understand what I say anyway. I nod, a jerky twitch of a yes to clarify, in case there is any doubt.

They attach the first bio-electrode as I scan the room. Despite the paralysis, I still feel the needle scratch on the back of my hand as I try to commit it all to memory – just in case. A bench mark – I might need that when I reconstitute. I end on the calendar on the far wall. Even the date is in on the joke today. Independence Day. Yesterday. The calendar is lagging behind, but I am forging ahead. The exquisite irony of it all makes me want to laugh but laughing is hardly the right thing to do when you're about to die.

Chapter 2

1st April 2029: Jason

'Coffee?'

The mug wafts in front of me, the sharp tang of Arabica almost fooling me into accepting it before I consider where it's come from.

'Man or machine?'

'Machine,' Matthew admits. 'But for God's sake, it's exactly the same as your precious barista's efforts.' He puts the mug down on the desk next to me and it sits there, steaming and gently tempting. Matthew's voice has a suppressed freshness to it, like the lab has when it's empty. Like it has today, surfaces pristine, equipment tidied, test circuitry stacked. A ghost lab – except for us. 'It's made with the same beans, to the same recipe, and with the same panache,' he's saying as he perches alongside it, grinning. I have known him since university, liked him ever since, and worked with him almost as long. He is the only man I would trust with my life, but still I won't drink his industrialised coffee.

'Not quite. It comes from a machine.'

Yeah, crazy, given what I do for a living. But whoever said I was sane?

'Which we designed to your precise coffee-making specifications, if you remember? Right down to the robotic arm sweetening the brew.'

I smile, remembering Matthew and the lab team's joke last Christmas: make a coffee machine good enough to stop 'the boss' going out to get his coffee. They'd even incorporated a version of our most refined cyborg prosthesis to sprinkle a token three grains of sugar into the cup, before presenting it to the recipient. Another joke; my insistence on attention to detail and a hatred of over-sweet coffee. It had been a minor triumph at the time – a breakthrough in the fine-tuning of motor control response and the precursor to the CyberArm 3.2, now crushing the market and making me a fortune. Nevertheless…

'But some things will be forever the province of man,' I object, gently dismissing the offering. '*Some*,' I emphasise.

'Christ, you're a difficult bugger.' But Matthew gets the joke, of course. He pulls the coffee towards him and drinks it in response, making a deliberate show of how good it is, and for a moment the old carefree Matthew is back. I watch him, smiling, enjoying the rare glimpse of the old Matthew, my cantankerousness – and my infamous reputation – until impatience gets the better of me. He didn't bring me in here to try to make me drink machine coffee, although the smell of coffee is in my nostrils and my mouth is moistening. I half wish I had accepted it now – except I never would…

'I'll get my own later. But what is so bad that we had to come in on a Sunday, just the two of us?'

'Oh no! Not bad. Good!' He grins and his face lights up and reminds me that when his enthusiasm takes over he's still the potential risk-taker he was when we first met 'You remember we extrapolated the CyberArm blueprint but weren't sure if we could ever incorporate it into a full-body build, given the limitations we kept hitting with it? Well, I kept at it because initial tests indicated it *should* be fully compatible with cloning and 3D organ printing, like we hoped it would be, even if it wasn't, and…' He grins again and waves towards a clone dolly in the corner of the lab, covered discreetly with a green surgical drape. 'Voila! Fred Mark 2.'

'Really?' I push my chair back and coffee – of any sort – is forgotten. I beat him to the clone dolly by minutes, but then I would even if he'd been trying. I've not always beaten Matthew but I do now – at everything. He's still perched on the desk, a remote in his hand, his grin stretching the width of his face now. Under the drape is CyberFred; our ForEver test model – but different. The shiny platinum plating normally covering the circuits and data transfer units on his lower face, neck and torso is part-coated. He has skin. 'Christ! That's amazing! How did this happen?'

'There's more.'

'More?'

'Touch it.' I touch the cyborg's chest and shake my head in amazement. It could be my own skin I'm touching – even down to the finest fuzz of hair. Matthew's grin is as expansive as his body language now. 'And this.' He manipulates the remote and Fred's head turns. Not like it used to – almost human, but not quite. Naturally. A soft slide to focus in my direction.

'Damn! That's good.' I probe gently, outlining sinews and muscle underneath the outer layer. 'But how? What fine motors have you modified?'

'Nothing. It's the CyberCute. It's done it itself, integrated with the outer shell and already self-modifying.'

'Christ, that's incredible! This means...'

We lock gazes. To say Matthew looks smug would be an understatement.

'Yup!' He nods, gleeful.

There is a buzz in my chest as I compute precisely what this means. Our latest development, CyberCute, is still under wraps – literally. Supposedly. The whole lab must have seen this though. In my absence... My inner demon grumbles. Matthew shouldn't have done this without telling me: ForEver was my baby first, not his. This moment should have been mine to share with him, not his to share with me.

'So when did you come up with this little gem – without telling the boss?'

Matthew doesn't miss the inflection on *boss*. His grin twists and turns rueful. He pushes the coffee mug out of the way and hunches over, folding in on himself. I know the gesture well. He's feeling insecure and now I'm even more irritated with his neediness and that I can't control Matthew's inability to malfunction, or conversely, to function independently of me when I can control almost everything else of his life in relation to me. Almost everything.

'Sorry Jason, it wasn't intentional. The test results only came back to me last week, and then we got caught up in that little flap over the original CyberCute degrade whilst you were away and... well, anyway, it took most of the week to sort that – as you know. We'd run out of prostheses ready for treatment by the time we'd cracked it so as a last resort I tested it out on Fred, and hey presto – Fred has become human!'

'He has,' I agree, still marvelling at what he's achieved, but without me. It grates, but I can't let it show – that would display MY neediness. 'And I was only joking.' I turn and smile warmly at him, whatever the ice inside. It's the best I can manage but I know it will work. It always has. The Jason effect, the girls used to call it when I was younger – whatever that was. Together we could have achieved world domination on just that and Matthew's charismatic craziness alone if he hadn't gone too far. He smiles back, his tentativeness emphasising – as if I needed it to – the distance between where he is now, and where I am. Briefly I regret how it's all turned out – all of it – but there's no point dwelling. It is what it is.

Now I've given him permission, he comes over to join me, still holding the remote, but still folded in on himself.

'Really? I mean, I didn't intend…'

I put my hand on his arm and his posture immediately loosens, unfurls like a fern opening at dawn. 'Yeah, really. This is amazing. The best!'

'Oh,' his earlier jauntiness returns. 'Then I need to run though everything it can do now, so you know the works.'

'So how much can it do?'

'Like I said, pretty much everything – eventually. Of course, I need to check the replication function properly, and I need to monitor brain function but…'

'Then *we* should press on.' The gentle emphasis isn't lost on him.

'Oh, yeah, yeah. Test it properly. What do you suggest first?'

'Well, have we got the cyborg and its cloned organs fully integrated?'

'Uhh, that depends.'

'On?'

'Well,' he scratches his head. 'What you intend doing with it now.'

That I hadn't expected.

'Now? I thought we'd agreed on that when we started the project? What we first started developing it for.'

'But we never went to war, after all, did we? So the full-body failures we anticipated never happened. We've had limb and body insufficiencies, but no full-body failures.'

'I beg to disagree. We have millions of full-body failures every year. The old, the chronically infirm, the terminally ill. Just think…'

'I know but, that's not what we're doing this for now, is it?'

'What?'

He frowns. '*Profit*? You're talking profiting from it?'

Yeah, Matthew - profit; what we always planned to make with our skills, but then he always was more the scientist and me more the entrepreneur. And more and more these days I realise I did more than reign Matthew in when I'd had to. I'd truncated part of him – the part that was ready for anything – including manipulating the market. I guess I'd had to at the time, but now… Matthew's expansiveness has gone into reverse throttle with his thoughts, as I should have known it would. I wait, anticipating the age-old argument about testing that always brings us back to square one, whatever progress Matthew's just made for us – but which wouldn't have posed a problem once.

‘Why not? We’re paying to develop it. What’s wrong with recouping those costs?’

‘Well, nothing, in principle, of course, but… I thought we were advancing science and…’ He tails off, but we are back in the loop, having the same debate we always do - now. I grit my teeth and hone my speech.

‘No, not just profit, although that is what we make from everything we do. Look, a lot has changed in ten years.’

‘Yeah,’ he agrees ruefully, lip curling and I know he’s remembering just like me. My oldest friend and trusted colleague – he’s as much boss as me in technical knowledge and ability, and should have been as much boss as me, except for his lack of cash and control.

‘Yeah,’ I repeat pointedly. ‘When we first started this, it was to avoid living in a world full of the maimed and deformed since another world war was imminent. That didn’t happen, thank God, but it prompted what we’ve developed. Instead we live in a world of adaptive and synergistic pacifists, but even that can be improved – for all of us.’ I still enjoy the words I used at the last bio-tech conference, but I am as careful now as I was then with the words I don’t add: *where there’s sufficient money to buy good health.* That’s the part everyone finds difficult, even if privately they acknowledge it. Idealist-speak works better on most people, including Matthew. ‘So if we can make that possible, shouldn’t that opportunity be available to everyone? To survive beyond whatever ravages time or damage wreaks on their body? To really enjoy what we’ve managed to achieve?’

‘I don’t disagree, in principle…’ He twitches his head to and fro, grimacing, to indicate he can see both sides of the argument – it’s another of his gestures I know well. But I also know it means he does disagree, ’But doing that would entail finding volunteers – and that would be nigh on impossible in the current climate. You know that. The government is just too cautious now.’

‘Maybe,’ I agree reluctantly. At least we seem to have avoided the money versus equality argument this time around. But we always do this bit too – him posing pragmatism, me conceding whilst repositioning to a point he can’t argue against; apparently backing down, but only in preparation for advance. ‘Finding volunteers for anything is always fraught with difficulties. If we go about it in the normal way…’ I caress the perfect skin covering. I can feel Matthew’s eyes on me, questioning. ‘But if there was a desperate man or woman, willing to take desperate measures to avoid the – until now – unavoidable…’

He's shaking his head, but not with any great vehemence. Underneath he's still as keen as I am, he's just struggling with who he has made himself be now.

'But… wouldn't it be unethical – since we don't know what the outcome would be of merging a human brain with a part-cyborg, part-cloned body. Would the brain even survive the transition?'

'Agreed. That's why we need to get moving on the testing now.'

'Well… but still, where would we find a volunteer – ultimately. I still think it would be nigh on impossible.'

'No,' I clap him on the shoulder. 'Very easy, if we asked around in the right quarters…' Matthew is looking at Fred, carefully, silently, but I feel his thoughts turning. Him turning. We may approach life differently now, but we are also the same. 'We don't have to have a full working unit before we can start tests anyway, do we? There's still a lot of single elements to test. Brain function for starters. The rats won't argue ethics with us, will they? And in the meantime, I'll put some feelers out – see what turns up.'

'I don't know…'

I twitch the coverlet back further from Fred's chest just as Matthew's phone buzzes. He grimaces.

'Jane?' I ask.

'Yeah, checking where I am. It's a Sunday, for God's sake! As if I would…' he pauses, remembering. We exchange glances. It had only been last Sunday I'd last bailed him out. I still don't understand his need to risk ruining himself every time he sits at a card table despite everything, but then he probably doesn't understand my need to control. 'Yeah, well, OK…' he shrugs.

'Maybe you'd better check in, anyway? She'll have the hounds on you, otherwise.'

'Hound,' he corrects. 'Bloody solicitor.' He turns out his lower lip and I have the urge to laugh, except I can tell he is genuinely glum. He pulls the drape back over Fred and returns the controller to the desk, collecting the coffee mug from it as he does so. He is short and burly to my tall and lithe, the bumbling scientist to my urbane entrepreneur. Not my words – Jane's, but he didn't hear her say them, or know why and when – nor any of my history with her, luckily. Any arrangements we have are only between him and me, as far as he knows.

'I guess.' He's reluctant. I give him the look, and he knows it's futile. 'OK, I s'pose I had better go and pacify the beast or I'll be on report. I wanted to show you the rest, though.'

He's deflated. Momentarily, I feel guilty – both for things past and for pulling rank on him earlier. I watch him amble towards the door, affable, kind, faulty – a genius in crumpled trousers and faded shirt now the radical go-getter had been expunged by time and misfortune. I follow him, brushing invisible creases from my trousers, and relishing the feel of my pristine silk shirt against my skin, even as I count my blessings. I may have lost Matthew the risk-taker, but Matthew the inspired scientist is still mine to deploy in the war against the world of bio-tech and all the would-be challengers to my dominance of it because of that small but fatal need he has to risk all on the turn of a card or the toss of a dice, whatever his principles might otherwise be. And I am the boss because he wouldn't be capable of being it. We're still a team – of a sort.

I hesitate. Conscience is a bastard at times, if you allow it, but I could ring Elise and tell her to book us all somewhere to eat out tonight to celebrate. That could be my apology too. Yes, and Matthew would believe even more so that I'm the god he tells everyone I am. The god with feet of clay, but who's to know that?

'Hey!' He turns to look at me and my interjection as we reach the door together, despite his head start on me. 'Why don't we catch up later and celebrate tonight?'

His face returns to the expansive grin he originally greeted me with. 'Oh! Oh, hey! That would be great!'

I nod and clap him on the shoulder. 'I'll get Elise to find us somewhere. We'll pick you up at seven.'

'Elise too?'

He is fully unfurled now, and as joyous as that freshly sprung fern.

'Yeah, why not?' Why not indeed? It's another sop to the starving, and I owe him, even though he doesn't know that – or would ever think it. He thinks he owes me! 'And now for some real coffee and a chat with Fred.' The smell of Arabica from the coffee Matthew made is long gone, and yet there it is again – tantalising and taunting me.

'Oh, aren't you going home, too?'

'In a while. But now I'm here, I think Fred and I should get properly re-acquainted over some *real* coffee.'

'Shouldn't I stay too then?'

'No, it's fine.' I push him firmly through the doorway ahead of me. 'You go and get yourself out of whatever hot water Jane wants to put you in and I'll see you later.'

'OK, boss. He doesn't take sugar at all though, or liquids – yet.' We both exit the lab laughing. 'And don't stay too long – you'll tire him out.'

'And you don't be my mother!'

He grins indulgently back at me, relishing the camaraderie and the endorsement that we are still best mates, whatever else we've become. 'The length of a proper coffee, that's all,' he cautions.

I watch Matthew amble away as I wait the requisite five seconds for the door lock to click behind me so that Crane Enterprises' latest secrets are contained behind a bullet- and laser-proof door. I find myself smiling contentedly as I exit the building. My empire. My best friend. My first real – and unexpected – breakthrough with the ForEver project, even if it is Matthew's success in reality. Today is no ordinary day. In fact, there should be bells ringing out its extraordinariness. And there are, the bells in the market square as I exit the alleyway and cross to the bakery and coffee shop, chiming mid-day – and the bells on the bike of the cyclist, passing me within a hair's breadth of my toes so that I curse her receding image – a large lady on a thin bike, a top-heavy T, all curvaceous buttocks and overly compressed.

'Sorry…' she tootles back over her shoulder. 'Not quite got the measure of the beast yet.'

The beast. Immediately I think of Fred – who Elise would no doubt call Frankenstein's beast if she knew about him. My rage deflates at that, descending into black humour and then a wry acknowledgement as I also recognise the departing top-heavy T as my cleaning lady – usually clad in flowery overalls and not astride a complaining bike. Who *has* got the measure of the beast? I know her, even if she doesn't know me – even aside from the personal connection; she is one of the many on my PC screen when I plot the demographics of our future clientele – the ageing crowd I've always had in mind if ForEver works out, even if Matthew hadn't realised that until now.

Despite it being a Sunday, it's still busy in the marketplace, with its jaunty candy-coloured canopied bakery, provincial stone square and requisite statue of a local dignitary, long since dead. The blowsy flower baskets, untidy now with overblown daffs, but originally intent on winning best spring town in bloom, festoon the railings between pavement and road and puffs of exhaust tangle with the drift of coffee from the coffee shop-cum-bakery I am heading for – my favourite, still brewing real coffee with a real barista, a throw-back to a less streamlined world I secretly enjoy, for all my futuristic drive. I am nose-driven, like a bloodhound on the trail, but with a million things to test out on Fred crowding in from all corners as I cross the road.

And that is my downfall.

I get distracted by the prospect of the impossible made possible whilst my senses are otherwise engaged. As my fat, tootling cleaning lady diminishes into the distance, a slim brute of a sports car, red and honking, rushes past and the backdraft catches me in that moment of distraction. I sprawl, ungainly and ridiculous, half on and half off the kerb as I miss my step. For a moment, the world spins and the gaudy, vintage carousel that has been set up in the middle of the market square in readiness for the local primary school fête becomes a whirling orb, spinning off its axis to collide with me. My head touches the pavement at the same time as my knees and I bend double, like a priest in prayer. Light and commotion fracture my vision and a kaleidoscope of images spins in front of me. I am out for perhaps a split second, then am rolling onto my back and staring up at the sky. It is so blue, so blue.

'Oh my God, it's Mr Crane.' My cleaning lady has returned for duty, even though outside my home. 'Is he all right?'

Hands tend to me, help me upright as I thrash around in the vivid aqua. They are connected to bodies I cannot see, only feel – but I *can* see the blue. So much blue. I am open-mouthed. How can the sky be so blue and so wide it takes over the whole earth? That is all I can think about. Voices question, sympathise, worry, as the marketplace bustles around us but all the sounds of the world collapse in on me, as I struggle to reply.

'Blue…'

I am upright again, but the earth is still the sky, together with the sky. I am upright and alive, but the world is completely blue. In fact, I can't see a damn thing but blue. That can't be right. I turn to the good Samaritan on my right-hand side to tell them so, but they are engulfed in the amorphous colour that seems to define everything. My legs buckle, and I fall back to the ground, sliding inexorably into the dark, dark river that is taking me with it.

'Oh my God! He's bleeding from his ear. Call an ambulance. This is bad.'

It echoes in the void.

This is bad.

Chapter 3

7th April 2029: Elise

He looks so peaceful – maybe more peaceful than I've ever seen him before, like a child. His eyelashes fan across his cheeks and his skin is pallid but not waxy. Fragile…

Huh! Now I want to laugh at myself. Jason has never been fragile. That is the last word I would ever use to describe him and yet he is. The fragility of greatness. And now I am crying, can't stop the hot tears burning my eyes, streaking my cheeks. All the time I have known him and loved him – much against my better judgement – he has been fragile; just waiting for this to happen. I desperately want to sweep him into my arms and cradle him, stroke his hair, whisper he'll be fine, but I'm afraid to disturb him.

They have removed the breathing tubes and only the ECG and pressure cuff remain hooked up. Old-fashioned and solid, they're somehow more reassuring than the fibre-thin probe Jason would have expected monitoring his vitals in the kind of facility he would have insisted on if he'd been conscious and able to do so. Funny how – with all our modern technology now – some of the old ways still seem the best, at least to me. Maybe I'm just an old-fashioned girl? Or maybe it's down to budget here – the nearest public medical facility around. Once here, no one wanted to move him again – least of all me.

Periodically the machine parts leap into life – inflating and deflating rhythmically, beeping and spiking, the readouts displaying automatically on the screen on the far wall, linked to the nurses' station. They're busier here too, monitoring the masses not just the elite few, but they will come immediately if anything changes. It doesn't. Those flickering spikes and numbers have become the rhythm of my life too over the last week, waiting for Jason to wake. And he will, they say. They are confident. There is no obvious brain damage, no apparent damage anywhere, other than minor cuts and bruises entirely consistent with the impact, despite the blood they originally thought came from a cranial haematoma that had burst. The MRI says no too, so we wait until he wakes.

I sigh and let my head drop back against the chair. It's one of those vinyl padded 'easy chairs' you only find in hospitals or waiting rooms. Not easy at all, unless you're exhausted or weak or as terrified as I am and barely even feel it beneath you. Only this morning life was normal Now it's a waiting game – waiting for whatever is going to sweep us all away. If I could pray, I would but no words seem to want to come to me. My eyes are aching so I close them but they don't feel any better closed, so I open them again. And wait.

Even the driver has come forward, horrified and obsequiously apologetic once they knew who it was they'd accidentally clipped in passing. But there won't be any charges. What's the point? They didn't do this. There is no real injury to accuse them of. Whatever it is, Jason has done this to himself – his own body has done this to him. That's what they told me; shut down in defence.

Defence against what?

We're waiting to see. And we will. When he wakes.

In the meantime …

I fumble in my bag for a tissue. I've run out. I must bring a box in the next time I visit. I wipe my nose on the back of my hand and pinch my nostrils instead, sniffing like a street urchin. I must look a state. I'm about to rummage in my bag for the little hand mirror I keep in there when the door swishes open behind me. The screen shows 'stable' but still we have the full attention of the medical team. This time it is from the kindest of the nurses – the little one with the cloud of dark hair and soft brown eyes. She is Buddhist or Hindu but I forget which now. She did tell me but my mind just doesn't seem to want to work at the moment. She even showed me some photos of her wedding. It was beautiful – all the brightness of the world encompassed in her and her husband's costumes and faces. I was that happy once. Once. I swallow hard to choke back the sob that would have slipped out otherwise.

'No change?' the little nurse asks gently. It is both statement and question. I shake my head. 'Give it time. Time explains everything.' She produces a clean tissue and hands it to me. I accept it gratefully and try to rub away mascara stains and blotchy make-up.

'But that's the one thing he might not have. What if he needs urgent treatment? Why would his body shut down like this if he wasn't even hurt?'

'It's difficult to know,' she agrees, 'but if time is what it takes, whether any of us have enough of it or not, we simply have to wait. Sometimes that is the only way we come by the answers.' She hovers by the ECG, adjusting the beep volume and taking a print of the latest reading. 'And he really is nice and stable currently,' she consoles me. 'That's good. It means it might not be much longer now and then we can find out the worst.'

I panic. 'The worst? Oh no, no!' I half-rise but she soothes me back into my seat.

'The worst in the sense of whether he needs treatment when he comes round. The doctors can assess him properly then. We can't do anything until they can examine him properly and, as this is brain-driven, they need him conscious for that. Would you like a cup of tea if I can rustle one up before I go off duty?'

'Please.' I put my hand to my head. My temples are tight and my head pounding. It's crying that does it. 'And some painkillers?'

She pulls a face. 'Probably not. But I'll pop back when I'm off duty and see how you're feeling then.'

She rustles efficiently, but quietly, to the door just as Jason's right index finger twitches. I jump.

'Oh!'

'What?' She's back by my side in an instant.

'He moved. His finger.' I find myself edging away from the bed and have to stop myself. When did I become anxious of being close to my own husband?

The nurse – Amarit, that is her name; it means God's nectar – lifts one of his eyelids. I watch, both fascinated and appalled. She told me her name when she was showing me her wedding photos and even then I thought the name was perfect. I would have liked to have been able to show her my wedding photos but Jason wouldn't have a wedding in the traditional sense. It was a registry office job on a Wednesday afternoon, straight from work just before they closed. Jane was one of the witnesses and Matthew the other because she had him in tow by then. I hated it – making the vows I'd always imagined making in a long white dress and veil and in church, in an office in a tweed skirt and jumper. But that's Jason. No nonsense. Pragmatic to the last. And I love him.

All we're doing is following through what we've already promised. What's the song and dance about? I'm not a hearts and flowers person, you know that.

I know that.

But still… I regret giving in over that more than almost anything. At least I'd have photographs of the two of us to look at, like Amarit has. But then I've always done what he wants – even about the child. No, actually, I regret the child most, but what's the point of mithering about that, as my grandmother would have said? I have Jason instead.

His finger twitches again. *He* is my child with his batwing eyelashes and transparent cheeks. The only child I'll have now…

'He's still out, but…' Amarit smiles at me. 'Looks like he could be back with you soon. Just hold on and press the buzzer if anything else happens. I've got to complete the drugs round but I won't be long and I'll come running back if I'm needed. OK?'

And now I'm the child, receiving reassurance. I nod, trying to pin a smile to my lips when all they want to do is droop. Clown mouth. Ironically, I wish Jane was here – and… but no, of course I don't. I wish Matthew was here. He couldn't do anything – would probably panic if anything happened in fact, but at least I wouldn't be quite so alone.

I needn't have worried, as it turns out. Matthew arrives shortly after Amarit leaves with one of the ward doctors. I wonder if Amarit had a hand in that. Matthew wraps an arm round my shoulders and I appreciate the heaviness of it when usually I would feel the need to escape.

'He moved. Twice.' I tell them both. The doctor nods. I feel Matthew's arm tense, tighten more firmly round me. I'd like to ask him to let go, but that would hurt his feelings. He's a good man – probably better than Jason, all told…

The doctor repeats Amarit's checks. Jason still appears lifeless, but when the doctor lifts his eyelid, he jerks suddenly and starts to struggle. I jerk too, shaking Matthew's arm from my shoulders as I scramble to my feet and the plastic hospital chair clatters to the floor behind me.

'This side, quick! Hold him rigid! Stop him hurting himself against the side of the cabinet.' The doctor directs Matthew round to the opposite side of the bed. Me, he pushes towards the ECG machine. I collide with it and it spins across the floor, detaching the electrodes and beeping hysterically. 'Don't worry about that. Hit the buzzer and then hold his head, like this.' The doctor sweeps the pillows out of the way and puts his hands either side of Jason's head, pinning him to the bed. From watching my husband lie like a corpse in a winding sheet, we are now attempting to subdue a raging beast, snarling and twisting, jaw locked in an uncanny similarity to rigor mortis. 'Don't let go or he might bite or swallow his tongue.'

I am sweating and my hands are slipping from Jason's skin by the time reinforcements arrive. Matthew and I are ushered politely but firmly aside by the blue-gowned team and I stand at the end of the bed, watching Jason arch and squirm, feeling every twist and wrench in my own limbs.

'What's happening?' I beg of one of the blue-gowned reinforcements as they swap sides with a colleague.

'He's fitting. It happens with this condition, but this is probably more a reaction to coming round than to the tumour.' He pushes me to the foot of the bed and pitches in with his colleagues again.

'Tumour?' I hear myself repeat, but not aloud. 'What tumour?' I ask aloud. No one answers me. I try to push between the swarming medical team. Matthew pulls me back and crushes my face against his lumpy jacket.

'It's OK. Let them do their job.' Matthew pulls me to him and I want to cry but my eyes are hot and dry. Matthew smells of must and chemicals, and Jason always smells of expensive cologne even when he's been playing with formaldehyde for hours, but for the moment that doesn't matter. I want to know what they mean by tumour.

'It's all right. He's calming down,' Matthew whispers into my hair. I can feel the heat of his breath on my scalp and it makes me nauseous. I manage to pull away and force myself to watch what is happening to Jason. He is calmer now but still twitching. The doctor who checked his pupils breaks away from the rest of the team and comes to stands with us. He observes what the rest of the team are doing for a minute or two and then turns to us.

'Well, Mr Crane is certainly now back in the land of the living. Don't worry. That wasn't unexpected, just came on a bit sooner than we anticipated. Once the sedative takes effect he'll settle right back down again.'

'No!' I am horrified. 'You can't knock him out again…' I grab his lapel. 'You said he has a tumour. He needs treatment!'

The doctor is shaking his head at me and gently disentangling my fingers, but I'm not letting go.

'We haven't knocked him out. We've sedated him, to help with the fitting, and also to enable him to have his condition explained to him now he's conscious. If we're to see how bad this is, we need him to be able to cooperate with our testing. Gaining access to the brain stem is a tricky business.'

'I don't understand. I thought this was just his body in defence-mode, but – '

'The coma, yes, but that's not the underlying condition.'

'What is then? You said there was no brain bleed.'

'No, there isn't…' he bites his lip.

'What then? A tumour someone said?'

'Well…'

He doesn't need to elaborate. It is all in his expression.

'Why didn't you say anything until now?' I can't decide whether to hit him or beg him to tell me he's making it up. He has hold of my hands and Matthew has his arm round me again. I am strait-jacketed with kindness.

'Because we aren't sure exactly what we're dealing with yet. And Mr Crane's medical notes don't permit discussion even with his next of kin. My colleague was a bit too free with his comments in the heat of the moment there.'

'But he has a tumour?'

'We think so.'

'You think so?'

'We know so.' He looks sad, and I know this isn't just any old tumour and that my husband isn't back in the land of the living to stay.

'How bad?' The question catches in my throat, but I have to know.

'That's what we need to establish – and can do now he's conscious.'

'What are you going to do?' I have visions of needles into Jason's brain and Frankenstein's monster-style experiments.

'Talk to him, initially. See what his symptoms are first hand. Then we'll have a better look at his brain stem with an MRI.'

'An MRI. But you've already done that, surely? When he was first brought in.'

I wish now I'd done what Jason would have wanted me to do and travelled the extra fifty miles to the Lanson facility – dangerous though the journey would have been.

'We have, but we need to see what's happened since then.'

'Why?'

Now spiders are crawling up my bones.

'Because we don't know how fast it's growing or what it's compromising. Or what we can do about it.'

'You know what it is, though. Don't you? I don't care what his notes say about not talking to his next of kin. I'll square that with him. You have to tell me. I'm his wife.'

The doctor looks anxiously at Matthew.

'I'll go,' Matthew says.

'No!' Now I am strait-jacketing him. 'You are his best friend, and I need you to help me face this.'

The doctor looks across at the bed. Jason looks as if he's asleep again.

'OK. If we have another episode like that, I'm going to have to revoke the patient's wishes anyway because we'll need next-of-kin permission to conduct any tests at all. We can't tell for the moment whether it *was* a bleed or the tumour that has caused the blindness…'

'Blindness? He's blind?'

'At the moment. It may not last. He may be recovering some intermittent sight and that's what may have caused the fit – reaction to light. What we now need to find out is can we operate to remove it, or can we stop it in its tracks if we can't.'

'And if you can't do either?'

'Let's not go there just yet. We need more information first. Then we'll discuss what's left.'

'What's left?' We all turn of one accord, to see Jason, eyes wide open, and jaw jutting, like he does when he's spoiling for a fight.

'Options for your treatment,' the doctor says smoothly, finally dropping my hands and slipping in alongside the bed. He perches on the now righted hospital chair and Jason has the attention I previously had. The doctor checks his pulse and shines a light into each of Jason's eyes. Jason continues to stare straight ahead, then turns his head woodenly towards the doctor's voice. I realise then he still can't see.

'Sounds like you've already figured out there aren't many.'

'That remains to be seen.'

'So what is it, this tumour?'

'Maybe now isn't the right time to –'

'Now is the perfect time!' Jason's voice is harsh.

The doctor dips his head in submission.

'With your wife and friend present? Your notes say…'

'Forget the notes for now. Sounds like something they're going to have to know about, so what the hell.' I slide in on the other side of the bed and Matthew joins me, pulling another lurid green hospital chair forward for me to sit on. I'm glad Jason can't see the colour of it, or his surroundings. Or judge me for bringing him here – not just yet, anyway. The doctor and I flank the colossus like two sphinxes. I take Jason's hand and squeeze it but it lies limp in mine. He rests his head back against the pillow and closes his eyes. The doctor hesitates. 'Go on,' Jason growls into the silence.

'Well, we think you have a tumour very close to the brain stem, and it has partially ruptured and possibly migrated – maybe when you hit your head after falling in the accident. Maybe of its own accord. It's rare, although potentially operable, but the bleed that may or may not have been caused by the car accident has complicated things.'

'I see. So what next?'

'Tests – of your reflexes, muscle strength, vision, eye and mouth movement, coordination, balance, alertness, and other functions. And we'll need another MRI. Then we need to compare the two MRIs to see the rate of growth and whether it has migrated.'

Jason's eyes are wide and staring at the doctor's face, but still unseeing, as if he can bore into the doctor's brain by sheer effort of will to extract what both he and I guess the doctor isn't saying.

'Migrated? You keep mentioning migrated. What makes you think it's migrated? Don't you mean spread?'

'No, migrated. The fact that you've suffered unexplained blindness after the – relatively minor – mishap with the car, and after no symptoms… I'm guessing you had no prior symptoms; giddiness, visual disturbance, unusual reflex reactions?' Jason's stony expression is its own answer. The doctor nods. 'No, I thought not. Well, in that case, we suspect something has spurred the tumour into life and either a cluster of cells has broken off and found a new home around the optic nerve, starting secondary growth there and causing your current blindness, or…'

'Or?'

Jason has closed his eyes and his head is resting against the pillows again. He looks tired, but with every muscle tensed. For a moment I am afraid he is about to have another fit, but he remains still as well as taut.

'Or it has migrated. It will be unlikely we will be able to do anything to stop it, if so,' the doctor concludes quietly.

'Nothing?' I can hear the panic in my voice. I try to moderate it – for Jason's sake. He is still prone against the pillows, skin almost transparent again.

'But we need another MRI to check against the previous one first.'

'So tell me, doctor,' Jason's eyes are now open, and he is apparently focused on the doctor's face again, 'which do you think it is, because you quite clearly have already given this quite a deal of thought.'

I can sense Jason's alertness, his straining to hear every breath, every emphasis in the doctor's words. I focus on him in the same way. As I watch him, I suddenly know what the doctor is about to say. I realise that so does Jason.

'It could be either,' the doctor demurs.

'But?'

'OK,' the doctor accedes, 'if you've had no prior symptoms, I think it is both the former and the latter. I think you have a slow-growing Parmensis tumour that trauma has set in action. The bleed has determined where it spread to first but now it may well be fully migratory.'

'But you can treat it?' I ask, the words riding on an outrush of breath.

'I...'

'No, Elise. He can't. That's what he's saying,' Jason interjects. He doesn't turn to me, but his fingers do squeeze mine for the briefest moment. He is still staring blindly at the doctor. 'Parmensis – explain.'

'Right, well, a Parmensis tumour can occur anywhere, but often the brain is where it starts. It can take years – decades even – to develop. Essentially, it's dormant until it's activated by trauma of some kind. Then it can do one of two things: grow and proliferate where it is, and then we operate to remove it before it spreads or moves. Or it moves. Once it moves – well...'

'Once it moves?'

'We can't control what it does after that. Even if we try to remove it from where we see it in situ, the nature of the tumour is that interference inevitably causes breakdown that enables it to circulate and proliferate elsewhere. Once it becomes itinerant it is no longer discrete – as most tumours are. We cannot remove it in its entirety – ever – and the more we intervene, the more aggressive it becomes.'

'I see.' Jason's voice is a low growl. 'So the second MRI will just be to confirm the original diagnosis. Am I right?'

The doctor nods. 'Yes,' he adds aloud for Jason's benefit. He continues, 'As I said, a Parmensis is rare. When we spotted it on the original MRI, we spent a lot of time studying it and what it could be doing. It has certain markers that we can use to establish its type. This looks like a slow-grower at the source point, but the section around the optical nerve is migratory, and fast-moving. It may even have already detached from there and be spreading into other areas.'

'Hence the fitting?' I'm surprised by Matthew's sombre voice from behind me.

'Hence the fitting,' the doctor agrees. 'But we still need to check, in case we are wrong.'

'How long?' Jason asks. 'How long do I have?'

Now all eyes are on the doctor.

'It's hard to say…'

'Try,' Jason's voice is quiet and ice cold.

'Maybe six months?' The doctor's words fall through a hole in the world and I follow them into the abyss beyond.

Chapter 4

8th April 2029: Jason

I am floating in blue. If I open my eyes, the blue recedes, but if I open my eyes, the real world intrudes too. I am not yet ready for the real world to intrude. Yesterday was enough for a lifetime. No. Change direction. I touch my face to make sure it's still here – I'm still here; not washed away into the bottomless blue with all the rest of me. My fingers outline soft flesh, cheekbones, lips, chin. My head, at least, has not disintegrated, even if my future has... Oh God! The panic washes over me in hot waves. I am not ready for this. I push the thought away, drown it, and go back to bobbing on the surface of blue, far above the undercurrents of illness and death. Damn! I've done it again. My breath is thready, panicked. I try to focus on something else. What? My brain won't work. It keeps coming back to…

This time I open my eyes to avoid the thought.

The room is pristine – and white. That is a relief. I was beginning to get sick of blue. I will never like the colour blue now, as long as I live… Oh fuck! As long as I live. I can't avoid it. What is the point of trying? Six months, he said. Six months they confirmed after the second MRI. Yesterday. Today it is six months minus one day. One hundred and eighty-two and a half days – say one hundred and eighty-three rounded up. Less one. I bite my lip to control the panic. What does one day more, or less, matter? In six months' time I will have stopped counting. The mass of misery in my chest threatens to crush me. Rolled up in it are all the things I will never now do. The summers and Christmases I won't see, the changing seasons I won't see change ever again, the successes, the challenges, the moments of quiet contentment. Now the tears fall and I make no attempt to stop them. I am entitled to this and there is no one here to see it – no one to protect. I can grieve for myself even though it doesn't lessen the pain of dying before I am ready.

I stay this way for an hour or more, until the clock on the wall opposite the bed ticks round to three-thirty. Visiting time. I could have visitors any time, but I don't want them. I feel shut off, alienated from everyone I would have said I hold dear until now. They are the living. I am the dying. I want their comfort, but I don't want their commiseration – not even Elise's. Especially not Elise's. I couldn't see her face when the doctor pronounced my death sentence, but I can imagine it even now – shock, turning to dismay and then pity. I have failed in the very act of living and I still have to die under scrutiny. It is almost too much to bear. Where is control now?

The tiny, but nonetheless, aggressive tumour around the optic nerve has shifted – moved on. It is now an indeterminate mass shadowing the brain stem, a susurration of starlings waiting to nest, a flock of crows fleeing the Tower, but until it settles my fate is unsealed; other than it is terminal. I have temporarily regained my sight, but without the ability to see further than damnation. The car accident was both a blessing and a curse in that at least I can do something with my remaining six months, which if it hadn't happened I might have squandered. That's what the doctor said – seeking that silver lining in what is undeniably a poison gas cloud. Yet, the tumour may not even have ruptured and may have remained slow-growing for years but for the accident. I try to recall the make and model of the red sports car that spun me off my feet and onto the tarmac. If I try hard enough, I can even imagine the blandly complacent face of its driver as I crumble to dust. I curse them, but the curse has no power. None of it has any power. Even the ball of misery has deflated into a small dagger lodged between my ribs and niggling at me but not quite polishing me off. And I am tired. It all seems so pointless now. Everything.

I close my eyes. The blue returns. I hate the blue but I am too tired to open my eyes again. I let it fold over me, enveloping the misery, the red sports car, the dagger. Damn them all. I won't die. I'm not ready to die yet. I have too much – too much to… The ECG monitor bleeps at me. A warning. I look at the wave form. Tachycardia. No! They've warned me I need to keep calm so the tumour doesn't get a kick up the backside and decide to head off somewhere else where it may do even more damage.

Although…

A small calm voice in my head points out that if I'm playing cat and mouse with the fucking thing, it's interesting to note that I may have an element of control over even the most uncontrollable element of my body.

I like that. There's a kind of twisted symmetry to it. Maybe I could even send the bloody thing somewhere by sheer effort of will ... The conclusion to the thought is lost in the blue that coats everything in a shiny plastic covering that slowly fades to pink. Skin-pink. And hair. A downy covering of hair that could be my own. Like Fred's.

Like Fred's.

My heart jolts again and I reach for the buzzer to call the nurse but the troops are already here, green-gowned and clustering around me like a swarm of agitated locusts. The prick of the needle sends me spinning back to blue oblivion but with that one intriguing, inspiring idea trailing after me.

Fred.

Chapter 5

8th April 2029: Matthew

Jason is sitting up in bed, cheeks flushed and eyes glittering. His laptop is balanced on his knees. I can tell he's had an idea. He has the look that precedes a demand – often impossible to fulfil, or near to – but I always do. It's a habit, coming up with the answer to whatever question Jason poses – it's the only bloody thing I can still do! That and make a mess of things… Around him the machinery bleeps and whirrs. The ECG machine shows a steady wave form and the blood pressure cuff inflates and deflates, recording near-perfect readings. I'm surprised he's not insisted on being moved. The equipment isn't out of the ark, but it is old-school, and Jason is anything but old school. Jason, by comparison, rises strong and determined from it, as ever Other than the rogue mass of cells in his head, he is a near-perfect specimen. I can't help the slightest twinge of envy at that – crazy though that is when he's dying and I'm not. I am the one that should be here, fat-gutted and out of breath as I am. Jane is right. I should lose weight, but I won't – just to spite her.

'What's happened?' I say, eyeing the chair next to the bed, a hard-rimmed shell designed for the svelte barely-stopping visitor. My ass only just fits onto that kind of thing these days. And if I think about that I'll sicken myself even more, so I won't. Easier that way. A lot of things are easier if you don't think about them.

'Nothing. I'm fine.' He laughs sarcastically. 'Or as fine as I'm ever going to be now. Sight back too – how about that? I've just got something I wanted to run past you before Elise arrives.' He gestures to the luminous green chair by the bed. 'Sit,' he instructs, pushing the trailing wires from the machines away from it so there is a clear space dominated only by him and his flailing hands. The machines continue to chirrup around him and for a moment remind me of Klee's twittering machine. I sit, tentatively and stiff-kneed, on the chair. My knees… that's the other reason to lose weight.

'I've been researching my condition. I imagine you have too.' He laughs at my expression. 'I know you too well, old buddy.'

I colour up, disliking the dull red feeling in my cheeks that I can never control – couldn't even as a kid, although it hadn't seemed to matter then. You'd be useless as a poker player – that's what Jane always used to say to me when we were first together. You might be able to calculate the odds, but you could never play them. I could almost laugh at how accurate she's proved to be – damn her. 'Yeah, well,' I mumble.

He sweeps on. 'I've also been reviewing the results of the Fred tests you've been doing this week, so you probably already know what I'm thinking?'

'Do I?' I shake my head, bemused. I have no idea what Jason is thinking. I usually do, but the one thing I've managed to keep smart and quick seems to have atrophied with the rest of my life now. I've been working on Fred – or variations on what we could do with Fred – only to keep my mind occupied, and with no real aim in mind or rationalisation of what any of the results have meant. 'But I'm so sorry –.'

'Never mind that.' He waves away my commiserations and as usual, I'm amazed at Jason's ability to move on. Whatever the problem. If only I could move on, be as self-contained, as self-controlled as he is. Maybe I would make a poker player then – with everyone and everything - but that's never been me. Over-react, over-do, overlook the consequences; that's me. I can calculate all the odds you like, but like Jane said, I can't apply them. I need Jason to do that for me. 'OK, well if you really don't know, I've had an idea.' Now he's leaning forward conspiratorially. 'And I'll need your help with it.'

'What?' I can't help it. I lean in too.

'Fred,' he says, and looks at me meaningfully.

'Fred?' For a moment I think he's lost it. The tumour must have reached his neural cortex and is impairing his cognitive abilities.

'Fred,' he repeats, eyeing me as if I am stupid. He grins. 'You know. Our project, dumbo.'

'I know who Fred is, but what about him? You want more of an update?'

My mind is full of all the things I could tell him but none of them are to do with Fred. More than work on Fred or any other project we might have in the offing, I have researched Parmensis, especially the migratory type. Extremely rare, and incredibly volatile. What is in Jason's brain today could be all over his body tomorrow, but not in his brain – or still in his brain *and* all over his body too. It's not only a death sentence, it's like having a death sentence that also requires you to ride a rollercoaster whilst completing it.

'No, but I do want to know what you think. So far.'

What do I think? *I'm so sorry, mate. I'll be there for Elise, I promise* – Oh God, no! That sounds terrible. *I'll miss you. God, I'll miss you so much. What will I do without you?* The tears prickle and my throat closes over.

'I, I… oh God, I'm sorry mate,' I mutter. I hang my head to hide my face. My nose is starting to run. Shit! I wasn't going to do this – not in front of him, anyway. What kind of man am I? I feel his hand on the back of my head, patting it like you would pat a dog. His voice is thick and indistinct too.

'SOK, I know.' We share the moment in misery and I realise he hasn't moved on, he's simply barricaded himself and his emotions in, just like me. He breaks the silence first. 'But I refuse to be beaten. That's why I want to talk to you about Fred.'

I wipe my eyes with my hand and rub the palm across my face. It's sticky with snot.

'Fred,' I agree, still not getting it, but this is Jason. Whatever he wants to talk about, it's OK with me. 'So – what about him?'

'We said it would be difficult to find volunteers. It won't. We already have one.'

'We already have one? Who? We haven't even started to think about trial subjects. And precisely who is going to risk death in exchange for, only maybe, whatever life Fred could facilitate?' Jason's expression has set, solidified. Then the penny drops. I know that expression – God, I've seen it enough times over the years, and Jason always gets his way. But not this time. It's impossible this time. 'Oh fuck, no! ForEver is nowhere near trialling – and definitely not on you! Yes, it might work – one day – but with what other side-effects? And, man, do you want to live forever inside a machine?'

'I won't. You said yourself, Fred's cloned organs are already integrating with the outer shell of their own accord and starting to modify themselves.'

'Starting. We don't know how they'll adapt in time. And what if there are problems? This kind of bio-engineering is only in its early stages. How long it will take for it to achieve full cohesion and integration is anyone's guess at this stage. It could take years – decades.'

'Six months,' Jason corrects. 'It will take six months, or I'll already be dead, and where will Crane Enterprises – or you – be then? Who will pay your debts and keep Jane at bay? Who will keep the place running and you in a job?'

'But Jason, it's… it's…' But I have no way of ending the sentence. He's right. I'm fucked without him and we both know it. Still I'm appalled – weak with horror at the idea of Jason…

'It's the future. My future.'

I recover my wits enough to protest. 'I was going to say it's madness. Anyway, it's in your brain, so…'

'Currently. But it moves, remember? I could move it. Out of my brain…'

'No, no… I can't let my best friend do this. It's madness.'

'Your best friend wants to do this. It may be the only option he has.'

'But…'

'And so does your boss – your boss who already owns all your assets and will release them only if you work with him on this.' We lock gazes and I know I am beaten. It's true. He owns me, right down to the last penny in my bank account – lent by him against salary due so I could pay this month's maintenance to Jane. I am beaten, and I am also relieved he's beaten me. What a fucking louse I am! We are both silent until his mouth twists in a pained smile. 'I'm sorry, old mate. I wouldn't have done this to you normally, but this is different,' he says eventually.

'I know,' I agree miserably.' I loathe myself for my weakness, for my manipulability, but Jason has me. I am his creation and he is my destruction, if he so wishes. He is not my best friend, as he always has been until now. He is someone else, but I can't blame him for that. In his eyes I see both desperation and determination and for the first time in a long time, I'm moved by something other than disgust at myself and what I've become. I am truly afraid, for him and for me. 'But I don't see how…'

'It can move,' he repeats. 'Do you get it?'

Oh yes. I get it. Move the tumour somewhere into his body and simply replace the part. Simple. Except it isn't.

'But what if you can't shift it or if Fred 's progress so far isn't sustained? What if we can't isolate it to one place? What if it doesn't work and you die anyway? Or worse still, become some mangled version of yourself that's worse than dying?'

‘Who is Fred?’ We both jump at the voice that cuts through our conspirator’s huddle. ‘And why might he mangle you into something worse than being dead?’

Elise’s face is powder white, like the genetically coded latex derivative I mixed into Fred’s CyberCute skin before it transformed; before it became something neither I nor Jason are able to explain because it has never existed until now – other than in our wildest theorising. A wild card, like I use to be. Symbiotic metamorphosis. Only a theory – and only mine at the moment – but that’s what might mangle him into something worse than being dead.

Chapter 6

8th April 2029: Elise

They are huddled together and turn as one. Their eyes are saucer-shaped with surprise. If I wasn't so suspicious, I would have laughed. They are like naughty schoolboys! I used to think of them as naughty schoolboys sometimes when we were all much younger and Matthew was still the cad to Jason's charming college boy, but knowing what Jason and Matthew do, this isn't naughty schoolboy stuff they are huddling together about.

'Elise!' Jason recovers first. 'Darling, I didn't expect you in so early. I thought you had a class or something.'

'Nothing I wouldn't immediately drop to come in to see my husband.' I don't mean there to be ice in my voice, but it creeps up from my spine, unwarranted. 'So? What could be worse than being dead?'

Matthew rallies too now. He pushes back his chair and it scrapes awkwardly across the floor. He steps aside, steadying it as he does so, and gestures for me to sit.

'Here… I was just going, anyway.'

I catch his arm. 'Not so fast! I want to know what you two are cooking up here.'

'Cooking up? I'm hardly able to even move, let alone cook anything up right now.' Jason smiles at me and his eyes have that look in them that he knows I can't resist. But this time I will, God help me! This time feels different – everything feels different.

'But you were. Who is Fred, and how could he hurt you?'

They look at each other over my head.

'No one,' Matthew says, simultaneous with Jason's, 'Or at least, nothing that matters.'

'If it's nothing, why won't you tell me about it?'

'Because it's nothing,' Jason shrugs, the epitome of reason. Matthew shuffles nervously next to me.

I have to admit that it hurts – that there is a secret part of Jason's life I can never share because it is entirely his and Matthew's province, and it hurts every time I am shut out of whatever they are locked in to. It hurts even more now I am about to lose Jason altogether. They've always been close – a duo, although the nature of the duo has changed over the years – and I want to say something cutting to Matthew, to make him feel as excluded as I do, but the decent part of me can't. He is such a puppy these days, tagging along at Jason's heels. Doggedly faithful. How can you hurt a puppy? And anyway, the fairer side of me argues, Jason is as much creator of this particular exclusion zone as Matthew, and he is my husband. It should be him I am hitting out at – even though I can't.

'And I really must be going,' Matthew adds. 'Leave you two to have some time together.'

The easiest thing in the world would be to do what I always do – let it go – leave Jason and Matthew their secrets and tell myself they don't matter. It's work, not play, that occupies them, and as long as Jason is faithful that is all that matters. But not today. Today that is the hardest thing of all to do because I feel so alone, so afraid of a world without Jason. I control my breathing and aim to keep my voice as low and reasoned as Jason's.

'You know, I never usually ask about what you're working on, but this time I think I need to know. Because this isn't just work, is it? It's something more. I'm your wife. You should tell me.'

There. Now I *have* invaded his and Matthew's province. I wish I hadn't said it as soon as I have, but it's out there and done. I search Jason's face for retaliation but he is calm – too calm, too composed. For God's sake, only yesterday he was told he only had six months… That brings panic in its wake and I have to swallow hard to stop the gorge rising in my throat. But maybe he isn't as calm as he appears? Under his left eye a tiny tic is throbbing, almost winking at me. An alarm, blinking – and his right hand is lying on the bed covers, the fingers curled tight, not loose and relaxed. I take his hand in mine and prise the fingers apart. Matthew hovers next to me. I can hear him breathing, short and staccato. Jason looks from me to Matthew. He is seeking permission. Oh my God! He has never sought permission for anything before in his life. Matthew shifts uncomfortably. No, not permission.

'Over to you, buddy,' Jason says wryly. 'You have the nay say on this.'

I twist around to look up at Matthew. His expression is pained, like internally he is being pulled in two. 'Matthew?'

'It's …' The internal contortions of his face intensify. 'Oh God, Jason, this isn't fair. And it's not up to me, anyway.' He shifts his weight onto his other foot as if he's hopping between two camps.

'I can't do it without you, so it is, I'm afraid, old friend.'

'What?' My voice is shrill in my ears. 'Just tell me!'

'ForEver,' Matthew's voice sounds unnatural, almost choking. Jason's monitors click and beep in the background and suddenly this is all too unreal.

'Forever?'

'No, ForEver; For-Ever.' Jason cuts in smoothly. 'It's something we've been working on more or less ever since the war threat. An extension to bodily prostheses.'

'Bodily prostheses…' I struggle to understand.

'Not just a limb or a body part. More – even a whole body.'

'But a whole body would be like a robot?'

'Well, of a sort – but far more sophisticated than that. A replica body, then, if you like. A combination of 3D printing and cloning. We haven't really got anywhere - until now.'

'But who's Fred?' I feel faint, like the world is closing in on me, and I am being encased by a bubble that includes only me. The very idea of a whole synthetic body makes my head spin.

'Fred's our prototype - the prosthesis we started with – without much progress until just over a week ago.' Jason looks across at Matthew. 'You tell her what we could do with it now. I'm tired.'

He leans back against the pillows and his hand goes limp in mine. His eyes are closed and his skin has taken on that transparent look again. I'm torn between concern for Jason and curiosity about ForEver. ForEver wins temporarily. Whatever it, is, it could do something worse than kill my husband. That's more of a cause for concern than Jason's exhaustion. I look at Matthew for clarification.

'It's…' he sighs and bites his bottom lip. It goes white from the pressure. 'It's complicated but, basically, Fred could become more than Fred. He's potentially capable of… transforming, shall we say.'

'Transforming? Into what?'

'Well, virtually human, or at least housing a human brain, so effectively becoming a human-hybrid.'

'But that's…' I can't control the shiver that starts at the base of my spine and spreads outwards in ripples. 'What the hell have you two been playing at? I never figured you for ghouls!'

'We're not!' Matthew still looks pained.

'So where would the human brain come from, then, if not a dead person?' I shiver again, this time revolted.

'It's nothing like that. And we're not playing with dead bodies, we're creating new ones – to replace the faulty ones.'

'To replace *my* faulty one,' Jason adds, opening his eyes and watching me carefully. 'It's what we do, Elise. You know that.'

'You make prostheses, not robots with stolen brains!'

'Fred's not a robot…' Matthew interjects weakly. 'He's already part human – the cloned parts at least…'

'Really?' I stare at him. 'That's human? We have a body we're given by God. It's not up to us to replace it.'

'We replace limbs and you don't have a problem with that. Why not a whole body?' Jason's voice is gravelly. I can hear the bite in it even though his expression is mild.

'A whole body is a person. A limb is merely a part. It's completely different.'

'And the brain? That's a body part too, but without it, are we ourselves? It's our brain that makes us human.'

'And the soul?'

He grins. 'Well, as I recall you telling me once I don't have one, so that's not really a problem, is it?'

He is deliberately needling me now. I know that but still I can't help but react. Jason has always known how to push my buttons. We have never agreed on religion or belief. He has none whereas I believe in the sanctity of life – of doing my best with what I have. I used to worry that it would pull us apart – that difference: he, the cynical pragmatist, and me the spiritual dreamer. It almost – and maybe it should have, except my need for him was too strong, and he knew that so it's something we have carefully avoided discussing in too much depth since… The trouble now is, where do I go with my principles when he knows I've reneged on them once already?

I flush with anger and the tears rush to my eyes. 'I've never said that. I…' I begin.

'I'm joking,' he adds hastily. He adds that smile, and that look, and my arguments falter, as they always do. 'Look, the reality is, I have a faulty body but now we have the potential to replace it.'

'But it's not your body that's faulty. It's the tumour in your brain.'

'That's where it started – but it has already begun to migrate. God knows where it will end up. Look, I really am tired now, but Matthew can tell you the rest, can't you, Matthew?'

Matthew grunts and we exchange glances. His eyes have the look of an animal caught in the headlights of an oncoming juggernaut, I wonder what mine have in them?

'Can you?' I ask acerbically to cover my sense of being pushed aside.

He grimaces. 'Well…'

'Good,' Jason closes the deal – and his eyes – and tunes out, leaving Matthew holding the baby. And now I wish I hadn't used that phrase to myself, because it merely brings back the sharpness of the loss I'd accepted in order to keep Jason, except now I will have neither – child nor husband. In the meantime, Jason proposes playing Creator with himself, yet I am denied creation? Anger and a sense of how unfair it all is floods through me in a way it hasn't for years. I'm about to push Matthew to explain when the bleeps from Jason's ECG suddenly go wild, then stop. I falter, the angry words gluing themselves to my lips. Jason is ashen-faced, teeth grinding, then he goes rigid.

'Oh no,' I murmur. I drop Jason's hand and dive for the nurse's call button. It echoes forlornly as Jason's face contorts and his back arches.

'Oh God! Oh God!' Matthew is wailing in the background, like a dirge.

'He's going to fit again. He mustn't swallow his tongue,' I yell at him. 'Help me hold him still!'

I try to remember what the medics did last time, but I can't. I can't remember anything, except what all the one-bit hospital dramas I've ever seen have portrayed as weeping and cursing, I pinion Jason to the bed whilst Matthew dithers in the background.

'Oh God, oh God,' he wails again.

'Help me, you idiot,' I shriek over my shoulder as Jason bucks and writhes. 'Hold his jaw shut so he doesn't choke.'

He flaps around me but does at least now take Jason's face in his hands and try – ineffectually – to hold his jaw shut until we are both shaken free by another violent tremor. I stumble backwards and into the chair, abandoned behind me. It screeches across the floor like chalk on a blackboard as I lose my balance.

'Shit!' Matthew yells as he ricochets off the ECG machine, detaching the remaining electrodes as he makes contact. 'He's too strong. I can't…' In a blur, I see him disentangle himself from the ECG stand and slink into the background.

'You coward, don't leave him, don't leave me!' I sob, but he pays me no heed.

'I'm not,' his voice fades into the distance. I know I am calling him names, horrible names, and I will regret it later, but for now, all I can see is Jason arching and bucking like he's a stallion being grotesquely broken by some midnight cowboy. I sink to my knees and despair threatens to overwhelm me but for the firm hands plucking me from the floor and steering me gently out of the way. It is Matthew and we have been here before…

'I got help,' he whispers. 'We can't do anything for him. They can.'

I wish we were back to that moment yesterday, before I knew; before Jason's fate was announced and sealed. I wish… The crash team sweep in around us, re-attaching electrodes and sweeping the pillows from under Jason so that he's lying flat. Now he's flaccid and floppy like a ragdoll. The cowboy has broken his mount and left. My stallion is defeated. One of the green-scrub army is rubbing the paddles of a defibrillator as two others are pumping his chest and bagging him and I realise with horror that Jason hasn't had a fit. His heart has stopped – or maybe the one has caused the other.

'Clear!'

Jason's back arches and thumps back down. Even those six months he was promised may never materialise. I watch the ECG monitor with dumb dread, my body as limp and useless as Jason's. He is still flat-lining, a long ghost line of nothing.

'Again!' someone shouts.

I watch the white line on the ECG monitor blip and then fade back to a straight line.

'One more time – on max please.'

It no longer matters what he and Matthew have been dabbling with. He is gone. I bury my face in my hands and try to cry but the tears have wedged in my throat and all I feel is numb. I feel Matthew's arm tightening around me, his apologetic voice saying, 'Elise, it's OK. It's OK.'

I throw the arm off, the trapped tears now turning to ire, a lava flow drowning my comforter. It helps that it's Matthew, who he was sharing secrets with instead of me. 'But it's not OK. He's dead.'

His face looms up in front of me, tense but smiling, a bobbing moon-face full of compassion. It wobbles and rights itself. He is shaking his head and the room is returning to normality, monitors chirruping merrily and the multitude of green scrubs previously buzzing around Jason fading away to just two; one fiddling with the knobs on the ECG machine and the other composing the crumpled sheet over Jason.

'They brought him back. Look.'

He guides me nearer to the bed but I hover unsteadily at the end of it. Jason is still ashen-faced but breathing, an oxygen mask marring his features. The ECG wave is in normal sinus rhythm and the blood pressure cuff is back on, inflating and deflating regularly. We are back to where we were yesterday, almost… I sigh heavily and noisily as the green scrub straightening Jason's covers makes way for me by the bedside. Jason's face is engulfed by the oxygen mask and he seems very small, very helpless behind it.

'Just for a few minutes, then you'd both better go,' the green scrub says quietly. 'He's going to be exhausted now, but he's OK. And I'll be here, keeping an eye on him.'

''I thought… is he… can he hear me?'

'I can hear you,' Jason's voice is a low growl, muffled by the mask. He reaches for my hand and I grab it like it's a lifeline. He waves his other at the green scrub and gestures for her to remove his mask. She protests but he's insistent.

'Two minutes then…' She removes the mask but hovers over him with it, waiting.

'Sorry about that. Didn't mean to cause so much melodrama.'

'Oh, don't be so silly!' I press his hand to my lips and can't stop kissing it. Now I'm crying and crying as if my heart will break. I so nearly lost him. Six months may be almost nothing, but it's better than nothing at all. I can feel his hand on my head, stroking my hair, then it drops away. I lift my head and gaze into Jason's face. He is smiling at me but it has a look of entreaty to it, and I already know what's coming.

'Elise. What we were talking about, before… Please… It could be my only chance.'

Chapter 7

8th April 2029: Elise

We leave shortly afterwards, me reluctantly, Matthew more obediently. On the monitor, Jason's signs are dropping again but I am assured it's just exhaustion this time and the best I can do for him is to leave so he can rest. I manage to hold on as we walk the length of the hospital corridor from ward 24B to the main foyer, but only just. Matthew and I are such fish out of water in this environment, meandering towards the entrance in a jet stream of awkwardness now we have been ejected.

'This way, I think,' he says, veering off towards the left. The sign says *Haematology.* To the right the sign says *All Departments and Exit.*

'No.' I take his arm to pull him out of the way of a porter and his trolley, aiming down the corridor like a ram raider targeting a shop window. '*This* way.'

I hadn't realised quite how much Matthew had changed until now. I only see him perhaps every few months or so now, and then only briefly when he drops some report or the other off for Jason to read. Of course, I've noticed the physical changes – more rounded, more blunted – every time I see him, and that impetuosity that implied he could do something completely unexpected at any moment; that's gone too. I hadn't noticed the lack of direction, like he's a child before, though. Was it marriage, fatherhood – all that kind of stuff? Or something more?

'Oh, right – yes. It is, isn't it? I didn't really look on the way in. Just too worried about Jason.'

I study him more carefully – not that I'm particularly interested in Matthew, but he's going to have to be my main emotional support for the moment. We have been coming here every day for the last week, ever since the accident, and he's a scientist with a sharp, logical brain. How could he not know the way out by now? And yet, not noticing is entirely in keeping with Matthew. He was always in a world of his own and oblivious to how what he was doing affected everyone else. Maybe that's the universal failing of the reckless? They have the impetus to do, but not the wherewithal to evaluate. A singular-mindedness that rules out the possibility of fear, failure or fault. To be fair, though, I have no doubt that his mind will genuinely have been on Jason rather anything else recently because there is also no doubt he's singularly-minded about Jason too. With those thoughts in mind, I reassess Matthew. I may not be a real scientist like him and my husband, but I was at least trained in the art of observation when I might have been one. I have known Matthew almost as long as I have known Jason, but I realise I now don't really know him at all – other than for the qualities I thought he had but no longer seems to possess, and the overall sense that he is basically decent. I've never bothered to find out that much about him. He was Jane's province, and he's always been somewhat shy and awkward around me anyway – Jason's shadow – even when he was being the maverick professor at university. And that brings it home to me just how much Matthew has changed! The maverick professor? This bewildered man allowing me to show him how to exit the hospital? How could I have missed such a change in him before? It shocks me that Jason has eclipsed everyone and everything for me for so long that the world and its people have passed me by without me even noticing.

When Matthew announced to Jason that he was getting married because Jane was, ahem, pregnant, I could have fallen backwards. That wasn't Matthew – not the Matthew I knew then, anyway. Matthew was never the sort to be tied down – even more so than Jason. Nor was it Jane, who I've known since school, but they did marry, – although the pregnancy was a false alarm – said Jane after the event. Doing the decent thing is very much Matthew, though, so whether it was really a false alarm or merely an invention to achieve an end, he would have responded to form either way. I never did work out what Jane wanted from it, even when we were so close we shared all our secrets. And then there was a real baby a while later anyway. I envy Jane both – Matthew's willingness to be manipulated, and the baby; two things I know Jason would never embrace, other than under life and death duress. And yet still I love him. And so does Matthew.

I cast another sideways look at Matthew as we make our way towards the exit. I feel sorry for the names I have just screamed at him now. He doesn't deserve them. I need to tell him that but don't know how to. Two doctors rush past, pagers bleeping and white coats flapping. They're on a mission to save the world, even though they can't save my husband. Matthew can though – according to Jason. What about according to Matthew?

We near the sliding glass doors of the main entrance and I pause. 'So you were going to explain.'

'Erm?' He looks confused.

'About ForEver.'

'Oh, yes, right.' He gestures to the doors and for us to exit. 'But not here.' Outside it is getting dark. I hadn't realised it was so late. We have been here, immersed in drama and tragedy, for almost four hours. It feels like my whole life.

'So where now?' I ask.

'Umm…' he hovers. 'I don't really know.'

'No avoiding, Matthew. I need to know what kind of moral monstrosity the pair of you are concocting between you.'

I know I'm not his favourite person right now – hell, I've just been calling him a bastard and a coward, and he's never been very forthcoming or friendly with me anyway – but I'm going to have to battle this through to the end, whatever his reaction. He hovers beside me. If we stand here for any length of time he will start to shift from foot to foot with nerves. It occurs to me then that maybe his awkward behaviour is deliberate – to fend off attention. Maybe the whole of Matthew is now designed to fend off unwanted attention?

'Oh Elise, it's not like that at all. I agree with you, really, I do. But Jason… I can't deny him a chance, can I? Please don't think so badly of me. I couldn't bear that. Not from you. I'm not a bad man.'

He looks as if he's about to cry and I am shocked. His eyes are beseeching and I suddenly see his discomfort around me from a new angle. He has always seemed so contained within himself – first as the care-less daredevil, and now behind that lumpy, uncared-for exterior, and I've never thought to peel the layers away to see what's really underneath, but perhaps I already know? Poor rejected genius, with as much brain and ability as my husband but none of the attraction for me. My heart bleeds for him and the revelation he's just brought me. Impulsively, I put my hand on his arm but he tenses, and I withdraw it as quickly.

'I didn't say you were a bad man, Matthew – and I don't think that either. I'm sorry for what I said in there. I was upset and afraid, but it was unfair and uncalled for. But what the hell is going on? I need to know. Please?'

The sensation that he's going to bolt at the first opportunity diminishes. He sighs, an outrush of tension.

'OK.' He rubs his chin pensively, and then it's as if he's made an internal decision. His body relaxes, and a glimmer of a smile plays around his mouth. 'I suppose I could take you to the lab and show you the project itself – the ForEver project. That might be easiest.'

I'm surprised at the ease with which he's agreed but I ride the wave and gesture towards the exit. Right now I'd go anywhere with anyone to find out what Matthew and my husband have been up to.

'Ok. Let's go!' I nod enthusiastically.

'Umm,' he hesitates again, and I steel myself to have to persuade him after all. 'Actually, where's your car? Mine's full of crap and you wouldn't want to ride in it.' He laughs awkwardly. 'I wouldn't want you to ride in it either, given the choice.' His face is a picture of embarrassment.

I sigh with relief and produce my car fob. 'Car park C, just across the road.'

We walk side by side, shoulders almost touching, to my car. There a scent of something sweet and floral in the air, crisp but pleasant – the kind of spring evening I would have enjoyed walking along the cliffs if Jason could have been prised away from his laptop or his engrossment in the various online battle games he plays. Ever the tactician – the manipulator; the victor but like a boy too.

The car gleams softly as we approach, haloed by the street lamp next to it. Its opalescent silver-grey sheen says money. Matthew hears it as loud as I do and momentarily now it is me who is embarrassed. Jason had mentioned only a couple of weeks ago that Matthew was struggling financially now that Jane was petitioning for divorce. She can be a mean one, there's no doubting that. I've always known that about her, despite being friends. I press my thumb to the handle and the door unlocks.

'Cool,' Matthew comments. 'Mine's still mechanical. But I like that, sometimes.'

'Sometimes?' I slide in behind the wheel as he hops into the front passenger seat.

'When it doesn't play up. Is this all-electric or hybrid?'

'Hybrid.'

'That's rare. Some of the old ways do still remain, then.' He grins ruefully.

'I quite like the old ways, actually.' I smile back as we share the joke. Jason's company logo has the strapline *'making way for the new'*. Matthew looks younger and less awkward when he smiles. I wonder how the hell he and Jason became such close friends and colleagues, but then, I wonder too how I fell in love with Jason – and, I remind myself, Matthew was different then. 'Which way?' I break the moment quickly, my chest tightening like someone's put a balloon inside it and blown… He reels off a postcode and I tap it into the internal satnav, setting the controls to *auto* and *drive*. I rest my hands on the steering wheel and it moves underneath them. I let it. The car knows where it's going now. I need to concentrate on other things. 'So…' I begin.

'So,' he agrees. 'I need to explain, don't I?'

'Yes.'

'It really is easier if I show you, but I can explain some of the technicalities on the way. Do you know anything about cyborgs and cloning?'

'Only the very basics. In theory you can take base cells and use them to reproduce an organ to replace a faulty one. And cyborgs are robots?'

'A bit more complex than that, but yes. We used the process to develop the CyberArm 3.2 and then some. You see, there are some mechanical and biological elements that are naturally symbiotic – carbon filaments, for example. They've been known about for years, but we made them work in a whole new way by encouraging the two to completely combine to create an organic whole. They've been used in treatments for torn ligaments and tendons for decades because, under the right circumstances, the body will regrow the damaged tissue using a carbon filament as a base. The carbon is then simply absorbed into the body when no longer needed so symbiotic metamorphosis has always been possible –after all, our bodies are simply an assortment of atoms, including carbon.' He smiles. He seems so pleased with it all.

'Hence the CyberArm 3.2?'

'Exactly. With the right processes, we knew we could manipulate specific elements to repair injuries or remove disabilities. The sheer extent of the limb impairment injuries after the Far East wars prompted the marketplace for replacements. We provided the expertise to develop them.' He peers sideways at me. 'You don't think that's a moral monstrosity, I hope?'

'No. It's a wonderful use of science and technology to repair lives as well as bodies. That wasn't what I meant when I said that.'

'I know. There is a difference, I agree.'

'But ForEver?'

'Is really just an extension of that.'

'But it's a whole body.'

'A body is just a shell, though – isn't it? It's not what makes us intrinsically what we are.'

'But where does the shell end and the intrinsic person begin? A brain isn't just a body part, is it? It controls our body, yes, but it's our thoughts and behaviours, principles, beliefs that make us. It's part of the intrinsic person.'

'Well, perhaps. But we weren't talking of replacing a brain here, just a body.'

'But how would that help Jason? The problem *is* his brain – with the tumour.'

'Currently.'

He leaves it there.

I wait.

'OK,' he continues eventually. 'Currently it is in his brain. Tomorrow it could be in his lungs, in his bones, his skin – anywhere.'

'So he will be riddled with it?'

'Well, that's just it. Maybe, or maybe not. That's the problem with this tumour. It may migrate in part to elsewhere, or wholly to elsewhere. It may leave his brain altogether, broken down to its basest cell structure – and reform in its entirety somewhere else. Or it may leave a section in his brain and simply expand to elsewhere. That's why they could operate and remove it in one place, but they know they could simply be providing the wherewithal for it to break down, disperse and reform somewhere else, quicker than it would if left alone. It's the very act of interference that seems to initiate growth or migration in a Parmensis.'

'So…' I try to draw on scientific skills I've long since stopped using. 'That's why the bleed caused the loss of sight? Seeding and VEGF?'

'Yes.' He looks surprised. 'How do you know about vascular growth factors?'

'I first met Jason at a biochem lecture when I was deciding whether to go into lab work or teaching. It was on cancer growth and metastases. It was only a trial lecture for me though. I decided then I'd rather work on growing bright sparks than trying to suppress fire-launchers.'

'Oh,' he nods, smiling. 'Well, now the tumour is on the move elsewhere – we guess – so that's why he's regained his sight. Currently, it seems to be more likely to be migratory than expansive, so that's good news.'

'So where is the tumour re-growing now?'

'I don't know without an MRI. His heart, possibly? That cardiac arrest was unexpected. But they got him back and he's stable for now, so it's quite possibly not stayed there either.'

'Oh God! You mean it's on the move right now? This is like Russian roulette!'

'Worse. You have five empty chambers and only one bullet with Russian roulette. With a Parmensis, every chamber is filled, just waiting to be fired.'

I reach onto the dashboard to re-set the tracking. 'We need to go back then. They need to do another MRI, urgently.' My fingers are trembling. I know he's noticed.

'No,' he puts his hand tentatively over mine. It's tense and I guess he's waiting for me to flinch so I control the inclination to snatch my hand away and wait. I need his support even if I don't want his attention. 'There's no point for the moment. If it's migratory, we need to wait for it to settle, then plan.'

I pull the car over to the kerbside anyway. 'Plan? What the hell can we plan?'

'Jason already is,' he reminds me quietly.

'But how can you plan if this thing can migrate to anywhere?'

'We track it and respond accordingly.'

'But what if it migrates everywhere?'

'That's where Fred could come in. If the whole tumour leaves his brain but invades across his body we could isolate brain from body, with the tumour trapped in the body. That's what Jason is preparing for – at the worst.

I can barely contain my shock. 'And could that really work?'

'That's the thing. It's largely theoretical at the moment, with a few early promises. The tests are really only in their infancy.'

'Then… Christ, this is horrible!'

'No, it's potentially amazing, but difficult. Let's go to the lab and I'll show you. Then maybe you'll understand better.'

We travel the rest of the way in silence, the miles between the hospital and the lab eaten up by the hybrid car, as easily as Jason's life is being eaten up by a Parmensis. Matthew jumps out and rushes round to hold the car door open for me. He avoids looking at my legs as I slide out and straighten with as much dignity as I can muster. He is barely two inches taller than me – and no one's idea of an Adonis anymore – but his smile is on the level with mine and that is comforting. It's been a long time since I looked a man in the eye and had a smile returned on the same level.

I haven't been in the lab since its grand opening two years ago. They were new premises then – big, swanky, high-tech. They're even more so now. The reception is redolent of inherent market sovereignty with its slick Crane Industries logo dominating the back wall. I imagine myself a client – or a customer, perhaps – entering this impressively minimalist facility. Would I be dazzled, or unnerved? Both, probably. Matthew seems strangely out of place here, even though he is one of the leading lights – a one per cent share-holder to Jason's ninety-nine, of course. The whole thing seems wrong for him, in fact. I want to ask him why? Why does he work with, or for, my husband? And why would he get himself embroiled in a project that is so against nature – this man who prefers the old to the new; the mechanical to the modern?

The corridor leading from the main reception reminds me so much of the hospital corridor I almost expect a white-coated doctor to brush past us as we make our way to the ForEver lab – but the place is as still and silent as you would expect at nine-thirty on a Sunday evening. Matthew stops outside Lab 10 and places his hand on the palm scanner, then stares into the iris recognition device.

'This is the ForEver lab. Only we work in here – with the occasional tech specialist.'

The doors swing open and he ushers me into his and Jason's secret world. My first impression is of space – wide white space bordered by storage and, above it, banks of monitors, their screens in various states of display, some blank apart from a bouncing screen-saver, others assiduously monitoring wave-form activity, not dissimilar to Jason's ECG monitor. Beyond them is a stack of cages full of tumbling bodies. White mice. It is a Cinderella setting, simply waiting for the mice to become men and the show to begin. Matthew pulls out a chair next to one of the monitors and gestures for me to sit.

'Would you like a coffee?' he asks politely. 'Barista Bev will make it for you.'

'Barista Bev? I thought we were the only ones here?'

Matthew laughs. 'We are. Barista Bev is the name of our coffee machine. Some of the team created it last Christmas as Jason's Christmas present. You know what he's like about his coffee. Got to be handmade by a barista or it's shit… Sorry, rubbish… ironic, given what we make here, but that's Jason for you.'

I laugh without humour and he hesitates – no doubt wondering if he's gone too far.

'It's OK. That's Jason, all right. Go on.'

He grins. 'Well, we were trying to convince him that there was no actual difference in reality. We made Barista Bev – to Jason's precise coffee-making specifications, but he still wasn't satisfied. It's been a lab joke ever since, pretty much every day. Barista Bev makes him coffee, he rejects it, we have to try harder, and he still gets his coffee from across the road.'

l cannot shake off the small stabbing pain under my ribs, the pain that comes from suddenly realising how little I am involved in my husband's life. Barista Bev is the kind of joke other husbands would share with their wives. Not so Jason, it seems. I am even more excluded than I thought I was.

'Is it good coffee – Barista Bev's?'

'The best. Better than the rubbish across the road, but if he admitted that…'

'He'd be admitting he was wrong too.'

'Well…' He grins awkwardly. We share the moment again. We both think we know Jason well. Now I need to find out what I don't know, because, clearly, I don't know the half of it with Jason – or Matthew either, and I suspect Matthew and I are going to have to become allies, whatever happens.

'So tell me what all this does – and how it fits into the ForEver project.'

I spin on the chair to which Matthew has guided me and survey the room properly. My first impression of clinical coldness is modified marginally by the postcards on the noticeboard at the far end of the lab and the odd-looking machine that I now realise must be Barista Bev. Matthew fiddles with it whilst I study my surroundings. They *are* white and pristine, but there are other more personalised touches too which I missed at first glance, nuances of the two people who work here. Next to one of the monitors is a mug, announcing itself 'Boss'. It sits alongside a neatly arranged array of pens and a notepad embossed with J. That must be Jason's station. Next to that is a monitor festooned with bright green post-its, and a curl-edged photo of a small girl, minus her front teeth grinning inanely into the camera. I stand and go over to read the post-its. My mission now needs to include finding out about the man who could hold such sway over my husband's life.

Jane called. On the war path about school run.

Jane. Maint?

7.30. The Whitehouse.

Sol called. Maint?

This must be Matthew's PC, with all the references to Jane calling – those are in Jason's handwriting – but what the hell is Matthew doing at The Whitehouse? The Whitehouse is a gentleman's club. Matthew returns with two mugs of coffee, the hot milk a frothy wave form of its own on the top. I take one from him and sip. He's right. It is good. He sweeps the post-its from the monitor and shoves them in his pocket. I bite back the question. It's too soon to be personal. I choose the impersonal instead, what I hope he will be comfortable with.

'You'll have to start at the beginning. I'm afraid. This has never been my strong point, hence why I apply what others do.'

'No problem,' he smiles. 'So we deal in cyborgs and using their blueprints in prostheses to make them as adaptive as possible; to merge with the recipient's life-style, routines, requirements – everything. To be their replacement limb in all possible ways. But that's not easy when you're dealing with what is basically a bit of metal attached to your body, so we looked for ways of integrating them using bio-engineering too. Like I said, it's not dissimilar to the surgery they did with carbon filaments back in the nineties. That's where we first got the idea to develop the interactive cyborg prosthesis; see if the two would interact like the carbon filament and ligaments did. Not just mechanical, but a combination of mechanics and the body's own cells. You see, for everything, 3D printing combined with cloning technology is potentially the key. We can't rely on finding a donor organ at the right time, but we can replicate one to order with the right technology.'

'And it's proved possible?'

'That's what the CyberArm 3.2 is basically – our first real breakthrough in full biological integration. The most advanced fitments are now symbiotic with the host. They're no longer a prosthesis on a limb, they *are* a limb.'

'You mean they've grown a new arm?'

'No, *we've* grown our patients a new arm, powered internally by cyborg circuitry, but that limb has then integrated with the body, voluntarily attaching itself to ligaments and tendons, developing capillary involvement, and eventually becoming part of the host body itself. Here…' He flicks a switch on the monitor and pulls up a screen linked to YouTube. The film it is featuring is of a young man demonstrating what his artificial limb can do, including picking up a hair-thin needle from a shiny surface. 'That's a CyberArm 3.2 before the skin modification. Now look at this one.'

I peer closely. He pulls another clip onto the screen and I immediately recognise the background. It is here, filmed in this lab. This time, a young woman is rotating her arm in front of the camera, up close and personal, downy hairs and freckles captured in fine detail.

'But that's a real arm,' I object.

'No, that's a CyberArm 3.2 with skin modification. A CyberArm 3.3 really, to be precise. We just haven't named or released it publicly yet. The join is just below the elbow. We shot that video only a few days ago.'

I peer even closer, the hairs on the back of my neck standing as proud as the hairs on the CyberArm 3.3. I can't see a join of any kind, just seamless skin. I want to squirm. I don't know whether I am immensely proud of what Jason and Matthew have produced, or immensely disturbed.

'It looks real.'

I look at Matthew. He is grinning like a child. 'It does, doesn't it? But that's not all. That's the limb we're going to release, but it doesn't just integrate in its immediate location. The skin modifier has done far more than that. It's both surface-effective and sub-cutaneous efficient. The skin modifier seems to kick start all the other processes as well.'

'What other processes?'

'Everything, really,' he shrugs. 'Vascular growth, cell reproduction, conductive nervous system signals – hell, it's even making inroads into connecting with the brain, proper! There was always the minutest delay in the electronic signals from the micro-computer that forms part of the control pack inside the arm reaching the part of the limb that was to be operated. Look, like this.' He flips screens and I am looking at a graph with *Command* on one axis and *Delivery* on the other. 'These are at most a few seconds delay, but they're still a delay.' I read the figures. They are minuscule, 2.1, 1.8, 2.4. Before I can complete the row, Matthew has switched screens again. The same axes are displayed, but in this version the wavering line that had bisected the previous graph is replaced by a virtually flat line. The figures written against it are unintelligible – to me, at least.

‘Zero point two,’ I start, ‘zero point four… They’re just figures to me.’ I look into his face, flushed and beaming. ‘I was only at basic level in biochem.’

‘They’re nano-second readings,’ he explains. ‘Nano-seconds between command and response with the CyberArm 3.3. And the only difference in spec is the skin modification. It’s organic. The CyberArm 3.3 has become organic. Capable of self-regeneration and self-control. It’s only the start. Now we can progress to all sorts of other organs, and that’s what we’ve been waiting for really; what CyberArm 3.3 means for everything else.’

It is only now that I notice the trolley that is poking out from behind the rows of cages – and I was wrong about the cages. They are not full of mice. They are in fact, rats. White rats with luminous red eyes. Matthew turns and follows my gaze. He turns back to me. I raise my eyebrows at him. Rats mean experiments.

‘So tell me the rest of it,’ I say carefully. ‘The everything else.’

The enthusiasm is still glowing in his face. ‘Well, the irony of Jason’s condition is that if he had cancer in a specific organ, we could potentially easily replace it. We could virtually replace his whole body that way, as individual organs. Theoretically we could even 3D print his brain – possibly, although whether we could duplicate what it does, specifically is another thing, of course. Brains are a bit tricky.’ He scratches his head. ‘What we can’t do – or couldn’t until about a week ago – is get it *all* working together.’

‘But now?’

‘Now, my CyberCute – the skin modification – seems to be making that a possibility.’

‘You developed the skin?’

‘I completed the tests that finalised it,’ he replies, ‘that’s all.’

‘I suspect you’re being modest.’

He grins again, clearly pleased I picked up on nuance in what he said. ‘Anyway, now we have symbiotic growth occurring organically beyond mere local attachment, we’re into a whole new ball game. I’ve been testing it out to see how far the symbiosis can extend on the rats. I’ve actually replicated a complete rat over the last week and set the CyberCute to work on it, then tested the brainwaves. After forty-eight hours the rat was apparently fully functional and remained that way, so then I took it a stage further. To check – ’

'And whose idea was that?'

'Oh, it was simply part of the original ForEver project plan.' He pauses. 'Jason's, I suppose, originally though,' he admits reluctantly.

'OK, and the step further was?'

'To mind-map the original rat's brain and compare it to the replica.'

'And?'

'Mostly the same...'

My mind atrophies. Surely a replicated brain would be completely the same as the original? Wasn't that the point of it?

'But?'

'Well, they say if you play with mirrors, you see a reflection of yourself, but the reflection is what you see, not what you are.'

'Somewhat metaphysical,' I reply, amused, in spite of myself.

'Everything we do is about the metaphysical. I mean…' He lowers his voice as if he's afraid someone will hear, 'sometimes I secretly ask myself, do we even have the right to do any of this?'

'If you question that, then what are you doing it for?'

'For the people who need it, I suppose.'

This side of Matthew is unexpected – and… nice. In amongst the general craziness at the moment, talking the semantics of metaphysics with someone who seems to actually appreciate them is comforting, if also a little strange. We are both quiet for a while after that, watching the white rats as they scurry in amongst their gnawed cardboard tubes and nestle into their billowing clouds of straw that are their sleeping places. Now they are gone, as if they were never there. I notice with surprise that they don't smell.

'They don't smell. Has that been genetically modified too?'

He looks at me, frowning gently as if I am speaking a foreign language.

'No, rats are very hygienic creatures, and we clean them out every day too.'

'It's OK. I was joking,' I reassure him. His expression smooths out across his face.

I wonder if they are hiding from us; rationalising that if they can't see us, we can't see them. Oh, were it that easy to hide from the world and its interference! But it's not – and rats aren't rational beings anyway. We are.

He taps one of the cages and a rat pokes its nose out of its bedding.

'So what did you conclude from your tests, then?'

'That we clearly had to consider whether the organs – and any of the body parts we replicate – perform precisely as they should do. After all, what's the point of giving someone a heart if it won't beat? That's why I picked the most challenging part of the body; the brain. I mind-mapped and recorded all of the synaptic processes I could and imprinted it onto the newly grown, but inanimate, rat brain, and then transplanted it into a mass of CyberCute. It was those results we were discussing just before you arrived today.'

Something cold and unpleasant is creeping over my own skin. I think I am beginning to anticipate what Matthew is trying to impart to me, very, very carefully so I don't freak out.

'Go on,' I say slowly.

'It seemed to produce identical results to the rat's own brain, functioning in its body, despite being our *version* of a rat's brain. I think it's the CyberCute that makes the difference. I can show you the test results if you like?'

'No, no,' I wave the idea away with something resembling revulsion. The thought of a brain sitting in a mass of artificial skin, feeling and thinking and pondering life, fills me with horror. The rat in the cage closest us reappears from its nest and stands on its hind legs, as if it's studying us. For one ridiculous moment, I imagine it reading my mind – it, or its counterpart brain doing so. Maybe having two brains both functioning identically or in mirror image of each other doubles brain power? That uncharted ninety per cent of it that may or may not encompass the psychic and the paranormal and be able to... I shiver. I know I am being ridiculous, but I can't help it. There is so much more to this than I ever imagined – ever even dreamed possible just over a week ago.

'I've never really asked you or Jason about all this stuff before,' I say, halfway between impressed and terrified. 'I guess to me it was all just too unreal. So can you now just 3D-print cloned body parts, put them all together with the CyberCute and it works?'

'Fred.'

'Fred.' My eyes skip past the cages and to the trolley. Fred. I'd almost forgotten Fred – whoever Fred is. I follow the outline of the shape under the coverlet. Fred. Now I am beginning to see where this is going. I am beginning to see what it is I don't know about my husband – and yet I've known all along. All those times we debated the existence of God, and man's responsibility to respect life, I heard him but still I didn't listen. Or maybe it's not been relevant until now? 'Is that Fred? Behind the cages?'

'Yes.'

Coldness creeps over me as everything Matthew has been telling me starts to fall into place. 'And who is Fred, really?'

'What do you mean?'

'Whose body blueprint have you used to clone and 3D print Fred, assuming that's what you've done?'

'Uh, maybe I need to explain some more about this first.'

'No, I want to see Fred.'

I get up and walk across to the trolley. Matthew hesitates behind me. I twitch the drape away from the prone form. It glides gently away from the face, slips off the edge of the trolley and onto the floor. It puddles around us like an inky red clot and I see Fred in all his glory. The face is part-skin, part-polished steel. Silver-bone protrusions form the nose, and the lips drop away from it, the same pink as of the freshly formed skin you find under a scab you've picked away. Above the nose are steel ridged sockets, and eyeballs, bright blue; alert. I try to imagine those eyeballs surrounded by skin, lids, eyelashes. Slowly they come into focus and I see. Only part of the face is skin-covered, like it is slowly proliferating from the jaw upwards, but it is enough to gain an idea of what it will look like when the covering has completed itself. The rest of the body could be human, skin and hair and sinew perfectly formed. I caress the chest, half expecting it to be warm. It isn't. It's clammy, but the texture is of skin, and the fine fuzz of hair springs rigid to my touch. I can feel Matthew behind me, breathing heavily and nervously. The cold has completely enveloped me now and I am as clammy as the body on the slab. I bend and collect the coverlet from the floor, arranging it back over the body, returning it to modesty. The intimacy of this body isn't for anyone else to share. This is my husband's body.

'Whose idea was it?' My voice is icy, even to me and I can sense Matthew behind me even though I don't turn. I can feel his intense discomfort, his fear.

'His… well… ours. It was a choice between the two of us. It's experimental, you see? We couldn't clone anyone else, so it had to be one of us. Jason was by far the more attractive prospect.

I could almost imagine it: the discussion, the agreement, the decision. Of course, it would be Jason. My husband's voice lingers in my ear, dry and amused, not exactly abrasive but challenging in that way that makes you want to rise to it – even if you don't. And then the look: those bright,

bright eyes, teasing. There was something about them you couldn't define – and yet it is in those uncloaked eyes hanging in the hollows of Fred's skull – that same provocative gaze. God knows how they'd recreated it – but then if they are cloned or 3D printed or whatever, they are a replica of Jason's. This body is a replica of Jason's.

I turn to face Matthew full-on. 'But it's still just a body, and only partially that too. A collection of parts that mimic Jason's but aren't Jason – or functioning yet, by the look of it. You can't just 3D-print a body and it works. It's only a possibility. You've just said that – or as near as.'

'Oh yes, there's a lot more to it than just 3D-printing and cloning. That's what I was trying to explain to you. Fred is just a control – initially to see if we could replicate a body shell effectively.' He produces a remote control and clicks it into life. Fred's body seems less prone. 'What is inside is a complicated combination of cloned organs and cyborg enhancements linking them together. The cyborg is controlled from Jason's computer – was mine, but as soon as he knew what Fred could do, he told me to swap.' He looks rueful. 'It's basic, but it works.' He operates the remote and the head moves, remarkably realistically. 'But only via the remote – and the PC.'

'And now you've found out what the CyberCute does…'

'Yes…' We study each other. 'It will get better – gradually metamorphose.'

'So if necessary you could remove the part affected by the tumour in Jason's body and replace it?'

'Well, simplistically, yes.'

I can hear him grinding his teeth with nerves. It sets mine on edge too.

'But if the tumour didn't shift? If it stayed in his brain?'

'That's where Fred comes in. Our test subject – for trial runs. But it's more complex than that. Jason's not a rat, he's a human being. We'd have to record and monitor every single reaction and electrical response in his brain to get a complete blueprint for it to ensure it connected properly once in situ. And then we'd have to successfully kick start it all once the transfer was complete and that's where these little guys come in, but who knows with a human being?'

'But Jason thinks you could do it? Even with a human?'

'Yes…' He pauses. I wait.

'But?'

'But it's still just mainly theory, despite Fred and the rats, Elise. Rats are simple creatures, with simple behaviour patterns. The human brain –

well... You see we can only achieve mind transfer by copy-and-transfer or gradual replacement of neurons. In the former, mind uploading is achieved by scanning and mapping the salient features of a biological brain and then by copying, transferring, and storing that on a computer. The downside of that method is that the biological brain may not survive the copying process.'

I can read between the lines as well as anyone. 'You mean your replicated rat died?'

'He grimaces. 'Well, ye-s...'

'And the other way?'

'Neural network emulation? A low-level structure of the underlying neural network is mapped with a computer system and then a blueprint of its source code is translated to another programming language. The human mind is then, theoretically, replicated by the emulated neural network.'

'But in a computer?'

'Well, we'd need to find a vehicle to make the physiological leap from mechanical to biological per se, then. I guess CyberCute could come into play there too? We haven't established its full potential yet, but it certainly seems to be extensive. But then, still, how can we be sure that we'd transferred everything – that the brain we transfer is the whole brain? That there's not something more we don't know about? We can't. So what we'd have to rely on is that the brain would extrapolate what we had transferred and grow new responses based on past memories and response patterns – which is what we do anyway. Back to symbiotic metamorphosis again. Our brain creates our world based on past and previous experience. That's what our little rat friends have done to some extent – taken basic patterns and extrapolated them – although even for them that's pretty simplistic too. For a more complex brain it would be a very risky business.'

'And what would Jason become if it didn't work to plan?'

'Most likely a vegetable – and that's what I meant by it would be worse than him dying. His brain might not actually die, but it might not function whereas his body would but with no purpose. Can you imagine doing that to him? Making Jason a vegetable?'

I go back to the chair by the PC monitor and sit on it before my legs give way. In my heart, I know the decision is right, but the pain of it is almost too much to bear.

'In that case I'm totally against it, even though it means losing him.

Life is a gift, not a commodity, and all the more precious because it is limited.'

'I don't think he intends that you have any choice in the matter, Elise. After all, why do you think that instruction is in his medical notes?'

'But it isn't the medical profession he is asking to do this.'

'I know,' he replies quietly, biting his lip.

'And if it worked?'

'Again, I don't know.' He is shaking his head. He looks bewildered – lost. 'More – or less human, I don't know. One thing I do know, though.'

'What?'

'This is immortality, if it works. That's why we called it the ForEver project. And who wouldn't want that?' He gives a little laugh that is more whimper than amusement.

'But we were never meant to be immortal, Matthew. Life is finite. To be immortal would be to become inhuman.'

The pain inside me intensifies until it is worse than being burnt alive. I could accept losing my husband, but potentially keeping him yet losing his humanity? Yet, to lose him altogether...

'Matthew, I have put up with a lot for Jason. I can forgive him all of it – the obsessive determination and blinkered drive for the top, the baggage from his childhood, even...' I can't bring myself to say it to Matthew's naïve moon-face; the fact that his friend is effectively a murderer and so am I – a child-murderer. 'But this would be a step too far … Please don't agree to it.'

'But this is Jason. How can I say no? How can we let him die?'

'Because it's wrong. Unnatural. I don't want Jason to become some kind of experiment. The very idea is obscene!'

'But he wouldn't.'

'Wouldn't he?'

'No. I wouldn't let that happen. I'd stop it before that happened. And symbiotic metamorphosis might not even be possible – ever – or not with the amount of time we have, anyway.'

'Then stop it now, or I will tell the doctors about it and that the tumour is obviously affecting his mental capacity. I'll get an injunction if necessary and get him or both of you – sectioned. Then you, Jason, and everyone else will have to get past the authorities before you do anything.'

With that, I flounce out, hating myself but unable to stay for fear I will cave in. I need time to assimilate everything I've learned and seen over the last few hours. I need time to examine me and my conscience and how I will look Jason in the eye and tell him I'm denying him life. I need to go to my studio, regardless of the time, and paint. As I leave I hear Matthew's plaintive, 'Elise, wait… You don't understand.'

No, I don't. I don't understand Jason, or me, or how God could have done this to either of us.

Chapter 8

10th April 2029: Jason

I didn't expect her back last night, but I knew she'd be here first thing this morning. Matthew's text made that quite clear – and her reaction, although I can't quite gauge his from the wording. I would have preferred the opportunity for a full de-brief from him before I face Elise, but hey, I've tackled worse. He may be inept at relationships, but his technical presentation is perfect. I have absolute faith in him to have said the right words to Elise in that sense. It's Elise who is the loose cannon here. The need to devise a strategy to defuse the cannon is almost a welcome distraction from the other – more unpleasant – thoughts I'm finding it increasingly difficult to avoid.

I close my eyes and allow the blue to invade temporarily. It's an aberration, the doctors tell me. My brain has learned to perceive blue. It's not really there to see, and the tumour isn't affecting the optical nerve at all now. It's merely a learned response I have to unlearn. I set my subconscious on unlearning it whilst I consider the problem of convincing Elise. She's a woman. She's emotionally invested. She's my wife. She's always deferred to me – even about the kid. Why wouldn't she defer to my decision now?

Because it's against her morals.

But so was the kind – and how is this immoral? How is it immoral to want to cheat death – live out a full life, not a mere fraction of one? A life potentially never-ending.

Immortality? But that's precisely what she'll baulk against.

God gave us brains to be able to rise above adversity – find answers where there were none. Isn't that one of these situations?

It's not that. It's about the sanctity of life – God's creation.

That was what Matthew's text had mentioned. Typical! She'd pick up on a bloody principle, not a fact. With ForEver I could survive. Without it

I'll die. I'll try that first. And if that doesn't work, maybe I'll have to give her a demo – what it will be like when I do.

Oh shit! When I do. I've been keeping that at bay quite well until now. Matthew's test results have kept me occupied and the nursing staff have obliged with sedatives when the thought has come creeping back since the cardiac arrest yesterday. Keep him calm. Bloody right! Keep me sane too! I can feel my heart start to pound as the idea pushes in on my rambling thoughts, all those smart-ass poets glamorising what has no glamour at all...

"Death, where is thy sting?"

"Do not go gentle into that good night..."

"Dying is a wild night and a new road..."

Oh fuck! I DO NOT WANT TO DIE!

And I bloody won't!

I push away the blue and look determinedly into the light. I have never given up before and I bloody won't now. And I'm going to need determination if we go through with the ForEver project.

WHEN we go through with the ForEver project.

I breathe out slowly and steadily, consciously calming myself and steadying my pounding heart. I mimic Elise when she's meditating. I close my eyes again and allow the blue to drift over me in waves.

Calm, calm, calm, calm...

The ECG bleep stops. I open my eyes and peer sideways at the monitor, trying not to eject my conscious thought from the calm, calm, calm mantra. It is back to normal, a steady drip-feed of blood through a normally beating heart, with the ghost of an idea riding atop it. Elise will never give up over metaphysics. That's why we've agreed to disagree all these years, and never discuss them. That's also why she steers clear of the lab and asking about what we're researching. If she doesn't know, she doesn't need to argue over it, and arguing with me is the thing she wants to do least. I didn't get it originally. She's feisty enough about everything else, but when she backed down over the kid, rather than split us up, I began to understand. Her principles aren't as strong as her love for me. I only have to press the right button and I complete all the emotional circuits for her – it's just determining which button it is that requires cunning.

The door to my room bursts open and a nurse pokes her head round the door. She stops short on the threshold when she sees me sitting up in bed, smiling at her. It's the little dark-haired Indian one. Pretty.

'Oh,' she smiles back uncertainly. 'I thought I heard your monitor go?'

'Really?' I feign surprise. 'I don't know about that. I was dozing but something woke me up just now. Maybe I had a nightmare? Dreamed I only had six months to live, or something like that?' I turn the corners of my mouth down and she cocks her head on one side, clearly trying to decide whether I am about to get upset or am a complete asshole who hasn't understood at all. 'Sorry,' I add, winking. 'Bad joke.' I give her my rueful face now. 'I'm trying to cheer myself up but it doesn't work very well.' She still doesn't look sure. 'I panic if I treat it seriously so I'm being a coward about it at the moment and joking, even though the joke's on me.' Now I turn on the miseries and she comes fully into the room and across to the bed.

'No,' she agrees sympathetically. 'You're very brave to even make a joke of any kind, actually.'

Her eyes are warm and kind. I enjoy them for a moment. I could turn on the miseries for real if I dwelt on my future – or lack of it – now, with those sympathetic eyes on me. I could do with a bit of warm and kind… Oh, I know Elise is warm and kind, but she is also *involved* – highly emotional, and I've always found emotional difficult. This warm and kind is impersonal and objective. It's easier to accept sympathy from a stranger than from someone you're invested in. This little nurse doesn't even know who the hell I am. Jason Adam means nothing to her. I've purposely insisted they exclude my surname from the outer cover of the notes so I'm a nobody in here. No press, thanks! I'll die – or live – in private.

'Better than wailing and gnashing my teeth, though,' I reply. I shrug and force the miseries down into my guts. I refuse to give in to them – or anything, come to that. I'm Jason Adam – terminal diagnosis on paper, but I'm still Jason Crane of Crane Industries in my head and heart until that diagnosis becomes fact. The thought brings iron back into my soul.

She looks into my eyes and I can see her pupils enlarge. Yeah, happens every time. Looks and self-image do matter, whatever they say. I could be the world's biggest asshole – and according to Matthew's Jane, I am – and dying, but charm and looks still get them every time. Her name badge stands proud of her uniform as she begins to straighten my already straight covers. Amarjit. Now I remember something Elise said about her. Her name means manna from heaven or something like that. And she has wedding photos on her phone. I look at the slim gold wedding band on her left hand as she smooths the coverlet. Elise had wanted wedding photos and a grand affair of a wedding. We'd done it my way in the end. There was no chance I was dressing up and walking down a church aisle – not even for Elise, but there is always an angle, no matter how awkward the spot you're in.

'I wonder if I could ask you to do me a favour?' I ask as ingenuously as I can manage.

'Of course,' she gazes earnestly back at me.

'Amarjit, my wife is due in any moment and I need to convince her about something, but I don't think I'm going to be able to without some help.'

The little nurse cocks her head at me again. I like it. She reminds me of a cheeky little songbird when she does that.

'Oh? How can I help with that?'

'You could help me convince her. Urgency is what I need – a sense of urgency.'

She looks unsure. 'Is it something she's got to do?'

'It's something she needs to let me do. My own choice.'

'Oh,' she looks worried. 'Maybe you need to talk to one of the doctors about that.'

'Oh, no, no, no, no – nothing like that!' I shake my head, laughing. 'I intend trying to live as long as I possibly can, but Elise is so averse to risk – won't try anything if there's any possible downside to it. I understand her caution, but basically – what have I got to lose, currently?'

'Is it some experimental treatment then? You'd still better talk to the doctors about it.'

'Oh no! There's nothing that could be done here, I'm afraid. The doctors here know there's nothing they can do for me, but I want to do something whilst I still can.'

'Well, OK.' She waits tentatively by the bed.

'Elise told me about your wedding and your fantastic photos.' I smile warmly, and she melts. 'We never had a grand affair. Too much going on at the time. We just wanted to be married so we dashed off to the registry office and just did it,' and to some extent it had been like that. I wasn't totally lying to Amarjit. The need to be married to Elise had been as strong as hers to be married to me – what is it the Chinese call it? *Yuanfen – the binding force...* Odd that... I drag myself back to my artifice, 'but I know Elise always regretted not having the white dress and the church and all of that.'

'And you want to do it now?' Amarjit makes it almost too easy for me and for a moment a sense of shame pervades me – but not for long. Survival beats everything, even Yuanfen.

'Well, maybe. But it would have to be whilst I'm still walking and who knows how long that's going to be for. Elise doesn't want me to do anything that would be taking a risk. Obviously leaving the hospital and getting involved in that would be…' I allow the idea to sink in.

'I suppose I could talk to her,' she says dubiously.

'I've tried that. Even my friend Matthew has tried that. Look – this is what he reported back last night.' I select Matthew's text messages and wave my phone at her.

'There's no way she'll go for it currently, it says. *Far too risky and she's afraid of losing you as you are…'*

Her eyes follow the lines of text until I flick the phone off.

'But say I could impress on her that I could literally die any minute so whatever the risk, it would be worth it for the moment? I've been racking my brains and that seems the only way to convince her – and allay her fears that she'd be doing me harm. I know it's manipulation of a sort, but oly done with the best of intentions.'

'Oh,' the nurse says faintly. She is looking uncertain again.

'All I'd ask you to do is to reinforce that idea. No lies or anything, just on my cue, maybe give me another sedative?'

'Oh dear.' She looks worried now. 'I don't think, ethically…'

'But you wouldn't be doing anything wrong because that's what you're doing anyway – when I need calming down. It's in my notes.' I look shamefacedly at the over-bed tray and she follows my gaze. *Sedate to keep the patient calm whenever necessary…* it said in the doctor's notes.

'Oh, I'm not sure you were meant to see that.'

'But I have.'

She purses her lips. 'Well, OK. I suppose…' She checks my chart and my blood pressure. 'You last had a sedative yesterday, so you *could* have another today if needed…'

'Please?'

'I don't know…' She looks over her shoulder.

'Cross my heart and hope to die.' I widen my eyes at her.

'Oh God!' Her eyes widen too, but in horror, then they crinkle at the corners and she is laughing with me. 'You are terrible!' Now they soften and start to tear up. I don't want that. She's no use to me as emotional as Elise.

'Always,' I agree. 'So this is our plan…'

By the time Elise arrives, it's all sorted. My notes are back in their rightful place and I am suitably disposed against the pillows, the tragic hero. To tell the truth, the strategising has helped a lot. You can't think about dying when you're planning how not to – and how to arrange it so even your opponent helps you plan it too.

Chapter 9

10th April 2029: Elise

I painted until almost dawn. By the time exhaustion overcame me, one whole wall of my studio was stacked with canvasses, sticky with paint and raw emotion. For all of her faults, at least Jane gave me this emotional outlet when everything fell apart. She suggested it after we terminated the baby. She simply turned up one day, bundled me into the car, dishevelled, despairing, lost, and took me to her studio, set me in front of a canvas with a paintbrush, a stack of paint tubes and left me to it, saying, *'I'll be back in about an hour. Just paint whatever you feel like painting.'*

'But I don't know how to paint.'

''Course, you do,' she replied with that haughty toss of the head she's so good at. 'Everyone knows how to paint, even if they're shit at it.'

'Then I'd be shit at it.'

'So? Be shit at it then but let it all out whilst you're doing it too. I promise you'll feel better for it.'

Then she waddled out and shut the door and I was left looking at the canvas she'd set up for me and the paintbrush she'd stuck in my hand without the faintest idea what to do with them.

Was she mad? I haven't a creative bone in my body. I'm a nothing – not even a mother. I became a teacher in the absence of a better idea, assuming it would only be a temporary position after I married Jason. It would only be a matter of time before we started a family and then ... I sank to me knees then, overwhelmed by the failure of my life. I curled up into a ball and lay there weeping for most of that hour, until exhaustion overcame me – much like it did last night. Or maybe drained would be a better word? I felt drained of misery, and when there was none left, anger replaced it.

And then I started to paint. I can't even remember what I painted that first time. It was all red and black though. Jane took one look at it and grimaced.

'We'll come back tomorrow,' she said, turning the canvas to the wall.

And we did – every day for a month. By the time the month ended I was painting in every colour under the sun, and Jane wasn't turning the canvases to the wall. She was seven months pregnant by then.

'You can have the studio if you like,' she said one day. 'I won't be able to come here anymore soon myself. You might as well make use of it. You'll have to pay the rent of course, but I can't see that'll be a problem for you.'

'But it's your studio,' I protested. 'And this was always your dream.'

'My dreams went when this happened,' she patted her bump. 'You might as well take them over. You're good, you know. You could even do something with it.'

'So ironic,' I heard myself saying before I could stop myself. 'You have my dream and I have yours.'

'Well, I guess that's karma, ain't it?' she replied, standing back to appraise what I had just finished.

'Karma? How?'

I wished she hadn't replied then or told me what karma she was referring to but what's happened has happened That was the last time I spoke to her. I had nothing to say to her after that, and I doubt she would have had anything more to say to me. I've never told Jason about the studio. It's the last link I have to a friendship that dragged me out of one abyss, only to throw me into a different one. And we all need a secret, don't we? I would have had to have told Jason about it soon – my first real exhibition should have been in six month's time...

Being good at something – something unique to me – was like becoming a mother of another sort. I gave birth to my paintings; intense and dramatic. The gallery owner described them as "a contemporary tale of death and resurrection." A bit melodramatic maybe, but I did die and resurrect that day Jane told me. I resurrected as someone who was going to be true to herself from then onwards.

Yet here I am again, in exactly the same seat by Jason's hospital bed as for the last ten days. You'd think I'd have got used to it now, but I haven't. What's worse, every day brings something more to worry about. First the coma, then the blindness, then the tumour, then the diagnosis, then the bombshell of last night. Then finally, this: the urgent call in to find... God knows what. Another emergency. Another close call with

Death so that Death has become more a lover to my husband than I am. I am sure Matthew will have reported back to him about last night but I have no idea what he will have said. I would have talked to him again before I came today but the message from Amarjit alone was enough to get me running, no make-up, no handbag even.

Everything appears calm right now but earlier I had to watch helplessly as Amarjit administered yet another sedative to stop Jason going into a fit. Now all I can do is wait – like she advised once before. Amarjit adjusts his tubes and the ECG machine continues its steady wave form. The blood pressure cuff fills and deflates. It's all routine to us now, with no routine at all except for the expectation of disaster at any moment.

'Will he be out for long?' I ask Amarjit.

She is red-faced and a little flustered. 'A while.'

'And do we know why this time?' She won't look me in the eye. Inside the jitters start. The little marching band full of percussionists march up and down my gut as they did yesterday and the day before. 'Is there something else I should know?' I ask, carefully.

'No.' She turns her back to me.

'Amarjit?'

'OK.' She turns to face me. 'You should let him do it. He hasn't got that long. Humour him. If it was my husband, *I* would.'

I am speechless for a while, computing the implication of what she has just said. Hurt almost outweighs surprise. He's talked about it to a nurse before he's talked about it properly to me!

'You know what he wants to do?'

'Yes.'

Jason shifts and murmurs in his sleep. We both immediately focus back on him. Amarjit takes the hand nearest her and checks his pulse. Instinctively I grab the hand she isn't holding – an ownership instinct I am immediately ashamed of. I am about to let go, but that gesture would be symbolic too. If I let go, it's like letting go of Jason forever.

'But it could do more harm than good?'

'Anything he has the opportunity to do now can only do more good than harm.'

'Would you let your husband do it?'

'I'd do anything for him in this situation.' She places Jason's hand gently back on the counterpane. 'He's OK,' she says to my enquiring expression, 'but unstable.' We both go back to studying him. He is deathly still apart from a flickering eyelid and his breath a little unsteady at times. The tiny veins on his eyelids stand out blue as I watch that flicker, both fascinated and in denial. Yes, he is unstable. My colossus of a husband is unstable and as vulnerable as a child and that destabilises everyone else around him. We need him to be our rock, our inspiration – Jason Crane, the man everyone looks to and follows. 'He needs you behind him all the way in this. It's a terrible thing to face,' Amarjit adds.

I'm about to snap at her that I know that only too well, but luckily the truth behind her words sinks in before my own leave my mouth. Yes, he does need me behind him. My colossus is falling and asking me to allow him not to. This must be the first time in the whole of my life with Jason that he has been vulnerable, and I am instrumental in that. Matthew's words ring in my ears. *'How can I say no? How can I leave him to die?'*

'Think about it at least.' Amarjit pauses to touch my shoulder sympathetically as she leaves. The gesture almost brings me to tears. Briefly I place my own hand over hers as it rests on my shoulder, the arguments I was going to use raging to nothing in my head. Now there were two people being more sympathetic to my husband's cause than me.

Yet it's so unnatural…

Amarjit presses my shoulder then her fingers slip away from under mine. 'I'll be back later to check on him. Got to accompany ward rounds now. Press the button if you need anything.'

I nod. I can't speak. I'm too full of self-reproach.

The door swishes shut and I sit in silence with Jason, studying his vulnerabilities. His eyelids are still flickering. I stroke his hand, hoping his dreams aren't too fearful.

'Don' wanna…' he mutters.

'Jason?'

'Don' wanna… no, please don't wanna…' A tear trickles from the side of one eyelid but he doesn't wake.

My throat clogs with dammed emotion. One word more and it will undam, a logjam of misery and despair. I swallow it back. He is vulnerable, and he needs me to be strong for him now the tables are turned. Usually it's me relying on Jason – indecisive, insecure Elise… I stroke his hand more resolutely and he starts to twitch. I tense, anticipating trouble again.

'Don' wanna die…' his voice breaks and he whimpers like a puppy. Both eyelids are streaming tears now and my sobs echo his.

How can I say no? How can I let him die?

'I won't let that happen, my love,' I say, the tears running in hot rivers down my own face as I try to brush his away. 'I won't. I won't…'

He stirs and his eyes open. 'Elise…' I throw myself onto him as gently as I can without disturbing any of the tubes and monitors. He sighs and says thickly, 'what's this? What's this all about?'

'You,' I reply into his shoulder. He smells of antiseptic and freshly laundered cotton, but also of Jason – musky, male, reassuring. His arms tighten around me and we stay like that for what seems like hours until he pushes me gently away.

'I'm being squashed here,' he says lightly. 'Don't want to be crushed before my time.' His eyes belie the joke though.

'You were crying in your sleep.'

He laughs, a short staccato burst. 'Isn't that a song?'

'Yes, maybe. But it's also true.'

'And you?' He sweeps the remaining dampness from my cheeks.

'I was crying in my wakefulness.'

'An awful lot of crying between us then.' His voice is husky. 'Does it have to be that way?'

'What has Matthew told you?'

'What do you think he told me?'

'That I was completely opposed to it.'

He pulls a face. 'And more. So that's me stuffed.' The face turns upside down – clown-shaped.

I take both his hands in mine. 'I don't know.'

He squeezes my hands. 'I know you don't. And I understand why. We agreed to disagree a long time ago. It's just now it means…'

How can I say no? How can I let him die?

'I don't have the right to deny you,' I qualify.

He shakes his head. His eyes are very blue, very bright – the way I remember them the first time we met. I saw stars then, as if someone had hit me over the head like they do in the cartoons.

'I don't know either,' he says quietly.

'You said you don't want to die.'

I am drowning in his eyes.

'I don't,' he says quietly. 'Scares the hell out of me. And I don't want to lose all that time we should have had together. But we can't always get what we want, can we – and that's a song too, isn't it?'

'But if you try…' I choke, 'sometimes you…' the sobs are making me breathless, 'get what you need…'

'Well, you know what that is, babe.' He sighs.

'Yes, I do.' The last vestiges of my principles tumble into dust. How can I be true to myself if it means letting the one person I love more than anything else in the word die? 'So I guess I have to let you get what you need even if it's not what I believe in, like… like when…' I can't go on but he knows what I'm remembering.

Chapter 10

10th April 2029: Jason

She is smiling, that smile that makes her skin glow like there's a candle inside her. I toss the pile of results Matthew has printed off for me onto the kitchen worktop and cross to where she is sitting, teetering atop one of the bar stools I like, and she hates. There is a smell of cinnamon in the air. She has been baking, but the worktops are pristine – the way I insist on them being. The only remnant of her day's activities is the small plastic stick that is lying next to her coffee mug. Her fingertips caress it whilst her eyes are all for me, brimming, iridescent. She is so beautiful. Even now she still takes my breath away – that strange nervous flutter in my stomach that has no rhyme or reason to it, other than that I'm looking at Elise.

I smile, despite my irritation at being summoned home before six-thirty. The radio hums softly in the background – some old seventies classics show. Elise likes the classics.

'What's so urgent?'

She smiles back, but it wobbles and tilts lopsidedly into a tearful grimace. Momentarily my irritation dissipates. She will always be an angel with golden hair to me, even if she calls me home early when I have work to do.

'Elise? Are you OK?'

I reach her just in time to steady her as she slides from the stool.

'Yes, yes.' She clings to me. 'Did Matthew tell you about Jane?'

'Jane?'

'She's pregnant.'

My stomach twists and the cinnamon smell becomes cloying instead of sweet.

'Pregnant? Since when?'

'Since a little while ago.'

She cocks her head on one side. 'You didn't know?'

I shake my head and use her as my excuse for steadying both of us.

'No,' I hear myself saying. It sounds awkward and abrupt. Harsh.

'Oh?' The surprise in her voice flows on into reassurance. 'Oh, well, don't be cross with Matthew. It might be because Jane had a bit of scare to begin with. Has to have some extra tests so maybe that's why he's said nothing to you, despite you being... I only know because I'm her best friend, and – well, women need to confide, don't they? Whereas men don't.'

'Don't they?'

Outside the sprinklers kick in and our garden is filled with artificial rain, heavily imbued with fertiliser to force on recalcitrant blooms. The soil isn't good on our plot, claggy and clay-sodden. I should have complained but it's too late now. One would think it hardly needs more moisture, so water-logged are areas of the freshly turned beds and newly bordered lawns, but Elise insists it just needs feeding. The oscillating spray patters against the decking and then fades to nothing as it reaches the lawn. The radio drops out – as it always does when the sprinkler kicks in. Should complain about that too. The silence is deafening, but the sprinkler still roars in my ears. She strokes my chest and then soothes my cheek but the tic keeps twitching. She will interpret it as irritation with Matthew.

'No, not really. Even though they should.'

'Up to him,' I say.

'You are put out with him.'

'I've other things to worry about more.' She looks quizzical. 'We've just started a new trial.' I gesture to the printouts. 'Our own new baby.'

'Oh.' She steps back and looks up into my face. 'That's good. Is it going well?'

'Not yet, but it will. That's what all that data is.' I shrug and my arms feel loose in their sockets. 'He doesn't have time for sleepless nights and nappies if this kicks off. I hope she realises that.'

I want to tell her that myself; shout it into her face; bitch! What is she playing at? She said she was covered.

Or maybe it's not mine? The idea calms me. Yes, don't jump to conclusions, and if she hasn't told you then...

'It does take several months to get to the sleepless nights and nappies stage,' Elise is smiling – teasing. 'You'll have his full attention for several months more and beyond, I'm sure.' The pause is infinitesimal. 'And

anyway, maybe your attention will be a little distracted by then too.'

'What do you mean?'

Her unsteady smiles settles and spreads across her face even while tears roll down her cheeks, yet the light within is unquenched by the downpour.

'Only that... I am too.' Her sentence ends in a half-sob of caught breath as she blossoms like a flower. The sun is at its zenith and it is streaming through the kitchen window, turning dust motes in the air to small spinning flecks of gold. I am hot, sweating. The golden dust motes settle on my skin and bind with the sweat that is oozing from every pore. It solidifies into a straitjacket of oppression as her words develop from information into comprehension.

'What do you mean, you are too?'

I don't actually need her answer. Of course, I understand – and anyway, it's written all over her face, as clear as the data in the printouts Matthew has just triumphantly provided me with. The inception of Fred. Faulty, but promising.

'I'm pregnant too.' The light inside flares. 'Isn't that wonderful'? She sniffs and gulps, clinging to me like a maiden aunt begging a kiss on a paper-thin cheek; like my mother on the rare occasion she needed our attention, or she showed my sister and I any interest. 'I wasn't sure until today, but I did a test like Jane suggested, and well...'

'Jesus Christ!' Another thought catches me off-guard. 'How far on is Jane, anyway?'

Elise frowns. 'Jane? Over three months now. She has to have an amnio tomorrow because of her age. She's been resisting it, but it's better to be safe than sorry.'

I look at the white plastic stick and it all starts to fall into place; Jane, her reticence, her absence, her careful avoidance of what she once chased. Matthew's smug face as he referred to the birth of Venus – or maybe Mars – when he handed me the Fred results and asked for tomorrow off for, 'something Jane needs me for.' I thought he was being bullied – like he always is where Jane is concerned, but no, he was being manipulated – like she'd manipulated me. Three months? Three months ago we'd been at it like rabbits – at every opportunity whilst Matthew had been hard at it in the lab, working all hours on Fred. It could only be mine.

Elise picks up the stick and brandishes it at me. 'But that's irrelevant to us. What's relevant are my test results.'

The breath is gone from me, punched from my lungs by the double horror of what she has just told me. A bee meanders in the open back door and lands on the counter next to where the white plastic stick was. It spreads its wings, heavy with pollen. Flaky yellow crumbs litter the worktop around it. Elise is breathless too, but for different reasons.

'Oh, look, it's like a blessing. Little drops of Ambrosia!'

I sweep the bee aside and grab the plastic stick from Elise's hand in the same movement. 'Pregnant' it announces.

'But how? You can't be.'

I stare down into her radiant face, blonde hair flax-silk around giant eyes and trembling lips. I have never seen her happier, or more dangerous. She nods, vigorously at first and then more slowly as her assumption of mutual delight begins to disintegrate.

'Oh Jason, I hope you won't be cross with me but when Jane told me... I did it on the spur of the moment. I didn't expect anything to happen straight away. I know I should have told you, but I thought...'

'Should have told me what? What have you done?'

I fling the plastic death sentence onto the worktop and stare down at her. She shrinks away.

'I... I stopped taking my pill – well, I forgot it one time and then I thought well, as I've already forgotten it once, maybe...'

'Because of Jane?'

'Because of Jane... no, no – because of me – us...'

'And when did you consult me about this? Ask me if this was what I wanted too?'

My breath is back now, acrid steam in my chest, a torrent of lava streaming from me and over her small golden head, bowed in misery. Angry words, I know I shouldn't say but she is Jane, she is my mother, she is the bitch who taunted me all the way through my childhood years, and worse – she is Elise, betraying me when I thought Elise would never betray me. The bee comes back for a second pass and I bat it away. It swings wide and collides with the cupboard door, tumbling onto the worktop in a stunned heap. I smash at it with my fist before I can stop myself and Elise's blubbing stops. We survey each other in wary silence, her eyes bigger than ever.

'Oh, I wish you hadn't.'

'I wish you hadn't too.'

She bites her lip. 'I'm sorry. It was wrong of me.'

'Yes, it was. So we'd better sort it out now, hadn't we?'

'Sort it out?'

The sprinkler makes an unexpected extra pass and the wind catches its spray, beating it against the kitchen window. The sun has gone behind a cloud and the temperature in the room drops from humid summer sweat to cold winter's night. The bee buzzes feebly and gives up, its pollen seed falling barren on the smooth grey marble of the worktop. Elise glances sadly across at it.

'You shouldn't kill bees. They help keep us alive.'

'So do lots of things. Something will kill it at some stage, anyway. It's life.'

'Not deliberately.'

'Deliberately – the world is full of predators.'

'Not until today,' she says softly.

The sprinkler passes again. It can only be turning the garden into a mud bath now.

'Jesus!' I cross the room and hit the off switch for the sprinkler. We'll be floating

away soon. The radio kicks back in almost immediately. A love song. 'You went a long time for me…' I return to Elise and the white stick and defunct insect.

'No, always, Elise. There are always predators, everywhere. Always have been, always will be. I don't want kids – we can't have kids. I told you that when we got married.'

'Why can't we?'

'We just can't.'

'But why?'

'Because… I don't want to talk about it. I told you no children when we married. I'm sorry. This can't happen. You'll have to have a termination.'

'No!' Her face is as grey as the worktop. 'Surely there's something…'

'No… No. We'll sort out a clinic tomorrow,' I say.

'And if I don't agree? I don't agree with abortion – you know that. It's a life. You don't just take a life because it doesn't suit you.'

'It's not a life. It's simply a cluster of cells and the start of a process right now. It has no independent life capability.'

Just like Fred – for the time being. She opens her mouth and I wait for all the old arguments to be repeated, but maybe something in my expression changes her mind.

'And would you say that to Jane too?' Briefly something like fire is in

her eyes.

'Jane isn't my concern.'

But she is.

I continue, 'You do understand, don't you, Elise? We agreed – we're enough for each other, aren't we? Or did I get that wrong? Did you not mean that when we married?'

'No, no, we are. It's just... I so wanted...'

'I know.' I pull her to me and smother her protests against my chest. 'But I don't need anything more than you. You are my world, you know that. I don't need anything else in my – our – world. Can't you just accept that?'

She resists at first, but the longer I hold her, the less the resistance. It's always like that with Elise. Eventually she weeps softly against me, all protest relinquished, and I am as water-laden as the garden. We stay like that until dusk begins to fall. She pulls away then, eyes bruised and face creased from the folds in my shirt. Her voice is dull and lifeless.

'I think I'll go and have a lie down. One of my migraines is starting.'

'My poor, poor girl.'

I stroke her face, fingers lingering under her chin as I tilt it upwards for a kiss. She smothers a sob and kisses me back and I know the future is settled. The radio plays her out. I can barely keep the irony from my face as I realise what the lyrics are that keep repeating.

'You can't always get what you want...'

Oh yes you can.

I leave Elise asleep or pretending to be, curled into a tight, round ball, like a child, in the middle of our super-king-size bed. She looks small and lost and for a moment I wish I could make the future different for her, but that can't be. I go downstairs and pour myself a brandy, close my eyes, remember the pain, the rejection, the betrayal – no! I won't do this tonight. It's enough my past affects my present so, but I won't let it dictate it. She has cheated on me – and yes, I have cheated on her, but it's different.

My eyes wander the details of the life we have built together over the years. It is perfect – comfortable, controlled, designed. Home, work and life all fit perfectly into the right parameters, from the encouraging data printouts Matthew gave me to review, to the moss-green silk drapes so artfully gracing the lounge windows that look out over our – just beginning to drain – garden, and on to the carefully casual flower display, refreshed daily, that adds just the right touch of natural shape to a room of angles and planes. I don't want any of this disturbed – the serenity, the isolation, the depth of it. It is mine. I have worked hard to get it this way.

But tomorrow, I will need to find out the truth from Jane.

***

I open my eyes. No moss-green drapes or artful floral displays here. Just sterile white walls and complex machinery I am almost as integrated with as Fred is with our test equipment in the lab. And the Parmensis. But at least I'll get what I want now. The right buttons. That's all you need. I'd like to close my eyes again, but if I do, I know I'll only have Elise's sad, lost face pasted to the back of them – and my regret that I hurt her so.

Chapter 11

19th April 2029: Matthew

'I still can't imagine how you got her to back down.'

'Women, Matt. They have buttons. You push them. Hey presto!'

'But she was so upset. I thought she was going to hit me at one point.'

'Well, I'm glad you were the messenger and not me, then.'

I hold the lab door open to allow Jason to be wheeled in. He is out, but on remand – in a wheelchair being pushed everywhere by a lackey to ensure he doesn't over-exert himself. Elise's conditions; endorsed by the doctors. 'Thanks, but you can go now,' he says curtly to the lackey.

'Oh?' The lad's fresh-faced youthfulness is flushed with both embarrassment and probably the latest acne preparation in the market. 'But I'm meant to… '

'I don't really care what you're meant to … '

'It's all right,' I step into the breach. 'I can manoeuvre him around the lab. You just wait in reception until we're done here.'

'OK,' the boy wavers, then sidles out. The door clicks shut behind him.

'He's only doing his job – and what the hell are you doing now?'

Jason is already half out of the wheelchair, throwing the brown fluffy blanket that had been spread over his knees onto the floor. It lies there like an old dog. 'What I'm meant to,' he quips. He looks far too cocky for a man with a time expire on his head.

'You're meant to be following the rules,' I reply, but I know it's pointless. When has Jason ever listened to reason – or me? But then, when have I?

'Rules are made to be broken.'

'Yeah.' I watch him move around the lab, checking the data I've already put up on the screens and finally ending up by his own PC. 'But you know there's a condition attached, don't you?'

He swings round. His expression is sharp and challenging. There's nothing of the invalid to him. I could almost believe this last fortnight has been a bad dream.

'Condition?'

'Elise put a condition on all this. If there's any suggestion it isn't completely tested by the time we need to think about doing anything drastic, then she'll do what she threatened originally.'

'Pull the plug? I know. So she'd better be convinced, hadn't she?'

He is scrutinising the data on his own screen now and ignoring me. I wonder if I should ask or let it lie. I thought a lot about Elise's initial response to Jason's plan in the intervening day but we haven't spoken about it since. Her sudden acceptance of it surprised me more than my own. Although do I accept it, really? I guess, in essence, I do. How could I watch Jason die if there was something that could be done about it? But in my gut, it doesn't sit right and Elise's words have murmured in my ears every night as I've drifted off to sleep since. I should talk to her, but I've become a coward. Yeah. I've become a coward in so many ways. Jason is still intent on the data, but I do need to know.

'So how *did* you persuade Elise?'

'Huh?'

'So how did you persuade her?'

'Oh, it was joint effort – me and that rather attractive little nurse, Amarjit. I told her some cock and bull story about renewing our marriage vows in a big white wedding do like the one we didn't have, but Elise worrying about the drain on me. She agreed to, let's say, stage a scenario to work the histrionics to a point where Elise felt obliged.'

'What the hell? How did you do that?'

'She injected me with sedatives in front of Elise because I am so stressed and that could send me into cardiac arrest again. Then she plays the 'I'd do anything for my husband' card, whilst I pretend to have a bad dream and mutter about being afraid of dying. Worked a treat.'

He grins at me and momentarily I both marvel at and actively dislike my best friend.

'But how could you have pretended to have a bad dream if you were sedated?'

'It was saline solution, old buddy. You think they dish out narcs on a whim, even to the terminal? I was wide awake all the time. Damn hard staying still and pretending to be asleep, though.'

'Bloody hell, Jason! You could have got her into trouble – the nurse.'

'Nah, she won't say anything if I won't. Got her old man a job in sales as a thank you, anyway.'

'Even so, you may have JC's initials, but you don't walk on water!'

'Neither did he, if you look at the evidence, but we won't go into that.'

'Christ!' I shake my head. 'Well, aren't you the Academy Awards star!' I don't like the sarcasm in my voice, but I don't like this – don't like it all.

'Yeah, aren't I?' he retorts. 'But in case it passed you by…' His voice has an icy edge to it now. '… I am dying, and I am bloody scared of that, so it wasn't all play-acting. When you're in the same situation, then you can judge, but not before. Can we get on?'

'Sorry,' I slide into the seat in front of my own PC. Yes, I am such a coward. 'What do you want to look at first?'

'The brain transplant rats. How are they doing now?'

'Good, but they've only been fully functional for five days. We need longer to check

their behaviour patterns don't change.'

'Why, if they've been the same for five days?'

Jason has accessed and is now manipulating precisely the data he asked me for. I can feel irritation building in my chest, like the vibration of a swarm of insects brushing my rib cage. Why ask me if he doesn't want to believe me? My reply is testier than it should be.

'The Blue Brain Project only went part-way there and the findings in 2020 left more still in development. Glial cell astrocytes and neurons have only minimal functionality in our rats too.'

'And?'

'Well, five days isn't long enough.'

'In the grand scheme of a rat's life it is. Five days in a life span of a rat is say…' he taps some numbers into the scientific calculator on his keyboard, 'about seven per cent of its total life, which would equate to monitoring a human for about six months…'

'OK, OK, it's a decent length of time to start with, but there are other factors.'

'Such as?'

'Such as behaviour transformation. That could take much longer to show up.'

'But we're not anticipating that will happen, so why look for it?'

Jason turns away from the screen and I can see from his expression he won't be dissuaded. I've seen that expression too many times in the past. Nevertheless…

'Because we need to rule it out or develop a strategy to counter it if it does happen.'

'Some behavioural transformation is always going to happen… The mirror effect – and experiential factors. Are you deliberately trying to stall me?'

His lower jaw is jutting, and the swarm of insects turn to red ants, crawling painfully into my gut. You simply don't argue with Jason, especially when he's… I catch the thought and detain it. But I should argue with him this time. This is important – life-shatteringly important, and he's my best friend. Even if I've become a coward, I need to brave enough to stand up to him now or… 'No, I'm trying to protect you!'

'From what? Living?'

I hadn't expected a stand-off quite so soon. Elise's original reaction had highlighted my own reservations, but her so rapid turnaround hadn't given me a chance to think them through fully – other than that it all needed more than six months to develop properly.

'I don't know from what. Whatever might flow from it, I suppose, initially. This should take years to develop properly – not less than six months. You know that too.'

'But I haven't got more than six months.'

'I know, I know.'

I can hear the weakness of indecision in my voice – like there often is these days – and hate it. How did I come to this? It's a question I've begun asking myself more and more recently. How did I lose the man I was, ready and unafraid to try anything, and become this sniffling, weak little shadow who jumps when anyone snaps their fingers? I fiddle with the fountain pen lying next to the keyboard whilst I try to put what I want to say in a format that Jason will accept. The pen is old and leaky, but I like it – like the way I have to moderate the speed of my writing to flow with its quirkiness and need to be refilled constantly and often. I've never really thought about it before now, but I use those enforced full stops as thinking time in the same way a writer uses punctuation to give their accumulation of words meaning. I don't think at the speed of light like Jason anymore. I plod, carefully testing out each possibility before giving it form. Jane is right. Who I am now will never set the world alight, but neither will I be the one to burn it down, and that gives me some comfort.

'And nor have you,' he adds quietly – so quietly I almost don't hear it. I look at him more on the suspicion of the words having fallen between us, the hush of threat. 'Crane Industries is me, Matthew. And so are all your assets, remember? I can't keep the creditors – or Jane – off your back if I'm not here.'

Anger races through me in the way it used to and I bite back. 'But nor will you keep the hounds off me if this goes badly wrong. I know you think you've got the worst of it, Jason, but if this does go wrong, where will the blame be laid for it? At my door. You won't be here to keep any of that off my back, will you?'

The pen has leaked, as it always does, and my fingers and thumb are now stained. The culprit is marked. And I am ashamed of laying that all on Jason, when, yes, he has got the worst of it. At least I'm not going to die within six months. Damn my leaky mouth and stained integrity!

'I see.' He leans back in the chair and studies me, blue eyes so intense they could be boring a hole through me and right out the other side. I feel every inch the traitor. I fiddle with the pen again. What does it matter if it stains my whole hand – my whole body even? He knows I'm a coward now. 'Let's examine this all again, shall we?'

'How?' I ask, the lumpen shame thickening my voice. I can't meet his eyes even though I can still feel them on me, steady and challenging.

'The controls so far have all been successful?'

'Controls, yes. But mice and rats, Jason… And we always said we'd test it first on a cyborg before anything else.'

'And we will. On Fred.'

'Fred's not a full cyborg. He's an experiment in putting body parts together.'

'*Our* bio-engineering…'

I shake my head, still avoiding looking at him. The pen's inky puddle extends to the edge of the free-standing keyboard now and my fingers are soot black.

'Is only in its early stages. How long it will take for it to achieve full cohesion and integration is anyone's guess at this stage. It could take years – decades.'

'But it can't, can it?'

He is silent. We are back to square one. I finally dare to look him full in the face.

'Like I said before, your initials may be JC but you can't walk on water – and neither can I.'

'Then we both need to start trying. I can only do this with you behind me, Matthew. You can make a miracle happen, and if you do, the hounds won't be tearing you to shreds, they'll be bowing to your success. I've always helped you in the past. Help me now or…'

'Or?'

He flicks off his PC monitor and pushes back the chair. The sun is already low in the sky and it filters drearily through the lab window behind him, turning him to silhouette.

'Or God help me, I'll see you and Jane facing each other in court, with all the gory details of exactly how and when I've helped you out in the past in her solicitor's papers.'

'But it would show you'd withheld…'

'It won't matter to me by then, will it?'

'You wouldn't!' I can barely speak with horror.

'I'm sorry, Matthew. I have no choice. I'm calling in your debts, old buddy. A life for a life.'

Chapter 12

19th April 2029: Jason

Calling in debts; this place is built on debts. You can smell them in the very fabric of the walls, the banks of equipment, the sumptuous leather of the furniture. Debts to society, to people, to principles, to me – but the debts themselves mean nothing to me now other than how I can use them. Poor Matthew. I don't like doing this to him, but there is no other way. He has buttons just like Elise. It scares me sometimes to see how vulnerable people are with their psychoses and angsts and worries. Jane, money, the kid, guilt. He has become imprisoned by all of them.

I turn away from Matthew so I can't see his expression, pretending to be immersed in the rat data again. I kick back in my chair and sprawl, allowing my limbs to dangle, loose and relaxed as those four prison walls of Matthew's morph into the walls that encase me too. Jane's face floats in front of me on the computer screen like a screen-saver, supplanting the rats – or maybe joining them. Well, of course, it doesn't really. There's no way either he or I would have an image of her in pride of place here. It's imagination, but imagination is an uncontrollable thing when it takes over and it's taking me over more and more, cooped up in here. I abandon the PC screen and stand and stretch to look out the window instead. I had the building designed with high-level windows purposely to keep straying thoughts inside and away from distract ions outside but, by God, I need a distraction now. It's there in the form of the distant fields swaying gently in the breeze, beyond the car park. The other side of them is a river and a pub, *The Dog and Duck*, or something equally inane. The beer's not bad. I can taste it now, sweet, with an undertow of hops, still fermenting on my tongue. I swallow, and the taste dredges up the memories.

'Jane wants a divorce.'

'Why?'

I stare at him across the table. It's rough – needs sanding down and repainting. Jesus, why don't these places maintain their furniture properly? Do they think customers like getting splinters in their hands and stain marks on their clothes? The rustic appeal. Huh! The sun is making him squint. Typical of Matthew to not even have the most basic of sunglasses to protect his eyes. My Raybans cut out the glare perfectly so I can study every detail of his face, the set of his expression as he delivers the verdict.

'She says we're just not suited.'

'Crap! You've suited well enough all this time. What's she up to?'

He shakes his head and peers down into the depths of the river flowing alongside the pub wall. A flotilla of duck and ducklings bobs past. Yeah, rustic charm all right.

'Nothing, really, Jason. It's been going down the pan for ages, really. It's not her fault. It's me.'

'Oh, crap again. When has anything not been Jane's fault? You let her get away with things far too easily.'

'I'm not like you, Jason.'

I study him more minutely. 'No,' I say after a while. 'You're not. Well, maybe it's a blessing. Get shot of the nagging wife, start again. You're not that old, pretty successful – dammit! You're part of Crane Industries! What else do you need?'

'Money…'

His expression makes me want to laugh. 'Well, you've got that.' Now his expression doesn't make me want to laugh. 'Oh no, don't tell me you've been doing that again.'

'No I haven't. It's not that. I sorted that, really. It's…' The table next to us is claimed by a middle-aged pair with walking boots and a snuffling dog. Matthew leans across ours towards me conspiratorially. 'I'll have to give her the house.'

'So? Buy a new one for yourself. You can afford it with what I pay you.'

'I can't.' His voice is rasping.

'Why not? It's not that wonderful – OK, but a bit old-fashioned. Needs updating, but if she wants it so much let her do that.'

'I can't give her the house. It's encumbered.'

'Encumbered. Oh Jesus, you have, haven't you?'

'No, really, I haven't.' His expression is that of a small child anxious for praise; simultaneously earnest and supplicatory.

'I don't believe you.'

I lean back and he leans yet further forward.

'Jason, I haven't gambled in ages. I promised I wouldn't and I haven't.'

'Then what?'

I lean forward to meet him. The duckling flotilla trickles into the shade of the reeds as a heron swoops across the water, sweeping low, targeting the unsuspecting tiddlers drifting too near the surface. It soars away with a wriggling unfortunate in its beak as Matthew explains. I watch the heron's trajectory into the sky until, even with the Raybans, I can't stare into the intensity of the sun any more. But I can't look at Matthew either. It is too much to have this power over him. Even I don't want the power to play God over him, but he is unrelenting in his confession. I close my eyes and listen to his voice and the gaps in the world around us that it's falling into.

'It started at university – well you know that – but you don't know how bad it got.'

'I think I do,' I counter ironically. 'Or my bank balance does.'

The river trickles by, small rippling sounds as the reeds impede and concede its flow. Somewhere nearby a bird is in full song, warbling its joy to an ungrateful audience. At the next table, glasses clink, the smell of cheese and onion crisps assaults me and my stomach demands food. I swallow a mouthful of my pint to quell the need and the sweet tang of warm beer slides down my throat, temporarily numbing other desires.

'No you don't. Really you don't. You see…'

I play out the scene in my mind as he describes it, the genius student with no common sense, straying into the tangled underworld of the no-hopers who can't stop themselves because gambling is as much an addiction as the need for alcohol or drugs. Oh, I'd known Matthew could be reckless – it was part of his charm – now sadly lacking at times, but I'd put that down to Jane and her stifling influence over him. But this? I stop him only when he gets to the security footage of him pointing a gun at a guard who wouldn't back down in the robbery he finally gave in to as a way of paying off his debts. I sit up straight and lean across the table, meeting him in the middle, nose to nose.

'But I paid those debts off.'

'Oh God, Jason, they were just a fraction. I couldn't ask you for the whole lot. Not then. You weren't that rich then. And this is from other things too. Since then, well, you have no idea… Jane's expensive, and so

is Katie.'

We sit in silence for a moment and the river world flows on around us, serene and tranquil. I seethe. The fool. Why hadn't he told me the truth to begin with? God knows what potential damage he could have caused by now – what liability he's become to me.

'So, you did the job in return for the rest of your debts being written off and got caught on camera. Bad enough, but you haven't been prosecuted yet, so what haven't you told me?'

'The guard got shot.'

'Fucking hell – and you shot him?'

'No! No! I didn't. One of the others took the gun off me because I was trembling so much I couldn't hold it still. He shot the guard, but I was the one on film. They bribed the security firm and got the footage to avoid prosecution, but I've had to carry on paying them ever since.'

'For what? You said you did the job to get rid of the debt.'

'For the guard.'

'The guard? Oh, I see. Presumably he wouldn't identify any of you then?'

'He died. Manslaughter they said, by person or persons unknown. They couldn't prove who, but guess who would be prime suspect if they could? Jason, I'm scared...'

'You are in a mess,' I agree eventually. 'But how did the house get encumbered though?'

'I borrowed to pay the blackmail. I gambled to pay the loan, and of course the two just fed off each other, plus Jane is expensive, like I said. The only way to deal with it all in the end was to sign the house over and that was supposed to pay off the blackmail in full.'

'You never pay off blackmail in full, Matthew,' I murmur dryly, thinking about Jane and how expensive she could be when she set her mind to it. Poor bastard!

'Well, no. But for a while at least – until I could get back on my feet. And I stopped gambling altogether after that. If Jane hadn't decided we're through, I could have maybe muddled through until retirement if they hadn't bothered me again. I suppose I didn't really think how it would all turn out eventually. Just how it was for the time being.'

'Well, you'll just have to break the good news to her now, I guess. Darling Jane. Of course, you can have the house – and the foreclosure on it... There's a certain dramatic irony to it, you have to admit. She thinks she's going to shaft you, but there's nothing to shaft you with.'

I can't help the small inner smile. There you are Jane. You thought you had him by the balls, like you thought you had me once. Oh no. Not either of us as it happens. Then I laugh out loud. Matthew looks hurt.

'Oh, she'll shaft me all right. She's got the biggest shafting tool imaginable. Katie. I won't even get to see her from a hundred yards if Jane can prove me unfit as a parent – and anyway, how do I explain how the house became encumbered without landing myself in jail, or in the gang's sights for grassing them up?'

'Ah.' I stop laughing. Katie might mean nothing to me, ironically, but Matthew is besotted, for some reason. And the gang's involvement is worse – especially as they might come knocking on my door as Matthew's business partner – even though I use that term in the lightest way possible. 'Yes, I see what you mean. You are well and truly in the shit, buddy. Well and truly.'

'Jason, I'm scared...'

'Christ,' I stare at him, at the whole sorry mess finally laid out in technicolour between us. This isn't Matthew. Rash, impetuous, impatient, yes – but not scared; not this quivering, quaking excuse for a man sitting across the table from me. And that means now I have no choice. I have to do something, because – God help us – I know he'd do something for me if the boot was on the other foot, damn him!.

I pick up my glass and drain it. His pint is as yet untouched. He sighs and slumps over it. Next to us, the table clears and the previous middle-aged duo sipping shandy is replaced by a group of twenty-somethings with bottles of cider and loud voices. Behind us a young family has settled in with burgers and chips and glasses of fizz. The kids are squabbling over who has the biggest chips. Slumming it by the peace of the river and the pub's rusticity – for all its hidden splinters and stained seats – has suddenly lost its appeal. And I can't think straight with kids around; ever. It's my turn to sigh now.

'Get that down you and we'll move on,' I instruct Matthew.

'Move on? Where to?'

'Somewhere more upmarket with no kids.' He swings round and watches the mock battles going on behind him.

'Oh, I don't mind them.'

'Maybe not, but I do. Come on, if you want me to get you out of the shit again.'

'Oh, I didn't tell you because...'

'Yes, you did. And what are friends for, anyway? Come on. At least

you're better off being in hock to me. Who's got the film now, by the way?'

He downs half his beer and deposits the glass on the table with a thump as I stand and head for the beer garden's exit. He stumbles after me as we leave behind the mêlée of unattractive general public and head across the less popular area near the car park.

'Eddie, I guess. Eddie was the shooter, and the gang leader, so I guess he wouldn't allow it in anyone else's hands anyway. They say the Krays are at the end of his family tree.'

'Nice. Always liked a bit of gardening. Life pruning.'

We are at the gate to the car park. He grabs it and holds it open for me. 'Oh, I wouldn't say that to Eddie. He'd take you literally.' He looks terrified again.

'That's exactly what I intend him to do, once we have that film footage safely in my safe and not his. In the meantime, let's pay off your cash debts so you can pay off Jane.'

In the distance I can see the kids from the table behind us have started a food fight. I shiver. To think I could have been subjected to that twice over if I hadn't curbed Elise and gagged Jane.

'God, thanks Jason. I owe you big time.'

'You sure do. A life for a life.' He looks shocked. 'But don't worry, I doubt I'll ask you to cash in your chips for me. No, I mean your life from now on needs to be the most exemplary, dull and dutiful life anyone could live. No more spur of the moment crazies for you. If you're going to get past this one, old buddy, you're going to have to become Matthew the mundane. Your high jinks days are done.'

He stared at me, then nodded, humbled. That was the day I truncated him. I can see that now. The day I put out the fire of adventure I need him to have now. I need to rekindle it somehow, but Christ knows how!

My arms are numb from reaching up to rest them on the window ledge as I look longingly towards the distant wheat field and the even more distant Dog and Duck. Christ, I'd even put up with a kid's food fight raging behind me to be there right now, pint in hand, splinters prickling the backs of my legs alongside the lucky rest of the fortunate unwashed world carousing their good luck, like pigs in shit. Even the worst of the outside world was better than being stuck here, destined to cash in my chips without ever venturing outside again if things didn't work out with Fred.

Chapter 13

19th April 2029: Matthew

I stare at his back as he stretches up to lean against the high window ledge and stare out of the window. I am still reeling at what he's just said when he abruptly abandons the window and walks to the door, ignoring me. He bellows down the corridor, 'Wheelchair boy? Time to go.'

I can't bring myself to stand. I don't think I could even if I tried. I can hear footsteps scurrying along the corridor, and I can feel Jason's gaze on me, but my body is numb. If it wouldn't seal the deal on me as a coward, I would cry, right now – right here, in front of Jason and the wheelchair boy and anyone else who cares to pass by. It's not just my body that's numb, it's my whole life.

'What will you start with?'

'Huh?'

'What will you start with? Single organ tests or multi-functional processes?'

I shake my head. The words are like a foreign language to me. The only words I'm understanding right now are the ones with which Jason swung the wrecking ball at my life. I put my head in my hands and allow misery to swallow me whole. Damned if I do and damned if I don't. And the man I've always counted my best – and only – real friend has just melted away, together with my future. I've happily watched him collect the plaudits for all the work I've done for him, forlornly abandoned all hope of the girl I would have died for in favour of the one who's ruined my life because Jason decided Elise would make him a suitable wife, and lived in his shadow for years now, because he's been my best and only real friend – the friend who bailed me out when everyone else would have abandoned me. But he's not. I know, even in my most extreme moment, I would never have betrayed him. Even my reservations about the ForEver project were only that: reservations that I knew one way or another I would have found a way to shelve for Jason, but for this.

And yet because of this, I *have* to shelve my reservations. God, I should have talked to Elise, really, I should. But how can I now?

'I…' I shake my head again, trying to free the still rational part of my brain from irrational thought. 'I don't know.'

'Well, you need to make a decision and get on with it. Time is money.'

We exchange glances and my head starts to clear. The rational part of it is angry and starting to think in a way I've never thought before. The wheelchair lackey arrives at the door and Jason settles himself into the chair, arranging his long limbs so his feet are astride the foot rests. He points to the brown fluffy blanket still lying despondently on the floor. I retrieve it and place it politely on his lap.

'Maybe you'd better instruct me then, as I am now your lab lackey.'

His eyes narrow. 'We're not going to fall out over this, are we Matthew? Elise needs your support too, not just me.'

I back off, though reluctantly. Mild-mannered Matthew, my rational brain is telling me. Don't rock the boat. You can't afford to. 'I was joking.' I smile, hoping it's convincingly pathetic. It should be. I am. 'You know what you want to achieve, so you tell me what you think we should start with.'

He waves the wheelchair boy away. 'Just stand outside for five,' he directs. 'This is classified.'

'But Mrs Crane, she's waiting…'

'Then she can wait five minutes more.' The boy looks scared and disappears round the door again. 'Has he gone?' Jason sits woodenly in the wheelchair as if he really is an invalid. I nod as the door clicks shut. 'Alright, start with testing full functionality of Fred, organ by organ, then, as a composite. In the meantime, we need to start some independent work on brain scanning. Mine. Tell Jane you're going to be working overtime for the next few months, so you can only see the kids on Sundays. That's always traditionally been God's day of rest, hasn't it? It'll be ours too. We need a medical facility set up adjacent to this lab too.'

'A medical facility? What for?'

'Me. I'm moving in. If this thing starts to play speedway through my body, I'm going to need twenty-four-hour monitoring and attention. Get HR onto it. And facilities. That should do for the time being. I'll be back in tomorrow to see how things are progressing.'

He signals to me to open the door and the wheelchair lackey timidly re-enters.

'Sir?'

Jason looks at me and winks. 'Yep, I think we could make Sir. New Year's Honours and all that. Don't you agree, Matt?'

I manage a smile, but it feels more like a grimace. It seems enough for Jason though, and I watch him and the boy meander the corridor in the direction of reception, where presumably, Elise is waiting. She could have come to the lab to collect Jason, but I suspect I know why she didn't. I close the door and relish the sanctuary of the off-limits lab. I have always been a man with one master – firstly science and then latterly Jason. Now I am a man with two masters: Jason, and the rebellion gradually gathering momentum in my head and heart. I have never been a selfish man. I am simple in many ways. Jane calls me soft, weak – soft as shit when she's being abusive. I am, but I have to learn how to be hard now or Jason may not be the only one not to survive past the next six months.

I mop up the ink now threatening to invade the keyboard and scrub the worst of it off my fingers using the test-tube brush by the lab sink. My fingers remain a mottled blue-black as I accept my fate – a man marked by both guilt and weakness. I did not kill that security guard, but I know who did, and if I had to defend myself in court, my fate would be as pre-determined as Jason's. I have lived with that guilt for nearly eight years, telling myself ultimately it would make no difference who actually pulled the trigger – not to the widow or the kids. Dead is dead, and no amount of apportioning blame ever changes that. That is the pragmatist's view – Jason's. But come to think if it, it was probably Jason's advice that planted that thought in the first place. Mine veers more towards eternally damning myself for my part in any of it but, then again, what would have been the good in condemning myself by coming clean? Instead, I have buried myself in work, Jane – and the alternatives to damnation that she willingly provides – and gambling. The only thing I am any good at is work, where precise thought and painstaking research pay dividends. I still calculate the odds – almost every day; the odds of losing my keys, the odds of the traffic lights turning red before I get to them, the odds of keeping my bank account in the black this month, but I can't make the connection between their mathematic value and its application in life. No wonder I always lose at cards – at everything.

My phone buzzes unexpectedly and I pull it out of my pocket. It is Elise. My fingers fumble to accept the call, small aftershocks making me unsteady, heart pounding.

'Matthew?' Her voice is quiet, hushed even. 'How did it go? How is he?'

I can't help it. I am still angry – but more with myself for getting into this situation than with Jason. The rational side of my brain accepts that his behaviour is initiated by the drive to survive. The irrational, emotional side feels betrayed and used – and scared.

'Belligerent, bossy, determined,' I pause. 'And afraid…'

I can hear the catch in her voice. She turns it into a small explosive laugh.

'Mainly the same then. He's clearly upset you though.'

'Not upset…' I am lying. 'Unsettled. I'm worried about this – where it's going.'

'So am I. But Matthew, humour him for now. Even if it can't work, he needs the hope it can offer to cope with this.'

'I know. I know.'

'Got to go. He's here now. Talk later.'

The connection clicks off abruptly and I am left staring at Elise's name on the screen, and a world of silence in between. She's right, of course. Whatever else is wrong, Elise is right about this, but she doesn't know the whole story. Not by any means. And I do. Talk later. Should I? Should I tell her what so unsettles me? That to enable someone to live forever is like granting them ultimate power; over themselves – but also maybe over everyone and everything too if they are the only one with that ability. Even a saint might find it hard to stay saintly in those circumstances, mightn't they? And Jason is no saint…

Chapter 14

1st May 2029: Jason

I roll over onto my side but it makes no difference. The bed still feels lumpy and my body tense and irritable. I have enforced rest times, but sleep doesn't come to order – only The Big Sleep, in my case. My suite of rooms is next door to Lab 10; an outsize bedroom with medilam flooring, ready for when wheelchairs and surgical trolleys will be more the thing than soft furnishings and cold comfort. It has an en suite bathroom – again with more space than would be needed to have a small party. *For access*, the designer insisted. There's also a lounge and kitchen area, framed in soft rose. The designer wanted baby blue until he saw the expression on both mine and Elise's faces. She was good though, the designer. It took a mere six days from concept to completion. A new world in less than a week. She beat God. Now I've got to do the same. There is even an interconnecting door between my rooms and Lab 10, drilled through on day one, much to Matthew and Elise's consternation.

'But how will you get any downtime, knowing all that's going on next door?'

I tempered my reply to the drawn look on Elise's face, her normally soft and pretty features sharp and shadowed. She doesn't understand – still she doesn't understand, but then why would she? The death sentence is once removed for her.

'I'll find downtime when I need it. The docs will make sure of that.'

And they would. The team engaged – also on day one – and housed on the other side of my new home are giants in their fields. They track every blip and bleep I make with the plethora of equipment attached to me during test times. I could be a man-machine already. They impose rest times to keep Elise happy, but at times I wonder whether the rest times are also to keep Matthew sane. I am pushing him. God, am I pushing him! He bends but struggles on. I push him again. I know I am being someone other than myself – or maybe someone more than myself – but if I don't, I will be nothing. And I hate it – would give anything to be back home, but I can't be. It's here or nothing.

The place has a clinical feel to it, despite the floral drapes and the over-plush chairs. The oversized TV was Elise's idea. Why, I don't know. I've never watched much TV when I had time to waste – why would I do so now when it's in such short supply? Luxurious terminality. Maybe that is what I feel in this opulent prison suite I have voluntarily inserted myself into – that the world outside is already ceasing to exist to me other than as a prize to hold on to. My rapidly diminishing allotted sprinkling of sand is running through the glass cup of my hands and into the sea of time far too fast.

I imagine what is going on next door, in Lab 10: the caged rats having their brainwaves monitored in exactly the same way as mine, checking for deformities of structure and malfunctions of basic behaviour patterns, rogue cells that will rampage and transform life into death. The Parmensis seems to be stable in my own brain for the moment. The arrhythmia was a false alarm, it seems. It hasn't moved recently, but nor has it diminished. After the first false alarm that it might have migrated to my heart and caused heart failure – which proved, after all, to be actually a dramatic drop in blood pressure, caused probably by the Parmensis' itinerant meandering in my brain rather than my body – it appears to have become static, inert, maybe even dormant again. Yet the underlying principle remains; I am on borrowed time and this lender does not give loan extensions. By contrast, the rats appear to be on ForEver time. They are healthy, vigorous, and behaving precisely to order – more so than a control model would suggest they should, in fact. They are model rat citizens, seemingly destined to reach a ripe old age without any intervention, according to the latest body function extrapolations. That is why I ordered the latest test – that Matthew should be completing now – during one of my enforced rest times. But I cannot rest because I need to know.

I swing my legs over the side of the bed and stand. That brings a rush of blood to, and then rapidly away from, my head. Dammit! I sway and then sit clumsily back onto the bed, body crumpling in ungainly fashion. For the briefest moment, I understand what it might feel like to be Matthew – bumbling, stumbling Matthew – with a brain working nineteen to the dozen and a body that now routinely disobeys the simplest commands to make him seem blundering and gauche when in fact he's far from that. I allow the waves of to and fro in my head to settle before I attempt further movement. It's like carrying a too-full glass over uneven terrain and watching the meniscus of the liquid slop high, first one side and then the other – almost overflowing unless I consciously control it. I close my eyes and it slows to a gentle swaying motion. Now I can stand again. Bloody Parmensis! If it has to invade me, it can at least wait out its time to control me. Six months they said and, by God, I'm having them!

My legs bear my weight and the world remains reasonably steady this time, but the after-effect of the slopping glass is nausea. It takes me as much by surprise as the dizziness – me who has never had a day's illness in his life until now and for whom the idea of physical frailty has always been an excuse, not a reason. I swallow hard, but the gorge continues to rise no matter how I try to stop it. It reaches the back of my throat in a boiling mass of spume and I retch, splattering the remains of my lunch over my bare feet and forcing the medilam flooring into action. Its muted beige muddies with unseen activity. The pooled contents of my stomach soak into the flooring and the army of microscopic bacterial agents inhabiting the medilam devour whatever was solid but leave my toes still wet and soiled. I watch the process with surprise and then revulsion as biliousness transforms into self-disgust. God, what am I becoming? I can't stop my lips twisting miserably and behind them, what had originally been the regurgitation of my guts, is replaced by something far worse. Self-pity. It overwhelms me, great gouts of misery rolling over me like storm clouds pierced by lightning so that the ragged gaping holes release hot tears I can't control, let alone stop. I shiver and sob and I am a child again, watching my mother turn and wave to me as she saunters jauntily down the path. I call to her to come back. She never does.

No!

I have never been a wimp. That departing wave decided for me long ago that everything had to be treated as an obstacle to overcome – using whatever means necessary – or life would grind me to my knees before it even began.

This, though… this threatens to take my soul from me.

Fuck it! The damn Parmensis may take my life, but it will not take my dignity.

I wipe my nose across the back of my hand and force myself to step away from the bed. Fuck rest, fuck illness, fuck women who dropped you in it – and fuck death.

I pad into the shower, abandoning my tracksuit bottoms, t-shirt and

Rolex on the floor on the way in; a breadcrumb trail to oblivion. I turn the water to Full and the temperature to Cold. It splinters over me like icy shards and I gasp, but the shock does me good. Yeah, fuck the lot of it! I will not die. I will not give in. You will not beat me, any of you.

I step out and grab one of the fluffy beige towels Elise has arranged in such an artful way – an attempt to make the unattractive attractive, knowing Elise. Wrapping it round my waist I saunter back into the bedroom and rummage in a drawer for clean clothes. Belligerence has made me feel more normal and, with defiance, nausea seems to have given up. Even the blue that persistently threatens on the periphery of my vision has faded for the moment. An idea pokes its way through the desert sands and sends out a shoot. Maybe belligerence helps? I rummage through my memory much as I rummaged through the drawer for clothes. What had they said in the mandatory psych module we'd been obliged to pass before being allowed onto the neuro modules at university? So long ago, but it will all be filed away there somewhere…

Encouraging empathy has an inhibiting effect on violence, and therefore vice versa. Stimulation of neuronal circuits in one direction reduces their activity in another and empathy and violence are bi-located.

So… an increase in violent thought could suppress weaker inclinations? Be productive, rather than destructive? I dress, still pondering that one – and what might it do to the Parmensis.

Matthew is clearly pondering his own reverse-theory as I enter the lab by the connecting door. It smells fresher than my rooms, but then I doubt he's just puked in it. The connecting door clicks shut behind me and Matthew jumps. His screen shows he's deep into the latest lay on whichever game he's currently into.

'Oh!' He swings round and stares at me. 'You're still meant to be resting.'

'And you're meant to be working,' I joke. He colours up.

'I am.' He flicks screens and a graph appears on it, replacing the green baize and card spreads he'd been studying.

'Results?'

'Ah, only just. I haven't examined them yet. I was just clearing out some old stuff whilst I waited for them to complete their last run.'

I slide in alongside him and twitch the mouse, minimising the current screen so the previous one is revealed. He has a good five card stud hand, but useless for Texas Holdem.

'You'll lose,' I say.

'Shit,' he says.

'To catching you out or to losing?'

'Both.' He bites his lip. 'I am working, really, Jason. I *was* waiting for the tests to finish. And I knew you'd want to be in on the evaluation of them so…'

'How much have you lost so far?'

'Nothing. Nothing. It's only a pastime now. I just watch and calculate the odds. We agreed.'

'I know we agreed, but we also agreed you wouldn't do it at all – not even calculate odds.'

'And you agreed… OK, fair enough. But it's not what you think. I was just watching whilst I waited, really.'

He flicks the screen off. The dollar sign in the corner was on five thousand, but it was green. He'd been winning. It will simply go back in the pot now and he will lose it. But the earlier empathy I felt for him when I imagined what it was like to be Matthew, lurching through life from one financial crisis to the next without even a good woman behind him for comfort, has gone. Belligerence versus empathy. Fight versus flight. Fight wins every time – especially now. There are a thousand things buzzing around my head that I could say to him, but I won't. Not yet. I need him. It doesn't stop me being fucking furious that he's gambling on my time – with my time – even if this is meant to be a bit of downtime for both of us. But I need him. I funnel the anger into direction.

'Whatever. Shall we get on?'

He nods and maximises the test screen. We both study it.

'The latest test?'

'On there too.'

'With all the results?'

He adds layers to the graph. It paints an impressive picture. We absorb it silently. I sit back first. He is still poring over them. I may have missed something or it may simply be – Parmensis notwithstanding – I have absorbed the meaning of them quicker.

'So?' I ask after a while.

'So… they're promising,' he concedes.

'Promising? They're more than that! The iPS cells did it.'

'Ok, the iPS cells do appear to have had a positive effect on the efficacy of organ acceptance, but we're only a few days in on the latest round. We already knew that stem cells facilitate encourage regrowth, but can we say for certain they're actually the reason for progress here?'

I contain my frustration with difficulty. Laboratory grown stem cells that could be turned into anything may not be the answer to everything but they were more likely to be so than anything else. The first phase of 3D-printed rat brains had suffered from short life expectancy after all. My initial jubilation had died along with the rats when we'd dissected the first terminal case and exposed its shrivelled and starved brain. It had aged prematurely in a dramatically short time. The same with the next, and the next. We tried other organs, and the rats carried on trundling happily round their wheels but the brain, each time the same thing. This time …

'Nevertheless, we've not got this far before. Time to move past rats, I think?'

'No. Let's see how long this one manages. If it gets past a week, then the longevity test will be passed.'

'But I haven't got weeks to waste, Matthew. We could be moving on to trials on Fred whilst we're waiting for that.'

'With what? We haven't got a human brain to waste.'

'We've got a human brain to 3D. All this mapping we've been doing…'

'But we have no control. We only have functionality as it's been mapped now – with the Parmensis.'

We have spent the last weeks – in between my mild seizures – with me hooked up to MRI scans, recording responses and memories and neuro-electrical activity, using voxels to track the 3D structure of processes. We've repeated and repeated. We've worked up and established, based on the Blue Brain Project from twenty years back – now long since outdated, of course, but relevant nevertheless because of the base use of rat brains – a complete low-level structure of the underlying neural network captured, mapped and emulated on our computer system and a blueprint of its source code translated into cCrane, our own programming language. The human mind and the personal identity can, theoretically, be generated by the emulated neural network in an identical fashion to it being generated by the biological neural network – in cCrane. In theory, but more than that too. The results have been the same each time. The functions recorded are the same as those recorded in the brain in my head.

'So we wait for the Parmensis to migrate and then we repeat the process, but in the meantime, we start testing what we have. A mock-up. 3D-printed.'

'In Fred? But what if the Parmensis in the 3D-print migrates into

Fred? And the brain functions? We wouldn't ultimately be able to use him.'

'Then we need two Freds. One for testing, and one for ultimate use. And we also need to look at how we can force migration when the time is right.'

'But that would be like, like…'

'Speeding up the dying process?'

'Well, yes. And what if it doesn't migrate? What if it proliferates instead?' He frowns and his face mimics Elise's when I've caught her watching me when she thinks I'm not watching her. Something revs inside me. I won't be pitied.

'We won't know unless we try, will we?' My voice is rough with controlled rage. 'But ultimately if we can make it happen, it speeds up the resurrection process too,' I remind him. 'Jason gets to walk on water.'

He grimaces. 'I'm not sure about the allusion.'

'Why not? And if it works, think about where we'll be at then.'

'You'd throw it open to everyone?'

'Oh God no! Think about what it would be worth! No, I'd throw it open to the highest bidders.'

'And the people who couldn't pay?'

'Matthew, there's always been the haves and the have-nots. We've had this discussion before…'

'But life or death – wouldn't we have a duty to make it possible for others like you to be saved?'

'We would. As long as they could pay for it.' I am irritated by his philanthropic naivety and the way he can afford it. I cover his debts, keep his grasping ex-wife off his back – and mine – and cover his and hundreds of others' salaries. I own him – and them. In return I've been providing the world with advances in bio-technology that alleviate disability and suffering for hundreds of thousands – the Far East war victims, for instance. They all benefit from Crane Industries' cyborg prostheses, just like he benefits from Crane Industries' control over his debt-ridden life. 'This is costing millions, in case you haven't thought about it. Every penny I have is being sunk into this. If it doesn't work, not only will I go down, but so will the company – not that it will matter to me then.'

'Oh.' His face is a soft smudge of surprise. 'I didn't think… I'm sorry, Jason. I'm just not very financially savvy. I understand, really I do, but we still need to test it more, take our time. Make sure... Well you know what I'm saying; ethics, and control models and making sure…' He nods earnestly as if reassuring himself what he's saying is right. He smiles nervously and it's almost supplicatory, an anxious child waiting for his mother to turn and wave and come back when he calls...

'Oh, for God's sake, Matthew. Ethics! I waive ethics – and I'm the poor bastard being tested on. Look, these results are more than promising. They prove functionality and stability. There is no pattern change. We can move on with them.'

'But only in theory – not in practice. We have no idea how it would work with Fred.'

'The rat brains made the transition.'

'They're rat brains, with different induced pluripotent stem cells to that of a human brain. Much less complex.' He was always so much better than me at the bio side. I can feel my jaw tensing. My ear starts to ache with the pressure of not grinding my teeth in frustration. 'We can target rat brains far more accurately because they are relatively simplistic, but we have no idea if we've successfully activated whatever the rat's thought processes are. All we're monitoring are standard behaviour patterns. With a human brain, we'd need far more complex co-translational mitochondrial protein imports.'

I study him, folded in on himself and awaiting absolution. He's such a tentative soul, always seeking my approval. Making sure… Making sure for me. I should be ashamed of myself, but if I allow that, I'll give in to empathy and swathes of self-pity will suffocate me. I park attitude and attempt appeal.

'Then what are you suggesting?'

'More testing. A lot more testing.'

'Taking a lot more time.'

'Jason, I know you haven't much of it, but…'

'But?'

'But the Parmensis is still there.'

'Then we need to prompt it to move and repeat the process.'

'But how can you do that? You can't. You have to wait. We have to wait. Make sure. Anyway, why are we concentrating so much on the brain. I thought the idea was to get the Parmensis to move and then replace what it moved to.'

'For Elise's benefit, maybe.'

He's silent. I glance across at him. His face – usually an open book – is unexpectedly closed. I sit back in my chair, still studying the graph.

There is something more to this than Matthew's natural inclination to caution. He can't pretend we were only looking at a single prosthesis. He knew from the outset when I suggested we employ Fred that I was looking at something far more ambitious and the tests he's displaying on the graph are definitive. He may better on the bio side than me, but I can still read these results and I know what they mean. Our breakthrough is almost here, on the screen in front of us. My escape from death and damnation is potentially right here. My ear aches. I consciously lessen the pressure on my jaw, letting it hang slack, but my eyes ache too. The lines on the graph begin to merge too. I have to look away. I minimise the graph and behind it is another screen. Not poker, not test results, not lab reports. Elise. Her face beams at us from the screen, intense green eyes full of compassion, mouth curving in a beatific smile, a stray wisp of flaxen-blonde hair whipping across her lips as the wind takes it and throws it away. I know the photo like I know the lines and textures of my own hand. It is from our wedding photo – and Matthew's screen-saver, it seems.

'Who's a rat brain?' I ask, my voice glacial, looking across at him.

He frowns. 'I don't understand?'

'You have my wife as your screen-saver?'

'Oh, oh…' his face is puce. The hesitation and unnecessary delay suddenly makes sense. If I don't make it, Elise will be a widow. Available. And Matthew always liked Elise, but I got there first. I feel my fists closing and the nails digging into my palms. I want to punch him, throttle him, beat the life out of him for thinking about my wife in that way. She is mine – whether I'm living or dying. I wheel the chair round in a half circle and nudge his so that we are knee-to-knee. He rocks as it spins, mouth opening and closing wordlessly.

'You want to fuck her?'

'Jesus, Jason…' His words are strangled. The blue on the periphery of my vision is a purple haze, staining slowly red. 'It's your PC, not mine. She's your screen-saver, not mine.'

Matthew is straining against the back of his chair, legs straddling it awkwardly as he leans as far away from me as possible, and I am half risen, towering over him, tensing for impact when his words sink in. I drop back, stunned and confused. The chair wobbles as I make contact with it again and the wheels skid me away from the desk. We come to a full stop a few feet away. In the background the rats chatter in their cages and their exercise wheels trundle round and round, squeaking and rattling.

I can taste blood, its bitter tang making my lip curl. Matthew cowers away from me as I stand and lurch towards him, but my feet go nowhere. I sway awkwardly, rooted to the spot with the chair nudging the back of my knees until the purple haze loses its red tinge and fades back to blue. My legs give way and I sit suddenly and sharply back onto the chair. The jolt jars up my spine and into my jaw, and then I realise the blood I can taste is mine, oozing from the split my teeth have opened up in my lower lip. Distantly I can hear a voice, calling me.

'Jason, Jason…' Matthew looms up in front of me, moon-faced and concerned. I struggle to hear what he is saying but it is lost in the rattle of the rat's wheels, grinding and squeaking until they make me wince and want to cover my ears. I put my hands over my ears and shout to make the rat wheel noise go away but it merely gets louder. Matthew is at the end of a tunnel. His mouth is opening and shutting but now there is only silence. No rat wheels, no screeching. Nothing at all. He comes into focus and the tunnel levels out – widens to encompass the lab, its ceiling lab, the overhead striplight a thin white line I have just crossed. And Matthew. Mouthing at me. I place my hands palm down on the floor and stroke its cold, hard surface. Gradually sensation spreads the length of my body. My shoulder blades dig into the floor and my head starts to loll sideways until I correct it. I am flat out. Flat out. This isn't me. This can't be it.

'Help me.'

I repeat it because it doesn't seem to come out the first time. My mouth moves and my tongue forms the sounds, skittering along the back of my teeth and caressing their serrated edges, but the words don't exist. They are without form and void – like the earth was before creation, according to Elise and the Bible. I say them again even though Matthew is already extending his hand, reaching for mine. He mouths something back and I read his lips.

'I am, old buddy. I am. Are you OK?'

No. I am not. I am deaf.

The Parmensis has migrated. This is either very good or very bad. For the moment, I can't decide which.

Chapter 15

1st May 2029: Jason

I watch Matthew mouthing at me. The arrival of the Parmensis in the superior temporal gyrus of my temporal lobe puts paid to hearing anything for the moment. Or perhaps it's settled in the parietal and frontal lobes of my cerebral cortex and is interfering with the processing of sound stimuli. Only an MRI will tell us for sure. At least I won't hear the bloody thing, which despite the claims, is uncomfortably loud even through noise-cancelling headphones. I have my own internal noise-canceller this time, if only of external sound. I attempt to stand but Matthew pushes me back down with surprising force.

'No chance,' he mouths at me. 'If it's moved, you're in the wheelchair until we know what's happening.'

I lie back, temporarily accepting this small part of my fate. It makes sense to be cautious because this migration was unexpected, to say the least. Lying on the cold floor of Lab 10, I wait patiently for wheelchair boy to arrive, marvelling at how I manage to do so. He arrives not long after Matthew's call, sheepish and anxious and I allow him and Matthew to heave me upright and position me carefully in the chair. Neither of them say anything – not that it matters – but Matthew avoids my eyes too. Or maybe I avoid his. His awkwardness has become mine for once. I can't hear myself, but I hope I've said it anyway.

'Kohn – you should tell her, just in case.'

Matthew nods. 'OK,' he mouths back, and fishes his phone out of his pocket. I can see his mouth working but my lip-reading skills are not yet good enough to work out the detail of what he is saying. That I'll have to address. I use the remainder of the journey to the MRI figuring out what Kohn is and isn't allowed to know if the news is bad.

I'd rather not remember Jane whilst trapped inside a machine, but there it is – you can't always control memories, and there is a certain similarity to being silently suffocated by a machine and silently suffocated by Jane. The silence of the Parmensis' making covers me like a blanket as I slide towards the mouth of the MRI machine and close my eyes on both the approaching cylinder and Matthew's silent posturings, the way Jane postured at me that day – the day it started with her. It was the same day that we first envisaged Fred, more or less, and she was mouthing instructions in the same way Matthew is at me right now…

'Turn it off!' It filters through the roar of the engine. 'For God's sa–'

I switch off the engine.

'SAAKE... Oh...'

'You were saying?'

She was ten years younger then, of course. Rounded where she's now angular. Soft where she is now brittle. Did Matthew do that to her or did she do it to herself in the process of destroying him?

She laughs self-consciously.

'I didn't expect you to turn it off so quickly. Matthew tells me you're stubborn. I thought it would take a lot more persuasion.'

'Oh, he does, does he? I'll have to have words with my best buddy then.'

She laughs again and her teeth are small pearls, neat and virginal against the red of her lips. She slowly licks her lips and I involuntarily harden as she does so.

'Your best buddy, huh? Oh well, now I have two men to persuade when I want something done. Matthew and his best buddy boss.' She winks salaciously at me and she is so unlike Elise I am intrigued they can even be acquaintances, let alone friends. The pearls morph into shark's teeth instead, threatening to split her lips and draw blood, equally – if not more – stimulating.

'And what do we need to be persuaded to do?'

'Oh, I'll have to think about that... carefully...' she winks again. 'I'm Jane by the way.'

'I guessed.'

She laughs, throwing her head back so I can study her long neck and the way her blouse falls away to expose her cleavage. Of course, I know Jane – Elise's best friend – but the Jane I've experienced up until now has always been eclipsed by Elise, or maybe muted by her? Or maybe it's just that I've never been alone with her before? This is Jane, full throttle –a harlot with precious jewels she is so clearly prepared to barter... She is so obvious I am both appalled and fascinated. Is it merely that you don't have something that makes you curious about it, or is there some other equation that causes havoc in the stream of logic at times? I don't want Jane, but the fact that she belongs to Matthew yet I can still have her makes me want her. She compounds it by slipping into the passenger seat next to me and crossing her legs so that I can see as far up the delicate inner thigh as I need to imagine what is beyond it.

'He's out at the moment. So you've got me.'

The promise is in both her eyes, and her voice so I rev the engine and we drive. Where, it doesn't matter. I let the engine have its head and we purr, throatily, beyond the suburbs and into the start of the green belt – far enough away to be anonymous and close enough to be easily recalled. The rows of red brick houses that surround the outer ring of the city give way to farther flung dwellings, not quite solitary, but surrounded by well-groomed shrubs and spreading oak and beech trees that look older than Methusalah. The kind of house I aspire to, one day. Moneyed, privileged, self-satisfied. Red and grey and crowded becomes green and pleasant and singular. Even the air seems thinner, lighter, more uplifting. I am driving a pearl-toothed harlot beyond Sodom, into Gomorrah, and it feels good. For the moment I don't have to check my principles, or watch my language so I don't offend Elise, golden-haired angel that she is. I can be a disciple of Mammon, a worshipper of all that is unwholesome and unashamedly enjoy it with this wanton slut.

And I did. There, in a field, under a tree, like Oberon with Titania, or a dog with a bitch. We don't even undress. It is quick, urgent, necessary and incredible. Do I smell the sharp sweetness of the crushed grass beneath our bodies? Do I savour the woody undernotes of the loam we lie on when we are spent? Do I relish the pinch of her pearly teeth before I move on to be mangled by her other more dangerously insidious mandibles? Do we talk, discuss, learn about each other? No. Do I care that this is Jane, my best buddy's woman, and my wife's best friend?

Fuck, no.

But here the suffocation begins too. Her of me and me of her. We persistently destroy each other and all that is good in our lives every day that follows, never talking, never sharing, never loving. Just fucking. It isn't love. It's furious sex.

Incandescent with rage? We've all heard that phrase before and it's perfect for the kind of sexual rage we act out every time we connect. If you imagine magnesium, flaring and brilliant, burning down to a white dust and then disintegrating, that is us. Now we are dust, burnt out, spent, destroyed, but the day we first met, and until Jane spoilt it all, we were incandescent.

I open my eyes and the cylinder still surrounds me, noiselessly spinning as it records where my karma is settling now. Jane would laugh so hard if she could see me in here. Maybe she would even mouth the words she should have said that day we first met. Whatever, all I have now is the memory of sweat and overhanging boughs and a dog and a bitch on heat. Do I deserve the day when, four years later, she threatened to destroy me by telling Elise unless I paid for the kid – whether it was mine or not? Of course, I do. I had just condemned my own to annihilation. I deserve much, much worse, and perhaps this is it now?

Karma.

Thank God Elise doesn't know.

Chapter 16

1st May 2029: Elise

The children are bubbling over, buzzing with impatience, or is that my phone buzzing in my bag? I'm torn. Check or keep in check? There are only fifteen minutes to the bell, but the TA, Candice, has had to dash to the loo and I realise now I've been relying on her all morning, not fully functioning as I should – as I owe to these kids.

'Won't be a minute – women's problems,' she mouths at me as she departs. That means she's unlikely to make it back before the bell – we all know Candice's women's problems of old – and I'm going to have to keep order on my own until they're allowed to rampage the playground. It's what spring does to them; March winds and spring sunshine send dogs and kids crazy. Normally I'd like that, but today my patience is as thin as their self-control. I dither near the desk, straining to hear above the classroom hubbub and wondering whether to simply grab my bag out of the bottom drawer and listen simultaneous with trying to control the rebelling forces. A scuffle is breaking out in the corner by the water play. There is water all over the floor and Esme James is crying. In the fraction of a second before her first howl splits the general babble, I hear it quite clearly. The phone is buzzing. Oh God, not now – please not now. I save Esme from the water monster and send Toby – the water monster – over to the Duplo.

'Build me a tower,' I tell him. 'A giant tower big enough for Rapunzel to let all of her hair down.'

'She's a girl.' His face twists in disdain.

'And for Iron Man to need his rocket boosters to fly over.'

'Oh, yeah!' Disdain becomes enthusiasm and I set Esme on mopping the floor and organising the other girls round the water play, the phone still humming in my brain. Calm is restored and the fairy story theme remains intact in both the classroom and my lesson planning. The girls set sail on a voyage to a far place where princes and princesses live for ever and I return to the one where they don't. I go back to the desk and my still buzzing phone. It's the one only Matthew uses because the other one is turned off – as it always is in class.

'Elise?' Matthew's voice is strident, the catch of panic grating it into snagging threads. 'You need to get in here quickly.'

The voicemail lasts less than ten seconds but it is enough. I do something I said I would never do – I abandon my class. Back hugging the wall just outside the classroom door and foot stuck sideways in the doorway to keep the door ajar, I allow chaos to reign in both the inner and outer spaces I'm inhabiting.

'Matthew. What's wrong?'

In the classroom, the noise level is steadily rising. It thrums in my chest alongside the alarm Matthew's voicemail brought with it.

'Oh God, Elise. This is incredible! It's shifted – the tumour has shifted. Moved on.'

'Oh my God! Moved on? Gone?' My chest feels as if all the breath has been sucked from it and my legs are barely holding me.

'Oh, no. Not gone. It still in his brain, but this is so exciting. Jason is hyped.'

'Hyped?' The thrumming in my chest changes vibration.

'That it's shifted. It means his theory is possible. If it moves far enough, we could isolate it from his brain, and then – well… They're organising an MRI as we speak. We'll know more then.'

'Oh.' A vision of Fred replaces the vision of Jason, prone and pale. I shiver. 'So where is it now?'

'Well, his eyesight is fine, but his hearing is affected now so it's clearly shifted or expanded from the occipital to the temporal lobes. Jason keeps going over and over it like he's obsessed. What did he do. What did I do. Short-term memory is controlled by the temporals too.'

'But he's hyped, not distressed?'

'Oh no, definitely hyped. This changes everything. And he's stable as far as we can see at the moment, but I thought you should know...' He trails off. Maybe he can detect my suppressed irritation. Maybe he can even hear the tumult from the classroom now. 'Do you want to come in?'

'I'm in school, Matthew. In class, in fact. And they're running riot in there right now. I'll come in as soon as I've sorted cover if Jason's OK.'

'OK.' He sounds surprised, and I feel judged.

'I can't just up and leave thirty children.'

'No, no, of course not. But Jason – '

'Did Jason ask you to call me?'

'No, but I thought you should know, since you're his wife.'

I kick the door wider and prepare to step back inside, before the chaos inside extends outside too. Whichever world I'm inhabiting, it seems I am out of sync with it. My temper flares. but Matthew doesn't deserve it and to be honest, it's probably not even aimed at him. although I don't know for sure who it is aimed at. Me? Jason? Fate?

'Matthew, Jason shuts me out of most things that go on there. I have to accept that, and I always do – jumping to whatever tune he calls but sometimes, my own personal commitments mean something too. I will be there within the hour, but now I need to go and stop World War Three.'

'Of co—'

I don't even wait for him to finish. I click the phone off and stuff it in my pocket just as the Deputy Head rounds the corner of the corridor.

'Everything all right?'

I know that phrase of old too – it's as euphemistic as Candice's, 'won't be a minute...' Our relationship isn't antagonistic, but it isn't comfortable either. Charlotte is my deputy, and this is one of my token classes for the week. It's hers the rest of the time, but I wanted to keep my hand in, just like she did; me to retain my hands-on skills, her to acquire management ones – and my job, if possible. All of life is an accommodation, isn't it? That's how we get by. Accommodating, sharing, caring. I just seem to do far more of it than I should.

'Charlotte, perfect timing,' I sweep her into the room with me. I haven't been married to Jason for eight years without learning some of his tactics, even if I rarely use them. Charlotte deserves them though, if not the lie, or my misdirected irritation. 'I've just been called in to a relative with a terminal condition and I need to go right now. We've been continuing the fairy story theme you started. Can you be the happy ending? Sorry.'

'Oh,' her face reflects the chaos of the classroom but under the circumstances all mileage is lost for her. Apart from goodwill. 'Of course, Elise. You go.' She smiles and her forty-something lines briefly pierce the carefully powdered make-up.

'Thank you.' I make my smile ripe with conveyed sentiment. 'I appreciate it.' And I do. Whatever her ulterior motives, I do need her – and even more so now. Accommodation again.

'I hope everything's all right,' she adds – I imagine as an

afterthought, given the sudden flit of awkwardness across her face.

'Who knows?' I shrug. And it's true. Who does know? If Jason's theory is possible, will it be all right? Not even Matthew was convinced of that, and Matthew is Jason's shadow. Of course, no one outside of Jason, Matthew and me know anything. If Jason is to resurrect, he can't be seen to die first – until he's ready to.

'Elise,' she calls after me.

'Yes?'

'I am here if you need me,' she adds more softly. For a moment I am so tempted to tell her the truth, but my fingers still smart from the burning Jane gave them when I trusted her. It seems safer to have no best friends these days – other than my paint and my canvases.

'Thanks,' I reply, nodding.I collect my bag and coat, instruct the office staff that I am called away, and head for my car. Their sympathetic looks send me on my way too quickly for them to see the tear-pricks their empathy causes, but they make me feel weak and unready for what I'm going to find when I get to the lab. It's always kindness that kills. I can take Charlotte's hard-bitten ambition any day, it's compassion that takes my ability to get through this from me. Luckily my stinging eyes could just as easily be attributed to the crispness of the wind, whipping up a mini dust storm from the road on this bright but blustery day.

The school car park – what there will be left of it – is still out of bounds because of the building work the local authority has finally sanctioned. Three new classrooms and an adventure playground will be engulfed by next year's increased intake of four-year-olds, and the overspill from our already bulging Year One in September. The class I've just abandoned will be one of the beneficiaries. Maybe World War Three will be less likely with better facilities? In the meantime, parking is wherever you can find it. I made a decision to make something of the dregs of my life when Jane told me – and I have. I was the youngest Headteacher in the county when I was first appointed. I suppose my staff would describe me as dedicated. If only they knew all I really am is hanging on to anything I can grab to maintain some kind of belief in myself. There had to be some part of my life that isn't overshadowed by Jason. My job and my painting have become what keep me sane, but I suspect not even they will help me with this.

I cross the main road and head for the side road I left my car in this morning. My head is full of what Matthew said. The tumour has migrated. Jason is hyped. The theory could work. Jason didn't ask him to ring. He thought he should—

'Excuse me!'

'Oh, I'm sorry.'

I almost collide with the young woman and the pram. How could I have not seen her? Usually my radar is set to red alert for any pram or buggy. We dodge around each other and she smiles indulgently as I can't help but sneak a peek at the blissful babe, fast asleep inside the pram. Baby blue. Oh, God, it's a boy. Soft brown eyelashes fanning out across porcelain cheeks, rosebud lips blowing tiny bubbles.

'Three months now,' she tells me proudly. My heart lifts and sinks at what will never be mine.

'Oh, he's lovely.'

The wilful tears return and I stumble away, head wobbling like a nodding dog in the back of a car. She must think I'm a crazy. I can imagine her eyes burning into the back of me as I flounder down the street, head down and eyes fixed on the pavement. She'd be right. I am – crazy with grief for all that should have been and isn't. I am crazy with grief for a little baby boy with batwing eyelashes and a blue bonnet on his head, for a noisy four-year-old who splashes water at little girls but runs to me when he grazes his knee. For a teenager who proudly shows me his exam results and shares his dreams with me. For the man he'd become. For the man I'm losing, and for whom I've already given all of that up. Jason and the child I might have had become one and I choke with misery for both of them.

With relief, I spot the sleek silver-grey of my car and fumble for the door. I can't see anything but a blur of monotone now – all grey: grey pavement, grey road, grey car, grey life. I find the handle and bundle myself inside the car. Jason insisted on tinted windows for the odd occasions he might drive it. My husband likes his privacy – even from me. Maybe especially from me, who knows more of him than anyone else. Much as I love him I thought it a pretentious idiosyncrasy even then – joked he wasn't *that* famous, yet – but now I'm grateful for it. Inside the car I am cocooned from the challenges of the world and for the first time since that day in the hospital when I found out what was really wrong with Jason, I cry. It is not the wild storm it was then, more a hopeless acceptance of what is, draining me until there are no tears left. I am a reservoir desiccated by the raw heat of an infinitely long summer, a desert in which the oasis has shrivelled, a brittle shell of a woman, a husk. I am not even sure how much I've cried when I stop, only that there is nothing left. I am not grieving for a man who doesn't even think to tell me when a major life event happens in the minuscule space of time he has left with me. I am grieving for myself, and I hate myself for that.

The phone in my bag buzzes again, and I fumble for it. Of course, it is Matthew. It can't – or wouldn't – be anyone else.

'He *is* asking for you now.'

'Are you telling me that on his orders?'

'No!' He is shocked. I can hear the dismay in his voice, crackling across cyber space to me. I am being unfair, trapping him in the middle of us, but the no-man's land isn't for anyone to inhabit but Jason and me. When I married Jason, I undertook with God to love and honour him until either of us died. However angry or disappointed I am now, I still owe on that promise.

'I'm sorry, Matthew. That wasn't fair.'

'It's OK. I do understand.' His voice is soft and kind, and it is going to bring me to tears again. And yet I am angry too – how ridiculous to be angry when in fact I am sad. 'And he really is asking for you. I've said you're on your way.'

'I am,' I rest my head against the headrest and the soft leather of the seat embraces me. 'I just need to gather myself a bit.'

'Are you OK?'

'I'm tired, Matthew. Tired and confused.'

'Confused about what?'

'What Jason wants to do.'

'Ah.' There is silence. I shouldn't have said that. Not to Matthew, Jason's best friend – Jason's all-but clone where scientific breakthrough is concerned. I am about to retract it and move on when he surprises me with, 'So am I.'

I sit upright. 'I thought you were all for this?'

'I'm all for him surviving. It's just how…' The words hang in the void between us. I wish I could see his face. 'Look, come on in and calm him down. He's getting agitated. We should have some results through soon too and we can talk more about this then,' he pauses again and adds meaningfully, 'when he's resting.'

'OK.' I rub my eyes and the make-up comes off on my fingers, tarry and black. I want to ask him to elaborate but I know I mustn't. This must come from him. I end the call and pull the sun visor down to check in the vanity mirror. My face is a blurred version of itself. I am a blurred version of myself. What am I becoming? I should be behind my husband all the way, desperate for him to beat this thing and survive, whatever that may mean – but here I am sharing doubts with his best friend who is being as hypocritical as me. I rest my elbows on the steering wheel and my head in my hands.

A clattering outside makes me straighten and I peer out of the windscreen to identify the source of the noise. In front of me, an old woman is hovering at the edge of the kerb. She must be ninety if she's a day, straggling white hair blowing around her in a fine chalky mist and legs as bowed as a Bosun's chair back. I'm surprised she can even stay upright. The slightest puff of wind looks as if it could blow her over, and yet she battles on. She's a tramp – a street woman – dragging her trolley behind her with all her possessions in it. Life in a bag. Something must have fallen from it and clattered to the ground because now she is easing herself double to pick it up. The effort must be immense, painfully immense, judging by the way her face contorts. I strain to make out what it is she is retrieving, but I can't. She grimaces as she pockets it and edges her way upright again, clinging to the handle of the trolley and panting. Suddenly it is the most important thing in the world to know what was worth so much effort, so much pain. What is ever worth so much pain? I'm tempted to jump out of the car and call her back from her tortoise-like progression along the road to ask her story, but then I'd have to tell her mine. And what is mine? The girl who was going to raise a brood of kids and live on a farm, but instead lives in a penthouse, with no friends, and broods over other people's kids whilst purging her disappointments in paint? Put like that, I'm horrified – how soulless, how sterile my life is! All the possessions and paintings in the world can't make up for happiness. I miss Jane! Even if she betrayed me, I miss having a friend to despair or delight to so much it hurts.

The old woman is almost out of view now. Ahead of me the road is empty. Whoever I am, I have to be more than this. I have to be Jason's wife for Jason and a whole person for both of us, even if Jason doesn't survive. However confused and disillusioned I feel, I can't even begin to conceive how badly he feels. And I need to watch Matthew, in case he is being Jason's ears now, as well as his eyes.

I arrive at Crane industries determined to be cautious but Matthew pre-empts what I'm planning to say when he greets me in reception. He is looking harassed, tie wonky and hair untidy.

'Look… What I said on the phone…'

'It's OK. I understand, too.' And I do. I really do. We are both faulty.

We are both weak and afraid. We don't have Jason's giant heart and enormous determination. That's why he leads, and we follow.

'Then, shall we agree not to say anything more about it for the moment?' He looks relieved, running his fingers through his hair and smiling awkwardly.

'Yes, absolutely. How is he now?'

'Rambling,' he grimaces.

Matthew leads the way and I see the guilt dripping from his shoulders – much as it must be dribbling from mine. I just hope Jason's senses aren't compensating for each other too much, otherwise he will see it too. I needn't have worried. Matthew is right. He is rambling. The lights have been dimmed and the curtains half-pulled, but the room still has a clinical feel to it. Even blush pink can't mask illness and imminent death. Jason is hooked up to an ECG again. I hadn't noticed it in the room before, but it must have been there. Everything Jason could possibly need has been incorporated into this suite of rooms. It's steady, though – normal sinus rhythm. That phrase will be in my dreams soon, I think. It bleeps gently, a continuous reminder that at least one thing about my husband's health is normal, even if nothing else is. Jason looks small in the big bed; small and white. His skin has that waxy look it had before in the hospital and I've come to realise since then that it is how it becomes when he is exhausted, but he isn't still like he was then; he is twisting and turning as if he's been possessed by a dervish.

'Oh my God, it's like a scene from *The Exorcist*!' I can't help it. Jason's love of iconic horror has long since stopped scaring me. Now it merely repulses. The words are out seconds after I've thought them and before I can stop them. I put my hand to my mouth, but they are already circulating the room. One of the medics gives me a strange look, then realises who I am and modifies it hurriedly.

'He can't hear you,' Matthew assures me. He nudges me forward as he begins to back away. 'I'm sorry, I need to go. Jane is kicking up again. School play or something like that. It will be awful, but she says I have to go with her, even though Katie wouldn't mind if I didn't.'

His expression is comical – an upside-down clown with attitude. A reluctant reluctant. That will be Jane's doing, though. I suspect Matthew would relish going if it weren't for her.

'Go and see the school play,' I say, wishing I had dire childish theatrical concoctions to claim to want to avoid in my world. Except I would revel in them the way I think Matthew is revelling in them other than that he has to attend them with Jane.

'Thank you.' And I know he means it. 'Sign language and lip reading.' He nods towards Jason. 'As you'd imagine, he can probably do both.'

I smile, even though it's not funny. 'Of course.'

The medic who gave me the dirty look makes room for me by the bed. Behind me the door clicks shut and Matthew has gone.

'Is it another fit of some kind?'

'No,' the medic shakes her head. Young, blonde, ice-cool pretty. No lines or wrinkles yet. Under other circumstances I might have wondered at the reason for her being hired, and whether Jason had ulterior motives, but I have seen all the medical staff's qualifications and they are all, without fail, specialists in their field – no matter how young or old. This one's name badge reads Frieda Kohn, Neurologist. The one in charge, if I remember rightly. She has a folder full of paper in her hand, 'He's just restless. Agitated.' Her Germanic roots betray themselves in her clipped speech.

'And the latest MRI?'

She glances at the folder she is holding. 'For discussion with Mr Crane when he is up to it.'

'Not his wife?'

She has the grace to look embarrassed. 'I'm sorry. Those are his instructions.'

'But has it actually moved? The Parmensis? Not expanded, but moved?'

'Yes.' She has a way of dipping her head as she speaks and it bobs up and down hypnotically as she replies. 'It has moved. And will perhaps move again, so we monitor him.'

'Why the ECG then? Will it show up on the ECG?'

'No, but his body's response to it will. We cannot track it as it moves, Mrs Crane. We can only identify where it's moved to via neural stimuli and the reactions they produce – or lack of them – then confirm with an MRI.'

She tucks the folder firmly under her arm as if she thinks I will try to steal it, and retreats to the anteroom attached to the bedroom that Jason had created for the medics to have their pow-wows in. Their accommodation is on the other side of it. I'm irritated that she will tell me this much but not explain the ramifications of what has happened. I sit alongside the bed and watch Jason twisting and turning. As I watch him, I begin to see a pattern to his movements. It's like he's dodging and weaving in his sleep, a subconscious boxer. It makes me want to cry again. He is fighting something he can't beat, but still he fights on. That is the remarkable thing about Jason – aside from his charm, good looks and intellectual abilities – he is so damned determined, he simply wears the opposition down. In all the years I have known him, he has never given up, and he has never been beaten. The only thing that ever beat him was his mother leaving him, and even that he would argue he rose above. The one and only conversation we've ever had about her comes back to me as if we were having it right now.

'You were talking in your sleep last night. Rosalie, you kept saying.'

He looks startled at that – even puts his coffee cup down – then pretends to fiddle with the e-post notifications to cover his tracks.

'Really? So, you've just found out the name of my mistress,' he laughs, putting the e-post back into its original pile after he's carefully distributed it between him and me. I leave it. I've learnt to do that. The more you push, the less you get with Jason. He looks up suddenly and catches my expression. I try not to let the cracks show, but they do sometimes. 'And that was a joke, Elise,' he adds softly. 'It really was a one-off.'

'I know,' I say. Funny, I hadn't even been thinking about that when I mentioned the name. He's never admitted who with, even though I know, of course – but he doesn't know I know. How do relationships - especially with people you love – get so complicated? 'Rosalie is your mother's name, isn't it?'

'How do you know that?'

I half wish I hadn't said it, but it is too late to turn back now. Sometimes the need for the truth is just too much to deny. He frowns and leans back; starts fiddling with his coffee cup instead. The e-post pile has my name on the top of it, and a notification from the local authority – "Re: building matters" – but it will have to wait. He's never actually acknowledged it before, but I know the reason our speedboat was re-named from 'The Rosalie' to 'The Elise', despite it being the name that first drew his attention to it. My old family solicitor made it his business to find out as much as he could about my husband once I knew for certain he was having an affair. Jason doesn't know it, but it's the same one who makes life a misery for Matthew on Jane's behalf now. But we approach things completely differently, Jane and I – even though she was my best friend. Jane thinks in terms of vengeance; I think in terms of forgiveness. The difference between us – and between me and Jason – is that I believe in turning the other cheek, in good overcoming evil; in God. And, after all, if I forgave Jane for having an affair with my husband, I have to forgive my husband, too, with open eyes. But Jason doesn't know that either. He only knows I know he was unfaithful, with someone. We left it there. He confessed, I forgave, we carried on. Me with my husband, but without my best friend...

'You must have told me.' I wait, watching his face close in, clam shut.

'I doubt it. I've never talked about her.'

'No, but maybe you should?'

'There's nothing to tell.'

'There's always something to tell about a parent.'

'Not this one.' He hands me the top e-post notification. 'Looks like you might have got your way after all.'

'No, Jason,' I reply. 'I haven't got my way on anything. Never. Not even in sharing your past, despite agreeing to forgive it.'

It's the most I've ever pushed him, and it's a dangerous game to play.

'Oh, I see. Tit for tat? Your forgiveness in return for another confession? You know I don't believe in that sort of thing, Elise. You accept me as I am. A sinner.'

'And I have, but can't you trust me even a little for that? At least I would feel I mattered more than... well, whoever it was...'

'You know you do! That's why I'm still here.'

He picks up the next e-post on the pile. It is for him. An invitation to something to which, no doubt I will be expected to accompany him. The nice little wife in the background. The bluestocking with the old family money that got him started in the first place. "She was a Capell, you know," they say behind my back – with that knowing look. "The family dates back to the days of Elizabeth the first and the Earl of Essex. The only reason he married her – to claim some nobility," is what they don't say, but it's not true: Jason married me for love, not money – his kind of love – and I took it gratefully.

'Then make me believe it, so I stay too.' To say that surprises him would be like saying Newton didn't come up with the law of gravity. It surprises me too. 'Tell me what is so bad about your mother that you never want to talk about her.'

And equally surprisingly, he does. All of it. It is probably the main reason I stay, because, finally, I understand. I understand what it is to be

Jason Crane and so rejected you can never find enough acceptance to make up for it...

'Where's Matthew?'

I jump. I have been so lost in the past I have almost forgotten the present – and the future. I stroke his arm. The merest touch until I know it's welcome.

'He had to go. School play duties.' He frowns at me and then I remember he can't hear me. I repeat it, overemphasising the pronunciations as he reads my lips.

'Oh.' He nods. 'Jane?'

I nod back. I let my fingers rest on his forearm. He hasn't rejected or acknowledged them yet.

He pulls himself upright, dislodging my hand, and studies the ECG still following its steady wave form. 'Back on that old malarkey, then.'

I nod again. 'How are you feeling?' I mouth. It seems stupid to say it aloud if he can't hear me.

'OK,' he nods again. He breathes in and out and flexes his shoulders, twisting his neck to loosen the muscles. I imagine all that shadow fighting has left him with an aching torso.

'You were very restless,' I mouth. 'Like you were fighting someone.'

'Yeah,' he laughs. His voice is overloud to my silent conversation. 'I was. Myself. Damn Jane. I need Matthew here. He needs to hook me up.'

'Hook you up?'

'Yeah, to the computer. Record some patterns for me. Monitor what's happening.' He taps his head. 'In here.'

'They've already done that. That young German doctor has the results.'

'The MRI? Not that. What's really happening. Matthew knows what I mean. Brain waves.'

'No, you need to rest.' I study his face – like a mother would. He looks tired despite the amount of time he's been asleep.

'What would you know about it?' His chin is jutting, and his eyes are steely. Jason in fighting form.

I rein in the hurt, reminding myself it's his natural form of defence. 'I know how you look, and you look tired.'

His expression softens like wax melting. 'No amount of rest will change that, Elise. It's not physical, it's mental.'

We contemplate each other. When all is said and done, we are all always only strangers who know each other intimately. I do not know what is going on in Jason's head, just as he doesn't know what is going on in mine, except now, maybe I ought to probe.

'Do you want to talk about it?'

'What, dying?' he asks roughly.

'I didn't mean that. About your fears, your hopes – anything.'

I can feel the tears prickling at the sharpness of his response, but I won't let him see them. I am good at that now.

'Sorry,' he says, testily. 'It's easier if I don't acknowledge it. Just pretend it's all fine.'

'I'm sorry, too,' I mouth. 'I shouldn't have asked.'

'I'm tired,' he says, suddenly.

'Do you want me to go?'

'Would you mind, hun? I think you're right. I need to rest. Tomorrow's another day – I hope.'

I gather my things and prepare to leave. He proffers a cheek and I kiss it, like a child kissing an aged uncle, lips brushing but barely touching. It feels warm and vibrant, full of life. I cannot quite believe I am kissing my husband in this way. We are more than miles apart, we are aeons, when we should be so close a slip of paper wouldn't be able to squeeze between us. Just as I stand, he catches my hand. 'It's OK,' he says. 'You'll see. It'll be OK.'

I nod, wordlessly. I can't trust myself to reply.

'Will you open the curtains before you go? I want to look at the stars until I sleep.'

Back home, I too leave the curtains open and watch the stars. But I don't sleep. How can I sleep when sleep brings nothing but nightmares – the same as living does. As a child, I thought of the stars as God's toys. Someone must have called them that and I latched on to it. A shooting star was one God had tossed to earth for us to play with. A blessing to thank him for. Now I see that was wrong. *We* are God's toys, and a shooting star is simply one that has been tossed aside to die. There are many things Jason has done wrong – some to me – but he is still the brightest star in my sky, falling, falling, falling; tossed aside to die. How can I thank God for that?

Chapter 17

1st May 2029: Jason

The lab is cool and anticipatory this morning, or maybe it is that I have a sense of impending drama waiting to unfold in it. It is silent too, but that is more to do with me than the place itself. It is too early for Matthew to be here, even with my early start requirement. I have time to gather myself and plan. What next. What next, Parmensis?

I flip the switch on my PC and the screen flickers into life. Unaccompanied by the usual pings and beeps, my calendar reminds me what day it is. Not only day, date and year, too but the significance is the day and date. I sit heavily on the chair and allow them to sink in. Of all the ironies, the 1st May this year is also on the same day of the week it fell on all those years ago. Tuesday 1st May.

'Mummy...' Anna tries to follow her, but she shoos her away.

'Not this time, Anna. Stay with your brother.'

Mummy is standing at the end of the path, halfway through the gate, hat perched rakishly to one side, tailored coat nipped in tight around her waist so she looks impossibly slim, one dainty foot poised toe to the ground, heel in the air, like a dancer. The sun is behind her and her face is in shadow. She moves and the sun blinds us as she closes the gate.

'But we can't stay here on our own. Daddy would disapprove.'

She shakes her head at me, a little toss like a pony shaking out its mane. 'You'll be fine. I have to go now. Just stay there, will you?'

'But Mummy...' Anna tugs at her.

'Oh for goodness sake!' She gives Anna a little shove and Anna totters unsteadily away from the gate. 'Go back to your brother, please. Now.'

Anna half turns to look at me, confused. I had been about to join Anna at the gate, pleading to go too, but Mummy moves, and she is out of shadow just long enough for me to catch her expression. My fingers curl round the envelope she has entrusted me with instead. I hold my other hand out to Anna like a lifeline. Hers, when she takes mine, is cold and clammy. We stand together, small and uncertain on the doorstep.

'Good.' Mummy smiles approvingly at us. 'Daddy will be home soon. Now just stay there. On the doorstep.'

'But where are you going?' Anna squeezes my hand as she asks.

'No matter. You just stay there. And Jason, give him that envelope when he comes back. It's important.'

I look at the envelope over in my hand. It is crisp and white with Daddy's name covering the whole of the front in long lilting letters. Mr Andrew Crane. When I look up again, she is gone. She's done many things – odd things – but she's never left us like this before. This is different. I squeeze Anna's hand back. She's crying now but I am the boy. I have to be strong.

'Where's she going?' Anna looks plaintive and afraid.

'I don't know. But we have to wait here, like she said. That's what she wants.'

And we always do what Mummy wants...

The air is heavy with the scent of the roses from next door. Early flowering climbers with bright blooms and sharp thorns, they tumble over the small picket fence between our two gardens; a small invasion into the pristine regularity of our path and front porch, broken only by the clumps of Michaelmas daisies that border one side, still to flower. When they're in bloom Anna and I like to run through them, deliberately brushing against them to make them bob and collide against each other. They are the one concession to irregularity Daddy makes. He is a tidy man, routine, solid, careful. Mummy – she's like the bobbing daisies. Neither Anna nor I are daisies, but we would like to be.

By the time Daddy returns from work, five hours later, we are cold and stiff and afraid, heads aching from the overpowering perfume of the climbing roses and hands clawed into fists. The letter is grubby and creased from my handling of it, but still unopened. Daddy opens it and reads it, then takes us inside without a word.

'Where has Mummy gone?'

It takes several askings, but eventually he focuses uncertainly on us .'Gone?'

'Yes. Where did she go? She's been gone a very long time now, but we waited like she told us to. When is she coming back?'

'Back?' His eyes waver and drift off into the distance. 'I don't think she is...' He gives a little shiver and then seems to come back to himself. He pats my shoulder. 'Shall we get you two something to eat, then bed, I think. Tomorrow, we'll see...'

Tomorrow she is still not there, nor the next day, nor the next, until I stop counting days and Anna and I have run through the daisies so many times their petals are all gone and Christmas is approaching.

After a while I no longer watch for Mummy at the school gates, but the rasp of disappointment remains. Every day Daddy is there instead, waiting, and we are singled out from the other children by that very fact. We are simultaneously unique and pathetic; small and overlooked and dishevelled in the buzzing playground because Daddy is no good at plaiting Anna's hair or remembering when we've been invited to another child's party or round to tea. Eventually that doesn't matter though, because the invitations stop coming after a while. Once or twice I hear one of the other mothers whisper to her companion that we have been deserted. I ask Daddy one day what that means, but he doesn't answer so I look it up in a dictionary at school, underlining the word to make sure I'm getting it right. Miss Ruben catches me and shuts me in the cupboard as punishment for defacing a book. The cupboard is dark and smells so of chalk, I think I will pass out. I count to ten thousand and fifty-three whilst I'm waiting, trying not to, but it is no good. My chest has an iron band around it and my head spins. I feel sick – am sick. It sticks to my shoes, lumpen and foul-smelling. I gag and heave again. My eyes water and my nose runs. I hold my hand over my face, covering both nose and mouth until I get to ten thousand and fifty-three but by then I am going to go mad.

I am going mad...

I shout and kick against the door, alternately screaming and heaving until Miss Ruben finally opens the door. Then I shoot out of there and push her over in my desperation to breathe fresh air again. I don't remember what I call her, but she deserves it, whatever it is.

'This is bad.' Daddy's face is elongated with worry. It's been like that ever since Mummy went, but now as he ponders what to do about my latest misdemeanour, it's longer than ever. 'You could be expelled.'

That cheers me up. No more Miss Ruben. But it hardly seems fair since she is the one who has been mean to me, not the other way around.

'What for?'

'For being so rude to her.'

'I wasn't rude.'

'You called her a bitch.'

'She is.'

'Jason, Jason, you should never call a lady a bitch, no matter how unkind she might be to you. Ladies are not to be likened to animals.'

He sits down heavily and cups his chin in his hand. His face flows over it like it has melted. That's the word I think of for him. Melted. He's disintegrated, whereas Anna and I are deserted. The dining room clock ticks into the silence as I wait to be punished. He reaches for the Bible and opens it. I cross my fingers behind my back and hope the admonishment won't be that applicable to a capital offence. It is pure luck where the book opens, but nevertheless...

'Let ye who is without sin cast the first stone...' He looks up and studies me. 'Indeed,' he sighs. 'That's fair. Remember that, Jason. We are all sinners. It is the human condition to sin – and forgive. Always be fair.'

He waves me away and I know the cane will stay in the under-stairs cupboard this time – not that he wields it with any relish or power. To sin and to forgive? Maybe. Maybe we all sin, but I won't forgive. I still see her tip-tapping away down the path towards the gate; the bitch deserting the pack. And Miss Ruben? If only Daddy knew how much better she is at wielding the cane than he is, maybe he wouldn't forgive either. I rub my ribs where the weal from the last thrashing she gave me still aches. One day, I'll do more than merely call her a bitch. The blood sings in my ears as I imagine it – what I will do to her and where I will thrash her with that cane. They pulse and throb and my head aches.

I let my head rest against the keyboard, imagining the nonsense of the imprint that will be on my forehead as the PC beeps at me.

'Invalid keystroke.'

Invalid keystroke? I sit up straight. I am clutching my fists and my jaw is still grinding at the memories of the sins of both my mother and Miss Ruben, but I am hearing too.

Hearing.

Christ!

It must have shifted again.

Chapter 18

2nd May 2029: Jason

The hope I had in the hospital the first time it shifted overwhelms me. If I shifted it once, I can shift it again. Maybe shunt it all the way round my body? What will it do if I'm really angry? I take myself back to my room and lie on my bed, absorbing the texture of the silk cover, the density of the mattress, the cool clarity of body against bed. The air-con whistles gently in the background, too cool, but I don't like it too warm either and finding that perfect balance – as with anything – is proving to be difficult. I feel vaguely irritated but that's not going to shift anything.

Focus.

Forget hot and cold, and think back to people, memories, situations. What makes me angry? I could revisit a recent memory but then that would be like going over old ground and I want to break out. I sigh. I'm not sure how much longer I can put up with being confined within these walls, even if it is a self-imposed isolation. They close in on me, like the cupboard in Miss Ruben's room closed in on me all those years ago. Panic starts to rise in me at the memory. No, that won't do. I stuff it to one side. Not fear. Anger does it. Anger. Jane, the kid – no, that's fear again… anger. I close my eyes and listen to the sounds of the room. Focus.

How odd it is that we miss all those infinitesimal sounds that surround us most of the time. It's not until we ignore all the other senses and focus on one alone that we realise how much of it we ignore. And sometimes it is the very absence of anything that enables something to fill the void. This time it's a name. Rosalie.

My mother.

'Rosalie?'

'Yes?'

She is as artful now as she was then, but older. Yet age doesn't seem to have taken her looks from her as it does so many elderly women. She still has a presence beyond her size.

'I'm Jason.'

'Jason?' She frowns. 'Do I kn… Oh…'

'Yes.'

Oh.' She eyes me the way she did that day. 'I suppose you'd better come in.' She pulls the oversized blue front door wider and I glimpse a hallway replete with antique hall table and oversized flower arrangement just as in all the glossy house and home supplements.

'Thank you.'

I step across the threshold and follow her through the second doorway off the hall. It is a lounge as perfect and stylish as the hall.

'Some tea?'

'Thank you, but no. I only came to talk, briefly, about what happened to you when I was a child.'

She straightens her shoulders and breathes in.

'I'm sorry. It was difficult at the time. I was only young.'

'So was I.'

She stared at me then, examining my face, my expression, my eyes. We are so alike – she the feminine, me the masculine aspect of our joint genealogical disaster. There is little of my father in me. I had thought it the other way round until now.

'I know,' she replied quietly. 'Again, I'm sorry. How is your sister?'

'Dead.'

'Oh!' Her face crumples in on itself. I watch it implode with the same kind of detached fascination Mengele must have felt for his victims. Even now I feel no remorse for the lie. It was small in comparison to the years of emotional implosion Anna and I had suffered. I picture Anna's serene composure morphing into surprised disapproval if she knew what I'd just told our mother. Very much the same as our father's would have been. Anna is more of Elise's ilk – forgiving; a soft compression of understanding.

I could see she wanted to ask more but dare not. I hugged the moment to myself with the same possessiveness as she took hold of the cushion lying artlessly scattered for maximum effect on the sofa next to her. She squeezed it to her breasts as if it were Anna she were squeezing there.

'Father too.' That much was at least true. 'I don't think he ever really recovered. I don't remember him smiling much, at any rate.'

'You've just said that to make me feel bad.' It explodes from her with venom. Oh yes, we are alike.

''Did I? Well, that's your opinion.'

'Why did you come here?'

I can see dust motes floating in the stream of sunshine flooding through the French doors out onto the garden. On the patio, huge tubfuls of Michaelmas daisies are nodding in the early autumn breeze. The artlessness extends from the house into the garden. Anyone else would have patio flowers – geraniums, fuschias, the last dregs of summer border flowers, but she – she has Michaelmas daisies as if to emphasise her lack of conformity. I have got her number now. I have her. She is shrine unto herself – just as I am.

'To see what you're like.'

'And what am I like?'

'Me.'

'What does that mean?'

'That now I know. I know what to do.' I get up to leave. She tosses the cushion aside and jumps up to stop me. The dust motes eddy and panic around her in agitated fear of what might happen next.

'You know what to do about what?' She follows me awkwardly to the door, shuffling behind my long strides across her over-plush wool flooring and along her minimalistic hall towards the heavy mahogany front door. Everything here is both over and under-stated.

'That isn't your concern.'

'But it is. You came here to decide about something because of me. That makes it my concern.'

'Would you like grandchildren?' The front door is behind me and she is silhouetted in the light from the lounge at the far end of the corridor. Now I can see the twist in her body as well as her spirit. She leans heavily on her stick.

'Ah,' her breath caught.

'Or have you already got them?'

'No, I haven't any grandchildren. Richard doesn't want them, and Maisie can't have them.'

Richard and Maisie – the two apple-cheeked inhabitants of the ornate frame on the mantelpiece in the lounge, its gilt edge militating against the sterner set of the mantel edge. Our replacements – Anna and me.

'My wife is pregnant.'

This time she says nothing, but I can sense her shift in perception of me in every withheld second, so I wait. The silence lengthens, expands into a chasm. I knew she would jump eventually.

'That is... wonderful.' The expelled breath carries the word to me just as I turn and slip the latch on the door. 'Jason?'

I walk through the door and down the path, through yet another Michaelmas daisy storm. I can hear her footsteps behind me, stumbling, faltering, but I don't stop. I don't need her now. I know what I needed to know. I've done what I needed to do.

I feel it moving inside me. We are symbiotic now. It follows my prompts and I track its progress. We understand each other. It will destroy me unless I destroy it first. It is a fair fight but I have allies on my side that the Parmensis doesn't have. Fred. And fury.

Chapter 19

2nd May 2029: Matthew

He is already in the lab when I arrive. I'm not surprised. After Elise's report of his mood when she left last night and his behaviour yesterday, I expected him to be capricious today. That, with Jason, is usually funnelled into work. He must have been here some while though; the system is already powered up and he is listing protocols.

'Early bird,' I comment lightly.

'Catches the Parmensis,' he quips back, without turning. 'Yeah, bad taste, but isn't it? All of it?'

I join him at the desk with some trepidation. After yesterday I am wary, but his mood seems buoyant – and friendly. He makes room for me and I pull the same chair up to the desk that I'd been sitting on when he threatened me yesterday. He maximises a screen and adds another function to the graph. Tissue cloning variables. 'Are you up to this? After yesterday?'

Something feels wrong, even though he is in good spirits. 'Why wouldn't I be?'

He finally turns and grins at me. Full beam. Then the penny drops. Of course! He hasn't been watching me as I've been talking. He isn't lip reading.

'Your hearing…'

'Is back. The army is on the march again, and I think I know how.'

'My God, it's migrated again? Why didn't you call someone?'

I am half on my feet, wondering who to call first – Dr Kohn or Elise.

'Relax,' Jason waves his hand at me in a gesture implying I should chill. 'I figured it out overnight.'

Fred is lying exposed on the clone dolly. A second dolly has been pulled alongside. The early morning light is streaming through the window onto the two dollies, putting them in a spotlight of crisp May optimism. There is something ominous about the two dollies, though – one occupied and one empty. Jason follows my glance. The lab smells different too – or rather like it always does, but more. Disinfectant. It reeks of disinfectant.

'It was May morning in Oxford yesterday.' Jason's tone is conversational, but Jason has a way of dropping significant things into conversation, so you agree to them before you realise the significance of what you've just agreed to.

'May morning,' I reflect, trying to figure this one out. I can't, other than May morning is in May. The disinfectant is bothering me though.

'The students will have been doing crazy stunts.'

'Oh.' I had almost forgotten that Jason got his first degree from Oxford. I am a lowly redbrick graduate, only scraping myself onto a DPhil programme there by sheer grind and good luck. Jason already had friends in high places by then; he's Jason, after all. 'I hope you don't have anything similar in mind?' I look meaningfully at the trolley.

He laughs aloud and the sound echoes around the lab. I am suddenly conscious of how empty the place feels today too.

'Me, a crazy stunt? When have I ever done a crazy stunt, Matthew?'

True, he hadn't. He'd left it to the rest of us to try out the crazy stunts in the past – me mainly. Nevertheless…

'And where has the Parmensis migrated to?' I peer at the PC he is loading with data. The tissue cloning function is for kidneys.

'If I'm lucky, somewhere we can isolate it – but not in my brain. That's what we need to do first. Find it.'

'Exactly. You need to be in there, being monitored.' I gesture towards the door that interconnects with his suite of rooms. 'Who knows what might be happening to you! An MRI…'

'Yes, an MRI will find it, but then we need to get back in here and get me hooked up. There's something I want to try. And you're going to have to do it without them being involved.' He jerks his head towards the interconnecting door. I am staring at him. 'For fuck's sake, don't you get it, Matthew? I don't need to waste time having another fucking ECG or my blood pressure taken and then being confined to rest whilst they mull over what may or may not happen to me next. I got them in to resuscitate me if they have to, not confine me to bed every time I twitch. I need to know where the fucking tumour's gone and if it's out of my head yet – and then we need to do something about it.'

'So an MRI…

'Yes, an MRI – and you're going to do it without anyone else being involved.'

'I've never operated an MRI on my own.'

'It's simple. You just roll me into it and turn it on.'

I shake my head. 'But it's in their lab complex.'

'In my building, which I own. Come on!' He switches off the monitor and stands. Now I see he is still in the t-shirt and jogging bottoms he was in yesterday. There is a tiny blood stain on the right-hand side of the t-shirt and his knuckles are grazed. He smells odd, too. He takes my arm and propels me towards the door. His rubber-soled shoes squeak on the flooring. There is no point in arguing with him, and I confess I'm a little afraid of him after yesterday's performance. I never thought I'd think that of Jason. I let him lead me because that is me – the weakness of me. Jane is right. I'm a blob of indecision.

We exit the lab and the smell of disinfectant comes with us. Then I realise it is Jason. The smell of disinfectant is as much on him as it is in the lab.

'Have you been scrubbing the lab?' I ask.

'Yeah, prepping.'

'For what?'

'MRI first,' he cautions.

We reach the door to the room housing the MRI. Money may not be able to buy happiness, but it can buy the tools that could lead to eternal life and all the trappings needed to get you there. When Jason had commissioned the medical unit to house him and his life-support team, he'd turfed out our least cost-effective research projects and staff, putting the staff on notice and the projects into the basement. It had caused an outcry, but he'd been firm.

'What would *you* do to survive?' was his only response to the mounting pile of unfair dismissal cases. What would I? I still often ponder that late into the night, long after everyone has gone home and Jason back to his suite of rooms inside the medical facility, when there is only Fred and me left in the lab. If I was Jason, would I do what Jason wants to do? Would I have the courage?

The MRI is one of the most expensive elements of the medical facility. It materialised almost overnight – the benefits of billionairedom; the ability to magic the most expensive and exclusive kit out of nowhere at a moment's notice when the NHS struggles to commission the same thing for delivery in two years' time. Yet even Jason's billionaire status must be running low, given the amounts he's been sanctioning for this project. I wonder too if I could study the company's current financial position, whether his threat that there would be no company if he died might be somewhat irrelevant. There might be no company if he survives either – except, of course, simply surviving will provide the company with its most exclusive and sought-after product ever. I hover nervously behind the MRI controls in the anteroom whilst Jason adjusts the head position on the scanner bed in the room housing the MRI. I watch him through the glass as he swings himself into a prone position and then gives me a thumbs up. The machine is already on and Jason has set it to full-body-scan. All I have to do is press the button and make sure it is working. The rest is down to Jason. And that is my life – do his bidding and the rest is down to Jason. If I weren't still so scared of what would happen if Jason didn't shield me from my past, I would find it soul-crushingly demoralising. But I don't. There was only one thing Jason did that I still find soul-crushingly demoralising. He married Elise.

Jason's voice blasts through the earpiece I am wearing to receive my instructions. 'Is the outer door locked?'

'Yes, Master.'

'Huh!' It's between an expression of irritation and an explosion of humour. 'Then we'll do two tests – the first is a control and check where the Parmensis is now. The second is to move it again.'

'Move it again? How?'

'Aggression. That's what shifted it before. I spent all night thinking about it and that's what I came up with. Both times I've been actively belligerent, there's been a shift.'

'But why – why would it be that? It could be a hundred other reasons and a lot more we can't even imagine. We simply don't know why this tumour moves.'

'OK, my theory. Focusing on something that causes anger initiates a flood of adrenaline and noradrenaline. They flow through the body providing a burst of energy. Heart rate, blood pressure and respiration all increase, powering up the body, and then the hyperlinks in the brain really get active. Do you remember that paper on direct and indirect occipital and temporal lobe connections?'

'No.' I am bemused. Since when had either of us had any involvement in hearing or sight issues – other than now? We are bio-technicians; gross and fine motor control at the rough end. Others provide us with the fine print for neurological interface although it is becoming somewhat more familiar to us these days.

'Oh, no. I guess you wouldn't. I only located it last night, when I was thinking, actually. It goes like this – MRI- based studies (5) first established that we have fibre bundles linking occipital and anterior lobes, arising in extrastriate visual "association" areas, providing fast transfer of visual signals to neuromodulatory back-projections from the amygdala.'

He pauses and waits, as if he has explained everything, head lolling to one side as he lays on the scanner bed, peering at me though the interconnecting window between the scanner and anteroom. I shake my head, struggling to place the words and theory into a sensible place within my – still infantile at times – understanding of neurology. He looks small and vulnerable, lying half in the scanner. Jason is a big guy, six-foot, ex-rugby player, broad shoulders, slim hips. He should consume the scanner bed, not it consume him – yet lying there, relating the technicalities of various neural pathways to me as if I am an idiot, he seems ridiculously ingenuous. What do we really know of the human brain and its functioning? Oh yes, we can record all kinds of complicated activity, build all kinds of models, duplicate all kinds of functionality. We can pinpoint this, stimulate that – but could we really, successfully, merge a man's brain with a machine's body? Even a 3D or cloned one that we could repeat and repeat and repeat, if necessary, until we got it right?

He's still waiting for my response, and I'm not even sure I know what the question is. Slow, faithful, plodding Matthew that I've become...

'I, er…'

'The amygdala!' He irritably supplies his own answer. 'It's all initiated from the amygdala. So what we need to do is establish what response is most active from the amygdala when we stimulate it and from that we can – just possibly – predict where the Parmensis might be prompted to move if we could generate enough impetus to shift it. It's nervous system-central that's the key, I'll bet. That's why the Parmensis targeted the auditory senses this time round.' I still don't get why, but I let him move on. Maybe the latest MRI results will make it all clear? He's clearly got this from somewhere. 'What I want to know is where it hived off to afterwards, and why. Then we can make a stab at directing it.'

His last words remind me of the rest of his plan. 'And you want to move it again?'

'I want to test the theory, yes.'

The anteroom is closing in around me, the lights and wave monitors suddenly blinding me. Everything is too white, too clinical, too out of my depth. What the hell am I doing? What the hell are we doing? I could be about to be involved in my friend's suicide.

'That's too dangerous.'

'So is living.'

'But you don't know where it will migrate to.'

'Let's find out, or do I have to get angry with you? You wouldn't like me when I'm angry.' He winks at me, grinning, and momentarily we are grad students again, picking apart the rationale to the Hulk movies, speculating about what we would do if it were us, joking about the impossible, which Jason knew I'd be just as likely to try out as to discuss – then; which was why he'd mooted it to me in the first place….

'Oh God, I can't do this, Jason.'

'OK, I'll get angry with you then. Getting angry with you worked a treat last time.' He swings himself out of the scanner and starts towards the door.

Something childish and irrational in me makes me want to rush to the door and lock it – him in, me out. He yanks the door open before I get to it. I steel myself. This is Jason, I tell myself. This is Jason, not the Hulk. 'How? By you wanting to beat me to a pulp again?' I ask, as if I'm completely at ease.

'If necessary.' He lounges against the door frame and flexes his fists. This is Jason, and not Jason any more.

'Let's do some tests on things as they are to start with – like you suggested, huh?'

'And then?'

'Then maybe we could see what happens using Fred.' The idea that has been in the back of my mind since I told Elise that the movement of the Parmensis changed everything starts to crystallise. But Elise would never forgive me. I would never forgive me. Oh God, I am such a coward!

'And then?'

'Well, maybe use iPS cells to control the replication of the Parmensis, but also replicate Fred so we have a clean model too if we can't… OR maybe, even get the Parmensis to shift into Fred…'

He is silent, eyeing me; weighing me up, and then he grins. 'OK.' He's understood where I'm going. 'The MRI first though. Ready? Or I'm gonna get very angry…'

Chapter 20

2nd May 2029: Elise

I am listening to Matthew's words but they aren't sinking in.

'Deliberately prompting it to move… Thought you should know… I'm…' he stops there.

We never did follow up on that half-admission we both made over the phone to each other when Jason was first discharged. We have both been afraid of what it says about us, I suppose. To wish death on someone you love, rather than see them live – in whatever form that is. What does that make you as a person?

'What are you, Matthew?' It comes out in a rush, too belligerent to encourage further confidences. 'I'm sorry,' I add, 'I didn't mean it that way. Talk to me. Talk to me properly.'

I can hear the hesitation in his very breathing. This is the moment – the moment we tell each other the truth. I hold my breath.

'It's difficult here, now.'

I can hear the distant voices of children squabbling, a banged door, a sharper voice intervening. Jane's voice.

'I understand,' I say. And I do. That makes it all the worse – for Matthew to be taking time out of his precious moments with his daughter so jealously guarded by Jane in her mission to screw him to the ground for alimony or revenge – although why the hell she needed revenge when she was the transgressor, God knows – meant this was serious. Dire.

'Meet me in the parking lot behind McD's in half an hour. I'm dropping Jane and Katie off there before I head back in. They'll walk home afterwards. Park out of the way though. We shouldn't be seen together.'

'I don't think Jane will think you're having an affair with your best friend's wife,' I say dryly, until the irony takes the breath from me. But Jason had.

'No, I'm hardly in your league,' he replies and there is something to his voice that makes me want to see his face and the expression in his eyes as he says it. I feel sad – and mean.

'I didn't mean it that way…'

'It's OK, I know you didn't.' Now there is humour in the pitch and timbre. 'Although Jane would be quite prepared to believe anything of me if it would increase the divorce settlement,' he adds. 'But no, I meant, in case Jason thinks we're talking behind his back.'

'We are.'

And I didn't mean that to come out in the way it did either, but I sense Matthew knows that.

'Yes, we are,' he agrees. 'Half an hour.'

Chapter 21

4th June 2029: Matthew

It is five am. As instructed, both Fred and I are waiting. His whole substructure has now integrated with the CyberCute and other than his head he could be human. We are two dummies awaiting direction. I pause to admire the perfection of the replication, right down to moles and freckles. In a moment of genius, Jason introduced some of his own DNA into the CyberCute and the skin covering is now an extension of him. Remarkable. This alone is Jason's certainty of wealth and success in the future, but I dare not say that to him. Every such comment is greeted with, 'but only if I *have* a future…'

Fred's face is lying in sections alongside his torso. Mandible, cheekbones and front cranium glisten in the lab lights. I could say they glow. The lab lights seem to do that to the high-tensile composite material we've used for Fred's internal structure, his bones. Inside, the hollow of his skull is cup-like, awaiting sustenance – my cup runneth over – but not how I expected it to. Our early dawn experiments – before Jason's medical team are on the prowl – have me mentally likening us to Burke and Hare, especially when we huddle around Fred, discussing which function to test first. Today is simply more of the same, yet different. Our attempts to force the Parmensis to migrate have so far been fruitless. Each day for the last two weeks we have been secretly repeating the charade of pushing Jason to the limits – literally infuriating him. His brain waves are off the scale – fury in the purest form, stimulated by any and every way we can make him feel badly used, or betrayed – but the Parmensis remains steadfastly in situ. The theory was fine; the practice has defeated us, as it so often does in life. But Jason is not a man to be defeated by theory not transforming into fact, and so we move on.

Our first test today is to see if Jason's brain can interface with Fred's body, and whether or not the Parmensis will shift whilst connected. I know it is because Jason wants his Plan B to remain on the table to give him alternatives. My plan – Plan A – to shift the Parmensis into Fred's body by hooking up Jason's brain to Fred's body is still only in the planning because so far, despite Jason's best efforts, whilst the Parmensis seems happy to make the rounds of various locations in Jason's brain, it has proved reluctant to move permanently from it. Our best efforts have only produced a temporary shift, but at least it has allowed us to create a Parmensis-free template to clone from. Any progress in any direction has been a long time coming, as far as Jason is concerned and at least the cloned brain is Parmensis-free, even if his isn't. For me any move forward from here is premature in the extreme, but at least my plan had some safety features inherent in it – and the benefit of keeping Jason – body and soul – all in one place. However, everything we have done so far has been pushing the limits, without any controls or background checks, so maybe *what the hell*?

Does impending death really make one so cavalier with life? I would have expected it to be the reverse, but Jason has become daily less cautious as this thing has progressed. Indeed, I now have a catalogue of situations and phrases that I know will 'push his buttons' where before, he was the personification of calm and control. The perfect entrepreneurial scientist – creative and innovative, with discretion. It worries me – what long-term effect this could have on his ability to control emotion – but his answer is always that he will deal with that when it arises; he has to survive this first. Every time Elise has visited, I have so wanted to take her to one side and tell her everything, but guilt has stopped me every time. Why am I doing this? Why would I not be doing this? My motives defy even me. Little things about Jason I have accepted without question over the years have begun to niggle – his authoritarianism, his unassailable self-confidence, his success, his good luck – even though that seems ridiculous now, considering his bad luck. But guilt that I should even be noticing them counterbalances his dictatorial behaviour. The man is dying – *dying*! How the hell can I complain that he is pushing too far and too fast? And anyway, it's his funeral – literally – if this doesn't work. *And your ongoing reputation*, the little imp in my ear whispers, even as I dither.

'Right, so all set to go?'

The door bangs behind me and I jump out of my reverie – the same one I have every day these days. Imp, conscience, imp, conscience, imp…

'Yeah, course.'

Conscience.

'Good, because today's the day!'

He slides in alongside me. He smells of spruce and open countryside, designer jogging pants and t-shirt – his everyday uniform now – pristine and crisp. Probably brand new. He looks sharp and debonair, even as he's dying. By comparison my wrinkled grey lab trousers and un-ironed polo shirt look drab and tired. I am drab and tired, even in full health. The spruce smell invades the lab – stronger than aftershave, lighter than disinfectant. I will remember that smell for the rest of my days.

'Today's the day?'

'We make history. We make Fred live. And maybe find another way to bypass the Parmensis. Who knows?'

The desk surface feels gritty under my fingers. It should have been cleaned but Jason has banned the cleaners. We have to do it ourselves. This is top secret. That means I have to do it because Jason can't. And I didn't last night, too tired from Jason's barked commands and his determination to do just one thing more…

'We're only testing very basic gross motor control today, nothing else.' I remind him.

It's a statement but I know it's a question too. This was *our* project but it's not any more. His expression is as much reply as his words: determinedly optimistic, mouth half-curving, eyes bright, teeth clenched in a would-be smile.

'Not *only*, Matthew. We're *starting* with gross motor control. We'll progress as appropriate.'

I know then that Plan A is still uppermost for him, but he cannot play God when God has no control, so we will see. His eyes stray to the replica brain on which we have been working. A next stage test model – what happens when it's in situ – connective tissue and neural bundles fumbling towards each other to create bonds? My eyes follow his. It's what I am afraid of most of all – with Jason out of control, and still playing God.

'Let's just start with that then,' I pacify him. We need to establish connections for either plan to be possible. I can see his jaw tensing. One of those push-the-button responses. If I could see his brain waves now, they would be cresting. I wonder sometimes if the Parmensis affects more than tissue and bone…

'Good.' He powers up the mainframe and then flicks on his monitor.

'With my brain.'

'Oh, but…' The wires trailing from Fred tremble and snake away from him as his circuitry fires up. 'I thought we were testing with the cloned brain from the command centre.'

'That is the command centre – or as close as. What's it is, is mine, and vice versa…' Jason doesn't wait for me to catch up. He skids his chair away from the monitor and scoots over to Fred. 'Hello old buddy. Shall we really get things moving today?'

He grins across at me and the tension is gone from his jawline. Briefly, I see a glimpse of the old Jason, the one with whom I conducted ridiculous experiments and dreamed crazy dreams. Not so different, after all – or maybe unrecognisable. He holds up two of the main leads from the cerebral cortex stimulator and spinal intersection, their neat circuitry gleaming softly in the lab light.

'Shouldn't we do a control first?' I ask.

'Why? It, me – we're the same.' His chin juts. Outside it is still barely light. The clock ticks over. Five-fifteen. I'm too jaded for an argument right now. It, him – what difference did it make in reality? It wasn't going to work anyway – too many potential complexities we haven't even begun to address yet.

'I need coffee first,' I say grimly. My face is rough because I haven't shaved and I feel as grisly grey as the outside light. It's going to be a long and difficult day, not least dealing potentially with Jason's ultimate disappointment.

'Good idea. Get me one too, will you?'

I turn and stare. He is busy checking Fred's leads are all intact and registering on the main monitor.

'They won't be open yet,' I say. He doesn't even turn, engrossed in correcting a minor misconnection. 'Jason…'

'What?'

Now he turns, two small crease lines like forks in the road between his eyebrows.

'The coffee shop won't be open at five-thirty in the morning.' He shakes his head as if he is a dog, flicking water from his ears after an unexpected dowsing. 'The coffee shop – for your coffee,' I persist.

'Well,' he still looks confused. 'I'll have whatever you're having then.' He grins at me as if I'm an imbecile. Maybe I am.

'Really?'

'Course. Come on, you're wasting time. Fred and me, we're ready to part-ay!'

'OK.' I brew two mugs of coffee in Barista Bev. Maybe it's the little things that go first when death comes calling. The finer qualities of man or machine-made coffee would surely be one of those. I take his mug to him and he waves at the desk top next to him. I place it there, all kinds of neuron connections misfiring in my own brain as Jason checks the status of the grey mass of the one about to interface with Fred.

Latterly, I am even more uneasy with Jason's initial plan of forcing migration of the Parmensis into his body, away from his brain and then interfacing his brain with Fred's body, than I was to begin with. It's not now that it's impossible, it's that it has the potential to evolve beyond anything I had considered before – with Jason driving it, that is. And I promised Elise I would push Plan A; that Plan A would be the plan we adhered to… On the tray next to the clone dolly is our first attempt to achieve it. Jason's replicated brain to be used to test Fred's responses, *but nothing else*. It is sheathed in a protective membrane and still floating in its embryonic bath, but the impulses it is sending out via the spaghetti of fibre-thin connections linking it wirelessly to the lab's mainframe are remarkable. Part of me is excited, with that breathless amazement unique to childhood and scientific breakthrough. The other part is terrified. What if we are creating precisely the Frankenstein's monster Elise once accused us of? Yet the responses from Jason's replica brain so far are identical to those from his real brain –with one notable exception: we have yet to identify any trace of the Parmensis within it. The iPS cells may indeed have worked. Jason's replicated brain may be tumour-free in a way he has not yet managed to manipulate his own brain to be. And that in turn has brought about Plan C on Jason's part – a development I certainly hadn't expected: Jason's cloned brain in Jason's body – cloned or otherwise.

'Cheers.' Jason doesn't even look at the coffee. He adjusts a couple of baseline functions then just picks up the mug and starts drinking, still studying the monitor. I watch the mug rise to his lips. Tip, sip, swallow, no reaction. 'I think we're good to go.' He turns to me and grins. 'Ready?'

The enormity of the whole business suddenly catches up with me and I am dizzy with fear. I lean against the desk top to steady myself, clutching my own coffee mug tightly but unable to do anything else with it.

'You OK?' Jason frowns.

'Bit tired,' I hedge. 'Look, testing the clone… why, exactly? Which plan?'

'Why? Why the hell wouldn't we? Isn't that the whole point of what we've been working on for the last God knows how many years? And who cares which plan? Any fucker that works!'

'But, it was…' I scratch my head, trying to find words that won't betray me and my thoughts. 'It was only Plan B. We aren't going to…'

'It was,' Jason nods slowly, his eyes scanning my face like a laser tool seeking out faulty parts to fix. 'But now it isn't.' He pauses. 'Are we not in agreement on this, Matthew?' The dry ice in his voice burns. The warning lurks just beneath it.

'It's not that I'm not in agreement. I'd do anything to keep you alive – you know that. You're my best mate, but… Oh God, Jason, there's so much we don't know, have no idea how any of this might work ultimately.'

'So now is when we start finding out.'

'But what are we finding out? I thought it was whether we could use Fred to migrate the tumour into, so your brain is tumour-free...'

He stares at me. 'But it's not,' he says eventually. 'Despite everything, it's not happening, is it?'

I look across at the cloned brain, nestling in its amniotic bath, and I no longer need to ask why we're testing it or why we're doing anything at all. I know Jason too well. Plan A is non-existent in his eyes, nor is Plan B.

'Oh man…' My heart is rattling at my ribs like they are a cage, containing it. 'Are you sure you want to do this? I mean, why don't we get Dr Kohn's input? She'd be able to check it over physiologically at least. Or we should do another fMRI first.'

'Why? We've cloned body parts before. We've already been there. We already know how to check for efficacy – and it's accurate. And anyway, what is an MRI going to achieve whilst it's inactive? ' His lips purse. The first signs of irritation will transmute into anger shortly if I don't mollify him. Pressing a button that we've deliberately developed over the last few weeks – to no avail. 'And we're the ones who developed the CyberArm 3.3 and its physiological integration – not Dr Kohn. Why do you want to hand it all over to some Kraut?'

I reel at the animosity and contempt.

'I don't, I don't. Just being cautious – you know me.' I smile and the sickly-sweet taste of obsequiousness makes me want to gag. I swallow to get the taste out of my mouth, but it lingers nevertheless. Saccharine with a sour aftertaste. I hate myself for the pretence, but it's necessary. I know what the result will be if I don't pacify him. He bridles but doesn't bite – yet. 'But to consider using a cloned brain…'

'Are you not sure you've got it right then?' He is squinting at me; the brain bore drilling deeper. 'You're the bio-technician.'

'Oh, yes, yes! It should be absolutely right, based on our extrapolations but, Jason, this isn't just a single limb, this is a whole body – and a brain…'

'And your point is?'

He stares at me, eyes delving into the flesh of my face, my skull, scooping out my brain to extract what I'm really thinking. I put the coffee mug down, slopping the contents as I do so. He shoves a handful of lab wipes at me. I take the wipes and start the mopping up job, uncertain how to reply. The volatility I can understand. We have deliberately worked on creating the neurological impulses that spark anger in an attempt to shift the Parmensis, and once neural pathways are learned they have to be unlearned. I knew I would have to expect him to be on a short fuse when we started the process, apart from the stress of the situation generally, the high-handedness – that I am used to – but not the foolhardiness. Everything we have ever done together has been carefully researched, planned in fine detail, tested, tested and tested again.

'It could go wrong, or not work at all,' I say eventually. I sound stupid. It sounds stupid, stating the obvious, and yet Jason doesn't seem to see the obvious any more. 'After all, how do we know about the soul… Is that in our brain or what?'

He stares at me, then bursts out laughing. 'Oh Christ, Matthew, you're priceless! You think I want to replace my diseased brain with a cloned one?'

'Well…' now I'm confused. 'I thought you were suggesting…'

'God, no! I want to see what will work since this bloody thing isn't shifting for the moment. Remember our formula… if it doesn't work the first time, piss off onto something else then come back to the problem with a fresh approach. This is the pissing off – making sure the end product of the process works before going back to the problem. It's no good trying to shift the Parmensis unless we can get Fred and my brain to integrate to make that possible anyway, so if we test Fred with this thing still in my brain then we see if we can successfully shift it into him and see if there might be another way to shift it too.'

'Oh, hence the cloned brain. A version of Plan A then?'

'Yup. If you like. What the fuck were you thinking?'

'Plan C or worse. A cloned brain and a cloned body, but I wasn't thinking straight.'

'Good job I am then, isn't it?'

He looks amused, eyebrows peaked, mouth pursed, and yet… the blackmail, the refusal to involve alternative expertise, the flippancy, the coffee… I'm trying to understand but I can't. Yes, he does appear to be thinking straight, but there are still the limitations, the likelihood of failure. How do I manage his expectations? Against that, the little voice inside me whispers *or the extent of his success – what about that?* I shiver involuntarily. But I will deal with that, will get that covered if I need to – I hope. In Fred at least. He is still smiling at me, all belligerence gone now and replaced by the earnest expectation of an excited puppy. How can I not go ahead with this? How was it Elise had put it? *'Humour him. Even if it can't work, he needs the hope it can give to cope with everything, God help me...'* And I need both the hope it can and the hope it won't. I bite my lip and buy into the charade as the most diplomatic way forward.

'True.' I pick up my coffee and drink it. It's cold and scummy, not unlike me. 'Let's crack on then.'

'Good.' He scoots across to the clone dolly. 'Gowning up, then?' He throws one of the sets of scrubs across to me and kicks the locks off the dolly. 'You bring Fred. I'll bring the control centre.' He drapes the scrubs over his arm and starts pushing the trolley housing the brain towards the lab's sterile area. I catch the scrubs mid-flight, juggling almost emptied coffee mug and conscience equally badly. The mug lands on the desktop and wobbles around noisily in concentric circles until it settles. This time it doesn't spill. 'I've switched to remote on the PC so it's already firing up in there,' Jason calls over his shoulder. 'Come on.'

I follow, the faithful dog responding to command, pushing Fred laboriously ahead of me through the swing door into the sterile unit. Jason is already scrubbing up, swathed in green cover-alls. I follow suit and we help each other on with our gloves. There is no holding back now. We acknowledge that silently to each other and high five with our elbows. We have done this so many times before, in partnership, with the CyberArm 3.3, the sense of déjà vu is so strong it almost overwhelms me, but this is the same without being the same. We leave the airlocked capsule where we've scrubbed up and enter the sterile chamber, the other side of it where we complete internal adjustments. Through the viewing window I can see the TV monitor that scans the corridor outside. The corridor is empty, shadowy and remote. It merely serves to emphasise our isolation as Jason takes his place on the brain side of the clone dolly and clicks the remote on the PC. All five monitors burst into life displaying limbic, neuro and bio-electrical recordings.

'Busy little beast, isn't it?' Jason grins at me. The brain responds with a burst of activity. Like it's laughing with him.

'Responsive,' I agree. 'But I thought you said it was inactive?'

'Ah, I fed the source code in when I fired the system up. It's me – or becoming a copy of me. Let's see what happens when we really start making connections.'

Jason lifts the lid on the tank in which the brain is idling. The spaghetti of minuscule fibrous connections shimmy like the tassels on a belly dancer as the fluid it is bathing in is disturbed. They are marked up in colours. Gross motor control is green, limbic system is red, central nervous system blue, and so on. Since its birth a week ago, we have spent every hour in the lab identifying and inserting the tiny probes that enable connection for the major sources of initiation. Its mottled grey surface is pin-cushioned with colour. Of course, we haven't found every possible connection. We have missed thousands, and quite possibly aren't even aware of hundreds of thousands more, but there is logic to Jason's argument. We missed thousands with the CyberArm 3.3, but the CyberCute did the remaining work for us. It was like we provided the people and the venue and the CyberCute created the party.

Jason flexes his gloved hands and lowers them into the tank.

'Wait! You're going to actually insert it into Fred's cranium?'

'Of course.'

'But I thought…'

That warning look is on his face again. I take a deep breath and shut up, thoughts reeling. The day is going to get worse rapidly now, but there's little I can do – or will do, I acknowledge with self-loathing. Instead I watch him deftly separating the brain and its rainbow of proboscises from the glutinous liquid of its amniotic sac. I am mesmerised by the ebb and flow of the tiny filaments as Jason's fingers detach and untangle. We have done this so many times too – with the CyberArm – but I almost forget what I am supposed to be doing myself in the significance of the moment. I am brought sharply out of my trance by Jason's unexpected expletive.

'Damn!'

'What?'

'Need three hands here. The brain stem is too embedded. Might have to cut into the host. Come on, get a grip, Matthew.'

'What? Oh wait – don't do that!' My voice comes out in a high-pitched squeak. 'Wait and I'll help.'

I scurry round to his side of Fred and squat so I can get a better view of where the glitch is through the transparent tank wall. The brain is nestling tight into a corner, with Jason's fingers encircling its base. I cannot see beyond them but, if the brain stem has embedded, we will risk damaging it and all the last week's work if we attempt to prise it free.

'And?' Jason asks, impatiently.

'I can't see, but you know what? I've had another idea. We're just testing gross motor functionality today, aren't we?'

'And anything else we can move on to.'

I ignore that. In my world, gross motor functionality is going to take most of a week to test, even in its most basic form. And even then… Best not to say that to Jason though or we'll be back to pressing the button again.

'Then why don't we leave the brain in situ and hook-up wirelessly to Fred. It'll take some modifications but then we don't risk damaging the brain or Fred with physical interventions for the moment? Especially if you've already uploaded the source code, such as it is currently.'

I don't dare look at him. I can sense his frustration in the tenseness of his fingers, the stillness of the fluid around the brain, the thickness of the air between us. Even the fibre connectors seem to be standing to attention as they await his response.

'We won't be testing physical connectivity with Fred's circuitry then, though. How will we know if we have created enough physical connection points?'

'It's not physical connectivity with Fred's circuitry we need to test, Jason,' I say quietly. 'It's the ability to make *any* neural connection at all. That can be done as well remotely as in situ. The brain is the key, not Fred. And if we're right about the CyberCute, that will eventually sort out the physical connectivity for us whether we've created enough physical connection points or not.'

He withdraws his hands slowly and oh so tenderly from beneath the brain. It settles back into the cushion of its fluid with what feels like a sigh.

'OK, you have a point. Let's see what we can do with that.' He dries his hands on some surgical gauze whilst I collect more fibre connectors.

'What do you want to test first?'

'Arms. We're pretty straight on them already.'

'OK.' I'd hoped he'd opt for something reasonably straightforward. I attach fibres to all of the green tendrils. It's a painstaking process and my back is frozen into a semi-humped position by the time I've completed the task. Jason has replaced his gloves with dry ones and stationed himself at the main lab console and the screens are gradually illuminating with wave-form graphs. I recognise some of them as the modular pattern for forearm connectivity – the extensor carpi radialis longus and so on, but upper arm musculature is displaying on some screens too – the biceps, triceps, brachioradialis, even the deltoids.

'Pretty good,' Jason says, flicking between the screens. 'They're identifying. Finished?' He swings round and looks quizzically at me.

'Apart from the ones that are inaccessible at the moment, yes.'

'In that case will they transmit?' He breaks off. Somewhere a bell is ringing. Insistently. It's the doorbell for the lab.

'Your medics?' I suggest. Hope wells up in me.

'No. I told them they aren't to disturb me before ten unless it's a medical emergency. That I need my sleep.'

'Oh.' I'd wondered how Jason had been playing it these last two weeks. Their lack of intervention had seemed odd. 'Elise, then perhaps?'

The clock on the wall indicates it is still only eight.

'Far too early. I told her the same thing.'

The bell rings again. The sound lingers and then is repeated even before the last strains of its first repeat have died away

'Well, they're not going away, Jason, whoever it is.'

'You go and see then. I'm not even meant to be here.'

'OK, but don't do anything without me, will you?'

'As if.'

He grins as I peel off my gloves and shrug myself out of my scrubs, dumping them in the laundry basket by the door, a deflated version of myself puffing itself into place at the bottom of it. The bell rings again before I get to the lab door.

'OK, OK, I'm coming,' I call ahead of myself. I open it cautiously, ready to fend off curios medics only to find Elise's worried face peering round the edge of it.

'I had this feeling…' she begins. 'Where's Jason? He's not in his suite.'

I open the door wider to allow her in.

'We're conducting some tests.'

'Not on him!' she gasps.

'No, no, on…' I think about the convolution of grey matter mushrooming tentacles like it's an obscene form of mythical beast, sending out waves of energy that might, just might… I cough and pretend to clear my throat. 'On some things we've been working on.'

She hears the hesitation even though I have tried to mask it. Her expression tightens and the hollows that have been gathering under her eyes over the last few weeks deepen. 'What things? Matthew, that sounds significant.'

'Maybe, or…' I cast a glance over my shoulder. I wonder whether Jason has waited, or the temptation has been too much. 'I should get back in there.'

'Not without me.' She grabs my arm and her fingers are like needles, piercing my skin. They stick into it like a grappling hook and I know there is no choice – just as there was no choice with Jason. I cannot serve two masters. At some stage the competitors must battle it out. Now looks to be that time.

'You'd better put some of those on, then.' I nod to the neat stack of scrubs in the cupboard next to where the clone dolly had been. I cross to the cupboard and pull out two fresh pairs. She watches me climb into mine and then copies. 'You'll have to scrub up on the way in too.' I pull the head cover on and pass her one for herself. Her soft blonde cloud refuses to be fully contained, though, and stray tendrils caress her cheek even after she has enveloped her head in the dull green bonnet. They are as fine as the fibre connectors vibrating with energy in the cloned brain, but more fragile, more precious. I want to tuck them safely away, but I dare not touch her or anything to do with her. I point to my own cheek instead and she understands immediately.

'Oh,' she stuffs the remaining strands of hair hastily inside the cap and joins me at the entrance to the sterile area. Normally the chemical tang of antiseptic would accompany me into here, but her perfume is stronger in a soft, diffuse way. I breathe it in and plunge deeper into chaos. She follows me meekly enough but that is where submissiveness ends. Jason has done what I feared he would do. He has activated brain impulses and Fred's arm is held aloft, waving at us. A cadaver with a welcome. 'Oh!' she repeats, but this time it isn't a soft explosion of apology. It's a firecracker of dismay. 'How is it doing that?'

I join her at the viewing window as Fred completes a full regal wave, like the Queen used to in the old film reels of royal outings, when they still happened. Damn!

'Brain impulses to the connective points within the cyber body.'

'You said it wouldn't work!'

'I said I didn't know, but I feared it wouldn't work – or would turn into something worse.'

She presses herself to the viewing window at precisely the same time Jason notices her. His expression freezes, and then morphs into triumph.

'It works,' he mouths at both of us. 'It bloody works!'

'But how?' Elise leans in towards Jason's jubilant face, which leers back at us through the viewing window. 'Whose brain?'

'The one in the tank.'

'Oh my God!'

'Cloned, of course,' I add hastily.

'Even so…' Her face twists with distaste and I try to imagine what Elise is making of what we are both studying as the brain trembles and transmits. She peers from Jason – now cavorting around Fred in a strange complicated form of dance as Fred waves furiously back at us all – to the tank, and back again. 'And whose brain has been cloned?' she asks eventually.

She turns to face me, and I hesitate, but it's clear she's already seen the answer all over my face. Slowly, so slowly, her expression changes to reflect the same dark reservoir of fear I have kept dammed up ever since Jason first decided to make ForEver his destiny.

Chapter 22

4th June 2029: Elise

It is macabre. If it was a film it couldn't be more crazy. A crazy sci-fi monstrosity. Matthew is just staring at me, not saying a word, slack-jawed and wide-eyed, but he doesn't need to. I can feel the intensity of his discomfort oozing from every pore. Or is it something other than discomfort? Behind the glass screen, Jason is cavorting like a demon and the robot-thing – Jason, but not Jason – is flapping its hands at us and twitching like a string puppet being jerked around by God. And I can't move. All I can think of is that this *thing* is partly my husband – how can it not be if it is his brain that is controlling it?

Jason's face is at the glass screen now. Flushed and excited, eyes wild with an inner light I don't want to see.

Or is Jason partly the thing?

Oh God! I spin away from the glass screen and slap into Matthew and his solid dependability that now I can't depend on at all. I asked him not to let this happen – this craziness. I begged him, threatened him – and yet here we are. I push him away, but he doesn't budge and I am a wild bird fluttering in a net, his arms the net trapping me.

'Oh my God, oh my God, oh my God…' I can't stop myself. All I can hear is my voice, high-pitched and wailing.

'Elise, it's OK.' His voice is in my hair, in my ear, in my head. 'It's only a test, to see if we can make it work. It means nothing.' Matthew is hissing, fast and urgently at me. 'You've got to stay calm. You shouldn't have even been here now, let alone seen this.'

'But this is obscene, Matthew! What does he think he's doing?'

'Testing the possibilities. Plan B – like I told you. Let him – you have to let him. Everyone needs hope even when it's hopeless – that's what you said.'

'But that doesn't look hopeless.' I disentangle myself from Matthew and the net, the trap, and turn back to face the awful truth still cavorting jubilantly behind me. 'That looks like it's more than a possibility.'

'It's not. It's a series of chemical and electrical signals being transmitted from one source to a receiving source via the cloned tissue and a computer. Take away the computer and who knows what we have – very little possibly. But Jason needs to believe, remember?'

I can smell Matthew's sweat. It's rank with embarrassment. And deceit.

'Not this much,' I say, the bile rancid in my mouth. I put my hands on the glass panel and lean against it. Jason is quieter now, more controlled, and has begun systematically testing reflexes. He sees me leaning against the panel, forehead plastered to it. He must take it for amazement because he gives me the thumbs up.

'My doppelganger,' he mouths at me.

I nod. I don't know what else to do, my forehead rubbing against the smooth glass. 'But you've let him get this far, knowing it's rubbish?' I say quietly back to Matthew.

'No. No one let's Jason do anything, Elise. You know that. I've gone along with it, yes. I've had no choice. You've had no choice either. Whatever we say to Jason, he isn't going to listen. And it's not all rubbish, it's just whether what he wants to do is really possible. I've done my best to rein him in, but he has the bit between his teeth. He would have had that brain inside Fred if it hadn't been for a technical complication he can't fix…'

I don't even look at him, but I can hear the unspoken words.

'But you can?'

'Maybe. But then we'd be another step closer again to insanity, wouldn't we?'

I roll my forehead across the glass until my cheek is resting against it instead, and the cold is cooling my flaming face but not the fire inside me. 'But if this is insanity, how can you let your best friend go insane? How can you let this abomination happen? You promised, anyway.'

'I know. But if I don't, he really will go insane with desperation. You know that. We agreed that.' He pauses, then adds, almost too quietly for me to hear, 'And I would be ruined.'

'What do you mean?'

'I'm sorry, Elise, but I had to.' He stares down at his feet. 'Jason owns me,' he mumbles to them.

I wait for him to elaborate but he doesn't. Just keeps his eyes steadfastly on the floor, staring at it as if it holds the answer to everything, clinical white and as polished as glass. It reminds me of something I can't quite remember – something from before Jason. Then I get it: *clarity*. It reminds me of clarity. There hasn't been clarity in my life for years now – from the moment Jason first entered it to the moment the doctor said he would be leaving it in less than six months.

'You work for him,' I say, trying to compartmentalise what Matthew has just said. 'And I know what I said but that doesn't mean you have to do everything he or I tell you to – not if it's wrong.'

'He owns me, Elise, not employs me.' He is still staring at the floor. 'My debts, my assets, my conscience. I don't own any of it any more. Jason does. I couldn't tell you before. I was ashamed.'

The silence in our airlock of space between the lab and the operating space Jason and Fred are occupying is stifling. My head feels like it's about to implode with the pressure. I peel my cheek away from the glass pane and put my hands either side of my face to contain the crushing mass of questions inside my skull, channel them into one single sentence that makes sense. I fail miserably.

'I don't understand.'

Matthew sighs. 'I've been stupid. In the past. Jason's bailed me out. But eventually you have to pay the piper, even if his jigs have always been merry reels in the past.'

'He's blackmailing you?'

'In a way.'

'No! I don't believe you.' I push past him and towards the door to the inner space.

He grabs my arm as I pass. 'You can't go in. You'll contaminate the area.'

'Do I look as if I care?'

'Jason will go ballistic.'

'I'm his wife. He'll forgive me.' Matthew lets go of my arm and forward momentum takes me almost to the door. I am almost opening it when I stop, hand on the handle. None of this is right, but most wrong is the way Matthew is no longer stopping me. 'Why?' I ask without turning. 'Why aren't you stopping me?'

'You're his wife. He'll forgive you.'

'And what else?'

'You will be his nemesis. Not me.'

'You're a coward! I fling round and face Matthew again. The fury I'd felt in the hospital room when Jason had collapsed the first time is back with me full-force, but even as I want to slap and smack and gouge at Matthew, I know my anger isn't at him. It's with life and how it's turned out.

'Yes,' he replies, and his eyes drop back to the floor. 'I am a coward, Elise, and I'm ashamed of that too. But I can't do anything about it. I am afraid for myself, I'm afraid for you, and I'm afraid for Jason.'

'But…' We lock gazes, and I see for the first time what is behind the intensity of fear in his eyes. It's not that he's afraid of what will happen to Jason if it doesn't work. It's what will happen if it does.

'What can you do about it, even whilst you're being a coward?' I ask eventually.

'What I've already been doing. Slowing it all down. But he's continually speeding it up.' He looks past me to the glass viewing panel. 'He wasn't supposed to start any tests whilst I was answering the door to you. Now we are both locked out of there unless we want to contaminate the area and invalidate everything he's done this morning. What do you think that will bring on?'

'Another seizure, I guess…' Misery crushes my voice so that it is tiny and weak.

There is a rap on the glass and Jason is leering through the window again. He gives us the thumbs-up signal and Matthew responds in kind. Jason grins and then raises his eyebrows at me. His voice floods suddenly into our little airlock.

'So, what do you reckon, Elise? Wouldn't Fred make a great pianist?' He waves Fred's right hand at us and then wriggles the fingers.

Matthew presses a button on the panel next to the door, and gestures to me. 'Go on, he can hear you now,' he says. His voice hangs in the stillness of the airlock.

'Jason… ' Words stumble over themselves in my head but dam up in my mouth. 'I don't know what to say.'

'Congratulations?' he jibes. 'I imagine Matthew has explained what this means?' He tilts his head like a coquette and raises his eyebrows at me. Classic Jason. Jason the wag, Jason the tease, Jason the in control again. I nod my head slowly. Yes, but not at what Jason thinks he will have explained to me.

'So Plans A, B and C are all systems go,' he grins.

'Plan A to C?' But I say it into our airlocked silence.

Matthew has switched the intercom off, and Jason has already moved on to testing Fred's left arm. 'Plans A to C, Matthew?'

Matthew rubs his hands over his face. 'Oh shit.'

'What?'

Behind us Fred and Jason are in synchrony, four-handed piano.

'Let me talk to him – when he's finished in there.'

'About what? Plans A to C? I know Plan A, but what are Plans B and C?'

'Plan A was to shift the Parmensis into Fred's body by hooking up Jason's brain to Fred's body and force a clean break between brain and tumour.'

'That's what I thought. And B?'

'Plan B was to work out how to isolate the Parmensis and get it to shift using Fred and more study because it wasn't moving.'

'Oh my God!' I pause, breathe choking in my throat, until I realise the horror doesn't end there. 'But why did you clone his brain to do that?'

'Because that's Plan C. Cloned brain and Jason's body.'

'But he wouldn't even be Jason any more then. Turn it off! Turn it off now!' I scream at him. I lurch towards the door again but this time he does stop me.

'I will, I will – but you have to trust me over this.'

'How can I trust you? You never told me my husband was planning on cloning his brain and using that. Your Plan A was bad enough. The rest of it… You said we should talk and we did, but you didn't tell me any of that.' Now I am pummelling him, beating my fists against his chest and shrieking at him, whilst the concerto beyond the glass panel reaches a crescendo.

'Stop, stop, stop…' I run out of steam almost as fast as the fury came upon me and we are left facing each other in the strange no-man's land of the airlock.

'Believe me, Elise,' Matthew pleads, 'I had no idea he was thinking about this originally. I would never have helped him clone the brain if I had. I thought it was purely for testing. Please, let's stop fighting and think about how to deal with this.'

'There's only one way to deal with this. Destroy it.'

'And then you'll destroy Jason, too. We thought it might have moved from his brain just for the moment when we created the clone template so cloned brain could be his only chance. Let's…' He breaks off, attention distracted. 'Oh…'

We are both distracted now. Jason is knocking on the viewing pane, his face drooping on the left side, mouth opening and closing like a fish underwater, eye twitching.

'What's going on?' he's mouthing at us.

'Oh shit!' Matthew spins away from me and slams his hand on the intercom button. 'Come out! Come out now!' he urges.

'M'OK, really, just tired…' Jason's voice is blurred, shaky. 'But what's up there?'

'Nothing!' I join Matthew by the viewing panel. 'But you're ticking. Come out before you have another seizure. Or I'll come in and get you.'

'No-oooh,' he laughs. 'I'm on my way out. Stand clear…' The airlock door decompresses and Jason slides round it, still in scrubs. 'Chair,' he demands as soon as he is clear. His hands are still stuffed into surgical gloves and a tiny green filament has attached itself to the cuff, like a snake stalking its victim. He collapses onto the chair Matthew wheels hastily across to him. I crouch down in front of him and start to peel the gloves off. He slouches against the chair back. 'Power down,' he instructs Matthew. 'Don't let it overload…'

'Don't worry. I'll deal with all that. You just get back to your rooms and lay down. Elise will call the docs.'

'Don't need the docs…'

'Yes, you do,' I say, trying to keep the anger from infecting my voice. 'Let Matthew sort this out now. You need the doctors.'

'Allllll-right… Good old Matthew!' Jason laughs. 'My best buddy… my two best buddies, Matthew and Fred. Good eh, Matthew? Good start. And Plan C. Just think what I'll be able to do with that – no holds barred!'

On the trolley in the surgical area beyond the glass viewing pane, the half-man, half-cyborg lies prone on the table. I can't bring myself to look beyond it to the glass tank.

Plan C seems to be partially underway already.

Chapter 23

4th June 2029: Matthew

'You made me a promise.' Her eyes are accusing; heavy coals burning in a white-hot face.

'And I'm keeping it.'

'Then what was all that about.'

Jason is sleeping now, sedated and cocooned by his team of medics. Elise is perched on the bar stool nearest the bar Jason insisted was installed in his private suite – although what the hell for? Alcohol is banned for him and that is one rule he won't break in case it interferes with his Plan. Plan B – now apparently ousted by the far worse Plan C. A cocktail glass is positioned in front of her. It could be a gin and tonic, without the ice and lime. It could be anything, just like everything could be anything at the moment, but knowing Elise, it will be water. Ice cold, and me in danger of having it dashed in my face. I keep the bar between us. It's not much of a barricade, but it's worthy of me, the heel, the pretender, the coward. A bar for a barricade, a lie for a life, a best friend heading for his death and his wife believing I was championing her when all I've been doing is covering my back.

'It won't happen, Elise. It can't. Maybe in five, ten years' time but right now there are too many elements we haven't documented – don't even know about. You asked me to go along with it without pushing it, so I'm going along with it. That's what that was.'

She pushes the glass away from her, eyes studying it, then sliding back to my face.

'Are we wrong, doing this, Matthew? Lying to him while he thinks he has a hope of surviving this?'

'What is life without hope?'

'What we are living now. What Jason is living right now if he but knew it.'

'Then let him carry on living it even if we can't.'

She fiddles with the glass again. 'You're right. I'm sorry. It's just… I feel so bad about this. About everything.'

'I know,' I say, without knowing anything of what she feels. How can I? I've never loved – except someone I can't have even when Jason is no longer here.

'I know you do.' Her eyes have softened to luminous fire points. 'And bless you for that. Bless you for being so… *good.*' So good? Christ, I despise myself! If only she knew – the reality, the possibility of how this could turn out – and what I have done in case… I spread my hands in supplication – mercy for my sins, God – please. 'But I do now need to control this somehow or it's going to get so out of hand we could all get destroyed in the meltdown. One of his doctors agrees with me – the little German one.'

She laughs, a small explosion of wry mirth. 'Of all of them, it was the German one who agreed, would you believe it?'

'Agreed with what?'

'That I might eventually need Power of Attorney on grounds of diminished responsibility.'

'Jason would never agree to that, and a fight through the courts would take you until he died – '

'I know. That's why he's signed it already. It was my quid pro quo for agreeing in the first place. Not financial, but health and welfare.'

'Why didn't you say?'

'I hoped it wouldn't be necessary. But just in case, Matthew, now you know – especially now I know where you stand.'

A part of me is relieved. The other part of me is disappointed. What does that say about me?

Chapter 24

5th June 2029: Jason

I have lain awake most of the night watching the shadows eddy and collect around me. I turned the light on once, but it made no difference. They were still there, waiting for me, pooling in the corners of the room, teeth half-bared in a sickly grin. Now I am resigned to staring into the dark, just listening to them and their whispers until the day breaks again – if it ever does.

Come on Jason, give in. It's easy. You just slip away. No more tests or disappointment or loss of control. No more humiliating weakness, or Elise watching you with eyes that are recording your minutest deflection from the norm...

I roll over. 'Fuck off.'

Why fight it? You can't win. This plan you have – it can never work.

'Why can't it?'

It's too advanced, too many variables you don't understand. Give in. It's easier...

'You don't know any more than I do on that score.'

Isn't that it, Jason, though? You don't know... Want to talk about it?'

'No.'

But now it's not the unseen fears I am answering. It is Elise, as she helped me back from the lab. I remember her soft freshness, her perfume – like lavender on a sunny day – and her eyes, asking, asking what I can't answer.

'You look so tired.'

'I'm OK.'

Her touch on my arm, feather-soft fingertips, stroking away the intensity of tiredness that is invading my body. Her shoulder beneath mine, edging me onwards, through the door, towards the bed. Her lips brushing across my forehead, as light and airy as a spring breeze, ruffling my face and then it's gone. I close my eyes and the desperation breaks through the hard, outer shell of my defences, just for a moment; but it is enough to allow her to as well.

'Do you want to talk about it?' Hesitant, almost inaudible.

'What, dying?' I open my eyes and wish I hadn't seen the look on her face. It came out harsher than I intended.

'I didn't mean that. About your fears, your hopes, anything.'

'Sorry,' I say, but it doesn't soften the blow. She doesn't understand. How can she? 'It's easier if I don't acknowledge it. Just pretend it's all fine.'

'Oh.' Her face is closed in like a lily closing to the night breezes.

I can't do this. It's enough that I hold myself together. I can't hold her together too. Suddenly exhaustion is complete. 'I'm tired,' I say. I can't think of anything else to add to that – whether the blow is hard or not. Inside me is hollow, empty – depleted beyond refilling.

'Do you want me to go?'

'Would you mind, hun? I think you and Matthew are right. I do need to rest. But tomorrow's another day – I hope.'

'OK.'

I can hear the hesitation in her voice but I will not give it space to develop. I close my eyes to end the conversation. What could I say if it was to continue anyway? I've already said more than I intended.

It was a moment of weakness before Plan B and I'm not going to repeat it, or it becomes real. I don't want to die. I don't want to go into that good night. I want more – more of everything.

And I'm afraid.

I watch her leave through half-closed eyes. It is a shamed, awkward leaving and I know I have done that to her. But I can't make it right, because I never can be and, God help me, I hate her for it. She is living on, but I am dying – unless a miracle happens. A miracle called Plan C unless I can shift the fucking Parmensis out of my brain.

I roll over again because the fears have started to whisper again. They don't believe in Plan C either. It's not possible, it's a sham. The cloned brain doesn't even exist – or if it does, it doesn't work like I thought it did. I try to ignore them because I know it does. I know it works.

Does it?

Does it really?

Or am I imagining it? Am I imagining it even exists? Am I imagining

Matthew's slowness, Elise's reluctance? Am I imagining death? Fuck no! I'm not. It's snapping at my heels like a Doberman on heat. And I will not be beaten. I will not die. I force the creeping dark out of my soul and my feet onto the floor. It is cool and calming. The underfloor heating is off. All the heating is down low – bad for sinuses and bad for the brain, according to Dr Kohn. Apparently even neurologists have complexes.

I stand and I am steady. Time to go. The digital display on the wall says 04:01. Four o'clock and all's well. It's not, but if I can keep things moving, maybe it could be. In the lab there is a brain that works without a fucking invader, and it's my brain or as near as damn it. My brain that I used to control Fred. What I didn't tell Matthew was that all the while Fred was waving and gesturing, it wasn't the system that was controlling him. It was me. I could feel it – I was thinking it – each minute movement was initiated by me. My brain. My *two brains* in harmony. And I could feel the latent power of the mass lying in the CyberCute jelly. I could feel it both in me and outside of me.

I pad across the floor, imagining my footprints, hot and sticky on the cool surface – a gingerbread trail to the witch's house. I can do magic. I know I can – whatever restraints Matthew wants to impose on me. The magic isn't in the technology or the CyberCute or our skill in connecting it all. It's in me and my will to survive. In the lab, I flick on the under-storage lighting, but not the main lights. They glow like aircraft emergency lighting, leading the way to the exits. The sterile area is shielded from the outside, so the lights can go full blaze in there, but here might attract security, even with my instructions to check with me first before entering. I make my way slowly across the lab, collecting surgical scrubs en route, and flicking on the lights to full brilliance inside the airlock. It feels safe inside. It isn't. Nowhere is safe for me but this is the safest I've felt in weeks. Scrubbing up meticulously, I check on the steadiness of my hands. Perfect. Not even the smallest tremor. The Parmensis hasn't found my CNS yet then, wherever else it may have diffused to.

Inside both the airlock and the sterile area, everything is exactly how we left it. Matthew must have walked away and locked up without a further thought. I think about that for a while. It could mean anything. Maybe best not to overthink it. It could be as simple as a flight response to the situation – and concern for me. I don't deny him that, whatever I may have done to him or him to me. Scratch that: whatever I have done to him.

My brain is nestling comfortably in the CyberCute. Dr Kohn would have been fascinated – amazed, even. Maybe even her Germanic stoicism would be replaced with childish wonder if I allowed her to see. That makes me laugh out loud. I've never been a stereotype, or prejudiced but there are types and she is one – but bloody good, the best.

I power up the computer, connect up the electrodes one by one to the cyborg brain and my own scalp and initiate the next round of tests we would have made on the cyborg brain alone if I hadn't flipped out. Gross motor control is fine. I even go so far as getting Fred to sit, then stand, then sit again. He perches on the trolley in an alert position, a gundog ready to retrieve for his master. I like that. No wonder Mary Shelley enjoyed writing Frankenstein. My creature. Except he's not a monster. He's me, potentially. I leave the computer console to examine him more minutely. His gaze is straight ahead – no eyes, of course, only the empty hollows of the orbits, patiently awaiting filling. That will be a challenge. Elise always claims the eyes are the window of the soul – overworked cliché though that is. There is something of the soul in her eyes, so maybe there is in mine too? Yes, maybe. If you believe in it.

We haven't cloned eyes in full yet, only the eyeball shell, but not the delicate optical nerve. Maybe Matthew was right and I should involve some of my medics after all. Kohn, at least, and maybe Pantov, the optical specialist; he could be useful if I ended up with Plan C. Or maybe there was a Plan D to be considered too. My brain and Fred's body, permanently? The best of both worlds. Fred is adaptive and designed to be integrated. Why re-invent the wheel? It had to be the future, ultimately.

I go back to the console and re-programme. Fine motor skills and CNS. The read-out in the bottom right-hand corner of the screen says 05.17. Still plenty of time. I can go slowly on these – make sure before I present Matthew with Plan C or D in full. Pincer grip is perfect, head and arm tracking perfect, co-localisation effective, and haptic feedback promising. Next, motor planning, sequence, timing, and precision… Choose the softest object for haptic perception… spot on. I adjust the parameters and change the direct control method. Now it's me via the Cyborg brain. I repeat the same exercises. They flow easily. I laugh and the laughter doesn't want to stop. I am thinking movement to Fred. I can route it directly or indirectly, through my brain or the brain vibrating gently in the CyberCute jelly, but either way, Fred and I are in tandem. Christ! And the cloned brain is free of the Parmensis! That brief moment of time when it shifted before settling back was our breakthrough.

Suddenly I am shaking and laughing and crying all at the same time. I can even feel what he's feeling. Not in my fingers, but in his – an off-centre, off-logic sensation with someone else's hand that is also yours. I pinch and twist and fumble and stroke. I pull a hair from his leg, I prod his thigh until the white impress of my finger – no, *his* finger – leaves a doughy dimple that blushes red when the pressure is removed. Can I feel that? Can I feel the pathological impact as blood rushes back into the tiny vascular pathways and stimulates the CNS response? Pain.

Shit! I can. I do it again. Extreme. And again. Oh God, I love that pain! I only stop when I realise Fred is bruising, his CyberCute covering tenderising like a hammered steak. Enough. Haptic response proven – and how! 05:56. One last test then, and I will have to decide after that whether to involve Dr Kohn and Dr Pantov. I come out of fine motor skills and select *Optical Response.* Immediately I am surveying the room through my own eyes on-screen. Great, but I need eyes through Fred. I disconnect myself and concentrate on the cyborg brain, stimulating the optical nerve connection and studying the feedback. It's active, at least. I re-route the stimuli so my lens and retina are routing to the cyborg's optic nerve connection. I have routed my own brain out of *vision* and I activate fine motor control and optical responses simultaneously. Now I am looking though my own eyes on-screen, using the cyborg. I laugh out loud and stimulate more fine motor control actions. Fred opens and closes his fist, pinches forefinger and thumb together, sticks the middle finger up in an 'up yours' gesture and I am childishly satisfied as I direct optical response to look at the rude gesture, the laughter rumbling around my gut like impending thunder. Then it blanks out. The screen flickers on and off erratically. I lean in to check the cyborg brain. A loose connection? No, all fine. What the fuck then? I disengage the rest of the electrodes from my scalp and go over to the cyborg brain and then Fred himself. One by one I check the electrodes and connections. The face is mainly metal and smooth plating, with only the merest covering of CyberCute, but one of the contacts around the orbital hollow seems to be pulsating. I watch it, fascinated, until it suddenly coils up and detaches and the screen behind me goes completely blank.

What the—! I peer at it. The electrode connector and the connection point is fine. I trace its line to the cyborg brain, and there I see why it has short-circuited. Around the optical nerve connection is a thickening mass that wasn't there before. Shouldn't be there at all. Damn! I disconnect all the electrodes and ignore the brain's reluctance to be detached from its CyberCute jelly. If this is what I think it is, it no longer matters what damage I do it. Nevertheless, I lift it tenderly from its nest and place it on the workbench near the console. It lies there, a grey convoluted mass of me – almost me, duplicate me, with – only just visible – a discolouring mass expanding around the base of the globe of the cerebellum. From its centre, a tube-shaped mass of nervous tissue a little over three inches long extends, and quivers as if awaiting its fate. Even as I watch the discoloured mass engulfs the brain stem and devours it. I step back, panting and repulsed as I watch the Parmensis we have cloned, subdue and consume all around it, as if it is an amoeba surrounding and engulfing paramecia.

'Damn!' I whisper. 'How…?'

But I know how. Our methods are failsafe – perfect. We replicate what is there. We have to. What is the point of cloning otherwise? And when we created the template, the Parmensis must have beaten us to it by maybe mere fractions of a second, but beaten us it had, nevertheless. I step back, colliding with the console chair, sending it spinning across the room into the trolley. Fred wavers and collapses from his sitting position, a redwood falling, as the dam breaks inside me.

'Damn, damn, damn!' I am screaming it, screaming at it, at me, at life and death, but who can hear? This hell is mine alone. I have a scalpel. It is impaled deep inside the brain and I don't even care that I can feel the sharp point of its entry viscerally into my very soul. I stab and stab and stab and only stop stabbing when someone – Dr Kohn, I think – calls to me through the intercom. By then the cloned brain is as crushed and useless as my own.

Chapter 25

5th June 2029: Matthew

I am on my way back from a ridiculously early visit to the corner shop with the lunchbox additions Jane forgot. The penance of delivering the kids to school is my blessing today, except Jane doesn't understand that. For her it *is* penance – although for what, this time, I don't know. I almost reject the call, assuming it will be Jane trowelling on another layer of demand, but it's Crane Security.

'Shit!' I pull over, tyres and brakes screeching, the range of awful possibilities vying with each other for worst place. 'Yes?'

'Best get back here straightaway, sir. The lab.' The voice is monotone. The lab?

'Is Mr Crane dead?'

'No, sir,' the guard's voice does have tone now. It is guarded. 'But – best just get here as quickly as you can. Dr Kohn's instruction.'

I barely hear the end of his exhortation as I slam the car into reverse and do a U-turn in the middle of the main road, ignoring the hooting and swearing from the car behind me. I just about manage to juggle steering wheel and phone as I make my apologies to Jane and attempt to not be seen by the roadside cameras aimed at the backward idiots like me who won't upgrade to autonomous vehicles and make the roads safe – their perception, not mine. I'd still rather rely on my own judgement than that of a road tracker even if I am fallible. And nevertheless, using a phone whilst driving at speed is still one of the safer courses of action I've taken recently. That almost makes me laugh, but for the reason I'm doing any of it – wise or dumb. Once I've finished with Jane, I try to raise Elise. I feel a duty to be acutely honest with her now, even if her appreciation of what I do is less than fulsome – except for one thing; that she doesn't need to know just yet. Her phone just rings out and goes to voicemail. Maybe she's already on her way and can't answer – except I know Elise does have the advantage of an autonomous vehicle, so the inference is that she's choosing not to answer. I know her phone is glued to her like Jason is glued to the lab. That can only be bad. Inside me, the threatening storm gathers momentum. This could be it – after all. This could be it… Maybe she'll never need to know?

I reach the lab in less than fifteen minutes, which, given it's a good twenty-five minutes' drive from home and I haven't caused any major incidents en route, apart from the enraged motorist behind me, endorses my view of road safety as opposed to the authorities'. Am I becoming as blasé as Jason about conformity? No. I can answer that without even thinking. I have always been a conformist. Afraid of my own shadow is how Jane would put it. Toeing the party line would be Jason's version – a good company man. Coward is mine. I don't even want to think about what Elise would call me if she knew the whole story. I abandon the car in the car park nearest the main entrance. It's the quickest way into the lab, the gamut of security arrangements notwithstanding. There is a back entrance only Jason and I use, but it is way around the other side of the building and I am no athlete. The reception staff have obviously been briefed anyway as I speed though security with barely a blink into the iris scanner, before I am popping out the other side and hurtling down the corridor towards the lab.

I can already see security guards positioned awkwardly by its door.

'Dr Green, glad you're here, sir. Go right on in.' The guard – he looks so familiar – swings the door wide for me to enter. He looks stern, downcast. I remember his name at the same time as I step over the threshold. Fred. I want to laugh aloud at that. Yes, Fred – we'd named ForEver Fred after him because of his more or less permanently lugubrious state – much the same as Fred's without features or personalisation.

'Thanks,' I say to the already closing door and empty lab. 'Hello?' I call. 'Jason?'

'In here.'

His voice is cracked and distant – emanating from the sterile area. It echoes hollowly, almost a whisper, it is so muffled by the cocooning safety of the sterile area.

'Do I need scrubs?' I call as I make my way towards the door to the sterile area. There is no answer, so I grab a pair from the cupboard and start to struggle into them as I reach the door. What greets me as I open the airlock into the sterile unit proper is carnage accompanied by the repulsive smell of decomposition. The unit has been trashed. Monitor screens smashed, leads trailing, instruments scattered. At first, I think there's been a break-in. 'Oh God, who did this?' Then I spot Jason sprawling across the workbench nearest the console we'd been working from yesterday. He is on his knees, both arms stretched out to his sides, as if he has crucified himself on the workbench. He is staring to the left of him, cheek welded to the work top, eyes wide open, lips moving gently with what sounds like 'damn, damn, damn.' All around him is a sticky, amorphous mess of grey flecked with white. It reminds me of the revolting jelly Jane made for the kids' Halloween party once.

I wade through the debris of destruction, sending pieces of mangled equipment spinning in all directions, the flotsam and jetsam of disaster.

'My God, what's happened? Who did this? Are you hurt?'

'Hurt?' His shoulders begin to shake and I'm afraid he is crying. I'm useless enough when Jane or one of the kids cries – ineffectual bastard that I am. When Elise cried in the hospital was the best I've ever managed in empathetic response – not that I'm not empathetic. I'm too much so. I swear their pain hurts me more than it hurts them. But if Jason cries, then I know this is the end. He is invincible, even in the throes of death.

But he isn't crying. He's laughing, quietly, mechanically, persistently – like the rattle of a well-oiled machine gun delivering its rounds one after the other after the other.

'Jason?' I draw alongside him now and realise the amorphous mass isn't jelly. It's tissue. I gag. The brain we had cloned – Jason's brain – has been completely eviscerated on the workbench. It spreads in a dripping trail from the smashed console to the small blackened lump Jason's left-hand fingertips are almost touching. 'Jason?' I say it carefully, unsure whether he can see or hear or understand me.

'The Parmensis… It could have migrated anywhere.'

He closes his eyes as if going to sleep and his giggling slows to a long, deflating sigh. I wait a while but he doesn't move or open his eyes. I survey the unit as I wait. There is barely a thing left untouched – except Fred. Fred is lying hands crossed over his chest like a corpse awaiting his winding sheet. Jason is as still and silent now too. The insects crawling in my chest cavity begin to buzz and panic takes hold of me. I shake Jason's shoulder, gently at first, then urgently when he still doesn't respond. Somewhere in the room a fly has got in. It buzzes in concert with the vibration of hysteria steadily growing in my chest. So much for sterility. Everything is compromised in here, everything – except Fred, it seems.

'Jason, Jason, what the hell happened?'

'Wha—what? Oh, it's you.' Jason rubs his face with his hands, smearing grey brain matter over his cheeks like an Indian war tattoo.

'What happened?'

He pulls himself and his arms drop to his sides. He breathes out, a huff of exhaustion. 'That happened,' he says, nodding towards the rapidly shrivelling piece of dark tissue. 'We grew the tumour too,' he adds. 'We cloned my brain but we cloned the bloody tumour too!' He stands unsteadily and retrieves the piece of tissue, rolling it along the worktop in front of us. It smudges the grey brain matter and leaves a snail trail along the workbench. It stops in front of him and he picks it up and cups it in his palm, thrusting it towards me. I recoil. 'There. That's the thing that's killing me. Shame we can't get the real thing out of me as easily as I got it out of my cloned brain!'

'Jesus!' I take a step back and collide with a broken chair, its arm hanging wounded almost to the floor. It tips and falls over and the clatter makes us both jump. I right it and push it away from us. It spins giddily away from us and the dismembered brain-worktop, until it hits the secondary console on the other side of the room, where it bounces and bobs as if it's a small ship that's found its harbour. I look around at the lab. 'And did you do all this?'

Jason leans against the bench and crosses one leg over the other at the ankle. He looks relaxed and unfazed, but his face is greyer than the muck.

'I'm sorry.' Suddenly he crumples and puts his face in his hands, sinking to the floor in a graceful single movement. 'But what does it matter now anyway? If we clone another one, we'll only do exactly the same thing again.'

He starts to tremble and I dither, wondering whether to go and put my arm around him or try to reason and offer platitudes. Before I can decide, the trembling explodes into another seizure and I am trying to remember what the doctor told us to do at the hospital whilst I scream for help. The hands that take over are practised and efficient. I watch and wait as Jason's medical team sedate him until the seizure subsides. We leave the wrecked sterile unit in procession, Jason on a gurney similar to the one ForEver Fred is lying on, and Dr Kohn casting a curious but non-committal eye over the holocaust we are leaving behind, taking in the decaying brain matter, the extracted Parmensis, and ending on ForEver Fred. One eyebrow raises and when she looks at me it is with her head slightly to one side, like a small garden bird, establishing whether it is safe to approach or not.

'It was me who told the guard to call you,' is all she says, then busies herself with Jason. 'I didn't interfere then. I just waited for you to arrive, but maybe an explanation would be in order soon?'

'That's up to Jason – Mr Crane,' I reply cautiously. We need her, but we don't need her involved too far. She merely raises her eyebrows and smiles before overseeing Jason's sedation.

When all is calm again, I sit down alongside Jason's bed and wait for him to come round. I realise then that Elise hasn't appeared despite me assuming she had been called at the same time as me. Jason's eyelids twitch and I know he is awake but feigning sleep. I know him far too well now and I also have in mind how he 'persuaded' Elise.

'Do you want me to call Elise?' I ask quietly.

'No. Don't tell Elise,' is all he says. 'Not yet.'

'And the good doctor? She wants an explanation. Apparently, she found you.'

'I will see to that.'

'OK. Look, we'll find a way,' I add, wondering what else to say. 'Plan B, it could still work…'

'Will we?' he asks. 'Will we, Matthew?'

'Of course, we will. You're JC. You walk on water. There'll be a way.'

'I'm JC.' He snorts. 'Goddamn wish I was now. Physician heal thyself. Physicians don't bloody heal themselves and neither do prostheses giants. That's the whole fucking problem!'

'Fred's still OK. That's something.'

'Yep, that's something. It's just both my brains that aren't.' Jason turns his face away from me and for a moment I think he is crying. Then, 'that Parmensis specimen, what happened to it?'

'I don't know. Do you want me to go back and find it?'

'No, no. Leave it for now. I need to rest, then think. Don't tell Elise. Leave that to me.' He closes his eyes and I know that this is my signal to go. I slide off the chair and push it as quietly away from the bed as I can. 'Tell Kohn to drop in, though, would you Matthew? Better start on some of those explanations now, before she comes to her own conclusions.'

'OK,' I nod. 'Anything else?'

'No.' He smiles then, a lopsided twist that I recognise from other, happier times when we and the world were younger, brighter and more hopeful. 'Plan D, maybe,' he adds. 'See you tomorrow.'

Chapter 26

6th June 2029: Elise

'Why wasn't I told?' I ask. I can hear the whininess in my voice and hate it. I should control it better or Matthew will stop telling me anything. Matthew doesn't seem to notice though. His hesitation clearly has other reasons that a phone call – unlike a face-to-face conversation – doesn't reveal.

'Jason said not to.' He pauses, and I am about to ask him – caustically – if he always does everything Jason tells him to or does he ever have a mind of his own? I pull myself up just before he begins to speak again. I don't like myself like this – and there's more to this than Matthew is letting on. He confirms that in his next sentence.

'Look, Elise, I don't agree with this – keeping you in the dark – but I'm tied. You know I'm tied, God help me.'

His voice is tired and splintered. Yes, now I know how he is tied and I don't know who that reflects on most – him for his deficient vulnerability or Jason for his ruthless supremacy. Neither sit well with me. And then there's me, and my predilection to judge… I claim to be able to accept and forgive, but when have I? With Jason, yes – but what about Jane?

'Why?' I ask in the end, shelving all the recriminations. They're as much of Jason and me as of Matthew's withholding of information. If Jason and I had a relationship of trust, there would be no withholding of anything; the small voice that over the years has reminded me of how far I fell when I fell for Jason, is there again, niggling. Oh, what a fool I have been at times! What a fool! But it is too late for that now. Choices are choices and once made can only lead on to other choices, not a remaking of history. Matthew's continued silence at the other end of the phone speaks volumes. It wasn't the episode I wasn't to have been told about. It's what is flowing from it. That's why. 'Matthew?' The whininess is gone now. I am in control again. Not of Jason, but then I never was –

Power of Attorney or not. He knows I wouldn't exercise it unless there was nothing left of hope in any format. The only control I can have is of my own life from now on.

Matthew's reply comes like a rush of confession. 'I don't know exactly, but whatever we were going to do, we aren't... I don't think… I won't know until tomorrow – and maybe not even then. But Elise, trust me… I made you a promise and I will keep it. I will keep this in check.'

'Well, if Jason won't tell me and neither will you, I haven't got a lot of choice, have I?' I hate the implied threat in my voice. I want to take it back. I am not like that. I am not a blackmailer. I am the blackmailed.

'Elise, I'm sorry. I know it goes against the grain, but sometimes not knowing is better – or pretending not to know. I've learnt that from Jason. Please just hold off on that for a while. It would be better if you held off…'

I want to ask him what he knows but pretends he doesn't. Or maybe it is better not to know? Yet I need some comfort, and if not from Matthew, who?

'And which are you currently?' I ask.

'What?'

'Blackmailer or blackmailed?'

'I'm only just finding out, actually Elise,' he replies, so quietly that for a time I'm not sure he's even spoken.

Chapter 27

7th June 2029: Matthew

The conversation with Elise stays with me into sleep and beyond. My jumbled dreams are filled with her face and then Jason's, morphing into grey rivers that turn out to be brain matter when I get close enough to peer into them, flowing away to some unseen point of origin or departure. Jane figures too, looming over me with chains that are made of the flowing grey, wrapping them round and around my wrists and then handing the two ends to Jason and Elise to secure, but when I wake, I know that is merely my subconscious inserting her into the scenario. I am trapped by all of them in different ways – Jason through debt and threat, Jane through domestic coercion and Elise through emotion. My legs are twisted in the bedclothes and my body sweaty and weak. Christ, I hate myself and my weakness – but not as much as I hate what I have done. But how else can I break any of these chains?

Coffee. I need coffee and something to lighten my mood, but coffee alone isn't going to do that. In a moment of inspiration, I step through the remains of yesterday and the half-eaten takeaway congealing on the plate by the iPlayer. Underneath it, the discarded, dog-eared newspaper telling the world and me about the next conference in Tokyo that heralds the latest breakthroughs in medical bio-engineering but which Jason Crane, as yet, is mysteriously not confirmed to be at. A puddle of grease and curry sauce has overflown from the plate and stained Jason's image and made him into a daguerreotype, all colour leached and stained sepia. Jason a thing of the past? I still can't believe that, whatever the facts now. I step over the conjoined plate and newspaper to the chest of drawers tucked into the corner of the room, the place I usually avoid as much as possible. I rummage through the drawer that contains all the detritus of my current life, mainly bank statements with everything counterbalancing on the wrong side for financial health and Sol's increasingly irritated written exhortations for me to give Jane what she wants and just get out before it gets really nasty. Too late, Sol.

The twist of marijuana left over from a long since forgotten party attended with Jane before it all went wrong is still there, right at the back. I pull it out and unwrap the brittle paper it is folded in. Both paper and marijuana crumble in my fingers. It would probably still work, though, a momentary high to counter the almost continual lows… But what would Elise think of me if she knew? Probably almost irrelevant given what else she will come to know one day, but nevertheless, the inspiration ends up flushed down the toilet and I make do with coffee. Madness averted – this time, maybe. I'm going to need my wits about me today, I suspect.

The traffic is mild-mannered on the way to the lab but the day is grey and unworthy of spring. It matches my mood perfectly. Even the air smells grey and musty. The end of the week and normally I would be relishing a bit of free time and maybe an hour or two with the kids, if Jane decided she wanted to impose on me or someone else. She never understands why it is no imposition for me, but then she never understood anything about me or me anything about her. This Friday, though, I have the feeling of impending doom, even more than I've had over the last month or so. Jason's Plan D, whatever that is, for a start. Yet when I arrive at the lab, all is serene and controlled. The lab itself is pristine – and empty. I retrace my steps to Jason's suite of rooms and they are empty too. I buzz reception from the internal phone and ask if Mr Crane has any appointments. The receptionist sounds surprised.

'No. I thought he was still unavailable for anything like that. You said so yourself only last week when the Tokyo conference people were being so persistent.'

The note of question in her tone sends me scuttling. Be careful. We've kept this under wraps for now but that move was stupid.

'Oh, no. That's still the case. Just checking in, that's all. My stupid absent-mindedness. You know me.'

'That's all right, Dr Green.' Indulgence is back in her voice and I disconnect before I can I mess up by saying anything else, but a sensation of dread dogs my footsteps back to the lab and to the one place I haven't checked but should have as my first stop.

The door to the airlock is closed and the place is in silence but instinctively I know. I collect scrubs and take a deep breath before I type in the release code and insert myself into the cocoon of whatever ForEver is now creating. The unpleasant smell of yesterday has gone, replaced by an antiseptic tang. The blind has been let down on the viewing window, but a small crack around the edge where it doesn't quite meet the edge of the frame allows light from the sterile area to pierce the intentional blackout. I hesitate, caught by what I'd voiced yesterday to Elise as a platitude: the choice between not knowing and pretending to not know. I know Jason is on the other side of the airlock and Plan D will already be evolving there. Do I want to know what Plan D is? The temptation to walk away – just simply walk away and to hell with everyone and everything – is almost too much. Jason's life isn't my responsibility. Elise isn't my wife. Jane isn't my commitment any more. Whether this experiment with God and immortality works or not isn't my problem, even though I'm curious but… No. Go and be whoever you want to be, that little voice of total anarchy whispers to me and, where I've always discounted it before, now I want to listen. Oh God, I want to listen!

The red light on the airlock door goes off. The intercom buzzes.

'Well come in if you're coming. Can't fuck about waiting all morning for you.'

So that is the mood for today, and my fight or flight will have to be fight. This time. I pull on the scrubs and settle in front of the wash area.

'I assume we're sterile since the light was on?' I call over my shoulder. Jason must have set the intercom to *on*, whatever he is doing, or he wouldn't have heard me enter, sequestered away as he is in the sterile area.

'Yup, sterile and rocking.' His voice comes back muffled but full of the old vigour.

The door releases and I step through the airlock into Jason's domain. Gone is the devastation of yesterday, the sea of grey matter, the trashed hardware. The sterile area is back to new – better than new – but with Fred still dominating the central space in his silent, anticipatory way. Jason is bolted to a brand-new monitor – one of the latest models from the CyberCute lab, it seems. Alongside him is an array of other – to me – new machines. An ECG machine stands off to one side of the workspace, plus a portable MRI – something I've heard of but not yet seen – and oxygen tanks stacked against the far wall. The trolley of surgical instruments has been replenished and they wink flirtatiously at me under the stark overhead light. The collection looks fuller – extended. I count up rapidly. There are thirty separate instruments where before there were seventeen, including bipolar forceps, a full set of dissectors and rongeurs, drill bits, wire and pin instruments, elevators and impactors. There is something suspiciously and worryingly medical about the whole range of new equipment – in fact, suspiciously neurological. Overnight probably most of the remaining liquid assets of Crane Industries must have been invested in the ForEver project.

Jason swings around. His eyes are hollow orbits and his skin has the waxy look that whispers lack of sleep, but his face is tight and his eyes are intense.

'New plan,' he announces. 'Plan D. We use the cyborg's brain but my body.'

'What?' My voice is as shot as my nerves. I had seen Plan D coming, but not this.

'Well, if we clone my brain we clone the damn tumour too, so let's capitalise on that. Clone the bloody thing and then remove it. It'll be easier to get to unconnected. Exposed that way. No cerebral cortex issues to get in the way. Dr Kohn can remove the tumour and then assist in the insertion. Forget cloning my body parts and getting everything to integrate around a cyborg base. Just use what we've already got.'

His jaw clicks and juts. Mine hangs slack. I knew he was determined but this, this is…

'Jason, this is impossible. Your brain, it… we don't know how…'

'Cyborg's brain, my impulses. We captured and directed them with the CyberArm 3.3. It's only the same process and we can do the same with a cyborg brain.'

'It might be same principle but it's not the same thing at all.'

'Then we need to make it so, don't we?'

'And how the hell can we do that?' My disbelief morphs into horror. 'There's absolutely no guarantee that what we clone is what is in your brain now – or even a fraction of what is in your brain now.'

'You've run tests. With the rats.'

'Basic functionality. And even that… well…' I think of the test results, and the grey area that had started to form as a result of my assessment.

'The CyberCute.'

'The CyberCute?' My voice has risen at least an octave with exasperation. Or maybe fear.

'Yeah, you said yourself that it's a catalyst of the most extreme sort. Symbiotic metamorphosis. That's what it is, isn't it? So, we clone my brain again and let the CyberCute integrate. Or with part of my brain perhaps. Like we did with the prostheses, but using nanocytes to disperse it. '

'But they were way different – and what part of your brain anyway? You need all of it right now!'

'I need the active part of it right now, but what about the inactive areas?'

'We don't know they're inactive. We're only speculating.'

'Then let's start testing. Immersion therapy. That will get maximum response. I got the idea from Kohn – clever girl. She doesn't realise quite how clever, actually.' Jason swings back to the monitor and is fiddling with the programme he is running, bringing up reams of recorded response data, whilst I attempt to take in the enormity of what he is suggesting. 'Any elements of my brain that are inactive during therapy are fair game. But we'll keep going with the other plans too. Safety in numbers.'

'Jason, are you mad?'

'No,' Jason swings round again. 'Desperate, Matthew. Desperate. And so should you be. Time is running out.'

Chapter 28

18th June 2029: Matthew

It is gone seven in the evening but Jason hasn't let up yet. We are watching the last section of a test report on-screen. Again. The data doesn't look any different to the last test we ran but I can see from the set of his jaw he's not going to accept no for an answer any time soon. Yet for the moment, no is the only answer his brain is giving us. From the extremity of fear this morning I have climbed slowly down as if descending a ladder from a high place, head still giddy from vertigo and lack of oxygen but levelling, as we've failed to identify any specific inactive areas to tap into. Over the last hour I've even been trying to objectively assess the feasibility of Plan D and the arrangements Jason may have already set in place to ensure its possibility. Does Dr Kohn know of Jason's plan? She must if he's progressing it this far, otherwise she wouldn't be prepared when the moment came. But would she be prepared? Prepared to go along with any of this? Surely her instinct for survival is at least as defined as mine – probably more so. If something like this went wrong, it would be her – and me – who would bear the blame and she's not approaching middle-age with an indiscretion so dark that the merest suggestion of it could wreak havoc on her personal life, unless… It occurs to me then that I've never checked out how Jason selected his medical team. Maybe they do have vulnerabilities other than the desire to make a name for themselves? Maybe they all have a fatal indiscretion to hide?

I lean back in the office chair and let its ergonomics support more weight than they should. Jane is right about that, I will admit. I am becoming fatter as well as weaker. Not the self-satisfied fat of contentment. The miserable fat of comfort-eating and not caring for body or soul because there is no comfort in my world and no point to it either. And that makes me piteous. But I'm not piteous – just fat and easily mismanaged. Jason, for all his inner frailty, is still lean and fit – hungry. For life, for challenge, for a miracle. Now I need his hunger, whilst he needs my white fleshed, flabby health. In fact, he's very little changed from how he was when I first met him: the fresh-faced, enthusiastic young bio-medic, in full flow on the subject of cryogenics and why freezing oneself almost to death wasn't the way but re-growing oneself was. Cloning and 3D-printing. Use what we already have to replace what we don't. Be the best version of ourselves we can be. Make the world and ourselves better. Live forever with the people we love. The bloody irony. The sheer bloody irony!

I drag myself back the twenty years that have intervened between then and now, superimposing the youthful then-Jason face over the strained and anxious now-Jason. I lose the image in favour of the now-Jason, talking to me...

'So, what's left?'

'Hmm?' My eyes slip back to the report on-screen, now complete. It is blinking a response at us – a summary. A conclusion. Or a preclusion. Which should it be? I can't deny him though, can't deny friendship or compassion. Or coercion.

'Kohn mentioned the neo-cortex at one stage,' he says.

'The neo-cortex? How much have you told her?'

'Nothing. Just made my excuses and pumped her for ideas. The neo-cortex,' Jason confirms, although there is more than a hint of question in his voice.

'But surely that's in use one hundred per cent of the time? Without the neo-cortex, consciousness wouldn't exist.'

'No, but it contains cavities without any brain cells, as well as considerable amounts of cerebrospinal fluid, white matter, blood vessels, blood and non-thinking cells. Perfect for nanocyte activity.'

'But it shouldn't be constituted as the mythical unused ninety per cent of the brain simply because pockets of it appear to be empty.'

'I didn't say it should, but those pockets are our best bet to extract brain material that we can use to integrate with a cyber brain, using nanos, without obviously damaging what functionality we know of. Look, the neo-cortex consists of a sheet of cells about two and a half millimetres thick. If we dive into one of those vacuums and extract cells, we at least have something to start with without extracting any real part of my brain.'

I pull the chair closer to the screen and give the back rest some relief. The chair is new too. Its heady plastic smell has been boring into my brain all day and now my temples and eyes throb with chemical odour overload.

Jason continues, 'We need a dynamic spiking neural network which reflects that the neuron fires only when a membrane potential reaches a certain level. We can't create that. It's too complex. All our mapping only maps. It doesn't create. Even the source code is limited. But if we could access neurons at source – the actual cells and molecules that provide the functioning of the neurons so that their quantum mechanical processes aren't affected, we would have everything we need. We've been going about this the wrong way all along, Matthew. We don't need to build. We need to extract and then proliferate.'

I have to grudgingly admit he could be right. *Could.* The results of the latest scan do tend to show pockets of non-reactive areas. Banks, or depositories perhaps of the type of material that IS the brain in its essence. Jason taps the screen directly over one such set of measurements.

'There. That's it.'

'But how can you be sure?' I ask, although I already know. We are pretty much of a level, intellectually and in terms of knowledge. He simply wipes the floor with me in all other ways. The intense emptiness of the area now highlighted on-screen is reminiscent of a black hole – the one I'm currently being sucked into alongside Jason.

'We've mapped it. It's a vacuum – or near as dammit.'

'So what are you suggesting?'

'We aspirate. Then re-insert using CyberCute as a carrier.'

'But what if we are compromising an area we haven't mapped within it? We can't be sure. And there *is* some density there, look. All those neuronal cell bodies and unmyelinated fibres we could damage…' I point to a small series of volumetric measurements.

'And all those higher functions like sensory perception, generation of motor commands, spatial reasoning, conscious thought, and language, of course that we would be directly accessing to replicate. Doesn't that make you happy, Matthew – that we first and foremost would be replicating my higher functions?'

'Or interfering with them… Jason… ' I turn the screen off. 'Are you really sure you want to go through with this? I know all your reasons why, but have you thought of what you might become?'

'Alive?' Jason suggests sarcastically.

'Alive, yes, possibly – and with the potential to repeat this over and over again and live forever, like we speculated, in a cyborg body, but is that really what you want?'

'Why wouldn't I?' Jason is still sarcastic. 'It's all right for you, you still have the rest of your three score years and ten to mull over the benefits of eternal life or not, but I have barely three months if I'm lucky – probably less. If I'm the prototype… others will follow. We'll build a new world where death isn't the end, just another form of treatable illness. And if I don't survive this, well, I wasn't going to survive anyway, was I? What have I got to lose?'

'Yourself?' We face each other out.

'Myself?'

'Your integrity – as a human.'

'Integrity. Now you're sounding like Elise. Remember, it's not me who might lose myself. Do we have to go all through this again – the money, the debts, the – '

'No! No…'

Jason turns the screen back on. 'The neo-cortex,' he says. 'Tomorrow.'

'And Elise? When are you going to tell her?'

'That's not your problem.'

'But it is – or could be. If you're not around. And, whatever you say, you still need my help to proceed with this in the meantime, and her permission.'

'Oh, for fuck's sake. I'll tell her, OK? I'll tell her.'

'Without the help of Amarjit?'

'Don't push it,' he says, his face a sheet of mild-mannered nothing. 'Just don't push it.'

Chapter 29

25th June 2029: Elise

Jason is sleeping. I am watching. And waiting. I'm reminded of that Christmas carol where someone – angels or shepherds – keep a watch over wondering love. That would be in exactly six months, though. Jason won't be here to keep watch over by then. I choke back the thought and redirect myself before the tears can prickle my eyes. I haven't been to church in a long time. It's difficult when you have to outride the kind of storm of sarcasm that Jason can whistle up – like the North wind icily wailing its way through your life – just to be what you are.

He still has a dressing over the point of entry, slightly larger, if anything, than before. Jason said the needle was tiny, but I don't believe him. He wouldn't let me watch either, and the dressing has remained in place since. Infection control, he claims, but if the needle was so tiny, even I know puncture wounds close over within hours. And he sleeps – a lot – in between equally lengthy spells in the lab – even more so over the last couple of days, as if some of his energy was extracted with the procedure, too. In the lab, there is frenzied activity. Here there is none. If only I could enter my husband's head as easily as that needle did and extract some sense of what is going on there, maybe I would be able to find some peace, some equanimity in what is happening to all of us, but I know that will never happen. Jason is complete in himself, even when he's incomplete. I accepted that long ago. I just still have yet to find a way to live with it all of the time.

He has only just settled in to sleep so I will sit here for three or four hours, just watching and waiting, if I follow the pattern of the last five days. I touch his face, so lightly; my fingertips barely make contact with his skin, yet he frowns and moves his head away from me. I withdraw. My husband is already a stranger to me – even without becoming one in the way he intends. I huddle back into my chair and fold my arms around myself. I need warmth even though it is hot today – already in the high twenties Celsius. I have an inner core of ice that has frozen steadily thicker as this project has progressed, each milestone, each experiment, adding another formation of ice crystals to the lower layers. One day soon, I will be frozen so solid that not even the heat of grief will thaw me. And in the meantime, I am watching and waiting, my watch over wondering love.

I can't bear it suddenly. The room is too cool with the air-conditioning on full blast and my inner ice and its outer cold are meeting in the middle. I need to get out into the sun, feel its heat, feel alive, and that there is another way this could all end – or at least get out of this room. I slip from the chair and tiptoe across the room – not that my footsteps would be likely to wake Jason when he's in this kind of deep slumber. I can feel the cool of the laminate floor even through my sandals, penetrating their rubber soles and freezing my toes. My extremities are dying from frostbite and my heart from despair. I will give myself half an hour in the sun. Half an hour to thaw a little – enough to withstand the oncoming winter, at least.

The door shuts noiselessly behind me and I make my way softly along the corridor like a cat burglar. Outside, heading into the sun and the sunlight glistening on the car roofs, life goes on for the rest of the world. It is only inside, in the cool, rarefied world of Crane Industries and its cutting-edge life, that it may not go on for Jason. Left or right? I don't know and there is no one else in sight to help me make the decision. It is eerily quiet as if a layer of silence has floated down over the whole building overnight and I wonder why, when it is Monday morning, the place feels so deserted. Have I missed something? I decide to investigate inside first and make my way along the corridor until I reach Lab 2. Hovering outside, I peer through the glass viewing panel seeking clues. No. I haven't missed anything here. Rows of white-coated backs are busy with test tubes and complicated-looking filtration equipment, just as they were every other day of last week and the week before. This is the CyberCute lab – the real source of all Jason's success now – and they are all locked behind the lab doors, seeking the elusive miracle Jason wants, even though they have no idea that is what they are doing. Matthew explained it to me eventually – as he now eventually explains everything when Jason doesn't. They believe they are working on a new hush-hush project to be released in a fanfare of glory next year, so time is of the essence. They need to beat the rest of the cyborg market. That's the power of Jason. He commands, they do.

'And, well, they are – in a way,' Matthew shrugged as he told me. He looked earnest, eyes saucer-shaped with childish appeal; trying to believe what he was telling me, but we both knew there was more to it all than belief.

'Really? And that's how you see this latest development?'

'There can't be any other way at the moment, Elise. You know why… And we agreed, since…'

We agreed. Yes, we'd agreed. Matthew would keep me informed and I would decide when it was time to pull the plug. It's remained unspoken between us since he told me about Jason's blackmail of him and I told him about the Power of Attorney, but I know it has made him feel more relaxed about allowing Jason's plans to evolve. The irony is that the Power of Attorney is more power over Matthew than it will ever be over Jason. In fact, I think Jason has completely discounted it, in truth. He knows me too well. He has given me control over his future, knowing I won't ever be able to wield it.

I move on, peering through more windows, but seeing nothing different to a normal Monday morning here until I stop outside Lab 10. Jason and Matthew's lab. The ForEver lab. If anything is different it will be here. I expect the door to be locked, but it isn't. The lightest touch of my hand sends the door inwards. Deliberate. It must be deliberate. I step inside, into the cool sterility of potential immortality and man's failure to achieve it – yet. The room is so white, so gleaming, it hurts my eyes. By comparison, Matthew looks as grey and miserable as I feel. He looks up from what he is doing, papers and graphs in print form stacked untidily on the workbench in front of him. Printouts. The portable MRI machine stands idle in the corner but with legs dangling from it. A truncated man, wrestling a machine. I stop and double-take.

'Is it being repaired?'

Matthew looks confused. He comes to greet me but I bypass him and walk into the centre of the lab, still eyeing the MRI and legs.

'Elise, what are you doing here?'

'I couldn't stand the just waiting. Needed to do something. I'm cold, too. Why is it so cold in here? Is the air-con on overload?'

'Maybe,' he shrugs. 'I seem to be in a permanent sweat, myself, these days.'

He dodges in front of me and my view of the machine and legs is blocked so I cross the room and perch on the chair nearest to where

Matthew is sitting instead – clear view of the machine re-established. The chair has wheels and swivels before settling, sliding easily over the bonded floor. Even the smell is cold in here. Fresh, crisp, empty.

'Really?' I shiver.

'Shall I turn it down in here? It's Jason's preferred setting, not mine.'

'Jason's preferred setting… No, it's OK.' I look around, now realising why the lab seem empty. No Fred. 'Where's Fred?' Then I bite my lip. Maybe I shouldn't have mentioned Fred with someone else here. Unexpectedly, Matthew nods towards the MRI machine and the legs.

'Resting.'

'Oh.' We eye each other, then I leave the chair and go over to the machine with its dangling legs.

'From?'

'From the latest batch of tests.'

'But I thought the plan didn't involve Fred any more?'

'No, but the others do. We still have multiple plans in place and Fred is still one of them.'

'So why is he in here? Really?'

'Monitoring impulse responses and comparing them to brain functionality, before and after the CyberCute hybrid is introduced. And checking general function, too, of course.'

'Is this to do with the neo-cortex material? Jason said you had a new idea you were trying out with it. What have you been doing with that?'

'That's what the CyberCute is hybrid with. Jason believes that in time, the two could bond and catalytically react.'

'To produce what?'

'Not to produce, to reproduce. His brain.'

'Oh God! In Fred?'

I should have caught up with all this sooner. My need to be an ostrich where this is concerned is still overtaking my need to be on top of it. Ignorance really is bliss, until bliss turns sour. I have that sour taste in my mouth now and it is my fault because I've allowed myself to be kept in ignorance with occasional bursts of explanation from Matthew – never Jason. Never question Jason… I touch Fred's legs and am struck again by how real, how so like a human body he feels. If I press through the thin cotton scrub trousers, I can feel sinew and muscle, in the same contours as Jason's sinew and muscle. I can't help but slide my fingers across his thigh, testing the sensation of almost flesh to flesh, skin on bone, heat on cold. Memories of Jason's skin and Jason's muscles tensed and hard as he pressed against me, into me, through me, make me shiver again but not from cold. How long has it been since we made love? Since his body was heavy on mine and we flowed into each other like lava flowing and consuming all in its wake until all that is left is the pumping, pumping and sweetness of the climax as it bursts in our heads and bodies? I snatch my fingers away. Christ, this is Fred, not Jason – even though it feels like Jason. I am disgusted, the gorge rising in my throat as swiftly as desire had pumped through my blood and engorged my body.

'No, not in Fred.'

The MRI bed slides smoothly out of the machine and I look down on the object of my lust. He is clothed loosely in green cotton scrubs, lumpily outlining his toned and muscled frame. God, he is so like Jason – in everything except face and being. And yet, my disgust isn't quite complete until the scanner bed reaches its full extent. Now Fred's face comes into view too. Or Jason's face, even down to the finest downy hairs at the nape of his neck and along his brow line. His eyes are closed but the half-smile on his face is redolent of Jason in repose – and disturbingly most so after sex, when the thrust of passion has de-tumesced to satisfied exhaustion. I recoil, even as I want to touch that brow, stroke that cheek, place my lips on his lips and slide my tongue between them to taste his mouth.

Matthew's words finally break through my fugue of self-loathing and amazed disgust and I swing round to stare at him.

'Where then?' He doesn't reply. He is looking down at his feet and wringing his hands. 'Matthew?'

'Oh Christ, Elise, you didn't know? You're not going to…' He stands as if readying himself to sprint to the door and escape.

'Whatever it is, you need to tell me.'

He falters. Nods. Holds out his hand to me. Slow motion. This is going to be bad. Worse than anything so far. I can already tell that.

I barely notice my feet moving as I cross the floor, but there I am: in front of the monitor Matthew has been sitting at, and which replicates the topmost printout on its screen. He gestures to the seat next to him, where I sat before. I sit, obediently, planting my feet firmly on the floor to ground me. The chair's wheels skitter but don't slide away this time and I swivel, smoothly, to look at the screen. The smoothness of the bench top counterbalances the rough texture of the chair's fabric seat that imprints on my bare thighs. My knees poke awkwardly in front of me. I try to tuck them away but the skirt is too short – designed for a carefree summer not this careworn descent into winter. I feel like a scarecrow in an assortment of designer clothes that were designed for someone else, even though they were Jason's choice for me and fit to perfection. Still they feel like they don't fit me at all, like nothing fits any more, not even my skin. Matthew looks at my over-exposed knees and looks away. I can see his cheeks beginning to flame but I don't care. I don't care if he is embarrassed or even afraid of me. I don't care. And then I understand what the ice layers inside me are all about. They are the only way I can cope – to not care anymore, even though I do.

'So, explain,' I repeat, my voice distant and lost in both the emptiness of the lab and of my life right now.

'OK.' He breathes out and composes himself. 'We extracted fluid from the neo-cortex to establish what might be possible with symbiotic metamorphosis. We've been trying to recreate Jason's brain using the methods previously used for digital upload – mapping, of neural network emulation and so on. It was possible. But the time it would all take... well... And anyway, the results were disappointing with the rats, so Jason wanted to push on – see if we got past the rats, different physiology might produce better results – and we already had Fred...' He glances at me. I stare back at him. He colours more, eyes dropping down, hitting my knees and bouncing straight back up to my face. 'We wanted to see... how far man and machine could meld, that is... so we could see whether it would be possible for a cyborg to house a human brain, if we could successfully reproduce one, and for the two to work in mutual co-operation. CyberCute seemed to do so much...'

'Plan B again.'

'Well a composite of Plan B and C.'

I shiver, remembering Plan C. 'And?'

'Nothing. Nothing at all.'

'Oh. But is that so surprising? All you're doing is mixing substances. Maybe they're incompatible or simply discrete in their own right?'

'No. I understand what you're saying but it doesn't correspond with the theory, because we've already tested it with the CyberArm 3.3 and what CyberCute achieved for it in terms of metamorphic bodily integration. So we decided there was something we were missing. We needed more neo-cortical fluid. A lot more. Jason said... We inserted a cannula – a bit like when taking drugs intravenously or – '

'I know what a cannula is,' I interrupt. And now I understand the dressing that is never removed or discarded. And growing. 'So you've been milking Jason of neo-cortical fluid on a daily basis – I assume?'

'Well, not quite like that – and it was his idea.'

'I'll bet it was. OK, go on.' My stomach is rebelling, rising up in mutinous waves of disquiet at what Matthew is telling me, but I can't let him see that. Not until I know the full story. I know Matthew now. He tells me, but not always all of it – unless he's not afraid of the reaction.

'Still nothing happened, whatever the mix. There was still something missing – some factor or variable that stopped the CyberCute from instigating a metamorphic reaction. Then we turned it on its head – literally. The CyberCute hybrid needed to be incubated in a live host not a dormant host.'

He stops, awaiting the storm. It rages inside me, but I don't let it break outside. I have learned, you see. Learned so much over the last weeks and months. Learned I am a fool, but that I can't help but be a fool, that I am smart, but that I don't yet know how to use that keenness. And learned how to lie.

I surprise even myself with my calm – and yet, am I really surprised? My husband is going beyond all boundaries in search of the myth. Why would he not go beyond this one? It is merely the step before the final one – to transform into another format. And don't we transform into another format anyway when we die? Ironically, it strikes me Jason has missed a very salient argument he could have directed at me if we had continued this discussion beyond the Power of Attorney and me agreeing to disagree but not to interfere, unless… When we die, we transform. Into what? Who knows, but we all do it. What is Jason doing but transforming in a way that is more obvious to the human eye.

But obscene, nevertheless.

'The neo-cortex and CyberCute hybrid fluid is being incubated in a live host? So, I take it that Jason is the live host?'

My eye is caught by the storage racking behind the portable MRI, now I am close enough to see the contents of the containers ranged within it. Liver 21/6. Lung: part 23/6, kidney 23/6, heart 24/6. Clones. Jason clones.

'Well, it made sense. No likelihood of rejection either.' Matthew is watching me carefully – oh, so carefully.

'And what are the results now?' I control the modulation of my voice with difficulty, but it works. I sense Matthew relax, open up.

'See for yourself.' He swivels the monitor so that I can see. 'This is time along the horizontal axis. This is exponential growth along the vertical. We started the process two days ago. Already we're seeing rapid cohesion and less free space where we inserted the hybrid mix. Those areas should have been blank space – surrounded by neuronal cell bodies and unmyelinated fibres. Instead they ARE neuronal cell bodies and unmyelinated fibres. We can only assume the CyberCute has kicked them into life.'

'You're saying Jason has more brain capacity now?'

'So it would seem, although of course we can't measure brain capacity. We can only measure volume and activity, if we know how to stimulate to produce a response we can record.'

'Isn't this dangerous?'

'Elise, what is dangerous to a man already in danger?'

I sigh. I should have expected that. And Matthew is beyond me at the moment: in one of those wavering moments he has wavered in favour of research. He and Jason have that alike. Tomorrow, he may waver in favour of self-preservation again. I no longer have the energy to cope with this today. Yet I must.

'So what will you do with it next?'

'Well, now we've set the chain reaction going, we'll get on with cloning. We'll repeat what we did before,' he pretends he ignores my involuntary shiver at the memory of Jason and Fred maniacally playing air piano via the last brain clone, 'but better. This time, we'll weed out the Parmensis before we do anything and then test using Fred. That's also why Fred's on a heavy-duty health check. He needs to be working to full spec for us to get reliable data back for analysis.' His cheeks are still flushed. But now with the excitement of achievement, not embarrassment. Oh yes, he and Jason have that alike, whatever else they don't concur on. That is where Jason truly has him – as much as with whatever he has on Matthew to coerce him.

'And the neo-cortical area governs the higher functions like sensory perception, generation of motor commands, spatial reasoning, conscious thought, and language, you know, Elise. We are replicating and increasing the better things about the human condition too, not just the baser instincts and bodily functions.'

'Maybe, but what then, when you've cloned another complete and Parmensis-free brain? And if you're going to clone another brain, why do you need the neo-cortical fluid?'

'Oh, well… we're cloning only the Parmensis-free area of the brain and supplementing with the neo-cortical hybrid to complete the process and replace the neural blue print we would otherwise have to map – which would take months, maybe years to do properly. So it turns Fred into a working model, not a work in progress.'

'And is that what all those organs are for? To keep Fred at high spec?' I wave towards the storage unit.

'Oh, those? Yes, replacements. We can grow pretty much anything now from stem cells. They were some test runs. All nicely compatible with Fred for a kick start, but of course the CyberCute could outperform them and self-renew, if what we think about it is correct. It's a whole new world, Elise. A winner's world, where the first man to win the immortality race wins everything. We just have to test it out a little longer…'

He stops abruptly. He is watching me again and I realise now that he has been carefully watching my reactions throughout. I just haven't been paying enough attention to him – until now. I wonder what he can read from my face. Is it a graph of dismay, a bar chart of fear?

'Come on,' he says suddenly. 'I think it's time to go. Jason may be waking soon, and you'll want to be there for him, won't you?'

He switches off the monitor and takes my hand to pull me out of the chair. He catches me off-guard and I stand before my body registers preferred refusal. I resist, pulling back against his grasp, but he holds on tighter. His eyes signal defiance and I waver. This is most-un-Matthew-like. Jason-Fred still lolls across the guts of the scanner bed, like a limp rag doll. As we pass him on the way to the door, for a moment I imagine he is Jason and want to rush back to him, lay him out straight and composed – dignified – but Matthew guides me firmly onwards and shuts the door decisively behind us. It clicks locked.

'Why wasn't it lock—'

He puts a finger to his lips and says loudly, 'Yes, it is bloody cold with the air-con on overtime, isn't it? Let's grab some heat outside for five minutes, shall we?

He leads me out of the building, still talking: nonsense about his kids, about Jane – that I know is nonsense because it is complimentary – about cars that don't work on rainy mornings and the summer scorch and gardens in need of watering and weeding until we exit the glass entrance doors having navigated the politely corporate receptionist and openly swaggering security guard. I haven't seen this kind of Matthew in years; calm, assured, determined – but outside, Matthew's demeanour changes again.

‘Sorry, needed to get you out of there before you said anything incriminating.’ This is the Matthew I know now, sweating, awkward, ambivalent, worried. He sets off at a forced-march pace towards the far side of the car park, the side that borders open fields that some developer will surely turn into a housing forest soon. ‘Look, I haven’t said this before, but I’m really worried now. I think he thinks he’s going to be a bloody God if this works.’

‘What do you mean?’ I am still adjusting to both the blazing sunshine and humid heat, as well as the changed situation.

‘Look, everything I said earlier is correct. If the CyberCute develops higher functions and we do clone a workable brain, it will be vastly more efficient than what we started with. That’s great. And if we can get Fred working properly and synthesising with a brain, amazing. We have the wherewithal to clone and replace anything that breaks down or treat any illness through gene therapy in much the same way with stem cell treatment and CyberCute. But what then?’

I don’t understand his sudden change. ‘Then Jason will survive.’

‘With darn near nothing that will ever hold him back. What would you feel like if you were nigh on indestructible?’

‘What are you saying?’

‘I don’t know. Most of the time I don’t know which way to go on this. I’ve just given you the party line – the Jason line. But as for mine? You’ve always known I’ve been ambivalent about all of this. The advancements that are possible are incredible – and yet… I keep thinking about what you said to me originally. It’s human to be faulty. It’s human to be mortal. But if this works – *really works* – then he won’t be. At all.’

‘Well, you know I never liked this,’ I say carefully, conscious this could be a trick, despite what we’ve discussed before. ‘So are you now thinking you should stop it? Because if you do, then…’ I break. But then Jason would be gone, never to return and strangely a part of me has even begun to come to terms with a much-changed Jason, if only he is also *alive*.

Matthew puts his arm round me. ‘No.’ He sounds uncertain, voice wavering into a question mark. ‘No,’ he repeats, more decisively now. ‘No, we can’t stop it, Elise. We both know we can’t. For all our sakes. Sorry, I said all of that – confusing everything again.’

His arm hangs around my shoulders but today I don’t find it oppressive. It isn’t comforting either, just an affirmation that he is there and I’m not facing this completely alone, even if his loyalties are divided.

And even as he demurs, his expression belies his words so that my own thoughts come flooding out regardless of whether it's wise or not to voice them now.

'Oh God – this is all so wrong! I can't bear to lose him but you know as well as I do that this is wrong.' I barely even notice that the words are tumbling out until they throng in the air and I can't take them back. 'I want you to stop this project. God help me, please, even though stopping it will mean Jason's death. Stop the project. I'll take the blame. I'll explain why to him. I'll use the Power of Attorney.'

In the fields, a brisk breeze stirs the waving corn and it ripples in a golden shiver.

'But… You, we can't. The Power of Attorney is for his best interests and… there are reasons… You know there are. And I – '

'Are there?' I can't take my eyes off the corn field because I know if I look Matthew in the eye I will see his condemnation and I will weaken. 'What are his best interests? To be a semi-human thing? We're not meant to live forever, Matthew. We're time-bound. We have our allotted time and when that's up, however painful it is, we have to accept it is over. You know that, too. I'll sort out your debts.'

'It's not that. There's worse.'

The sun is burning my face. I always burn at the slightest hint of sun. I should have put sunscreen on – but why would I have needed sunscreen in the ice of the facility?

'Worse?'

'It's not just debts. It's a situation I got… embroiled in.'

I turn to him as the corn stalks wave their warning. Then he tells me the rest of his miserable tale. Our five minutes in the heat pass – long pass. Mid-morning becomes mid-day and the sun is at its zenith. Jason may already be awake, but I cannot face him yet. The catalogue of his abuse of this kindly, naïve man leaves me ice cold, even in the blaze of the sun.

'And yet you've remained friends – loyal – all this time?' I ask at last.

'He hasn't not been a friend to me, Elise. I would have been sunk years ago without him. This is just me honouring my debt now. So, you see, whatever you say and however much I question it all, how can I let him down? He's never let me down or betrayed me. How can I do that to him? What you do has to be up to you, but I can't do it – and I have too much at stake here.'

I can see from the set of his jaw that he believes what he has said, whatever his errant principles. It won't be moral reproof that propels him forward in step with me this time. There and then, I decide – God help me – what I have to do next. I am so sad. So sad that it all comes to this. That Jason must die. That I must kill him and that Matthew must be forced to be complicit.

I tell him about Jane then. Jason and Jane. Just as with death, sometimes there is no choice with life either.

Chapter 30

29th June 2029: Matthew

'Jesus fucking Christ! Are you sure?'

'I'm sorry, Matthew.' Her eyes are shadowed, half-covered by the hand over her eyes, blocking out the sun. In the distance, the corn quivers and dances in the field. I feel its movement into my gut and down to my groin.

'You mean, all that time, she was… with Jason?'

She nods. 'It wouldn't have meant anything. It would have been purely physical. I couldn't believe it to begin with myself, but eventually I came to accept it – what it meant to Jason – but for Jane, of course… I don't know…'

Her shoulders quiver like the corn beneath the weight of my arm. I withdraw it. I need both arms to steady myself now – an acrobat on a trapeze wire that's spread across the ground, but still leaving him high and dry in thin air.

'Katie is six.'

'I know.'

She turns away. I move round to put myself in front of her but still she turns from me.

'When did he have the snip?'

'When… Six years ago.' I can tell from her rigidity that there is more she could say but won't. And I know I shouldn't probe, but we are one in betrayal.

'When?' I prompt gently.

She swings round and faces me. Her pain is naked to the world, arms hanging loose by her sides, eyes unshielded. Her lower lip trembles.

'When I had the abortion.'

The words hang in the air, as heavy as the sound of the lazy plane overhead. I can feel them circling with the drone of the plane.

'So, after Katie…' The breath leaves me and for a moment I can't speak, can't even breathe.

'After Katie,' she agrees, eyes slanted with pity.

'Oh God…' My self-pity becomes pity for her too. 'I didn't know.'

'You wouldn't.'

'Did you want – '

'Of course, I didn't!' Her eyes are small and angry. And of course, the reply was obvious before I even asked. I can't believe I did.

'Oh…' I feel like I should take a step away to allow space for her pain, but it's too late now. 'I thought you didn't want kids – were too engrossed in school... Stupid… is that why you kept away from Jane when she was pregnant with Katie?'

'No.' She shakes her head and the anger has gone. 'Yes… There are many things you don't know, Matthew.' Her lips twist as if savouring the sourness of belladonna.

'Clearly.' My voice is distant even to myself. 'Oh, Elise, I'm so sorry…'

'Well, it's done now, all of it, but if we're talking betrayals…'

'Yes, I see what you mean.'

We stand silently watching the corn.

'We should go back,' she says after a while.

'Why?' I ask. The belladonna is on my lips now.

'Because we have to. Whatever we do from here on in, we have to go back.'

She takes my hand and for a moment I could imagine none of this happening, no past, no future, only present, with Elise's small hand in mine and the sun beating down on us, blotting out everything but the heat I can feel pounding through my body at the sensation of it lying there, offered, accepting, welcoming.

'Elise, I…'

She shakes her head. 'No, Matthew. You don't. Maybe you did, maybe you would, but right now, you don't. We are simply two people facing a crisis in our lives and we will face it together like that, but only as that. Two people. There is nothing else to consider or worry about for now.' She gives my hand a little squeeze and then shakes hers free. 'Come on.'

'But you don't know what I think now…'

'About?'

'About… any of it. Jason, Jane… Katie…'

'I don't need to. Like you said, I have to do what I think is right, whatever you decide to do. I have the Power of Attorney. I will exercise it at the right moment if I have to. You have full knowledge. You will exercise that however you see fit at the right moment, too.'

She steps ahead of me, away from the waving corn. Her body sways and shimmers in the heat. I follow her back to the door from which we exited, and we slip back into the cool. I shiver as the door closes behind me and we walk side by side along the corridor back to the ForEver lab. We pause at the door.

'So,' I start.

She puts her fingers to my lips. 'So, I should check in on Jason. Come with me if you like?'

I know it is a signal but I'm too numb to be able to decipher it. I need time, and I don't need to spend it anywhere near Jason currently.

'I'd better tidy up the lab, actually. There are things to finish off before tonight. Jason will be back in action by then, I imagine.'

'OK.' She nods. 'I'll drop by tomorrow.'

She walks on into the whiteness of the corridor, fading out of sight round the bend that leads to Jason's quarters without a single glance backwards. I notice now that she never uses the connecting door between the lab and Jason's quarters, as if she needs to separate them with the walk along the corridor between their two independent entrances. I remain at the door of the ForEver lab, computing the possibilities. Elise is both more and less than I thought she was – yet isn't that true of all of us? No, I haven't said what I am going to do now, but she knows. She knows better than me what I will do, even though how I will do it hasn't yet been formulated. All this time, and I have been such a fool. Talking betrayals, we are all guilty of them now, except me – yet. My time is coming soon.

'Dr Green?'

I jump. Dr Kohn is standing directly behind me, close enough to rub her neat Germanic precision against me, yet distant enough that worlds could slip through the space between us.

'Dr Kohn! Can I help you?'

I twist round and take a step back all at the same time, stumbling over my feet – clumsy and clod-like at the best of times, but doubly so in the face of this minute power-house of ambition and analytical aloneness. She puts out a hand to steady me, even though there is nothing that she or anyone could do to set me back in balance; nor would she, I suspect, if she could. I have the sense that Dr Kohn's input would always be to further destabilise me if anything.

'Not really. I was just passing and was curious how things are progressing with Mr Crane's pet project?'

'Pet project? Why do you think he has a pet project? He's hardly well enough to...'

I leave it there, realising that Dr Kohn knows precisely how well Jason is, and how that current state of well-being is being determined by other influences she has nothing to do with, and what is beyond the airlock into the sterile area – or was once a few nights ago, at least.

'No, he isn't, but he is, isn't he?' Her eyes have narrowed. 'Oh, Dr Green, I know. And I could help...'

I shake my head and try to look dumb, not secretive. 'That's up to Jason, not me.'

'I know it is. But I'm not asking him, I'm asking you. Do you not need my help too? Now?'

I hesitate, picturing Fred, lying half in, half out the MRI, stalled in our latest test because I need to research neo-cortical responses to substrata electrical impulses before I risk blowing Fred or Jason's minds with more CyberCute. And research it I might, but applying that research was yet another thing. Dr Kohn would probably know the answers to my questions straight away or, at the very least, know where to go for them. She would certainly understand the ramifications of the theory and how to put it into practice in a way I would labour to establish. No need for the hours of painstaking and tortuous research I hadn't mentioned to Elise in my party-line enthusiasm for Jason's latest ForEver plan. Until now, we'd winged it on the basis of our own expertise – but the neuro-cortex? That was pushing me to my limits, other than what we had achieved up to yesterday when the latest Fred test had stalled. And if this latest plan was going to work – really work – the one person we should have on board now was a neurologist, yet still Jason consistently refused it – or had he?

I back away and bump up against the ForEver lab door. 'Best talk to Mr Crane about what he wants your input on.'

She steps forward in time with me and we are wedged together on its outer facet. She peers up into my face, eyes narrowing, then makes a little clicking sound with her tongue and wheels away as suddenly as she had appeared. 'I will,' she calls to me over her shoulder, 'but remember I could help you too.' Her neck barely twists as she marches away, also in the direction of Jason's quarters.

I watch her disappear around the bend in the corridor, wondering what she and Elise make of each other. There is an inner core of iron or something with which I can't even begin to compete in both, and it occurs to me that maybe there is yet another betrayal I hadn't considered until now. Dr Kohn hadn't simply observed Jason's comings and goings. The majority of the time she and the rest of his medical team were banned from his personal quarters other than for emergency access or routine checks, carried out at times determined solely by him. Yet she knew he was involved in something specifically with me, me who she'd barely come across. And she'd known where to find Jason on the night he destroyed the cloned brain, and even when to look for him there.

I dither, part of me wanting to sink back into the seclusion of the ForEver lab, examine what Elise has just told me and decide – really decide – what to do now, whatever my gut is prompting me to do. The other, self-preservationist part of me, wants to follow the same route as the women and find out what is going on with Jason. What is he doing without telling me? What else is he doing, has done, is going to do without telling me, this man who had called himself my friend whilst sleeping with my wife? I can feel my scalp prickle with anxiety whilst beads of sweat form at my hairline and trickle in tiny rivulets down my temples and into the fold of my neckline. My shoulder blades ache with tension. He is lying to me – has lied to me. What is he getting me into? He has me trapped – damned if I do and damned if I don't. Where will the blame lie of all of this goes wrong – if he dies as a result of the experimentation, not the Parmensis? With me. Me. Me…

The sound of voices echoing further along the corridor send me backwards into the lab whilst I decide. I push the door firmly into Lock position and stand with my back pressed against the inside door face. Fred's legs look to have moved, but that isn't possible. I go over and check anyway. They haven't. I breathe out and my breath cools in front of me. Out of the heat of the sun, the ice of the over-active air-conditioning calms me, turning logic back on – and if the encounter with Dr Kohn is anything to go by, I'm going to need cool, calm logic more than anything now. I need to change, become who I once was. I wasn't always a coward.

I settle myself back at the PC and open up a new incognito browser – a temporary solution. I'm going to need Tor for this and to access the dark net – a secret place for a secret damnation. And I'm going to need some very specific software and a new PC, one that isn't linked into the Crane Industries system or Jason. Then I'm going to need a very specific limitation for Fred and I already know what. It will simply mean some minute adaptations to the CyberCute formula – so simple, and so inescapable. Symbiotic metamorphosis or not, there has to be a limit even to the limitless. Damn Jane and her call over every penny going in and out of my bank account. I'll have to go overdrawn to do this in secret, the kind of overdrawn that is in the bank of the soul.

Chapter 31

29th June 2029: Elise

He is still asleep, but restless, when I return. I slip back into the seat I left a mere hour or so ago as if I had never left and nothing has changed, but I know it has. I didn't push Matthew after I told him about Jane. There was no need. I am enough a student of humanity as I'll ever need to be teaching the kids that I teach – a ragtag of the needy, the privileged, the lost and the power-brokers of the future. Ours is no ordinary school. It caters for the rich and their putative company CEOs, the movers and shakers of the modern world. I took the job thinking I could make a difference to what social conscience meant to them when they eventually moved into their adult worlds. Maybe I did – do – at times, but it is an unforgiving role, and not one to foster spirituality. Perhaps that is why I took it after I had the abortion? What spirituality did I have then? A soul full of sourness that had to be depleted before it could refill with forgiveness. Expending myself daily on a thankless task was just the thing for emptying that vast reservoir of rancour. I turned it into energy and pushed myself to the top with it; Head of Department, Deputy Head, Head. Now, six years on, I am ready to forgive, ready to look into the future I have accepted for myself, only to find that future being stolen as surely as my child was. I can't help the tears welling up in my eyes and tumbling down my cheeks in hot resentment and self-pity.

Matthew…

And self-disgust.

What am I doing? What the hell have I done?

Jason's eyes open at precisely that moment. I rub my hand over my face and smudge the tears into my make-up.

'Hey, you. Are you crying?'

'No, no – just a little tired, and the air-conditioning makes my eyes ache.'

'Never heard that before. Air-conditioning hurting eyes.' He is smiling, but in that half-joking, half-needling way he has at times. I owe it to myself not to rise to the bait today, though. I smile, and shrug, leaning in to caress his face, careful to avoid the dressing on his forehead.

'There's so much I've never heard before that I'm hearing recently, why not air-conditioning irritating eyes?'

Mistake. I've given him a lead in to contrariness. I know he will take it even before he opens his mouth to reply.

'Such as?'

He nuzzles his cheek against my hand and the old familiar surge of love overwhelms me momentarily. I feel dizzy with emotion. I want to cradle that cheek, that face, forever. The tears threaten again and I have to swallow hard.

'Oh,' I shrug again. 'Everything, you know… So, are you hungry now? You've slept for hours.'

'Maybe.' He pulls himself upright, abruptly dislodging my hand. 'But first, I want to know what you mean by everything.'

He takes my hand in both of his and pulls me in towards him, capturing my other hand at the same time so I am pinioned against him and the bed. The Parmensis has done nothing to weaken his physical strength, that's for sure. I can feel his breath on my cheek and my pulse quickens. How he has this power over me, I'll never understand. Some call it chemistry, some call it karma – the call of one soul to another. It is more than love for me; it is need. I need Jason, and yet I must let him go – push him away into the void where I can't follow. I try to stop my body tensing. Can he sense my betrayal?

I nestle my face into his cheek and breathe in his smell, musky, compelling, dominant. I want to suffocate in him, drench my senses in him whilst I still can, the longing, the need – and then, unbidden and unwelcome, the memory of Fred's legs dangling from the MRI ousts all other thoughts. Desire turns to disgust and I want to gag but Jason continues to hold me so tightly to him that now I am struggling to breathe at all. Eventually I push him away as gently as I can and take in a deep gulp of air-conditioned air that is full of nothing but ice.

'So?' he persists.

I shake my head as if I don't understand.

'So what has Matthew been telling you?'

'Why would Matthew have been telling me anything?'

'Because he's soft – on you. You know that. Anything you ask him, he'll eventually tell you. He can't help himself.'

'Nonsense.'

Jason leans back and rests his head against the headboard of the bed. It is at an awkward angle and it reminds me of Fred again. It is the kind of angle Fred's head would make, whereas a human's wouldn't.

'Of course, it's not. Don't deny it. It's been an unacknowledged thing for years. It doesn't matter. It's unrequited and we all know that but, nevertheless, there's one person you can claim ultimate power over, Elise. How does that jive with your ultra-fair principles?'

'Whether that's true or not, I would never take advantage of someone because they have a soft spot for me.'

Oh God, please don't be listening to me right now. Please don't be watching what I'm doing right now. I'm so sorry, Matthew. What am I doing? What have I done?

'Really, Elise?' He laughs. 'My lovely, lovely Elise, who would make me a better man than I am, if it were possible.' He turns his head and the awkwardness of the angle intensifies. I am thinking *The Exorcist*, *Alien* – all those old horror movies he loves to watch when we have what Jason calls a vintage film night. 'But it's not, other than via Fred.' Involuntarily my eyes flick from his strained neck to his forehead and the bulky dressing. Now he is watching me closely. 'Ah, so he has. What has he told you?'

'Only that you're continuing your research with Fred. You have other plans, too, now.'

'Neuro-cortical plans. Do you understand what that means?'

'Of course, I know what the neuro-cortex is.' The snap in my voice comes out before I can control it. Unexpectedly I identify its root cause even as I am dismayed by it. I don't like my husband. I don't like him at all right now.

'Good. I thought you did – all that long-ago scientific logic can't have been completely lost. So, you'll know what it means then – progress in that area.'

'Growing the neuro-cortex won't make any difference to the Parmensis though, will it?'

'Maybe not, but if I can lose the area the Parmensis is currently occupying and other areas of the brain can be developed to replace it, that's an option. Just think about it, Elise – being able to manipulate brain development. Not that you will like that one bit, will you, with your *to err is human, to die is divine* philosophy. At least I could make Godhead in your eyes that way, I suppose.'

'That's not my philosophy,' I protest, so loud it feels like the room reverberates with it and I realise too late, I have tripped over the deliberate device. The grin is all across his face, emphasising the awkward neck angle even more so it looks as if his throat has been cut and his head is now lolling precariously on a small skein of skin holding head and body together. I calm myself forcibly. 'You know that's not my philosophy,' I repeat, more quietly. 'Let's not argue. Now isn't the time to argue.'

'I'm not arguing. I'm asking you what you know about the current research so I can fill in the blanks for you. You are my wife, after all. Don't you want to know?'

The very reasonableness of him makes me want to shout. I choke it back.

'I would very much like to know. I love you and want the best for you.'

'OK, we are currently incubating a small amount of neuro-cortical material combined with CyberCute in my frontal lobe. That is totally riskless unless my body chooses to reject it as a foreign body – which it won't because it is essentially still my own brain material. We did it to counter rejection and non-progression in Fred. As a host, he clearly doesn't yet have enough biological cell matter to encourage growth. We are slowly rectifying that by replacing his cyborg processes with cloned organs reproducing the same functionality, but that will take a while longer to complete.'

'How much longer?'

I sense a watershed is coming with Fred's preparation.

'A week perhaps? Maybe less.'

'And then?'

'Then we will transfer the neuro-cortical material back into Fred.'

'To what end?'

'To grow a complete brain, hopefully minus Parmensis.'

'So you're thinking of a brain transplant now? From Fred into you? What plan is that?'

My voice has peaked in pitch, and he bursts out laughing.

'God, no! I doubt if even the semi-divine Dr Kohn would be able to accomplish that yet.'

'But you were playing air piano via Fred and the cloned brain…'

'Yes, but we couldn't transplant the brain *into* Fred. It was in vitro.

The connections were too complex. We could test compatibility and response using it, but we couldn't incorporate the two. And cloning the whole merely reproduced the original, Parmensis and all. No, the way forward with my brain isn't to clone. It's to regrow it.'

'In Fred.'

'Yes.'

'And then what?'

'Then Fred has a shiny new brain, and I have a shiny new body around it.'

'So that's the plan…' It comes out on a breath that dies away almost before it combines with the atmosphere it is expelled into.

'That's the plan.'

He straightens himself and now he looks normal again. He is still watching me closely. Serious.

'Will it work?'

'You tell me.'

'How would I know, Jason?'

'All right, will it work for you? Me alive.'

'Of course, I want you alive. How can you ask that? I just don't know that Fred can be called alive.'

'What is alive?'

'Well, human…'

'And won't my brain and my organs make him human?'

'Your organs?'

'Cloned.'

'He'll still basically be a cyborg.'

'Being transformed into a human. Here, hand me my pad. He gestures to the iPad balanced on the bedside unit nearest me. I palm its sleek secrets and hand them to Jason. He settles it on his knees and gestures for me to slide on top of the bed alongside him. I do so gingerly, hoping my disinclination to be close right now isn't showing. He taps the screen and it opens to a film clip.

'This is film of our latest fitment – a half-arm prosthesis built using the same technology as Fred and CyberCute. CyberCute is the catalyst as well as the covering by the way. CyberCute is the breakthrough in all of this. Whatever we add CyberCute to, transforms – as you'll see.'

He taps the screen again and I watch the young woman demo-ing the arm as she puts it through its paces: fine pincer grip, full rotation, extension, flexion, and finally gross motor control as she takes a tennis ball and slowly crushes it until it bursts apart within her grip, sending shards of tennis ball, like pulverised flesh, spinning off in all directions. They spray the camera crew and onlookers, who all duck and dive and laugh delightedly at the display. The unease within me grows. I look away to recover equilibrium. He grips one of my hands and pins it to my leg, his covering mine and pressing it down flat. The pressure is approaching that of the girl in the demo film as he says, 'Keep watching. You tell me what is human and what isn't now.'

I focus back on the screen, trying to ignore the force of his hand pressing my hand into my thigh. The cameraman is homing in on the girl again, closer and closer, until we are being treated to an ant's eye view of her arm, her skin, the hairs on her skin, the pores; macro-photography at its most extreme.

'And now what lies beneath,' the voice on-screen says. The cameraman pans out and we are now watching the girl's arm being sliced open. White-gloved fingers reach in and peel away the skin to reveal a tangle of circuitry and bloodied flesh. The pristine white of the fingers smear with red.

'Oh my God, Jason. What are they doing to her?' I rip my hand from under his, but he grabs it back.

'Watch!' he commands.

'They're torturing her!' How could you allow this?'

Vomit is rising at the back of my throat, hot and sour. I am shivering all over, my flesh crawling with imagined red ants, pinpricking fire into it as they cut and serrate, blood speckles from the ant invasion freezing almost immediately as they appear by the ice-ice cold of the damn air-conditioning.

'No, they're not. Watch!'

I watch with pain, but apparently she doesn't. The camera pans out to show her, Madonna-like, serenely watching her arm being dissected, and the circuitry and bloodied flesh slowly resolving, combining, becoming a mass of what I vaguely recognise as muscle from my years-ago sessions in the university lab when I first met Jason. From time to time, the cameraman pans out from the transforming morass of red and white and silver to encompass the girl's lower wrist, and after a while I realise why: he or she is deliberately showing us the time. It has gone from around ten o'clock when I first notice it, to mid-afternoon, with small, blurred phases in between.

'The time,' I murmur.

'Time-lapse,' Jason agrees. 'It took about thirty-six hours in all. I won't make you watch all of it.' He fast-forwards to near to the end, based on the time line running under the film screen. All I can see now is muscle mass, then the same gloved fingers, or maybe another's in fresh gloves, because they are pristine white again now, stroking the opened flap of flesh closed. It lays, mountainous for a while, then starts to subside, soften, smooth. The bloodied edge of the cut diffuses, turns pink, then white, then fades away altogether. According to the time displays it has taken a total of an hour for the skin to close over as if no one had ever sliced into it. The film ends by panning away from the now non-existent cut and focusing onto the girl's face. She looks tired, small shadows creeping in hollows under her eyes and her hair is dishevelled, but otherwise she is still smiling serenely.

'It was a long trial,' Jason he taps the screen and the film shuts down. 'But now you tell me – what of her arm is and isn't human.'

'Is that really what the CyberCute does?'

'Yes. It symbiotically metamorphoses. Whatever it covers or comes into contact with, it initiates cellular change to morph into the biologically functional version of the cyborg process. So the 'wiring', if you like, of electrical impulses carried from the brain to the muscle becomes muscle fibre, the outer covering for the prosthesis combines with the dermis to process itself into skin and the tubular structures carrying fluids to oxygenate or energise functioning parts become veins, arteries, blood. Of course, the larger the structure or process, and the more complex, the longer the metamorphosis will take but, in time, theoretically the CyberCute, combining with enough of those processes and structures, will enable a cyborg to become a biologically functioning unit.'

'Fred will become human.'

'Yes.'

He lets go of my hand and I slide off the bed. I need space. Time. Have I been wrong? Am I wrong? 'But only if he also has all of the things in him that makes us human.'

'He will have. He'll have my brain re-grown too. He'll be me.'

'But how do we know what it is that makes us uniquely us?'

'Oh God – *the soul*, you mean? You're saying Fred will have my body parts and my brain but not my soul? What if there is no such thing as a soul, Elise? What if we don't have one? What if we are purely the sum of our parts and God is the manufacturer of our neediness?'

'God isn't the manufacturer of neediness. He's the central core of belief. My belief.'

'But not mine. Why should you impose your beliefs on me? You claim that I am dogmatic and dismissive of your right to have your beliefs. What about you? Aren't you doing precisely that to me?'

'I'm not. I'm simply saying that is what I question in all of this – what life is?'

'Life is what you have whilst you have a vehicle for it. Well, I want more of it than I appear to be about to get. The vehicle for it is disposable, but now it's also potentially replaceable.'

'God, Jason! Is life really only that – dependent on a body to be in? Isn't it about what you do with it, how you treat people, what good you can do too?'

'No, Elise, it's about getting what you want while you can – but I don't disagree that if it's not in short supply you can afford to give a bit back too. It's not such a mad scramble to have as much as you can within a finite time. There, isn't that a reason for immortality, if ever there was one? You actually have enough time to be able to do some good, not just scramble to survive? Live long enough and you get what you want and do good unto others too. Job done!'

'No matter how long I live, there's one thing I will never get though. You saw to that.'

The pain of loss suddenly comes back at me as sharp as the initial cut in the girl's arm. Fingers are peeling back the grown-over pretence that I can live with it, forgive and forget it even as I am struggling to stuff the raw and bloodied flesh of my dismembered child back into the tiny white coffin we buried her in. Jason reads her in my eyes. No, he hasn't forgotten either. Now I know.

'Elise…'

'It won't make any difference what you say. It's done now.'

I turn away. I can't look at him at the moment. I love him, but I can't bear him either, not remembering as I am now. Then his arms are around me, pulling me to him so my back is pressed against his chest and I can feel his heart pounding into my shoulder blades. He wraps his arms around me and I am imprisoned, a wilting flower, draped over the edge of its cut glass vase. He murmurs into my hair.

'I'm sorry, I'm sorry, I'm sorry…'

I start to cry and this time I can't even try to hide it. It is all too much. I gave up my child to have Jason, and for what now? A cyborg man metamorphosing into some kind of biological replica of him? If that?

He pulls me round to face him and tucks my cheek against his chest, stroking my hair.

'It was the only other thing I wanted.'

'I know. But you know it would have been a disaster, under the circumstances. She was sick.'

'There are treatments.'

'Not for what was wrong with her.'

'You don't know – you don't even know that whatever it was would have been a problem.'

'We discussed this all at the time.'

'Not enough. You never told me enough.'

'You didn't need to know any more.'

'But I do. I did.' I pull away from him. 'Why? Why won't you tell me the rest?'

'There's nothing else to tell.'

'But…'

'Oh God, Elise, can you never leave it?' He walks away from me and paces the room. His bare feet make small padding sounds across the floor, like time ticking away. 'I told you, my mother had a sickness. I couldn't risk it coming out in a child.'

'There are genetic work-ups we could have had done.'

'Only with genetic material to work with.'

His pacing is to and fro between me and the bed. It is the closest we've ever got to discussing this.

'We had you and we could have asked your mother…'

I hold my breath as he turns and walks towards me. Pit, pit, pit, feet padding out the distance between us. We need to deal with this, whatever else happens. Our immortal souls need to deal with this and I need to forgive.

'Don't you get it?' He stops in front of me and the spittle from his words hits me in the face. 'We couldn't ask her anything. She walked out on me, when I was a child. She abandoned me, Elise, left me and my sister on our doorstep like an abandoned litter. My father said she was ill. Couldn't cope with motherhood. I found her later when I was in my twenties. She wasn't ill. She was happily shacked up with some other bloke, surrounded by more kids. You don't need genetic material to diagnose cruel indifference.'

I reach for him, to soothe his pain with mine.

'Maybe she was ill. Post-natal depression, that sort of thing. It happens. Did you ever speak to her?'

'Yes, I spoke to her. Later. I asked her why. She said she simply hadn't been ready for kids then. I'm sorry… *I'm sorry…* Hoped life turned out OK for me anyway.'

'When was this?'

'Six years ago.'

'When…'

'Yes, then.'

'But why didn't you talk to me about it?'

'I did.'

'You said it was a genetic problem, but it wasn't, Jason. We could have sorted it out.'

'We did. You had the abortion. I had the vasectomy.'

'But she wasn't ill. There wasn't a genetic illness to avoid.'

'Yes, there was. Genetically she was a bitch and my father was too weak to admit that. I wasn't perpetuating those genes under any circumstances. You and I are all I need.'

'What about what I need?'

'You have me. And your God. Isn't that enough?'

'You made me murder our child because of this?'

'Murder? That's going it a bit, Elise. It was just a bundle of cells then. That's not murder. It would need to have developed a long way from that for it to be murder. Fred is more progressed than that.'

'Everything is just a bundle of cells to you, isn't it? Me, our child, Fred – a bundle of cells that either serves or doesn't serve you. To be moved around and manipulated to serve the will of Jason Crane, kept, discarded, symbiotically metamorphosed to suit.'

My armpits are soaked despite the cold of the air-conditioning, and my legs feel as useless as Fred's. I am trembling, but I cannot feel my body moving. I am ice and I am fire. Life and death. Damn him, damn him for what he has done to me!

'Like your God…' He reaches for me but I push him away so violently he loses his balance for a second, stumbling sideways before he corrects himself.

'There is nothing wrong with my God, other than you're trying to act like him.'

'Ah, now we have it!' He grins. 'But I'm not, Elise. I'm very much in the hands of your God, and you. That's why you have Power of Attorney,' he adds. The grin has gone now, replaced by baby eyes, wide and trusting. 'To do what is best for me if you ever have to, based on medical advice and my wishes.'

'I know that, Jason.'

'I know you know that. That's why I've told you what we're doing for me with our current research, so you can see how incredible it could be if we progress it.'

What a fool I've been. The Power of Attorney is a puppet show. I am Jason's puppet. Now I know the script, I understand that. We stand a mere stride apart but we could be on the other side of the world to each other. Maybe we always have been. I don't know whether I hate or pity him now. Or love. I shiver. He steps towards me and encircles me within his arms.

'You're cold, love.' Out of habit I lay my head in his shoulder and we stand, entwined for what seems like hours. I haven't the energy to move, nor the will to stay. 'I'm sorry. It'll be OK. You'll see,' he says into my hair.

'Will it?' I mumble into his shoulder. He smells of heat and power and determination. Like he always does – in that he is unchanged – but there is something else indefinable hovering in the mix too, and I am afraid of it. I am afraid of everything today, but as I eventually pull myself away from my husband and he releases me, I realise that now I am more afraid of who and what my husband already is than what he might become.

Chapter 32

29th June 2029: Jason

Today my forehead feels tight, complaining. I touch the dressing. It is intact, no weeping or heat, but I seek out the mirror in the bathroom anyway and peel it away to check. The tap Matthew inserted looks neat and uninfected, yet I feel uneasy. The exchange with Elise hasn't helped, I suppose. We've never argued like that before, not even over the baby. I lean in over the washbasin and study my face. No discernible change at all, really – except for the minute tap protruding from my temple. I imagine the fibre-thin tubing threading from its entry point to my neo-cortex, snaking its way across my forehead like a worm boring in and invading me. Better than the Parmensis invading me…

Why did she question me now? Damn! She caught me unawares, or I wouldn't have told her about Rosalie. Rosalie – I can't call her mother. She's not. I peel away from the washbasin because I no longer want to look at my face. It is too like hers.

'I'm sorry, Jason,' she said.

I'm sorry, I'm sorry, I'm sorry…

No, you weren't. You were never sorry. You were just embarrassed that I found you. Embarrassed that I asked. Embarrassed you had to answer me.

I slam on the tap and the water bursts from the faucet. It splatters against the basin and splashes onto my hands as they grasp the basin edge. The water globules spread across my hands like cells, growing and dividing. I don't want to remember, but I must. All the research says I need to be deliberate about this – remember the good and the bad. Deliberately renew and refresh the playbacks in my mind as the CyberCute does its job catalysing with the neo-cortical fluid, building and defining what is in my brain as the microscopic mass we inserted there grows. We'd never attempted cloning inside a host before this, hadn't realised that the more electrical input there is – because that is all my thoughts are – the faster the response. Probably why it failed inside Fred – apart from there not being the right biological conditions, there was no baseline activity to develop from. But this – I wonder how Matthew explained this aspect to Elise. And she didn't object. That was strange. I park that and re-apply myself to the unenviable task of remembering that meeting again, six years ago.

'I'm sorry. It was difficult at the time. I was only young.'

'So was I.'

I look at myself in the mirror again. No, I am unchanged – unchanged even from then in many ways, and yet so different already, the change is immeasurable. I can feel it growing inside me – depth, substance, more of… I don't know what yet, but more… I should talk to Matthew about it but something holds me back. Gut instinct is something I've never been strong on, but this feeling is deep in my gut, but not *of* my gut. I know I have upset Elise more than merely telling her about Rosalie should have. Of course, I have – even my emotionally truncated self of six years ago would recognise that, but there is something to her upset that disturbs me in a way it wouldn't have six years ago. My heart feels unstable in my chest and my stomach crawls with small biting insects. I have never experienced this sensation before, even though I know its name: anxiety.

I throw off my sweat pants and t-shirt and climb into the shower, turning it to pulse. It spatters over my head and hammers onto my shoulders in an alternating flow of pummel and soothe. It mimics my own pulse and its oscillation between calm and concern. I let the water slowly beat my shoulders into relaxation and set my mind to examining why I should feel this way. Elise has no power over me, despite the Power of Attorney. That is a sham, and she knows it. She would have to prove that halting all research was in my best interest – and my preference – if she was called on to exercise it. The anxiety isn't because of that. Then what is causing it?

I step out of the shower and towel myself dry. The towel feels like sandpaper against my skin. I leave it on the floor as I would if it had been a hotel bathroom and pad back into the bedroom. The soles of my feet stick to the floor with the compulsive attraction of iron filings to a magnet. I peel them away from it with each step, wading my way through an unseen cloud of nitrogen, oxygen and carbon dioxide that, nevertheless brushes my skin with featherlight touches as it flows around me. I half-close my eyes and I see the particulates in the air, swirling and settling:

droplets of water, dust, dirt, skin cells… The feeling of anxiety intensifies. I pause, naked, in front of the floor to ceiling mirror Elise suggested, falsely assuming she would be inhabiting my cocoon here with me. I scrutinise myself again, head to toe, touching and probing. The dressing has come away from the small insertion site on my forehead but the wound is neat and healthy. I touch my forehead, but my skin is smooth and cool. No fever, so I am not ill; no infection has wheedled its way into my brain. And I find I am logical and objective when I examine the contents of my mind, churning and chopping the ideas that are forming in it until they become concepts and plans. There can only be one reason for it, then: perception is expanding, and my body is struggling to process it. It started this morning in truth.

'My God!'

Matthew's head looks like an amorphous lump, scattered with baby hair, fine and wispy – although of course it isn't. He is thinning, and his head is a solid lump engrossed in readings he doesn't fully understand but knows they mean something extreme is happening. He is a child amongst men at times, biddable and ignorant for all his ability. The lab clock records 7.35am, Monday 29th June 2029; a mere nine hours ago.

'What?'

'It looks like we're seeing rapid cohesion and less free space where we inserted the hybrid mix. Those areas should have been blank space – surrounded by neuronal cell bodies and unmyelinated fibres. Instead they ARE neuronal cell bodies and unmyelinated fibres.'

'You're saying I have more brain capacity now?'

He turns to stare at me. The solid lump of forehead is wrinkled, crumpling into confusion.

'Well, we can't measure brain capacity.'

'Then we need to.'

'Jason…' He pauses, pinches the bridge of his nose. 'We can only measure volume and activity if we know how to stimulate and produce a response we can record. How would we do that?'

'What I can do now compared to what I couldn't do before.'

'But there's no way of knowing that with brain function. We haven't a baseline, to begin with…'

'Who needs a baseline? It's working, Matthew. The CyberCute is working – growing capacity. Growing independently. Who knows what I will be able to do as it expands. Who knows what Fred and I will be able

to do?'

I laugh with the sheer elation of it. I may have a Parmensis in my brain, but I also have the capacity to grow a replacement too. My laughter echoes around the lab, bouncing back at me off the walls, rising and swelling in a crescendo of sound that I can see as waves, atom by atom, rolling and twisting as they spiral towards me. My laughter rises and surges with the realisation until even to me I sound a touch deranged. I rein it in and join him at the monitor, addressing the graph on screen.

'Cortical plasticity.'

He swivels in his chair and addresses the monitor with me.

'Synaesthesia? You're saying you've developed synaesthesia? You can't develop synaesthesia. You're born with it.'

'Maybe we're all born with it, Matthew, but only a few can access it.'

He is still frowning as I leave, but he's got the picture. Solid, reliable Matthew has got the picture. Where it goes from here potentially has no limit. Potentially I have no limits if I can make it into Fred before the Parmensis makes it into the rest of my body.

And we do have a baseline, Matthew. We have what I perceived six years ago and what I perceive now. Or even further back, as a child, when Rosalie abandoned Anna and I, and I had to plod through childhood, with the finger of pity continually pointed at me. All the dull, useless self I was then, rejected, abandoned, wondering what was so wrong with me my own mother walked out on me. Every day until today I still felt that – every day, whatever I was doing, however many plaudits I received, however much money was in the bank. How could I possibly pass all of that – my legacy of rejection and the genes that went with it – onto a child? But now? Oh yes, I am very different now. Very different, and becoming more so even as I reflect on it. I stretch out my hand and touch the mirror. Our two hands touch, me and my alter ego. They touch and combine. There is potentially no limit to what I could do if the cortical plasticity keeps stretching and growing and Fred and I become one.

Behind me a shadowy figure has entered the room and is hovering just out of sight. I know, even though the whole building's doors are designed around a noiseless open-close system to minimise distraction when processing tricky procedures, because I can sense their eyes on me. I address them without turning, registering their surprise and their intent before they answer.

'Dr Kohn, what do you need?'

Chapter 33

3rd July 2029: Matthew

I'm surprised Elise hasn't been back in to see me since our conversation overlooking the wheat field. Surprised, and also relieved in some ways. In the meantime, Jason has been pushing our experiments on at a pace, and I have silently observed. We haven't discussed further the anomaly I noticed in the readings on Saturday. Strangely, he hasn't seemed to want to. He has been distracted and distant, but that, too, has suited me. How can I talk to this man as a friend, knowing what I am doing? Fred, on the other hand, is getting disturbingly closer. As the CyberCute works its magic on him, his face has taken on Jason's with worrying ease – even at times seeming to mimic Jason's expressions.

My eyes linger on the storage racking behind the portable MRI: liver 21/6, lung – part 23/6, kidney 23/6, heart 24/6, pancreas 1/7, lung – expanded to bronchiole 2/7. The growing stock of cloned organs has reached abundance level and sits in silent condemnation of me and my contemptible plan. At least faulty internal parts could be replaced… I turn away because Fred is still recumbent on the MRI bed, awaiting today's full scan to ensure everything remains in good order, but he has been turned onto his side so he looks at me – eyes permanently open and staring. They haven't been upgraded yet, either. Their budding stand-ins are currently blossoming in a dome-covered petri dish in the inner lab. The glass eyes are reproachful. Wherever I move they follow me. Who the hell moved him anyway? I get up, pushing the chair away from me with a screech as it catches on a stray paperclip that has fallen on the floor. The chair spins away from me as I rise from it and ricochets against the worktop. The disturbance unsettles me as much as Fred staring at me. We don't use paperclips in here. It's a pet hate of Jason's. So, who has been in the lab apart from me and Jason – and Elise four days ago?

I cross to Fred, still chewing on that one. The air-con has gone up a notch and today the temperature is almost warm. That, too, has thrown me as I have taken to coming to the lab in thick plaid shirts or sweatshirts, so today I am sweating instead of freezing. My armpits rub uncomfortably against the inner seam of today's plaid offering and my crotch grinds in moist reciprocation against my thick winter jeans. Fred, by comparison, when I go to manoeuvre him to reposition him onto his back, facing the ceiling where his staring accusation can't harm anyone, is cool but pliant. I step back and reconsider before I heave him about. Why this position too? I circle the MRI bed and crouch behind it and Fred, peering over his shoulder. However paranoid I am feeling, it can't have been to make me squirm under his appraising gaze because Fred's view is actually focused on the place Jason normally sits when reviewing data. I have been hot-seating it, peering over Jason's shoulder, in effect. The data has been streamed to his PC for the last three days, diverting away from mine with Jason's claim that his machine processes faster, it's operating system being based on quantum mechanics principles. Mine is bog-standard; take that as a commentary on the two of us, too. So now I have a mystery – a paperclip, a repositioned Fred, redirection from Jason and, after some thought I add, absence from Elise.

I complete Fred's repositioning, increasing my heat and dampness in the process. It's not so much that he resists, as that he fails to cooperate – if that can be said of an inanimate object. In the silence of the lab, my grunting and complaining is comedic except that this situation is anything but funny. I finally abandon Fred to his usual reclining position with relief. And presumably Jason has been redirecting all that data on purpose – so I don't have first-hand access to it, only when he is here and logged onto his PC. I have been canny, generally being able to download copies whenever he has been wired up to Fred for us to complete compatibility checks, but it's always only the data of the day before. The data of the current day can't be downloaded until it's complete, so I don't know yet what yesterday's said about Jason's neo-cortical plasticity growth or the state of the Parmensis in his brain or what development that might produce today – or what new plan Jason might have – E, F, G, H – wherever he's got to now. I can't access that until Jason has, so the sooner he does so, the sooner I can too – directly or by more nefarious means. The data before that, though, has been showing a trend. One I can't quite figure out at the moment, but I know I should. It makes me think of something quite specific, but I can't quite pin down what.

Jason should have been here long ago, too. It's gone nine. Outside, the sun is already beginning to heat up, glowing royally as it rises on its arc across the sky, and Jason's team will be checking in on him in just over an hour and a half. What we can do in that time is so limited, it's almost not worth doing. Now my unease gets out of hand. Something must be wrong. I dither between the MRI and the door, sniffing the air like a bloodhound, unsure which trail to follow. The trail is cold in here, no smells except the antiseptic tang of the lab cleaning materials and stale coffee dregs. I seek other clues in the lab itself and the only two occupants it has – me and Fred. Fred lies lumpenly in situ where I replaced him, still accusing, but it's more in the implication than the actual now. No help there. And me? Gingerly I test my conscience. Something *could* be wrong but do I want to know about it? If something *is* wrong, it means I don't have to do what I was setting out to do. I can back away, pretend there was never a conflict, never the resentment and anger and betrayal. Never the treachery that now lingers in my heart. I am still between Fred and the door when it bursts open and Jason takes ownership of the room. He is dressed in t-shirt and shorts, as if he's going for a day on the beach, but he looks diminished – odd though that sounds.

'Man, what are you doing round there?' His tone is light but suspicious nevertheless.

'Ch-checking Fred.' I don't mean to stammer but the words choke in my throat.

'Oh,' he crosses to his work station and switches it on and then immediately off again, still eyeing me. 'Thought you and Fred might be ganging up on me. Or you and someone else?'

'Jesus, Jason, why would I do that?'

I can feel my cheeks flushing that awful dull red I so hate: port-wine stain; indelible ink stain – guilty stain.

'I don't know. Why would you, buddy?'

Now he's looking at me curiously and I struggle to recover. I am not doing anything wrong. I am merely limiting the limitless. Holding back Icarus. I'm not a bad man… But that direct challenge. Does he know? He snorts with laughter at what must be my pained expression and the old Jason is back momentarily. 'Anyway, whatever you're doing round there with Fred – and far be it from me to get in the way of any form of *special* relationship – '

'Christ, don't be disgusting! I'm not like that and Fred's a… Fred's a…'

'Guy?'

'A cyborg!'

'Well… ' Jason shrugs. 'Maybe not forever…' He winks at me. I'm taken aback. He doesn't suspect anything. It was simply a lewd joke, and yet…

'Stop it!' I run my fingers through my hair and catch my breath. 'Stop it,' I say more quietly. 'This isn't a joke.'

'Oh no,' Jason's voice has dropped a tone and it spans the distance between us in a deep, dark admission. 'This is no joke, Matthew. This is for real. Yesterday proved it.'

'What yesterday?'

My voice is sharper than intended and his demeanour changes again. He walks carefully across the room, feet making soft splashing sounds on the pristine floor. He is barefoot, legs lean to the point of thinness. I frown. Shorts, t-shirt, barefoot. In the lab?

'This yesterday.' He switches the PC on and adjusts the brightness of the monitor, waiting for yesterday's data to load. 'See?' He is pointing to a spike in recorded electrical activity during one of the routine fMRI scans we had carried out – not of Fred, but of Jason. 'That's bigger than ever before.' I join him, scanning the graph over the top of his head but I am distracted by his nearness and the small round spot of baldness I have never noticed before on the crown of his head. It looks stretched, shiny – as if something is pushing against it from the inside. I want to touch it to see if it is. The Parmensis or the neo-cortex? 'And it's following a pattern,' he adds after a while.

'What's the pattern?' I tear my eyes away from the bald spot and focus on the screen, eating up the data. There is no pattern I can see, except in that it has a randomness that could be a pattern of its own – a growth pattern.

'Well, directly correlating to CyberCute injection of course, but also correlating to other functions. Brain function up, bodily function down – as if the brain is expanding into the body. And specifically…' He stops short. He is staring out of the window. 'Yes, that's it…'

'Are you OK?'

'Yes, oh yes. I'm fine.' He closes down the screen and logs off. I am tempted to stop him, hold my hand over his and force a restart. Never before would I have challenged him, but the glimpse of what he called a pattern lodges in my mind. It mimics another – in reverse – but without both sets of data, I can't check – or at least not right now.

'Oh, aren't we doing anything today?'

'No. Not enough time now before the quacks want to check up on me. You do the usual with Fred, make sure he's still in tip-top… How are the eyes going by the way?'

'Fine, I think. Probably another few hours before they're functional, but no apparent problems.'

'Good. Well, in that case I'll go and lie on my bed like a good patient and check back in later. Bit out of sorts today, actually, so that check-up might be a good thing.'

'Oh? Specifics?'

The unease that I was feeling earlier is changing, mutating into something I cannot put a name to; a sense of the divine intervening on humanity, perhaps? Or the divine overtaking humanity.

'Just… Who knows? Going to lie down anyway.' He stands, and the chair does its wheelie like it did for me. He stares at it and it corrects itself, this time gliding over the top of the paperclip and hiccupping to a stop a foot away. He smiles. I watch, unsurprised, ideas slowly tumbling into place like a Rubik's Cube being manipulated. One face completes green and an idea fights its way to the top of the heap of all the others. Standing, Jason's stature is little more than it was sitting. He is hunching over, as if he has been deflated and the bag of complexities that is Jason Crane has been looted, leaving little but the outer casing.

'Actually, you do look a bit crock.'

'Yeah. Well… You and Fred carry on, and no more hanky-panky.'

I would have taken exception except the jibe seems to have lost its power. I eye the blank computer screen and then Jason as he makes his way across the lab. Gut instinct is working overtime – and mystery solving. It occurs to me that, God help me, I really need to get my hands on that data, check what it shows, bury it if necessary if its impact on me will be negative after the event. Oh God, I disgust myself.

'What about that pattern you mentioned? Want me to check the data in the meantime?'

He is at the door, heading for the corridor. 'No, be fine… I'll look again later myself.'

The door closes behind him and clicks onto 'lock'.

Who uses paperclips? Dr Kohn.

I do something then that I've only ever done once before: ring Elise to sound her out rather than inform her. I tell her what I know – and what I suspect.

'He's worse?' I can hear the panic in her voice.

'I don't know. Worse bodily, but maybe that's not the real picture.'

'What then?'

'His brain... that data... he mentioned a pattern. I think he thinks there's a miracle in the making.'

'Or a nightmare.'

'Well... But maybe you should come in. See if he'll talk to you.'

'He won't talk to me, Matthew. He doesn't need to. Pull the plug.'

'But if there is something? If I could just see what he was talking about...'

'No. Enough. He's destroying himself in pursuit of an illusion when it's bad enough he's dying anyway. Pull the plug.' Her voice is of the same timbre and pitch as when she told me about Jane. I don't need more reminding.

'All right, I'll pull the plug tonight. I can't do it now because he may come back during the day once the medical team have finished with him. I'll do as he says as if there's nothing different today, but meanwhile I'll put the block I've already envisaged in place. If you're sure, that is.'

'I'm sure.'

'Even if there is a miracle that could really happen? To ruin that would be...'

'You won't ruin a miracle. I want a miracle as much as Jason, but this isn't it. You know that or you wouldn't have told me about what he's doing now. This is against all laws of nature, and I don't want to lose my husband before I have to lose him.'

'OK.'

'I'll come in later, too.'

I know what she means: to check.

She ends the call and I retrieve my laptop from my backpack, the laptop that isn't registered on the Crane Industries system and so should be rejected like incipient bacteria, invading the healthy bloodstream of its research body – except it isn't. I have gone to great pains to enter the Crane Industries system via the back route thanks to Tor. I am a weevil burrowing into its knowledge core, undetected, unsuspected and undermining. The CyberCute formula is mine anyway. Why shouldn't I adapt it? Jason's body might be declining as his brain activity increases but however strong his body, or Fred's is, it is only as strong as CyberCute. I can slow things down if nothing else, give me time to quantify what might happen if there *is* a pattern developing. And if there is? Christ; then we're in trouble...

Chapter 34

3rd July 2029: Jason

It's late. Elise has been and gone. We hadn't much to say to each other. What is there in words now? And I didn't make it back to the lab as I'd originally intended. After the usual round of checks from the medical team, the fatigue that was already setting in when I was reviewing yesterday's data with Matthew spread its languor and sealed me to the bed. I look along the line of my body and still it is unchanged, yet inside I feel the metamorphosis. Do I fight it or let it take me? Time is short now. I haven't told Matthew or Elise. It has come on me suddenly but strangely I'm no longer afraid. Death comes softly, creeping like a mouse tempted by the prospect of sustenance, but it will find there is none here.

The cold creeps along my limbs, curling its tendrils around my skin and bones, twining insidiously into sinew and cell. I tense, consciously control the muscle contraction and it releases, but it is followed by another, and then another. I reach for the call button behind the bed and collapse back from the effort, sweat beading my face and making my t-shirt stick to me like a second skin. The wave of contractions carries me into the mouth of the beast and on into its gut. I gasp and fight it, waving my arms and shouting, but inside I am calm, clear-headed in a way I haven't been since the Parmensis invaded. Through the haze of sweat now threatening to blind me, I see Dr Kohn, advancing on me with gag and shackles as my back arches and my heels skitter against the sheets in a desperate attempt to walk the plank off the sinking ship and into the shark-infested water.

'It's OK, it's OK,' she says as the needle pricks my arm and the gag opens my mouth wide. 'Bite down on it. The sedative will work in a minute.'

I close my eyes and Dr Kohn and everything else fades in the dwindling light of the beast's closing mouth.

I am in the depths.

Awake.

Clear-headed.

Sure.

Sure as never before.

'Mr Crane, can you hear me?'

I open my eyes. Dr Kohn is bending over me, her sharp features poking into my face. I focus past her. White. Gleaming white. We are in the lab.

'I can hear you,' I hear myself saying. It is garbled, but I understand what I mean. I hope she does too. I blink at her – the code we agreed just in case. Three blinks, wait, three blinks.

'Good,' she withdraws, and I feel less claustrophobic. 'You are paralysed from the chest down. It was the last seizure that did it.'

I nod my head, although to her it must look more like a ship rolling leeward at sea.

'Scan,' I articulate with difficulty. I direct my eyes towards the MRI. Fred is still comfortably recumbent partly inside it. He will have to make way. New resident coming through…

'The MRI? Why?'

'Moved.' It's barely more than a whisper – a moue.

She frowns, then her face opens up like a flower. 'It's moved? You think it's moved?' I nod frenetically. 'OK, let's see.'

I close my eyes and allow my numbed body to drift, rudderless and functionless, but not hopeless, as I am manoeuvred and man-handled by Dr Kohn and her team. They are green and scrubbed, and only lack one person as they manipulate me into position onto the scanner bed with ease. I allow the machine to subjugate me to its whirring, clattering intrusion as I have so many times recently, but this time with joy, not fear, at what it will show. I cannot help them but Dr Kohn has already been briefed and I already know what she will see. My expanded neo-cortex has already juggled all the scattered parts of the data into a coherent whole. Twenty minutes later my fate is acknowledged, if not sealed.

Dr Kohn is hyped, cheeks flushed and eyes glittering. 'The Parmensis has migrated.'

I nod. 'Where?' I manage.

'It is now running along your muscle fibres, hence the paralysis, but it appears to be clear of your brain.' The tears are rolling out of the corners of my eyes and down the side of my face. I can hear them pounding on the scanner bed in steady rhythm. At last! 'Mr Crane?'

I nod again. 'I'm OK. I'm OK.' The words are clear to me even if they're not to Dr Kohn – but they do appear to be. 'It's now, though.'

'Now?'

I can hear the tension in her voice where before there was only blind arrogance. Yes, her team needs the one it is lacking. I need the one it is lacking even more.

'Now.'

'Are you sure?'

'Matthew. Phone. Pocket. Speed dial. One.'

It is all I can do to expel the instructions. Staccato bursts like machine gun fire. I feel her fumble in my pocket for the ever-present lifeline to Matthew, hands trembling. The sheer irony of the fact that Matthew doesn't realise the importance of himself in all this. Dependable, biddable, safe Matthew holds the key – always has. Him and his CyberCute. She drags the phone from my pocket and holds it in front of me. I blink, and the screen opens wide-eyed for my iris. She speed-dials 'one'.

No answer. I hear the tinny rebuff of the voicemail message.

'He's not picking up.' There is a hint of panic in her voice; cool, calm Dr Kohn. It communicates itself to the tingling fibres of my extremities with the energy of a fated event.

'Without Matthew then.'

There is no time left. The tingling in my extremities is travelling inward. The Parmensis is approaching its apex as my bodily functions decline.

'But…'

It takes all the energy I have, and the darkness begins its descent even as the last word thrums the air between us.

'No buts. This is our moment, doctor. Yours and mine. Just follow the instructions.'

Chapter 35

4th July 2029: Matthew

I am stealing into the building like a cat burglar on the stroke of midnight. This is ridiculous, but since the moment I left here early evening, I've been on the verge of retracing my steps – all my steps – and reversing what I have set in motion. That saying 'vengeance is mine' is all very well in melodrama, but in reality? Christ! How could I do this, even to a man who has been wronging me for years?

I can't. I can't allow this crazy situation to become even crazier. Jason will die, and I will look back on this time of heightened emotion and despair with a kind of disbelief, years from now. And will any of it matter then: the rights, the wrongs? No, but I will forever know that if he hadn't died, I would have been the instrument of his death anyway. I can't reverse the process now. It has already started. Fred will have to be re-set, the CyberCute reprogrammed, but that requires a total shut down for me to access the Crane Industries formulaic records via the dark net – unseen.

It's eerily quiet tonight, like the whole world is sleeping, excepting one small geographical portion of it. The Crane Industries lab building stretches squat and flat like a giant incubating insect across the area between car park and corn fields, but in one corner there are pinpricks of lights. Anxiety engulfs me in a dark unguent wave. The ForEver lab. But no one should be there at this time of night – not even Jason in manic mode. My pace quickens, heels clicking out my presence like the clicking of mantis legs just before attack. A soft breeze ruffles the intensity of the black sky, broken only here and there by a smattering of stars. It is clouding over – maybe a storm brewing to break the viciousness of the heatwave we've been suffering. There is something electric in the air as the breeze surrounds and tugs at my loose t-shirt, sending a trickle of something close to fear down my spine. I can smell anxiety even on the wind. Oh God, if something has happened!

I drag my phone from my pocket and its vacant screen suddenly fills with missed call after missed call, silently screaming at me.

Jason.

Shit! Why? Is it not working properly? I turn the phone sideways in confusion, then remember I turned the ringer to mute in preparation for my nocturnal excursion. Damn! I access the last missed call and it directs to voicemail. All I register is Dr Kohn's normally cool voice high-pitched with tension, but the rest is beyond comprehension. They can only be the words I have dreaded hearing ever since this nightmare started. I break into a sprint – as much as my soft and ill-conditioned body can, stumbling, lumbering and staggering towards the lab side door outlined in an ethereal yellow glow that softly marks out the entrance to hell in the murky night. No time to backtrack. No time to reverse anything now, only stop it – stop it dead before it's discovered. But if Jason is in crisis, there'll be no powering down now either. The best I can hope for is that it's not discovered for now.

I slam my palm against the security scanner next to the entrance and wrench the door open. Inside, the corridor is ringed in the same soft yellow glow, small beaded lights outlining the intersection between wall and floor. I steel myself in readiness for throwing myself onto Jason's mercy – or his funeral pyre, for that is all there will be left for me if what I've done is discovered. My rubber-soled shoes squeak piteously as I lurch to the end of the corridor, towards Jason's quarters with their never-open door gaping wide and displaying a room full of emptiness. Empty? Then this really is bad. I stagger on towards the surgical unit attached to his quarters and backing onto the lab, but before I reach them I encounter the lab door. It too is wide open. I hover there, sweating and panting, heart hammering in my throat. Someone has been in here. Someone could have looked. It is almost beyond me to walk over that threshold, but know, *I must*. Slowly, my guilty feet take me into the room, and I register a sense of abrupt abandonment – of hurrying from here to somewhere else – as I also register the ON status of the MRI, and the small red dot glowing 'on' at the edge of Jason's PC screen… The small trickle of fear running from my shoulder blades and down my spine to pool at the base of my rump and into my crotch tells me this is worse than bad.

If what I have done has been uncovered there can never be redemption for me. I cross to the monitor and flick its switch. It is the PC on which Jason keeps all the data. It revs into life with venomous glee, displaying not only the most recent MRI scan results, but something that stops me in my tracks. It's not yesterday's data. These are timed 22.57 today and are a whole-body series. I peer at them in confusion. They do not make sense. Interwoven amongst muscle and bone are the tendrils of what could be some great sea creature, rising from the depths to entangle and drag its victim down to the gloomy sea bed, there to ebb and flow with the detritus from ancient shipwrecks and the bones of long-dead sea monsters. The patient's name stares back at me from the top of the screen, and it takes me almost precisely the same time as it takes me to realise that Fred no longer lolls languorously across the MRI scanner bed to read it.

The patient's name is Jason Crane.

I do not need to know now what the details I couldn't understand in that garbled phone message were. I do not need to know why Jason's quarters were empty or why Fred no longer curries favour with the MRI scanner, I walk like a member of Fred's kind towards the sterile lab unit and enter the code to gain access to the outer area but the door is already unlocked. This is mine and Jason's domain. No one else should be in here, but I can already feel the intrusion – the invasion. My senses are on full alert now. There is the merest trace of perfume on the air, overlaid by antiseptic. One of the taps drips, flip handle not quite flipped fully off, and the very atmosphere is charged with bustling people and anxious activity. The automatic spray has been activated too – the norm before any procedure is undertaken in the inner sanctum.

I gown up and pull the blind open on the viewing window. I stand as far away as I can to observe, a ghost lingering in the shadows as death makes its case for victory. A thousand, a million, a billion moments I have shared with Jason wash over me, tumbling me over and over as the magnitude of what I have done drags me down into the depths of my soul. I am lost beyond all trace, even as the voice finds me.

'Dr Green!'

I focus on the viewing window. Hell. We have created a living hell and Jason is about to enter it.

On the slab are the two bodies, the living and the dying. Fred lies exposed in all his masculine glory. Jason is more appropriately covered by a green surgical drape. He is hooked up to the computer by a tangle of wires attached to his shaven scalp by shiny silver electrodes, giving him the impression of wearing a metallic hedgehog cap.

'Dr Green, we need you. Come on through, please.'

Her eyes are beseeching. I have never seen Dr Kohn beseeching before. Her eyebrows arc over their wide-eyed desperation, and the perspiration on her surgical cap plasters it to her forehead. Fred dangles, slack across the slab, mouth agape and arms slopping over the sides and onto the floor like tentacles, like the alien thing inside Jason. He too wears a cap of electrodes.

'What are you doing?' My voice is harsh, an iron filing grating of disbelief over dismay.

'He was dying – *is* dying. He insisted.'

'But you don't know… you don't…'

'No, I don't. That's why I rang you. The Parmensis moved. There are instructions, but they need you to follow them properly. You didn't answer so we had to do something – start the process, at least. He's in stasis for the moment – somewhere between living and nowhere, but conscious.'

The Parmensis moved. The tentacles. The string wrapping itself around sinew and bone on the MRI. Of course; of course, that was why Jason had seemed depleted, fading this morning. God! How could I have overlooked this possibility? I'd though it was the neo-cortex starting to edge out gross motor control but it was the bloody Parmensis! The thing we'd been trying to make happen was happening of its own accord even as we ignored it.

'What have you done?' I don't know whether it is an accusation or a question, but I can see Dr Kohn takes it as both.

'He's hooked into the cyborg for main organ resources and we've made a partial cortical connection, but we don't know how you were going to initiate the first stage of transfer, and he can't tell us. His speech is gone.'

'Fuck!' Neither do I. 'You mean they're already connected?' My brain rapidly digests the fact that Dr Kohn knows about Fred and Jason's plans – whatever letter of the alphabet they have now reached – but all my mouth wants to issue is expletives. 'Fuck!' I repeat, grappling with what to do next. OK, so we'd made the connection before in the abortive attempt to clone Jason's brain and integrate it with Fred, but we'd not managed to actually place the brain in situ, and how could a man walk around without a brain in his head?

'Notionally I understand you managed it in part with the clone, but we now need to get Mr Crane's brain into the cyborg or it won't be many hours before the connection degrades and then the organs will fail in both bodies.' Dr Kohn is sweating even if she sounds calm. 'He wrote it down

– what to do – but it requires a specific item that only you have access to.'

'Specific item? What the fuck? I don't know! We weren't ready for this, Dr Kohn.'

I'm backing away from the viewing window as she's approaching it. I turn off the intercom and her words are mere openings and closings of her fish mouth. What do I do now? What the fuck do I do now? She is right up against the glass now, banging her fist on it. Behind her, Jason twitches. Simultaneously Fred mimics him. *He wrote it down – what to do...* I turn on the intercom again, just long enough to hear her diatribe, for what it's worth.

'Are you scared? Are you a coward? This is his moment; this is the moment you've been working towards – shutting me out – and now you're scared? You are...' her anger dissolves into Germanic abuse that I don't understand but can guess the gist of.

'Shut up!' I snap at her. 'You have no idea what we were doing – no idea what this entails!'

The Germanic abuse continues and I shut off the intercom again to give myself a chance to think. Oh shit, oh shit, oh shit, oh shit... Then I am saying it aloud. Louder and louder and louder until I scream it and Dr Kohn is still mouthing silent Germanic insults at me that cut to my very soul.

'Shut up! Shut-the-fuck-up!' I scream at Dr Kohn. She can't hear me, but she shuts up anyway, probably because of the fury on my face, backing away from the glass and eyeing me balefully. The smell of antiseptic is unbearable and I want to gag. On the slab beside her, Jason twitches again. My friend. The man I've known more than half my life, with whom I made my biggest and most inspirational discoveries, made my worst mistakes. The man who made me and could ruin me. I begin to shiver and sob. My friend, whatever he has done to me and I have done to him.

I sit heavily in the chair to the side of the viewing window and face the PC screen that displays what is happening in the inner sanctum if the viewing window is screened. We've only used it for review in the past because the programme records as well. Now I can see both Fred and Jason in fine detail on its monitor. They are Siamese twins in all but humanity. And Jason's eyes are still open. Oh shit! She's right. He's still conscious and hearing everything we're both saying. This is what we've been working towards for the last – Oh God, for the last most of our lives – but I don't know what to do. *He wrote it down – what to do...* What did he write down?

I leave the PC monitor and go back to the viewing window. Dr Kohn is still statue-like in the centre of the inner sanctum, her two patients either side of her. Her green-gowned team float vaguely in the background, afraid but awed by what is going down. The bank of monitors behind them on the far wall display Jason and Fred's vital signs in duplicate, the one notably stronger than the other. Jason is fading even as I watch. I flick the intercom switch and peer through the glass at him. Dr Kohn approaches, blocking my view.

'He's conscious. Can he talk?'

'No. I told you. Paralysed. Neck down and vocal chords.'

'Then what did he write down?' I ask her quietly, as calmly as I can.

She breathes on the glass and laboriously writes backwards. The words angle downwards and are malformed but legible. *In the report.*

In the report? But I can't access today's yet and using my system I have to wait until the next day to do so secretly. I glance at the time stamp at the bottom right-hand corner of the monitor. 11:49. I go back to the viewing window.

'Can he last another twenty minutes like this?'

Dr Kohn breaths in and draws herself up to her full diminutive height – daunting nonetheless.

'I will do my best. If he does not, I will report why. You were on call but didn't respond.'

I ignore the threat and go back to the monitor, plugging in my own laptop and preparing to bypass the Crane Industries security system the moment the clocks ticks over to tomorrow. One access per day, that is all I can have without the system noticing the virus-like intrusion my peeping eyes represent. Those eleven minutes take eleven hours to pass but the moment the digital clock twitches onto 00.00 I am in. My delving around brings up not only yesterday's test results but two reports. The first, the last report I'd seen – from the day before yesterday, with Jason's tentative transfer procedure outlined in it. The second, linked to what was now yesterday's data – is the last one Jason ever wrote, time and date stamped a mere four hours ago.

He wrote it down – what to do…

By God, he had! He had written down exactly what the results from yesterday inferred, and how simple, really the CyberCute made the whole process. Terrifyingly simple if it worked – and terrifyingly faulty if I used the wrong CyberCute.

'My God,' I say it low, under my breath – not that it matters who hears now. Yes, I know what they mean, but only because Jason's report makes the quantum leap from fact to application – the pattern I could perceive but certainly not otherwise understand. It has to be the CyberCute's interaction with the neo-cortical fluid that has enabled his leap of comprehension. I push the chair back with such vigour it careers across the room and collides with the washing area, clattering angrily behind me as I address the viewing window and Dr Kohn.

'Yes, I know what to do – whether it will work, who knows, but he has left instructions. You are my witness, though. These are his wishes, not mine.'

She nods slowly. 'You mean we are all exonerated if they don't work?'

'Huh. Exonerated? None of us will ever be exonerated. This is life – and death…'

She stares at me and then shrugs. 'OK, tell me what we have to do.'

After I tell her, I pull my phone from my pocket and dial Elise's number.

'You need to get down here, and I'm sorry.'

'Wh-what is happening?' Her voice is soft from sleep.

'It's now. What we've been waiting for. The nightmare or the miracle.'

'Oh!' Slumber has left her and her voice pitches down the phone at me like the first rolling boulder precipitating an avalanche. 'You said— '

'I know what I said, but I can't now. I can't condemn Jason to death. He found a way and I have to try for him. Just get down here now.'

The click of her rejection is simultaneous with the click as I turn the intercom back on. Dr Kohn stands to attention.

'Dr Green?'

'I need to scrub up and there's a formula I need to access to manufacture more CyberCute, then I'll be with you.'

'We have some here already. That was the only thing I knew to have on hand.'

'From when?'

'Today.'

I hesitate. The new formula couldn't have been put into production that quickly, surely?

'That's probably OK then…'

She gets the uncertainty in my voice and I can see the light of curiosity is in her eyes even through the viewing screen.

'Or is it not OK?'

'What's the time stamp on it?'

'No time stamp, unless you'd count it as when we synthesised it.'

'And when was that?'

'Tonight. On Mr Crane's instructions.'

On Jason's instructions? Then that must have been before I'd uploaded the new formula because he'd gone to lie down before I'd accessed the records myself. In that case I still have time to do my best for both Jason and cover my tracks too.

'All right.' Dr Kohn is watching me carefully – too carefully. I square my shoulders. 'Just keep him stable and have a series of ten-mil syringes ready for each of the electrode sites on the cyborg because we need to withdraw fluid from the tap in Jason's forehead. We can't transplant the brain completely intact but we can help the points of connection to stimulate growth within. We've been working on Jason's neo-cortex. I think there's a pattern we can mimic to produce the same results in the cyborg, but you'll need to access yesterday's MRI data for me to look at it.' I look at my watch! 2.11. The twenty minutes Dr Kohn had promised were already up. 'Do it whilst I scrub.' I reel off the access code and leave her to it.

I don't even wait for her response and I don't even question my logic. There is none to this. It is all in the gut and I suspect that's how Jason felt about this pattern too. But he *knew*. I can see now that's why he went off to lie down. He knew what was coming. The pattern had already completed itself for him – it just did so quicker than he'd anticipated. I complete the scrub process in record time and enter the inner sanctum with almost a feeling of peace – the same one I'd felt earlier when I'd felt the hand of the divine on my shoulder.

I stand over Jason and his eyes focus in on me.

'We're ready. Are you?'

He twitches and makes a whining noise, like gas escaping a corpse. I touch his arm and then nod to Dr Kohn. She treats me a long hard stare.

'The CyberCute we have, then?'

I nod vigorously. 'And come on. Time is running out.'

The stare shifts from me to Jason. If this works, she's his problem to deal with and that stare tells me she could be a handful, but then an ambitious subordinate is the least of Jason's problems right now. And if it doesn't, she'll want to be as quiet as me about it all.

Dr Kohn inserts a cannula in the back of Jason's hand and pushes the anaesthetic through. I try to stay in eye contact with him, but his eyes roam the room and settle in the distance until his lids droop. I mouth goodbye to his unconscious face. Whether it will be hello again later, who knows?

We start by pumping Jason's blood through Fred's venous system , supplemented by plasma, and shocking his heart into action. For a time, they are truly Siamese twins, blood brothers. Fred's heart beats steadily in rhythm with Jason's. We watch the physiological transfer of Jason with astonishment as the other cloned organs placed inside Fred gradually slip into rhythm too, but I am too afraid to do anything more. It is like that for maybe twenty minutes, me silently monitoring the steady throb of life through Fred's body and the slow decline of life in Jason's. When the readings have remained constant for over half an hour, I take the syringes Dr Kohn has prepared and that now lie, silvered and potent on the surgical trolley nearest Fred, and wave her away. She resists, but I don't want her to be any part of this last moment I have with my oldest friend. Out of the corner of my eye, I see a movement at the viewing window. Elise has arrived but cannot enter. I have made sure of that, engaging the locks from the inside. She leans in against the glass and her breath steams a small patch on it. Her eyes watch me sadly above it, misty and diffuse. I imagine her sharp intake of breath and the pain on her face as I withdraw fluid from the tap on Jason's forehead and then plunge the needle of the first syringe into the site of one of the electrodes caressing Fred's cranium, linking directly to the partially connected cloned brain, but I cannot turn to look. I repeat the process until they are all spent.

'Now what?' Dr Kohn asks, baleful eyes sulky above her mask. 'Where do I need to operate?'

'Nowhere,' I reply, fatigue beginning to take over me.

'But you have simply suspended the brain in the cavity,' Dr Kohn is incredulous.

'Yes. Now we wait.'

'For what?'

'A miracle.'

I sit down on the floor between the two slabs and put my head in my hands. I am no longer sterile. I am no longer clean. I am no longer decent, but I am at least true to my old friend.

'That all?' she asks dryly.

'Isn't it enough?'

Chapter 36

5th July 2029: Elise

I'm in the studio when call came through. I haven't been here in weeks. My refuge hasn't felt like a refuge anymore – nowhere and nothing could be a refuge from what is happening. Or, maybe that's wrong. Once upon a time, Jane would have been my refuge; my confidante. We were always opposites; she wayward, wild and from the wrong side of the tracks, me the polite English rose with the cut glass accent and impressive ancestry – not that it did Robert Devereaux, Earl of Essex much good. My famous ancestor might have been the queen's favourite, but it didn't keep him his head, and now it feels like I'm losing mine.

Why do we set such store by status? Have I been guilty of that? Standing on ceremony because of who I am? I find my mind drifting back to this morning and how I've ended up here today, when I should have been at work.

'Eleven-ten,' Charlotte is peering round my door. I jump. Eleven-ten – is that significant? Is she trying to trip me up over some meeting I've agreed to but forgotten to mark in my diary? We stare at each other. She frowns and steps into the room. 'Are you OK?' she asks.

'I... why wouldn't I be?'

'Because you should be taking 2B. I've left Candice in there, setting up the easels but you know what she's like. She could be off anywhere the mood or her physical problems take her.'

'Oh God!' I just continue to stare at her. I'm numb, legs like stumps of tree, mind full of cotton, exhausted. I didn't know I was so tired – so beaten until now. I can't face 2B, but she is right. This is only one of two classes I still take during the week and I relish it, like water in a desert, but not today. Today the sheer enormity of what is happening to me, to Jason, to our world has overcome me and I see now I have been sitting at

my desk doing nothing since I first sat down here after whole-school assembly.

'You're really not up to it, are you?' Charlotte asks, approaching my desk and sitting in the chair in front of it. She crosses her legs and I register for the first time how long and slim they are, how tall and commanding she could be if she were me ... I don't know what to say. The truthful answer would be 'no', but then I will have lost the fight I've been having with Charlotte ever since I was appointed Head. 'Look, I know something is going on, Elise, and tell me to mind my own business, but if you need time out, that is what I'm here for. We don't have to be at odds, you know. I know you think I'm after your job, and under other circumstances, I would be, but not if there's something going wrong in your life. I'm ambitious, but not ruthless.'

'Oh dear,' I say eventually, 'am I such a dragon?'

'Not a dragon, in fact you so rarely breathe fire, Elise, sometimes I wonder if you ever get fired up at all – except for recently. But today, well... One thing I do know about you – even though I barely know anything about you except for the fact that your husband is rich as Croesus so you hardly need to work at all – is that you never let anyone down, so to not turn up for 2B this morning, something must be very wrong.'

Normally I would have assumed she was trying to trip me up with a statement like that, but today there was something else in her eyes as she waited for me to reply. Sympathy. Maybe it is that which makes Jericho's wall's tumble at last. My jaw drops and I can feel the tears forming in my eyes. Before I can reign myself in, they overflow and start to roll uncontrollably down my cheeks. Charlotte jumps up and rounds my desk, draping an arm around my shoulders and pulling me to her so I am blubbing like a child into her angora jumper, its fur sticking to my cheeks and lips as I sob.

'I'm sorry,' I manage when the worst of the storm abates. 'You're right, there is something going on but I can't talk about it.'

'OK', she withdraws to the chair the other side of the desk and I can sense disappointment in her.

'No, I don't mean I won't talk about it. I mean I really can't , no matter how much I'd like to – I'm not allowed to.' And suddenly I desperately want to tell her everything – as if she was Jane. 'It's top secret – my husband... and... oh...' the tears threaten again. 'I would really like to be able to talk to you,' I add miserably because I can see

that maybe I've been wrong and Charlotte isn't my rival, she's my support. Yes, she has aspirations of her own, but what is so wrong with that? All this time I could have had a friend in her, not a competitor. My world takes another tumble with that realisation and I am left bewildered by the new perspective.

'Well,' Charlotte says, leaning forward conspiratorially, 'I can keep secrets, you know – like I haven't told you about the surprise party we have planned for your birthday...'

'Oh!' my look of horror has her roaring with laughter.

'Only joking. I know you'd hate that, but if you can't talk about it – whatever it is – you can talk about how you feel about it and why you're so upset. Do you want to do that? How about I provide moral support for Candice to stop 2B turning into a painting bloodbath and you take some time out for the rest of the day to get your head straight. Then, if you'd like to, we could talk about it after school over a glass of wine.'

I nod vigorously. 'Yes, I'd like that – over a glass of wine. Can't leave Candice to a painting bloodbath.'

'OK,' she smiles and stands, unravelling her long body and squaring her shoulders as if for a fight. 'Once more into the breach...' she winks, then pauses. 'I know we approach things differently, and maybe we even have different principles and beliefs, but we're all the same, basically – just struggling through life, hoping to survive against the odds.'

'That's very profound,' I say, in an attempt to prove I am valuing her, and I will open up to her.

'My dad,' she says as she turns to leave. 'We never agreed about a single thing in life, but he was right. I should have listened better to him at the time. Should have agreed to disagree, but I suppose at least I learnt from it even if I didn't get it right at the time. He was killed in the war. He said sometimes you had to fight fire with fire. I criticised him at the time, until I found out he was part of the peace process and was killed trying to protect the politicians who brokered the accord. Always two sides, aren't there?'

'Yes,' I agree softly. 'There are always two sides and it is all about survival.'

I can't face home, with its empty rooms and echoing memories so I've taken refuge in what is no longer a refuge, but a revisiting of all the pain and confusion of my past recorded in my paintings, Charlotte's and her father's words revolving around and around in my head. Two sides to everything. I had never found out either with Jane or Jason. I'd simply cut Jane out of my life and fashioned Jason into a demon in my head. And that was how he'd remained all these years – still loving him but hating him too. I could see that in every brushstroke, ever swathe of colour and distorted image. No wonder the art agent had said they were extraordinary; they were extraordinarily tortured and iconic art is all about torture, isn't it? He'd gushed with delight about Munch, and Van Gogh and de Goya when he'd looked at them. I would be a sensation, he'd said. *The contemporarily tormented soul.* I'd wondered what the hell he'd meant at the time, but the desire to do something that would stun Jason – get back at him for all the times I'd felt excluded and isolated; left out – well, that had superseded any need for explanation.

I stand back from the easel and survey the canvas I have been attempting to fashion into something that represents my feelings as they are now – a tumble of regret, anger, despair, paralysis. Its reds and purples stain my fingers and make my eyes blur. The central figure is being castigated and flayed bloody by the angel rising up in a fiery blaze. That's me. Oh god, that's me – the angel is me. I drop the paintbrush I am holding and cover my mouth with my hands. That's retribution too! So is my determination to stop Jason going through with whatever he thinks will assure his survival punishment rather than protection? I am just trying to come to terms with that, and the gorge that is rising in my throat at the realisation that this could just be me being vindictive for how Jason has wronged me in the past when the phone rings.

'Elise, something's happened. You need to get here fast. I'm sorry…'

I grab my bag and run from the studio, paint staining everything I touch en route red and purple, and leaving the door swinging wide open behind me – a window onto the soul of the damned.

The diffuse inner blind Jason and Matthew can draw across the viewing window to the inner lab area is clear. My heart feels overlarge for my rib space, crowding my lungs so I can barely breathe. It is a repeat of the last time I stood here, hands sweating and clenched, legs atrophied and feet glued to the shiny lab floor, except this time Matthew is the other side of the viewing window, instrumental in birthing the sick parody of life that I am watching. They are almost inseparable, Fred and Jason, except one is a mere husk, devoid of life. The other? The other has his eyes open and is looking straight up whilst the husk is following the movements of Dr Kohn and Matthew with an intensity that is frightening. But I can't be there, holding his hand and soothing him. I can't do anything, trapped here as I am. I look to Matthew for guidance, but he avoids my eyes and busies himself with the complex paraphernalia of syringes and sterile tubing linking Fred to Jason – or Jason to Fred – and the bank of monitors behind the trolleys on which they are lying. He says something to Jason and Jason's head lolls to one side, twitching, eyes now fixed on Matthew. I lean closer to the glass and my breath creates a small cloud of confusion on it.

'No, no, no!' But I am silent to the world on the other side of the glass.

Matthew nods at Dr Kohn and she inserts a cannula into the back of Jason's hand. His eyes flit around the room and stare into the distance until they close. Now I peer through the condensation and watch Matthew as he angles one of the syringes into an electrode patch on the shaved scalp of Fred. It must be Fred. There is no need to inject anything into Jason. I place my hand against the glass in mute protest and pull air tight into my lungs to hold back the scream. It is cold and antiseptic but doesn't cleanse the wound Matthew is piercing in my soul as he completes the procedure.

No!

He draws another syringe of fluid from Jason's head and again transfers it to Fred. He is mechanical. I see that in his face. He has shut off and is simply following through a process. There is no help from Matthew now. No help from anyone. Slowly, miserably, I watch my husband's life being drained from him until he is no more than a shell. Matthew completes the last syringe transfer and then sits down heavily on the floor between the two trolleys, head hanging almost to his knees. There is something of the husk to him too. And I am still plastered to the glass viewing window, steaming up its all-seeing eye with my panted-out pain, hopeless and hopeful all at the same time.

Dr Kohn says something to Matthew but I cannot hear because the intercom is off. Matthew has made sure I can see but not hear nor stop what they are doing. I am a goldfish in a bowl, swimming and swimming and drowning. He lifts his head briefly to answer her, lip curling derisorily, then lets it hang again.

And then we wait. It seems like hours, but it isn't. The wave forms on the bank of monitors behind Jason's trolley slowly wane but there is no corresponding rise on the others. Deep inside me, the weight of my pain deepens and expands to fill all the cracks and crevices of my existence with misery. Jason is dying but Fred is not living. I stop scanning the monitors for changes and allow numbness to take over from pain. It hasn't worked. Whatever monstrosity they thought to turn Jason into hasn't worked. I rest my cheek against the window pane and cry until all the numbness in me has drained away and there is only empty space and the cold of the glass becoming warm and the warmth of my cheek becoming cold. This is how I will feel forever now without Jason.

And there I stay. There everyone stays as night turns to dawn and dawn turns to day, until the wave form on Jason's monitors is almost flatlined. I watch it tail away until it is a mere trickle. Matthew watches it too. So does Dr Kohn. Their faces tell the story, but I don't care how they feel. If there wasn't four-inch thick glass between us I would have torn and bitten and scratched them to shreds like a harpy by now. Time to go. I turn, intending to go back to Jason's quarters and curl up on his bed, at one with the last indentation his body made on it, immersed in the male smell peculiar only to him. Then I will cry again – but I don't make it even as far as the outer door. The sudden whirl of activity in the surgical unit makes me jump. The monitors behind Fred's trolley have begun to go wild, spiking crazily. Dr Kohn is pushing a surgical instrument cart out of the way and Matthew is scrambling to his feet. The room is ablaze with flashing lights and punch-drunk green scrubbed bodies as everything bursts into life. I can see Dr Kohn's mouth opening and closing, shouting rapid-fire instructions. Matthew is on his knees staring up at Fred like he is a god – and maybe he is. Out of the ashes of my husband, another, unknown life form is rising phoenix-like. Its hand twitches and grasps Matthew's wrist, then its eyes open and stare first at Dr Kohn and then as he tries to rise, directly at me. A flurry of green scrubs restrain him as I hammer on the glass viewing window until my hand is bruised. It is only then that I hear the shouting.

'Let me in, let me in, let me in…' but it is all in my head and the world this side of the viewing window is as silent as the grave, whatever hell is breaking loose on the other side. Matthew points to a green scrub and they approach the viewing screen. I hear the tumult from the other side simultaneous with the acknowledgement of my own silence. The intercom buzzes and then blares at me.

'Oh my God, Elise. It's worked. If I let you in, can you stay calm?'

'I won't do anything. Just let me in!'

My voice is cracked and scaly, a monstrous reptilian birth of sound. I slide away from the viewing pane and to the inner door. It resists me momentarily, and then caves in. I tumble into the surgical unit as the door swings opens and have to grab at a green-scrub team member to regain my balance. He holds me firmly until my feet steady, but I know he is restraining me too. I hold on tight whilst my head steadies, chest aching, heart pounding, throat closed over with fear. Jason is fading before my very eyes, but I can do nothing, nothing… I feel the cry building in chest long before it makes it out of my mouth but, even so, it is strange and haunting, the cry of a wounded wild animal, echoing around the packed surgical unit and reverberating off the flickering monitors and surgical instruments. The green-scrub team stops in its tracks and so does Dr Kohn and Matthew. We are frozen in time, a set of ghostly images paralysed by what should never have been – but is. As the sound dies, the main monitor behind Jason flatlines and on the periphery of my vision my worst fear finally crashes out of the void as Fred sits abruptly upright, sending tubes and wires and electrodes and unprepared green-scrub bodies flailing in all directions.

'Oh my God!'

Dr Kohn is the first to reach him, grabbing handfuls of disconnected wires and desperately trying to reconnect them. The green scrubs swarm back around him like a haze of greenfly around a new bloom, sticking, uncoiling, re-attaching as Matthew rushes to the monitors, now flickering like strobe lights.

'Blood-acidity levels acceptable… glucose saturation range 5.5… Normal… Oxygen saturation 95.3… ' His voice is shaky, like an old man's.

'More enhancement required?' Dr Kohn is hovering by Fred, hands flapping like a bird, filling the room with nervous energy.

'No.' Matthew's voice is breathy, staccato. 'The bio-medics all check out. We'll leave it for now.' He looks at me. My wild animal cry is no more than a garble in my throat. I read what he is thinking in his eyes. Oh God, please no, please yes…

'Jason?' I can barely hear myself. 'Oh my God, Jason!'

I switch backwards and forwards between the sitting Fred and the prone body of my husband. I want to ask but can't because I already know the answer.

'How do you feel?' Matthew is hovering in front of Fred now, head thrust forward like an inquisitive insect.

'Aa…' the sounds are guttural, indistinct, but they take over the room.

'Don't rush it. Just yes or no to begin with. Or your name?' Matthew is like a child, stepping from one foot to the other. Nausea fills my throat with thick bile.

'Ja – so…nnnnn.' His voice hums, fillingthe room with a low but vibrant note like that of a stringed instrument.

'Oh my God!' Dr Kohn is at Matthew's side, eyes wide, mouth open like one of the children in my class when I showed them the butterfly opening its wings – oh God, if that was all this was – a child's delight. I catch my breath. I want to cry, shout, scream, wither. I don't know. I don't know what I want to do any more.

Fred ignores Dr Kohn and turns slowly and deliberately to look at the empty shell on the trolley next to him.

'Ja – so…nnnnn.' It is half statement, half question. My choked breath becomes a noise, a rasp, a low whine, pained and painful. Fred turns to me. Jason turns to me. Fred – Jason – Oh my God what is he? Who is he? He tells me, eyes beseeching mine, locking them into his. 'Ja – so…nnnnn.'

I break free of the green scrub who has been restraining me and reach the trolley before anyone else can react. My hands are on his legs, his torso, his face, pulling and pinching and clawing, red marks rising livid on his skin where my nails dig in until Matthew and Dr Kohn pull me away.

'You promised,' Matthew is hissing in my ear but the only words I am listening to are the thing's; the thing that is both my husband and some cyborg monstrosity.

'Ja – so…nnnnn.'

Chapter 37

5th July 2029: Jason

Noise. Then sensation.

Movement.

Upright. Re-orientate.

Sensation...

It's not that you're cold. You're just... You haven't yet identified a word for it. Come back to it.

Something in front of you. Mirrored surface. You are looking at someone you know. Who is it? That face...

It is yours.

The monologue of check, counter-check in your head pauses.

It is you.

You?

The running narrative is an irritating background noise.

'Oh my God!'

Female gender voice? Familiar. Not yours.

'Blood-acidity levels acceptable... glucose saturation range 5.5... Normal... Oxygen saturation 95.3.'

'More enhancement required?'

You?

'No. The bio-medics all check out. We'll leave it for now.'

Is there a concept called 'you'?

Referencing psychological and socio-psychological theories.

No theory. 'You' is a sense of being. Check.

You. Me. They. Us.

Me. Not you, me. I.

'Jason?' *Curious face. Puffy. Contorted.* 'Oh my God, Jason!'

Same voice. Female.

'How do you feel?'

Not female. Male, high-pitched. Visual correlation. Matthew Green. Chief Scientific Op, Crane Enterprises. You are meant to reply...

I am meant to reply.

'Aa...' *voice quaking and cracking. Nonsense. Rubbish, a string of disconnected sounds.*

'Don't rush it. Just yes or no to begin with. Or your name?'

'Ja – so…nnnnn.' *Interesting resonance. Your name.*

'Oh my God!'

Female gender voice. Definitely female this time. Visual correlation. Dr Kohn. To your side. Turn, look. Across from you, another slab. Another body. Data upload.

You?

Also you.

Ah. Was you.

The eyes are open and staring, the mouth loose. The previous you looks surprised. Vacant.

'Ja – so…nnnnn.'

Another woman's voice. Broken. Turn again. Straight ahead...

Pain.

Pain... Upload, upload! Visual correlation...

'Ja – so…nnnnn.'

You say it to her, the female. She is crying. Grasping at you. Clawing at you. Dr Kohn and Matthew Green restrain her.

She is Elise Crane. And you are...

You are Jason Crane.

ForEver.

Ah.

Chapter 38

6th July 2029: Jason

It's dark. Cross-check dark and light. Orbital changes. Earth rotation around sun produces periodic changes in light and dark. Dark is night. Light is day. This is dark so this is night. Turn on your side. The mattress is soft. Sinking in, nice. Soft. Like soft.

Elise is soft.

Elise.

Elise Crane.

Wife.

Soft.

'Jason?'

Male voice: correlation Matthew Green.

'Yes?'

Turn on other side, reposition. Away from him. Access data.

'Is it OK to come in?'

Data processed. Friend. Respond accordingly. Jason words.

'Yep, old buddy.'

'Christ, never thought I'd hear you say that!'

Proximity level: three feet. Close. Eyes watering. Emotional response? Strong...

More data needed.

Like Elise?

More diffuse. Old buddy. You said that. Jason said that.

I said that. I.

Old buddy... Access more Jason words. Turn over. Face him. He expects that.

'Never say never.'

Even closer. Touching close.

'No… So, how are you feeling now?'

How are you feeling now? You? Jason. Me.

How am I feeling?

Hard. It's hard. Everything coming at you at once... coming at me at once.

'Different... and the same.'

'Yeah.'

He's so close now you could stretch out a hand and touch him. What would he feel like? Skin, hair, bone, sweat, tension, exhilaration. He's smiling, a smile that twitches his lips to and fro. Comes and goes, asks and answers his own question.

More data required.

'How'd you think I'd feel?'

'God knows! I didn't even think this could happen. Well... maybe I did, right at the last, but not until—'

'Until?'

'I saw the pattern.'

He licks his lips. There's sweat on his face but it's not warm in here. The air-conditioning is cool – too cool. Something... there's something...

'The pattern.' *Data?* 'So when did you see the pattern?' *Data accessed. Pattern. Date stamp.*

'Yesterday – whenever. When everything was kicking off.'

Sweat, anxiety, fear.

He's afraid. Why is your old buddy afraid?

'It already had by the time you arrived, I understand.'

Time frame data accessed. No access Matthew Green at time stamp.

He couldn't have seen the pattern. Jason didn't allow him access. Not until afterwards.

'Yeah, pretty much – yeah, and oh my God, what a kick-off. This is so amazing, Jason.'

He stops. You smile. He smiles back. Jason. Yes. I am Jason. I am, old buddy. So tell me...

'Dr Kohn says she couldn't reach you. Good job you came back anyway.'

'Yeah. Well...'

Raised blood pressure, increased sweating. Yeah. Well...

'Yeah.' *Wait. No response. He's afraid to tell you. Wait. He'll tell you when his guard is down.* 'So, where from here?'

'Onwards I guess. You've been out nearly sixteen hours since...' *Shoulders shrug. Relaxing. But still anxious.*

'What about Elise?'

'Elise?'

'Yes.' *Wait...*

'Well, she's here. Sedated.'

'Why sedated?'

'To cope – with the transition.'

'Shouldn't that be my problem?'

Irony. Like that.

'She was… upset… understandably…'

'Understandably. OK. Well, we'll need to talk. What do I need to tell her?'

Eyes widening, jaw taut. Yeah. Well... I get it. Jason got it. I get it. We get it.

'God, Jason, I don't know. Maybe that you're still Jason even though…' *He hovers, fingertips brushing the bedclothes.* 'That inside you're…'

'Still the same?'

'Yes, even though you appear different.'

'Appear different? Outside I'm the same too, aren't I? As we planned?'

Watching. Tension in jaw and fingers.

'Yes, oh yes… I mean to her you might appear different because she watched you… well, you know… die.'

We both wait. Significant moment for him. Let him process.

'OK, I see. When will she be up to talking then?'

'Well, soon, I guess. It wasn't a strong sedative. Just to calm her down. I'll send someone to see how she's doing whilst I do your vitals, if you like?'

'Or you could go.'

'I don't think she wants to talk to me at the moment.'

Interesting. What have you and Elise between you, then?

'Even less than she wants to talk to me?'

'Oh, well, I have no idea. I'm sure once she…'

'So I could go.'

'Oh God, I don't know if that is a good idea. She might…'

Face askew. He's grimacing. Bad. Bad reaction.

'Reject me?' *Shrugs. Face still askew.* 'Or attack me? I'm pretty indestructible, aren't I?'

Like that irony a lot.

'Well, of course… It's more the emotional impact I'm worried about.'

'I'll manage.'

'For her actually.'

His irony. Yeah. We both like irony. Is that friendship? Similarity? Swing legs off bed. Touch floor. Feet cold. Sensation. You like sensation. We like sensation. Always liked sensation, skin on skin, sliding, slippery skin. I like sensation. I. I. I.

'Right.'

Laugh. Look sympathetic. How is that done? However it's done, it must have been. He's smiling again.

'And you should be monitored for a while. To make sure…'

Look at him. He looks away.

'Monitored?'

'Well to make sure… Look, if you want to go, we'll go together? We can both suffer her wrath and get past it together then. I can be back-up if need be too – you know, with what to say… But not now, not yet.'

'Now.'

Stand, move past him. He is behind me, doggedly following me to the door.

'Oh, right. OK. Well, I'll come with you. This time...'

OK. Come with me. This time. Additional data is always useful, and I can read you like a book; raised respiration levels, chemical toxicity, neuro patterns. Manage this transition. For now. Then...

Chapter 39

6th July 2029: Elise

I know I'm asleep because this can't be real. I roll onto my back and stare up at the ceiling. It is dark again now but still I can see its smooth nothingness – a blank canvas worthy of Michelangelo's interest. Could he have painted the Sistine Chapel ceiling anywhere else but in a chapel? Can the mysteries of life and death be depicted anywhere, or do they need a spiritual space worthy of them? Can life be created anywhere? The start of life can certainly happen everywhere, in whatever situation humanity is currently in – soft bed or backstreet alley. Life can be lost anywhere too – is lost everywhere, from the sound and chaos of battlefields to the quiet desperation of a curtained hospital bed, the surge of pain to the subsidence of it. If I close my eyes, Jason's desiccated body as it lay, drained and useless on the trolley in the surgical unit, is imprinted on the back of my eyelids. Despite the sedative Matthew injected I have managed to keep my eyes open throughout the last ten hours because of that. Now they feel gritty and stretched at the corners, bloated with tears that won't fall.

There is probably a guard on my door. I haven't checked but it's the sort of thing that Kohn would insist on. Keep the crazy wife at bay while the medical miracle convalesces. And Matthew? Despite all he promised, he assisted, facilitated. Collaborated.

Do I hate him?

I have no feelings left.

I would merely like to close my eyes and sleep and forget now, but I can't close my eyes and I won't sleep. I refuse to.

At least it's dark in here, blinds drawn, lights off. Nothing to see to remind me of…

The vaguely antiseptic tang of lab cleaner lingering in the room is overlaid with the equally chemical attempt at reproducing summer florals.

I concentrate instead on smells to distract my thoughts. If I looked, I expect the name of the aroma on the room enhancer is something similar. It's not completely unpleasant. It just reminds me of the artificiality of everything here and then I'm back to… OK, something else then. Sounds, not smells. It's quietest here at the back of the building so I'll imagine: the routine clatter and rumpus of children on their way between classrooms that I hear every hour on the hour, at school, as they swarm past my office door. Then the hoot and whistle of traffic at rush hour: the rhythmic tick-tock of the grandfather clock I inherited from my parents that lives in the hall at home – even though Jason hates its chime. Jason. No. Think of more sounds: the drone of a stray plane overhead on a lazy Sunday afternoon in summer. The insistent swish of uncut grass as it eddies and whips against the wind: the—

A soft knock on the door interrupts the logical follow-through of that one – and maybe fortuitously as I already know it will take me, inevitably, to the last conversation Matthew and I had against a backdrop of swaying, whispering corn, and I don't want to remember that it was me who deliberately hurt him then to achieve my own ends. It's probably only food, though and I don't want to eat.

'Elise?'

Oh God. It's Matthew – as if my guilty thoughts have summoned him. The betrayer summoned to the betrayed. Or the guilty to the guiltier.

I roll onto my side and try to ignore the second knock. The door opens a crack and a thin line of light from the corridor bisects the room, cutting my body in half as I lie on the bed. What is this room anyway? I haven't thought about that since I was brought here yesterday, half-senseless with horror and disbelief. It smacks of a guest room in a medical facility, but I never knew it was here until now.

'Elise, I have someone who needs to talk to you.'

'I don't want to talk, Matthew, especially not to you. Please leave me alone.'

'It's important.'

I imagine his face close to the crack, whispering through it like Pyramus to Thisbe.

'I don't want to talk.'

The light line widens.

'But I do.'

Jason. No! Impossible!

The new voice pins me to the bed. It is *his*, but not his. The timbre not quite as husky, and yet… I try not to move, not to roll onto my back again so I can see. But I know what I would see if I did.

'Elise?' Matthew.

'I don't want to talk. Not to anyone.'

'Please try. Just give it a chance.'

'It? The thing?' I curl into a ball, tucking my knees up to my chest and clasping my arms round them.

'I know. This is hard, terribly hard for all of us. But a miracle has happened, even though we didn't expect it to and there's only one person that matters to me now to share it with.'

That voice: that voice again, but it isn't him! Yet his voice is drowning me, seeping round me, cradling every curve and angle, until I am submerged. But it isn't him. It isn't Jason. It's… I can't bear it any longer. I can feel his eyes on me, caressing the ridge of my spine, coiling around the barbed spikes of my elbows, soothing the rigidity of my limbs. Stop it. Stop it.

I roll over and straighten out but don't want to lie prone on my back. The bed seems to thrust me out of it, so I sit up. The light is streaming in around him from the corridor behind the partly-open door. He is the Angel of Death come to claim me, a fiery Azreal. Instinctively I scuffle up the bed away from him until my back is hard against the wall. I hadn't expected to be frightened but I am. He advances towards me and I press my spine flat against the unyielding cold of the wall until it aches, and still he approaches, softly, sinuously – almost cat-like – until he is standing over me.

'Elise?'

'Please don't. Please go away.' My voice is a half-sob.

He ignores the plea and sits on the edge of the bed. It sinks with his weight. So there is substance to him. He isn't a vision, a nightmare, a chimera. He is real, solid, unavoidable. My body inclines towards him as the bed settles to accommodate him and I put out my hand to stop myself lurching clumsily into him. He takes my outstretched hand in both of his before I can draw back and it is encased. Electric eels crawl the length of my arm from fingertips to shoulder and I shiver, but I cannot pull away. This is Fred, not Jason, my brain is screaming. This is Jason, not Fred my senses are screaming.

'Elise,' he says again, and in the gloom I can see the gleam of white as he smiles. The eels quiver as the electricity flows between him and me, a Sistine Chapel spark – God to man, man to God. I breathe out and the very act makes me shiver again. His hands are warm, soft, gentle. They are Jason's hands in the act of love and now I want to cry and cry and cry as if it would be impossible to stop. My bloated eyes release their tears and they cascade down onto my chest, dark splotches of grief. One hand releases its grip on mine and caresses my cheek, smoothing the tears into a flowing river.

'But you're dead,' I moan. You're not real. You're not Jason.'

'No, I'm not dead. I'm here. I'm still here. I'm here forever now.'

'This isn't you. This is something else. Something I don't know. A machine.'

'Do I sound like a machine? Feel like a machine? Could a machine talk to you like this?'

'No, but…'

'Then I'm not. I'm Jason. I'm still Jason, just the same as before.'

'How can I…'

'Trust me. Just trust me. Accept me. I am the same. I'm the same, just like I've always been.'

'Jason…' Matthew's voice is whispered but cautionary. Jason waves him away without even turning.

'Later, Matthew.'

At first, I resist the gentle pull as the hand on my cheek slips round to the back of my neck and propels me closer to him, but the closer we draw, the less I can stop him – and the less I want to stop him. His lips on mine are tentative, searching, tempting. I can feel my resistance melting with my disbelief and the hot bubble of desire starting in the cauldron of my stomach as the pressure of his lips on mine increases and his tongue probes and gains entry. His skin rasps against mine the way Jason's skin always did, and his breath flows into my mouth and his fingers tangle in my hair. The blood is coursing round my body now, pounding and throbbing – denying all that my brain tells me about impossibilities. And I want him – whatever and whoever he is, I want him in the same way as I have always wanted my husband. When he eventually draws away I cannot move. My whole body cries out with disappointment, hungry for more.

He puts his forehead against mine and we rest against each other. He breathes out slowly, the desire inherent in it as strong as mine.

'So,' he says, heavy-breathed.

'So,' I echo.

'Am I real?'

'Yes, but... But I don't understand. Your skin, your touch... how can this happen so quickly?'

'It's the CyberCute. It's what it does. It transforms, transitions – creates where there wasn't. We didn't even need to clone my brain after all. It was all in the neo-cortical fluid. It just took a while to achieve stasis and then go on to develop as we'd projected it could.'

'Is that what I saw Matthew injecting?'

I pull back from him and touch his shaven head. It is smooth and unblemished.

'Yes. I had no idea until the last round of tests we did. Not even Matthew knew. But, luckily, I wrote up the details and, when the moment came, Dr Kohn and Matthew tried it as a last resort.'

'So what has it done?'

'Reproduced me inside the shell that was Fred, but which will now transform into me.'

I pull further away. '*Will* transform?'

He pulls me back. 'Has already transformed in the main. There may be one or two finer points that will take a little longer... complex activities, complete assimilation of nerve function, repair of genetic structures – a bit like having someone go round and make sure everything is perfect – but, other than that, what you see is what you get.'

'You really are... ' I touch his arm, assessing the texture of his skin, the way the hairs stand away from his forearm and the vein in his wrist stands proud.

'I really am, but better. Or will be. No malfunctions, no disrepair, no faulty systems, no integral damage from life or any other kind of abuse.' He laughs, and it is Jason's laugh that I have heard a thousand times, a hundred thousand times, a million times. 'And no Parmensis! Everything functioning perfectly.'

He strokes my cheek and squeezes the hand that he is still holding. The electric eels crawl again, but not unpleasantly this time. I touch his face, follow the curve of cheek to jaw, along the line of his lips and back onto his cheek. My hands hugs the curve, and revels in the raw joy of renewal. It is Jason's cheek I am stroking, Jason's jawline I am describing with my fingers.

'And are you really already...'

'Biologically human? Yes, I am tissue and cell and complex ridiculous illogical emotions. Organic material, just like you – or I will be, given sufficient transition time.'

'How long is transition time?'

'A few days, a few weeks? Depends on how fast the CyberCute works, but essentially, it's fine-tuning, Elise. Just fine-tuning. A miracle, if you like?'

'You don't believe in miracles. This can't be real.'

I pull away again. He reaches across me and flicks on the small bedside light. It showers us in a warm peachy glow and there is my husband, on the bed beside me, smiling with that lopsided smile he has when he is waiting for me to be persuaded – and knowing that I will be. The only difference is the shaved head, lending him the spiritual look of a Buddhist. It makes me want to laugh but I don't. Never in a million years could anyone call Jason Buddha-like.

'Oh Elise, of all people not to believe, when you have the strongest beliefs of us all! How am I not real?'

'You are real, but this is just incredible – beyond believable. I saw you die.'

I can't help the harshness in my voice. He draws back and places my hand back on the bed. It feels lost and lonely there. I want him to take it back in his and never let it go.

'And I'm sorry about that. You shouldn't have. But it was a necessary part of the process though. The Parmensis was never going to leave the body it was in, so I had to instead. Maybe you need more time?'

He starts to stand.

'Oh!' It is the cry of the wounded animal again – but softer than before. He sits back down. I start to cry again.

'Don't,' he says, pulling me close to him and this time I don't resist at all. The tumult of emotions is a mess of everything I have ever felt in my life. He is warm and solid and he even smells like my husband, that unique smell that is Jason. I bury my nose in him and suck breaths of his scent in to fill my lungs with him.

'I'm afraid, so afraid.'

'There's nothing to be afraid of. It's all fine now.'

His lips are in my hair kissing and nuzzling and my lips are on his skin, devouring the taste of him as if he is the only nourishment that can keep me alive. I thought I had lost him but now he is here again. The need is too strong. I have to believe. I have to accept. Maybe miracles do happen.

'Jason?' It is Matthew. 'You really need downtime. Nothing extreme, remember? We didn't check your vitals before we came so perhaps…'

'OK, just a bit longer.'

After a while he gently disentangles himself from me. I stroke his face and touch his body again, afraid that he might disappear before I have checked every part of him.

'Matthew's right,' he says reluctantly.

'Nothing's wrong is it?' My heart starts to pound with anxiety again.

'No, no. Early days though. We need to keep a check on me for a while. I'll go and subject myself to their prodding and probing and then we'll have some proper time tomorrow. You look tired too.' He touches the hollow under my eye. 'I doubt you've slept much over the last few days.'

'No.' The gift of proper sleep hasn't been mine in a while.

He stands, my hands slipping slowly out of his as he does so until he pauses, his fingertips still holding onto mine.

'Paint?' he queries. My eyes follow his gaze. I am still emblazoned with red and purple paint.

'Oh, yes.' Our eyes meet. 'I paint – have done for quite a while now. I was going to tell you soon because there was to be an exhibition, but it doesn't matter now.'

He frowns quizzically at me. 'but it does – everything about you matters to me. I'd like to see your paintings, if I may?'

I nod, wondering what he will make of them and how I will explain them – but that is a matter for another time. He nods back and we are mirroring each other for a moment, then he moves quietly back to the door and Matthew. I follow him, snatching a last embrace before he slips out into the corridor.

'Back to Dr Kohn's gentle ministrations,' he quips, smiling at me in that way that always twists my heart into a knot. I laugh, jealous of her for the time she has with my husband, this intimate stranger who I have no choice but to welcome into my life. Matthew ushers him away but I jump up and catch Matthew's arm as he turns to follow Jason and squeeze it.

'Maybe I was wrong. Maybe you were right after all.'

'We'll see. Too much too soon isn't good though, Elise. Baby steps. There's a lot more to come, I suspect.'

The knot of jealousy mutates into anxiety. 'Matthew?'

Matthew looks over his shoulder and shakes his head. His expression leaves me cold. I watch their two figures merge as they round the corner in the corridor in the direction of Jason's quarters, and I am left marvelling and wondering at what I've seen. And at what I don't yet know, but Matthew implies he does.

Chapter 40

11th July 2029: Jason

Rumbling discontent...

Shut up!

I am not the invasive element in the cyborg-Fred. I am the inhabitant of the cyborg-Fred; the owner of cyborg-Fred...

Of course, what you said to Elise wasn't quite the truth. You are not yet you. Agreed. But you are a work in progress, and you… no… I – I must become operative. Control this beast. Own it. It is yours. Mine.

Indeed, the cyborg-Fred and I are working together more as a cohesive unit each day. The CyberCute is undeniably amazing – surpassing even what you – Jason – I, had considered possible with it, but meshing consciousness with it is a challenge. You – I – hadn't expected it to have consciousness, but it has – in a basic form, as basic as the lab mice perhaps. Which reminds me, I, yes, I, should check how they are progressing – the last experiment I conducted as Jason, the day of the transfer. In case.

I have been kept away from the labs until now with battery after battery of tests and checks. Biometrics, electrocardiograms, MRIs – as far as I will allow them – and rest. In between there has been Elise – sweet, surprising, soft – and hours of prowling the facility, just testing, practising, absorbing, controlling. I never knew you had flat feet before until now. Of course, now you don't have flat feet, you have perfect arches, but who would know except me? Us. Nor do you – I – have a sensitivity to heat. My internal thermometer works perfectly – automatically adjusting to the temperature without even the need for air-conditioning here. And my hand to eye coordination improves by the day. Who would have thought you – I – would develop an eye to draw from this, yet I have. The angles and distances, planes and curves of an image are no longer block-solid shapes to me, but flowing lines and intriguing cadences, full of musical notes and elusive fragrances. Paintings have only ever been of interest to me if demonstrating carefully thought out mathematical structures and form. Now, however, they are like the full swell of a sweetly tuned orchestral work. The appearance of a well-known piece I did quite like in a TV documentary on iconic art and artists I lighted on, merely through absence of anything else to occupy me in between this biometric and that, occasioned that particular epiphany. I have become synaesthetic. What a joke, when before I couldn't draw a stick man without it looking broken or listen to a piece of music without impatience if it lasted too long.

So what else are you becoming?

Not you. Me. What else am I becoming – remember?

I wonder.

I test my reflexes. No, not the kind of tests Dr Kohn and Matthew preside over. *My* tests.

I can catch a fly in flight. I squash it, of course. I haven't that much control yet, but it's coming.

I can hear everything that is being said in the next room, merely by shutting out all other peripheral sounds.

I can see across to the far side of the wheat field still glutted with burgeoning corn stalks, to the dog walkers and kids playing at its edge where it runs into the first line of spruce trees that mark where the woods begin. Estimated distance? Half a mile.

And I can heal. Just like our test subject in the film clip I showed Elise.

I discovered that by chance. I had no real inclination to cut myself, but fine sensations are still muted in some areas, so the missed shard of glass from the tumbler I dropped the second day as me-Fred found its way into the sole of my foot without sign or symptom apart from the smear of red on the floor last night. The evidence of it was completely gone by this morning though, so I experimented. The results were illuminating. So today it's time to visit the lab, whatever my doctors say.

The cages are stored on the far side of the ForEver lab, behind some newly installed racking designed to shield the working guts of the lab from the sensitivities of the less pragmatic – Elise. Matthew is glued to his PC as I enter.

'Oh!' His cry of surprise is like a small imploding pop. I ignore it and propel my torso steadily towards the racking. Despite the other advances, nothing is yet instinctive, but it is becoming more so as my synaptic pathways link with the cyborg-Fred's circuitry. I haven't told Matthew or Dr Kohn about this inner struggle. The daily MRIs they insist on merely show a continued interface between organic and manufactured material – no rejection, and that is enough for them. I have avoided an fMRI until now. I know Matthew is looking for anomalies, so I tell him nothing. I can't admit to an issue with consciousness to Matthew or Dr Kohn or it is a whole new ball game with ethics bouncing around between us all, higher than a pro-football game. I cannot become a study of the archetypal question: what constitutes life? The lag between initiation and response will fade away completely as the cyborg-Fred's lesser consciousness gives way to mine, and then it will be irrelevant. Fred will have been absorbed by me, but for the time being we are symbiotic. I need Fred and Fred needs me, but the longer we are merged, the weaker the resistance and ultimately I will preside. So far we have contained all of the events of the last few months within Crane Industries' walls but if ethics becomes an issue, God knows what will happen. Fred is merely a cyborg prosthesis I have been housed in, and the only consciousness we are dealing with is mine. At the end of the process, there will simply be me – with a blanked-out history of a few months that no one needs to know about.

'Jason? Where you going?'

Progress requires focus, and some days, negotiation with Fred. Today is one of those days. I ignore Matthew and focus on my target, on succeeding in my challenge for overall control today. We test my neuro responses daily and that is a challenge too. I have to be in complete control then or cyborg-Fred's electrical impulses might be recorded. So far, my automatic responses have been identical to the ones recorded for Jason before the transfer – exactly as it was with the mice – so that is enough, for Matthew's purposes. We are simply proceeding to plan with the same meshing of biological and mechanical functions, as experienced with the CyberArm3. He doesn't question that. He doesn't even question the more sophisticated functionality that is being established, but I am careful with that in case Matthew makes the leap for himself. My brain is never part of the MRI scans so I can only *feel* the impossible has actually happened without being able to check, but I am acutely aware of all Matthew's fears now about longevity whenever I feel drained or Fred's consciousness gains the upper hand and mine fades with exhaustion. It's not over until the fat lady sings – isn't that what they say? Wait for the last tragic aria to die away before the happy ending can be pronounced.

Maybe the mice will give me a clue to the type of happy ending it will be for me.

'Hey, old buddy? Is everything OK?' Matthew's voice follows me round to the other side of the racking. Now, I can't ignore him.

'Yep, fine.'

In theory, these mice could be my equals, chock-full of my neo-cortical fluid. What will I say to them? Hello, old buddies? I locate the correct cage amongst the rows – D35 – but no one's home. Typical mice, sleeping on the job. I ping the wire mesh to entice them from their nest, but nothing happens.

'Saying hello to the zoo?' Matthew asks. He is behind me, his faintly greasy smell reminding me of the lardiness of the human race; carbon and grease, that's all humans are, really. That's Fred. I bat him away. *Yeah buddy, carbon and grease and superior consciousness.* That shuts him up.

'Yeah, just checking in. These little guys – where did they go?'

'Dunno. Cage has been empty for several days now.'

I touch the catch on the trapdoor. It is shut tight, but a small shred of wood shavings has been caught between it and its mesh counterpart wall. It has been opened and shut and the shavings scuffled over the edge in the process. A human hand wouldn't do that. A mouse foot might. I laugh, a small snort of amusement. Well, there's my happy ending, if not theirs. I wonder if they're canny enough to survive outside in the real world. But then, why wouldn't they? They've taken my neo-cortical fluid with them and therefore an understanding of all the dangers they'll meet and how to overcome them.

'Oh well, we don't need them any more. Good luck to them.'

I can sense Matthew's expression without turning to see it. That's another thing I can do. He will be frowning, still processing the problem – where the mice have gone – and not yet attaching my comment to any logical assumption. He is a clever man, but not clever enough. Not as clever as you. Me. Not as clever as me. I click the trapdoor open and flick the captured wood shaving back into the cage, not anticipating the nick of an unexpectedly sharp edge to it – more a splinter really, but it punctures and then falls away from my finger tip, leaving a small round globule of red forming on it. Instinctively I wince at the prick and rub forefinger and thumb together, smearing the red globule across both tips.

'Jesus!' Matthew grabs my hand. 'You're bleeding!'

I try to pull away but he holds on fast.

OK, maybe it's time for this too. Maybe. We'll see…

'Nah,' I study it. 'Probably just food dye or something in the cage. We used cochineal once, remember?'

'Not with these ones.' He squeezes my finger and it obliges again but now with only a tiny speck that disappears almost as we watch, fibrin proteins already clumping to form a clot, collagen gathering behind it to start the repair process. 'See, you are… were… bleeding.'

I shrug. 'Yeah, maybe…'

'Aw, come on, Jason.' We lock gazes. 'You know what this could mean!'

What settles in me then is a sense of calm. The fat lady is singing. The aria is almost finished and now it's time to acknowledge that. I retrieve my hand, gently disentangling it from his and gesture towards the main part of the lab.

'OK, yes. I do.'

'How long have you known? And when did it start? You have to know. You're living inside this thing. You must be able to feel the changes?' He cuts himself off short, clearly embarrassed by his clumsy terminology.

The human has more sensitivity than assumed.

Of course, he has. He's human.

'Perhaps. More that I could see some possibilities of them from this morning's scan.'

'Christ! Why didn't you say? Show me!'

I shrug again. There are battles you can fight and battles you forgo. This one I must manipulate.

He follows me meekly back to the PC monitor where he had been working. It is already displaying yesterday's MRI results. I smile to myself. So, Matthew, have you been wondering too? I gesture for him to pull up a chair and he skids in alongside me, bringing his lardy solidity into too close proximity. *Gah! Foul! His smell is…* Yeah, yeah. That is the cyborg-Fred's take on it. I push the cyborg's objections aside. For me it is reassuringly human. And Matthew. And then I am surprised by the sudden rush of something I can only describe as… I don't know… It takes several seconds to process that. Things fire somewhere in my head. Good things. Bad things. Negatives? *Delete negatives.* A rush of images flood my mind. I breathe out and push them aside. Later. This is now. Identify what this is now?

Love.

Christ! Something in my core squeezes tight.

'So, these results… What did you see?' He is peering closely at the monitor, engrossed in an area that showed nothing new, unseeing of the real picture. I am struggling with the overwhelming need to reach out to him and embrace him. I contain it with difficulty, insisting that the cyborg-Fred swallow and then breathe slowly until I can control the urge. I zoom out of the imagery, noting with curiosity as I do so that Matthew is intent on the CyberCute, not the inner workings of me. OK, let's look at that, since I've just demonstrated to him what's going on with it anyway. I refocus on an area of proliferating capillaries. They are easy to spot, if you know.

'That's what I saw – not on my hands, on my upper arm, but presumably the whole limb has been modifying since yesterday.'

'Oh my God, you're developing a full-scale venous system – not merely using the basics that we 3D'd.'

'It seems so, yes.'

'My God, Jason. So what we thought was possible really is…'

He swings round to stare at me, open-mouthed and round-eyed like a child.

'Don't go too fast. It's only one example.'

'But it's what we predicted.'

'I predicted.'

'Well… yeah, OK, sorry – YOU predicted.'

'Yes.'

The idea rankles, then pings into place.

That is what you have been uneasy about.

I watch as he scoots out of the chair and hunkers over another monitor. His hunched back tries to keep his secrets intact as he wrestles with them for the rest of the morning, but I snapshot the screen anyway and contemplate my lacerated finger, now pristine and completely unblemished, and the time stamp of Matthew's access of my report on the last MRI I underwent as Jason Crane, human.

00.01.

And before that, a system interruption the day before at 00.02.

And before that, a system interruption the day before at 00.01.

He asked me if we could wait and keep you alive in the meantime. We had to wait more than ten minutes.

To when?

Just after midnight…

My report on the 3rd July only went so far. It took the fMRI results on the 4th to make the final connection – and complete the procedure for transformation. But that couldn't have been read by Matthew – could it?

'What is a system interruption?'

'Bit like a virus attack, Mr Crane.' Bob's wary. He hasn't been in charge of our cyber security all these years for nothing. He knows a loaded question when it's asked. He deflects it easily. 'We get them all the time, but our bots scare 'em off.'

'Routine attacks – as in regularly orchestrated?'

'Sometimes.'

'At roughly the same time each day?'

'Oh no, virus attacks are random. Never the same time or even near it or the system would already be geared up for them. It's quite interactive in that way.'

'So if they are at roughly the same time each day?'

'They're not a virus. They're a person, trying to have a look...'

'At what?'

'Anything. Whatever they think is important, I guess? Is there a problem, Mr Crane?'

'No, no, just filling in some blanks for myself...'

What would a person want to specifically look at? Crane Industries' biggest secret – other than me?

Products.

Formulas.

CyberCute formulas.

Periodically Matthew straightens, checks if I'm still there, then dives back into his work, presumably waiting for me to go. Is this the time to ask? Are you far enough along that you can abandon Matthew? Eject him if necessary? That interplay of emotion would be a serious obstacle if you have to wait on this. That rush of love, or whatever it was is weakness, it will grow, uncontrolled. *You can't have weakness. You are strength. You are ForEver.*

Shut up. This is mine to handle... 'Actually, I've been meaning to ask you about that whole evening.'

'Which?'

'The evening I transferred.'

'Oh, right.'

I can smell it too this time. Not the lardiness of humanity, the lardiness of fear. The same fear I detected before.

'How did you know what I predicted?'

'What?'

'How did you know what I predicted? How to complete the transfer? Only I had access to that report that day.'

'Dr Kohn.'

It is almost too quick, hard on the heels of my question in a way Matthew never is. Rehearsed.

'I don't recall giving Dr Kohn access to that kind of information.'

'Well, no, but she said you'd written it down – what to do – so I… ' He won't meet my eyes.

'I had, but only I could access that.'

'I don't understand…' His eyes glaze then clear. 'You left instructions. I read them…'

'Yes, but I didn't complete them. And you weren't here earlier either, according to Dr Kohn.'

'I was! It was just she couldn't raise me, that's all. Problem with my phone. But I was checking in anyway, so it wasn't a problem, was it?'

'And how did you figure out the last stage?'

'It – it was obvious from the extrapolated data, wasn't it?'

'Extrapolated data?'

'I mean, from *extrapolating* the data – the other test results we'd seen. It was the only logical conclusion…'

The lardiness is back.

Access data.

No, don't access data. You need to be human. Read him. Read his body language.

Lying.

'No,' I clap him on the shoulder. 'It wasn't a problem. It was inspired. Thank you, old buddy.'

'Yeah, well.' He avoids my eyes again. 'Glad to have been there.'

'Exactly.' I make a show of closing down the MRI records. 'But now, you have work to do.'

'Work?'

'On the CyberCute. It has more than just a future, it has a ForEver future. Shall we see what we can do to improve on the last formula that was used?'

'Oh, well, I think it's going OK, actually.'

Sweat.

'Show me. I've been out of action for far too long. I need to get back into things.'

'Oh God, maybe best to wait…' He looks at me, eyes beseeching. I wait. The sweat is a sheen now, sparkling across his face, neck, palms.

I wait, absorbing his discomfort.

'… I mean, that's fine… but if you want to check it over, how about we schedule it in for tomorrow and I'll make sure all the data is up to date by then.'

'Up to date, huh?' His eyes widen again and the whites in them glisten. I wait… then I laugh. 'I thought you'd learnt your lesson about keeping things in hand and up to date. You're the untidiest scientist I ever had the pleasure to work with.'

'Oh, right!' His expression loosens, hangs around his face like a bloodhound's. 'Yeah, you know me and report-writing. Always was more your forte than mine. I'll get onto it right now.'

'OK, you do that.'

He settles back to his monitor, but his shoulders are tight and set. I watch for a while then decide it *is* time. For some of it, anyway.

'Matthew?'

He swings round, forehead creased into a frown. Over his shoulder I snapshot the screen he's working on and compare it to the one he was working on an hour ago. It hasn't changed.

'What?'

I leave my chair and go over to the bench that still houses a Bunsen burner. I turn it on full and its blue flame shoots heavenwards. His expression alone will be worth it even if the performance falls flat. It doesn't though. I position my hand in the flame and wait.

'Jesus! Stop it!' He's on his feet faster than I've ever seen him move before. 'What the fuck are you doing?'

'Showing you.'

He reaches me at precisely the same time as I shut off the burner and show him my palm, blistered and raw where the skin has bubbled and then burnt away and the flesh beneath begun to char. Third degree at least. Yes, it hurt, but I can control pain. The smell is disgusting, roasted meat gone off, but the response time is impressive.

'Fuck me!' he says, jaw hanging slack and eyes popping. The skin softens and smooths over, charred area furring into a soft pink, then white, then nothing at all. Healed.

'Actually, I think I am indestructible. I just thought you ought to know.'

'Jesus!'

'If you like. JC for certain. A miracle man for real. Take up thy bed and walk.' I can't help laughing, sick though the joke is. Yes, he needed to know. Whatever he's been devilling away at, it won't work now. 'We picked a good name when we called it ForEver.'

Chapter 41

11th July 2029: Elise

Jason seems in a particularly pensive mood this evening. Since that fateful day I have been sent back home but have spent most of my time in the lab, slowly getting to know who or what my husband now is. No extreme interactions yet, Matthew has advised. Just straightforward everyday contact in the company of others. *Get used to him and let him get used to you…*

When I look at him, he is Jason, just as he's always been – outwardly. But inwardly? Can it be that simple? Can such a complex organism as a person combine with a cyborg and remain human? Of course, I don't share those thoughts with anyone, not even Matthew. I wait and wonder, barely daring to believe Jason is the same, monitoring his every mood, every word, every expression – and yet he is, apparently, the same, but more. The same old private jokes surface, the same old feelings overwhelm – and the same old issues provoke, but do I care about those differences now if it means he is here, with me, instead of a mere memory? I don't know. If pushed, I would say it is ironically comforting to find we still disagree on ethics because, of all things, it means he's intrinsically the same. Yet I know that isn't all of it. There is another side to him that I have glimpsed recently too, a surprisingly gentle side: creative, soft – dare I say it – spiritual even. I am watching it now, in fact, as I loiter at the door, uncertain whether to announce my entry or to clutch this moment to me a while longer: a chance to study the clean regularity of his profile, the athletic tautness of his body. He doesn't know I am here yet, bent low over a photograph of us taken, oh, perhaps five years ago? We were in Italy; a surfeit of sun and pasta and simple pleasures, to make up for what happened the summer before. It was unspoken between us then, the acknowledgement that it was a sop to satisfy me, to fill my sadness with artificial contentment – as if you can ever fill an empty vessel that has a hole in the bottom of it. But it did, in a way. Being the centre of Jason's world – even if only for a week or two – has a quality of magic to it, just as he does.

For two weeks, reality was forgotten, depression was overcome and he and I – we – prevailed. The sun beat on our backs and the sand trickled through our fingers with no thought to the passing of time, and how important that would be one day. The thrust and enthusiasm of so much *life* surging through busy Italian markets and bustling village streets swept me along on its tide of live now, live well, live fully. And I forgot. Indeed, I could almost have thought myself back to that naïve girl who'd watched Jason, starry-eyed, on the podium delivering his inaugural lecture on a subject, the basics of which, even then, open-minded and youthfully sharp as I was, I was struggling to make any sense of. So far removed from my natural inclinations was it that I might as well have been making an attempt on Mars single-handed and without a spacecraft. Cloning, or *The Cloning of Small Organisms*, to be precise. See, I even remember the title!

I left the degree programme the following year and settled for a BEd, teaching little ones the wonders of butterfly metamorphosis and how frogs grow legs – with play props. Far more my style and reach, even though I understood the concept, if not the specifics. And I just don't have the mind to apply them. That day though, Jason explained them purely for me – me alone – front row and hypnotised by this handsome young lecturer who seemed to be delivering his unintelligible presentation on cloning small organisms directly to me – and in words I understood, albeit only momentarily. And for him, centre stage, there was apparently only an audience of one – me – amongst the hundreds sitting in that auditorium.

Is that how love starts? The unexpected eye contact, the sudden spark, the string that grows instantaneously and simultaneously between two separate souls? It's a romantic notion, to be sure, and yet that is how I always think of it for us. The air-conditioning droned, the bench had chewing gum stuck underneath it, rough and nobbly, and the waxy polish on top of it was sticky and unpleasant. The seats were hard and the opposite of ergonomically designed and some of the floor tiles were turning up at the corners. The place smelt of stale ink and old professors and unforeseen delight, and I was transfixed. I waited at the end of the lecture, shuffling my non-existent notes and dithering because he was barely ten feet away from me surrounded by an enthusiastic buzz of students similar to me, but knowing, knowing, that he was as aware of me behind his wall of admirers, as I was of him beyond it. I slid my notepad and pen into my bag and fiddled with the pen, uncapping and replacing the cap until I'd lost count of how many times, but in the meantime the crowd around the speaker thinned and as I stepped onto the steps leading up to the exit to the auditorium, he fell in alongside me.

'You seemed intrigued,' he opened with. 'Is it your subject?'

'Not really. It's probably a bit too complex for me, but you made it fascinating.' My knuckles were white as they clutched my bag tight to my chest; so tight they ached.

'I was pretending I was telling you all about it. That was why.'

'Oh,' and then that rush of blood to my cheeks and that little stumble as I missed my step and he caught my arm. We both turned, looked, knew. From that moment onwards we were fused together, red and blue glass dissolving and combining to produce midnight purple. Or that is what we would have produced.

'It was a good holiday.' He calls it over his shoulder now. I catch my breath. His voice is unchanged from then, even though that was over fifteen years and a lifetime ago. He turns around to face me, slow smile teasing his lips apart. 'It's my hearing,' he adds apologetically. 'It's so much more acute now.'

'Oh.' I step out of the shadows and let the door slide shut behind me. That rush of blood is in my cheeks again now and he is holding his hand out to me. This time the room smells of lilies and light and intensity. He walks towards me, collecting me en route and diverting us towards the bed. 'Oh,' I say again. We sit on the edge, the way we sat on the edge the first time we ever made love. The light is behind us, streaming in the window, a golden glory of setting sun and falling twilight, but I can see his eyes nevertheless. They are kind. I am surprised. I have never thought of Jason's eyes as kind before. They draw me to him. I touch his face. It is warm, soft, skin-like. I draw away. Skin-like.

'How much of you now is…' My tongue falters and sticks to the roof of my mouth. How clumsy can I be? 'Oh God, I'm sorry. I didn't mean it like that.'

He laughs, tongue making a small clicking sound like an admonishment. His teeth are white, pure white. 'It's OK. Better to be honest with each other. About seventy-five per cent. The basics. The rest is still fine-tuning, like I said. Has Matthew told you?'

'What?' My head is shaking on my shoulders, but I am mesmerised by the whiteness of his teeth. And his lips. The way they twitch into a smile and out of it again, tongue slipping easily over them, making them glisten, then slipping back into his mouth. I'd wondered what would it feel like? What would it feel like when he kissed you, that tongue?

It had felt real.

'What I can do now.'

'What can you do now?'

'Heal, Elise. I can heal.'

'We all heal.'

'Not a cyborg. A cyborg is repaired, maintained. I heal. Cut me and I bleed, care for me and I heal.'

We haven't been intimate beyond that kiss on the very first day – not even a repeat of it. We have talked, compared, watched, discussed, even touched briefly – the tentative touch of one endangered species of another – but never lingering. And I have assessed and categorised that touch, reviewed those discussions throughout – carefully keeping the me that fell in love with Jason Crane behind the glass viewing window as the sceptic me collates the data and feeds it into the jigsaw puzzle entity that is now Jason Crane. His hand is suddenly on mine. I jump, but he doesn't remove it. It is warm and gentle. Like skin. Skin-like.

Real.

I stare at him.

'You bleed? You haven't been doing anything bad to yourself to test that out have you?'

Now my heart is thumping in my chest at the thought of Jason deliberately cutting himself to prove he is human.

'No,' he laughs again. It is comforting. 'It happens though – like it happens for you. Minor mishaps, small injuries.'

'What? You're hurt?'

Now I grab his hand with both of mine and turn it over and over to examine it. It is unblemished.

'I was, but I've healed.'

'When?'

'This morning. I cut myself by accident and I bled, then I burnt myself but I healed.' He sounds like a little boy boasting to his gang members.

'But there's not a mark on you.'

'That's what I mean, Elise. I seem to be very good at healing.'

'Did you expect that?'

'Not entirely. But it does make sense given that the CyberCute encourages MS.' He smooths away my frown with the fingertips of his free hand. 'Metamorphic symbiosis. The organic transformation of one substance into another by use of a catalyst.'

'So which way is the transformation going?'

'Well, I bleed and I heal. What do you think?'

'And there's no Parmensis at all anymore?'

'Nothing.'

'You really are…' I examine his hand again. The hairs on the back are the same as Jason's. The fingernails are the same as Jason's. I trace a line from fingertip to wrist, across his palm – a favourite to tickle him. He cannot help but react – has always done so. His hand curls automatically. Even his spontaneous reactions are Jason's.

'I really am.'

I look into his eyes again. The kindness is still there, but so is something else – something I haven't seen in Jason for a long time.

Love.

I allow my fingers to trail past his wrist, onto his forearm. I like the sensation, the stubbly hairs brushed against the grain prickling my fingertips. I watch the progress of my fingers along his forearm and upwards. I pause at the crease at his elbow and we look into each other's eyes again.

'I am me, Elise,' he says. And just like that moment in the auditorium when we fused, I know he is.

'I know,' I say. I don't even want to breathe in case this moment dissipates, disappears. His lips brush mine and I close my eyes. They brush again, but this time they linger, and I linger too. Our tongues touch and his is probing, first gently, then more avidly. He tastes of aniseed and star drops. I relax into the kiss and it envelops me, enclosing around me like a sigh as my heart expands to outsize my chest, and the old familiar sensation of desire flows through my stomach and along my limbs. Tonight I want intimacy, whether Jason is seventy-five per cent human or one hundred per cent. The rest doesn't matter.

We slip backwards onto the bed until we are lying limb to limb, arms entwined, kissing and caressing. He is peeling my clothes away from me, layer by layer until all my layers are gone and it is only me, laid bare, naked to the soul, that is left. His body is hot, sweet, hungry. The slip of sweat on skin and lips on skin and his hands caressing every inch of me create ripples of desire that stretch my muscles taut. The throb of need tunes me like an instrument and I thrum to his touch, coiling and snaking around him until I can no longer avoid the only thing I don't dare touch. He slides between my legs and I wait, eyes half-closed, terrified and yet longing too, the heady desperation to feel him deep inside me, possessing me, almost too much to bear. He enters me abruptly and the shock is as violent as my orgasm, sudden and intense and leaving me gasping and clinging to him. He arches above me so he can look down into my face and his sinews are mine and my ecstasy is his.

'Elise,' he murmurs then surges hard into me and the waves of pleasure erupt a second, third, fourth time until I am sobbing and begging him to stop, don't stop. I shudder and he pushes harder.

I grasp his shoulders and my nails dig into him, soft, spongy flesh that gives to my touch and then burst opens under the pressure from my manicured nails – my one vanity. The red of his blood is the red of my fingernails and I exclaim. 'Jason, oh God…'

He kisses me and I swoon into it, forgetting momentarily that I have made him bleed. Then he draws away and thrusts hard before melting into me in a convulsion of gasped air that sounds like agony. He collapses on me and I am pinned under his dead weight, body still vibrating with the throb of blood through me. He mumbles against my shoulder and I nuzzle into him, this man, this… this… man.

We lay like that for a long time, until I am numb from his weight. His ribcage crushes mine and I breathe in low shallow pants, but I don't want him to move. Slowly he shifts, withdraws, and then pulls me into him, curling us into a joint foetal position. I whisper into his neck but he shushes me.

'Just hold me, Elise.'

So I do, until we doze and the evening passes into night and we are still curled in a tight ball as darkness falls. I don't know when we fell asleep fully. It must have been somewhere between night and day, but when I awake, we have separated, slipped apart and are lying alongside each other, face to face, his nose only inches from mine, his breath fanning my cheek. His eyes are already open and he is watching me, those orange whorls that have always fascinated me in the deep blue-grey of his iris, shifting and changing like light does.

'Hello, stranger,' he says, smiling.

'Stranger?'

'No more,' he adds. We laugh together and he pulls me close to him again. I coil into him and we lay nose to nose, chest to chest, hip to hip.

'Jason…'

'No,' he says.

'You don't even know what I was going to ask you.'

'The answer is still no. You don't need to ask anything. Our bodies told us all we needed to know, didn't they?'

'I guess… but where do we go from here?'

'Forward.'

'What is forward?'

'What was forward?'

'Well, life together, husband and wife… but no children…' I say the last softly – almost silently.

'No, no children.'

I expect him to let go then, turn over, avoid the issue like Jason always did. He doesn't. He kisses my forehead and nuzzles my hair. His words, when they come are disjointed at first, but I know immediately the story they are going to tell.

'Rosalie. Marchant. She was a Marchant.'

'Your mother?'

'My mother, not that she was. Or she was, but she wasn't.'

'I don't…'

'You had a mother. What was it like?'

'Like?'

'To have a mother?'

'Oh Jason, I don't know. It just was. You don't think about it. It just is.'

'I think about it.'

'I'm beginning to understand that.'

'I don't know what it would have been like and I wonder about that. Is it better or worse to have had a mother?'

'Well, it's always better to have someone there to care about you.'

'Yes. I suppose it must be. I don't know. But I didn't.'

'Well, you have me.'

'Do I, Elise?'

'Yes,' I say it through lips pressed against his neck. I can feel the flutter of his jugular, bleating against them.

'And who do you think I am, that you have?'

I search for the right answer. Jason, or my husband? Or something else? Something new and terrifying, but dear nonetheless? None are quite right.

'You,' I say in the end. He seems satisfied with that. So am I, it seems. We curl in closer.

'She left when I was small,' he says suddenly. 'Just off to school. Imagine that. No one to take you to the school gates or collect you from there.'

'But your father?'

'Did. But he wasn't a mother. All children should have a mother. It's the right function.'

'I'm so sorry, Jason.' I want to cry at the image of him as a small child, walking lonely into school and even lonelier exiting it.

'I was less than all the other kids, you see. Lacking.'

'You weren't. It wasn't your fault.'

'No, it wasn't. But still I suffered it, whether it was my fault or not. They called me names.'

'Children can be cruel.'

'Yes.'

His arms tighten around me and I struggle to breathe.

'Jason…'

His grip loosens.

'Not just children,' he says. 'Adults too. But they will learn.' He pauses and kisses my forehead again. 'I am sorry. You wanted children.'

'That's in the past now,' I laugh at the ludicrousness of how in the past that was. I have almost lost and now regained my husband. The past is so far past it can never matter so much as the present or the future.

'It was too late, don't you see? I could already see her in me and that I wouldn't ever duplicate again.'

'But you *are* duplicated now,' I tease gently to shift his black mood.

'That is different. I was already created. And now there is the possibility of improving on me – taking the blueprint and modifying it in a controlled way. With a child there is no control. However the genetic make-up occurs is out of our control – until we physically control it ourselves. That's where cloning can come in – *after* modifying the blueprint. To make us better people…' He rolls onto his side. 'Tell me about your paintings and why you've never admitted to them before?' The change of subject is so sudden I'm lost for words. What can I tell him about them that won't damage the fabric we've been weaving together again over the last few days.

'Oh, there's nothing really to tell.'

'But you mentioned an exhibition?'

'I'm not sure about that now.'

'Why? Don't you want to show off what you've created? Your finest achievements?'

I sense there's more to that than meets the eye, after all, Jason is now created not born… I don't know what to say. I don't want to start an ethical debate now, not in this most intimate of moments. I've settled for something that challenges all my ethical principles, and yet isn't that what should happen if we are being truly open-minded – allow for change? My ethical principals have been challenged, defeated and proven wrong; changed.

I touch his shoulder in gentle acknowledgement and my fingers slide over where my nails had dug into him last night. There is nothing there but smooth unblemished skin.

'Maybe,' I say in the end.

Chapter 42

11th July 2029: Jason

Fully functioning! I would like to report that to Matthew, but instinct – hah! That's ironic! Instinct tells me not to. Accessing data reminds me why. Interface and suppression – not controlled yet.

Elise is asleep. I am reluctant to leave her when she is so inviting, curled up like a downy chick… There's a good line if I were a poet. Maybe I could be? It is not something that has appealed until now, but there are so many facets of life and living I haven't explored yet. Perhaps I will explore poetry over time, like Elise has been doing with painting? Painting; I'm intrigued – both by what she's painted and why she's kept it to herself. I perch on the side of the bed, careful not to let the redistribution of weight disturb her. I will find out soon enough, I'm sure. She seems to have completely accepted me as I am now – the new Jason - and there is no need for secrets anymore. I watch her for a moment as she sleeps, eyelashes resting against her cheek like a smudge of grey-gold, skin burnished from the ministrations of the past summer's sunshine and, just latterly, me. That makes me smile too. That sensation. It was extreme and exquisite in a way I have never considered before. Fred would certainly not have. How about that, Fred? Who has the upper hand now? Even the complex interaction of finger to skin, lips to mouth, limb to limb, took less effort this time. Just a few hours have made a significant difference – or maybe it is the knowledge that I am evolving, fully assimilating. This body has become MY body. I am what I always was, but better.

The high drives me out of bed and into the wet room, powering my body like a sleek limousine until I am standing under the splintering droplets of the shower. They bounce off my CyberCute covering with something akin to glee. But it is more than CyberCute now. So much more. It is interactive and self-processing. I even enjoyed the pain from the prick of Elise's fingernails into my shoulders last night – although not as much as the rush of the orgasm – because it also signified a peak in performance. I don't just function. I perform. High power… And now I'm too fired up to laze. Too jittery. My whole body is still tingling – hyper-sensitive. Elise was the last test. I can do anything now – ANYTHING! And I NEED to do something to take my mind off this sensation or it will implode. My mind is working nineteen to the dozen on all kinds of ideas I've never had before – solutions, possibilities, inspiration…

I leave the wet room and slide into yesterday's tracksuit pants and t-shirt, despite their unpleasantly used smell. Human smell. Sweat, skin debris, the minutiae of bacteria acting on shed particles. The human process. I'm still delighting in it – although it will pall. I already acknowledge that, so it will need to be refined. Humans will need to be refined. I don't want to have to put up with this constant fug that accompanies my companions for the rest of my life. I chuckle. The rest of my life? The rest of forever! Maybe I should put on fresh clothes – trousers and shirt, look the part now I am Jason Crane again? No, for the moment, I am actually enjoying being part of the human stench. The sterile crispness of perfection can wait for the moment. I will be a pig in shit for a while longer whilst I celebrate life. I eye my phone, lying dejected and abandoned on the dresser and reject that too. Why would I need it now? There are no potential medical emergencies to factor in, no function failings, no need of repair. I am my own man now, and the feeling of not needing to rely on anyone or anything is good.

My limbs glide effortlessly along the corridor. No struggle to direct them today. Bye, bye Fred. This is just me now. Need to get to grip with everything here now. It is all mine, after all.

The first lab is a minor genetics testing area. I power up the nearest PC and swallow the last report on it whole. Small fry, but interesting. I can see some areas that could be developed once I have reasserted my control over the divisions that Jason created when he carved up manufacturing from pure research and inserted artificial controls to stop one burrowing into the other before test results had been approved. I will come back to that. I shut down the PC and prowl the rest of the lab. It is pristine, as I would expect it to be: surfaces gleaming: written notes neatly filed and indexed and pens and pencils tidied away. Its emptiness breeds a stillness in me. Quiet. Calm. I like that. Ordered and identified. It feels good after the nervous energy I've been feeling since waking. Even the smells are muted in here, the usually overwhelming aroma of antiseptic and floor polish subdued into a tight layer that is only vaguely detectable to the finely tuned olfactory system. Most of my staff in here wouldn't even smell a smell, except their own. And probably not that. They haven't the instincts to notice anything other than the obvious. That is something I am rapidly absorbing about my human counterparts. I laugh, a small explosion of irony to accompany the irony of earlier. But I do, even though I have none.

But now I am bored in this lab. It has too little of anything to interest me. I'm back to wanting fecundity, proliferation, over-weaning ambition, propagation – reproduction, after all.

I want the ForEver lab.

I leave the lab door to shut behind me without waiting for the lock to click in place before setting off. It will. It's a protocol Jason – I – set in place when the facility was first built. Jason was nothing if not a perfectionist on that score. And I will hear it when it does anyway and by then I will be almost to the ForEver lab. I hear the distant click five paces away from the ForEver lab door and smile with satisfaction. Auditory systems are firing on all systems too. I give a little whistle to celebrate, pursing my lips and filtering air through them in the way I have seen Matthew do when he is pre-occupied. The sound it produces is clear and high. It could be bird-song. I test it again. A perfect high A. Good. Better than a violin. I whistle it again as I enter the ForEver lab. It makes me happy. Accessing data on happy? A slide show of imagery that I already know. Yes, I understand happy. Elise was happy last night. The test was passed with flying colours. Colours. None here either. White, clean, well-organised. Lab benches the only dark amongst light, the deep rich brown of mahogany. I cross to them and rub my fingertips across their surface. Smooth, but not the same smooth as Elise's skin. Which is nicer? Difficult. Skin is subtle, has texture, responds, but has that vaguely repulsive spongy quality to it too. The wood is solid, substantial, unyielding, smooth. Conclusion. Different purposes. Both acceptable. But here is the one place the lab is untidy too, notes from one of Matthew's rat reviews, no doubt, lying untended by the Bunsen burner tap I'd availed myself of yesterday to demonstrate my newly developed healing abilities. Next to them, a beaker of cloudy solution, unlabelled, suggests he was disturbed in the middle of an experiment. What? Now I am curious. The enjoyable buzz generated by the prospect of investigation replaces the nervous energy buzz that has been energising my limbs until now.

I reach across the bench and collect notes and beaker but am distracted by the first sentence on the top page of the notes.

Elise, I am sorry I…

The writing descends into illegible scrawl, but it is undeniably Matthew's. I squint at it, trying to decipher the loops and tails of the scribble as I perch on one of the bench stools. It slips sideways as my buttock settles too far to one side of the seat and I lurch forward, spilling the beaker's contents over both the notes and the bench. 'Damn!' Fred is getting his own back in my distraction.

I deposit the beaker on the bench and fumble for something to wipe the worst of the spillage from the paper before it completely invades the scribble I was about to disentangle and translate. It might be scribble to Matthew and anyone else looking at it, but not to me, not now. The only available help is my t-shirt. I blot the paper gently against it and then spread the paper back out across the bench to dry. The scribble is intact despite the fluid's ingress but as I watch the wet spot spread, fingers absent-mindedly paddling in the little pool of spillage, the sensation distracts me as well. It is nice. I splash in it like a child playing in a muddy puddle. I taste it out of curiosity – everything seems to create a sense of curiosity in me these days. I grimace. It's saline solution. Now I laugh. What is Matthew doing experimenting with saline solution? More to the point though, what is he apologising for to Elise? I sweep the puddle away with the side of my hand and concentrate on the paper and its secrets.

'… I am sorry I … fail… ou… ut…hav … bu..t..in…a fa..safe. W… te… y…'

My hand is stinging. What the hell? I rub the edge of it against my wet t-shirt and the stinging eases. I go back to the truncated words, mind trying out combinations in rapid fire until I have a selection of words beginning to fit the jigsaw puzzle. My hand stabs suddenly with a pain like that of a bee sting and I drop the paper to waft the insect away, but there is none. I rub at the sore spot and it feels gritty – as if someone has been systematically rubbing at it with sandpaper – and the CyberCute skin is red and angry. The fingertip of my index finger is smarting too. I flex my hand and rub it against my chest as a red ant army starts its determined march from fingertip to side of the palm, but there is no relief and now my chest feels tender too. I pull my t-shirt up to reveal a patchy red weal stretching across my chest like someone has been brushing acid on me in small circular motions. The aggravated area corresponds perfectly with the still mildly wet patch from drying my hand and the soaked paper on my t-shirt earlier.

'Christ! What is that stuff then?'

I pick up the beaker again and sniff it. It must be saline. There is nothing except the vague intimation of something salty that I had noticed before, yet the angry patches of CyberCute belie that because my hand is now bubbling into blisters and my forefinger steadily swelling to the size of a meaty pork sausage part cooked, the skin popping into tiny ulcers. I drop the beaker and rummage for my phone but of course I have no pockets. I run to the intercom between the lab and the medical facility. I should have put trousers on so I had my phone in my pocket. And where was Matthew anyway?

'Jason?'

It is Elise.

'Where is Kohn?' I shout at her. 'She should be there.'

'She is, she is,' she says soothingly. 'I'll get her. What's the matter?'

'And Matthew!' I shout down the empty line.

'Mr Crane? Dr Kohn here.'

'Find Matthew Green. He should be here. I need him here – now!'

'Where are you?'

'The ForEver lab.'

'I'll come.'

'I don't need you. I need Matthew Green. Just find him.'

The pain is becoming intense now. This isn't right. Why am I not healing? I rip off my t-shirt and squeeze my good hand around the wrist of the other, willing the pain to go, but it merely increases. I let go and lurch across to the lab sink and hang over it, running my hand under cold water. Slowly the pain subsides to a dull ache as the cold numbs it. My chest still roars with pain though and I am panting like a dog.

'Jason, whatever is the matter?'

Cool hands are on my back, but the fire still rages in my chest and hand. Elise is dressed in only the flimsiest of nightgowns – the type designed to seduce. The outline of her breasts and the sweep of her belly to her pubic mound is obvious through the diaphanous material – to me at least. It must have been for my benefit for when I returned.

'Something is wrong. Where's Matthew?'

'He's on his way. He got called away – his daughter…'

'I don't care about his fucking daughter. I need him here.'

I sense, more than feel her pull away, then her hands are back on me, caressing and comforting.

'What can I do to help in the meantime? Let me see – oh God, have you burned yourself?'

'I don't know. Not that I know of, but something is wrong. The water has helped a bit but…'

For a second I can see the fear in her face, then she recovers and bustles about me, locating medical pads and a bowl.

'If the fresh water has helped, let me bathe your chest whilst we wait for Matthew to arrive. You keep your hand under the running water. Here, sit.' She pushes the lab bench stool in behind me and fills the bowl with water. Oddly she doesn't smell of the human condition. She smells fresh and clean.

'What's going on?'

We both turn and Matthew is at the lab door, Dr Kohn behind him.

'Just you,' I say. 'For the moment.'

'OK.' He half turns to Dr Kohn and she scowls but melts into the darkness of the corridor.

'Where the hell were you?' I growl.

'Home. Katie was ill. I got called back last night but I thought you were fine – with Elise…'

They exchange glances. His eyes drop to the outline of her breasts and he blushes.

Elise, I am sorry I... fail... ou... ut... hav... bu..t.. in... a fa..safe...as...you...a... W... te... y...

'What's going on?' I demand.

'Nothing.' He looks from me to the spilt beaker and the scattered papers. His jaw is tight and a nerve twitches under his eye.

'Then what's this? Something's malfunctioning. The bio-repair system isn't working.'

'No, it's fine – you showed me yesterday… why should it fail today?'

'Why indeed? What's in the beaker?'

'Beaker?' He frowns and the confusion is real. He is hovering close now, mingling his fetid odour with Elise's fragrance. 'Let me see?' he asks quietly and she stands aside. He reaches across and turns off the running water.

'On the bench. I spilt the contents of that beaker on the bench and it went over my hand. I rubbed my hand dry on my t-shirt and you can see the result there too.'

His eyes are fixed to my now pin-cushioned and pockmarked hand

and chest. The blisters have burst in the main, leaving small pustular craters.

'Ah,' he says. His eyes glaze and then refocus on me, my cratering skin – CyberCute – and my fury.

'Ah, what?'

If it wasn't for the pain – albeit lessening now, but nonetheless still severe, I would have punched him to the ground.

'Well, I don't know… there were one or two things we were still working on when you transferred, but…' We lock gazes. His eyes drop first. 'I – we can figure it out. It's not a problem.'

He takes a step backwards, eyes darting from me to the papers.

'Not a problem? 'So why would saline do this to me?'

He grimaces and rubs his hand across his eyes – that Matthew gesture that tells me he knows what the problem is but doesn't want to worry me.'

'Why would salt do this to me?' I repeat, but quietly, silkily. 'Matthew? Remember what there is riding on all of this…'

'Yes,' he gasps. 'Well… salt can be corrosive of course.'

'Salt has never been corrosive.'

'Not to a hu—' He stops short.

We eye each other.

'To a human?' I watch him redden but there is no sympathy in me. 'And me?'

'To you, maybe it is.'

'Explain.'

'Oh dear…' He pauses. 'Well, the iron in the cyborg bones could react through the CyberCute. It's a catalyst, after all. Remember we had to look for something that would have rapid cell division for coverage and longevity, but osmotic because of the chemical activity arising from integration. Well the CyberCute compound is catalytically reactive to oxygen to enable cell manufacture and growth so it's also theoretically reactive to substances that may oxidise.'

'But how does iron in the cyborg bones inside Jason's skin cause this?' Elise asks.

'Oxidation.' I answer before Matthew, cutting him off, now I see where this could go – is going. 'Oxidation is an electrochemical process that acts like a battery, exchanging chemicals and small amounts of electricity. A solution helps the process by allowing electrons to move more easily between the two elements. Different solutions work better than others. Water takes atoms and changes them into a form of acid as the oxidation process continues, which makes metal rust faster. Acidic transformation occurs with pure water, but with salty water it is already a minor acid and so becomes an even more powerful electrolyte. Pure water forms an acidic solution and enables the oxidation process to happen slowly, but salty water is a catalyst – hypersensitised by coming into contact with another catalyst – CyberCute. Am I right?'

Matthew nods. Elise is staring at me without comprehension. 'I still don't understand.' Now Elise is frowning.

'Neither do I, actually,' I agree. 'So when did CyberCute become a catalyst, Matthew?'

Matthew looks like he would like to run as far and as fast away from me as he can but I'm not letting him off that easily. I gesture to him to continue. He shifts from one foot to the other.

'Oh dear…' He sighs, and the rest comes out in a rush. 'Jason's skin covering currently contains a high concentration of iron atoms because we needed iron as a component in bone formation and his blood is carrying iron atoms around because of the chemical exchange going on whilst the cyborg bone and human bone integrate. Contact with salt water initiates the oxidation process with that iron.'

'Or to put it another way, I'm rusting away,' I add sarcastically.

'But you're already mostly transformed, mostly human?' she says, shaking her head.

'Mostly, but not enough,' Matthew takes a bunch of medical pads and tries to dry my cratered hand. I rip it away from him and complete the job myself.

'But what about salt every day? Elise asks. 'And water. How is he to drink or wash? How has he drunk and washed without harm until now?'

'Small amounts of pure water are fine. Pure water is so slow in causing the oxidisation reaction, the most Jason would feel is like he's been sunbathing too long if he soaks in the bath. Internally, water and salt are going into his digestive system – and that we'd cloned, so there is no cyborg bone interaction involved. But of course, at the moment, his sustenance is still mainly intravenous as that matures…'

She looks at me. 'So that's why we haven't eaten together yet?' I ignore her and concentrate on Matthew, but she's persistent. 'And sweat and so on?' I shake my head to signify she shouldn't go on, but she does anyway. 'How can he touch someone if they're sweating?'

I stand and walk away, deliberately knocking the clutch of medical pads from Matthew's hands and scattering them to the floor as I pass him. I don't want to see his expression, but I still catch a glimpse of it before I turn away fully. It is frozen. The diaphanous night gown and its purpose has fully registered – and the fact that I haven't heeded his warning.

'Ahh… no,' Matthew replies slowly. I imagine him watching me as I walk away. He will be frowning a little, trying to figure out whether I have ignored him or was about to ignore him. 'That's so dilute and diffused into other chemical particles too, his bio system can neutralise it by treating it as an antibody. But something like salt solution in concentrate or volume, or a deliberate and direct immersion would be corrosive. So, say – don't swim in the sea…' There is a silence. 'Or dangle your fingers in saline solution,' he adds as I turn around to face the pair of them. 'That's too much to be treated as a random hostile element and if it gets past the bio-defence system and into the cyborg system before it has been able to assimilate the effects and calculate how to fully neutralise them, it will shut down.'

'What then?' Elise asks. I can hear the catch in her voice so I guess she's already worked out the possibilities. For her sake, I shouldn't walk away now, no matter how angry I am with Matthew. This is it. This is what the security incursions were all about. Adapting the formula. How was it that I never checked it? Trust? I trusted him? I am sure this has never been highlighted as a problem before. I turn on reaching the door. Walking away won't change facts anyway. Elise reminds me of a wraith in her floating robes – a wisp of smoky day on the horizon, foreshadowing dawn…

'Then he might be at risk of dying.'

… or twilight.

'My Achilles heel is a pillar of salt,' I joke, 'in a water column. Empires have been won and lost over blood, but I can be tumbled by a few grains of salt?' Matthew doesn't answer. 'Why didn't you say when you were first trumpeting how wonderful CyberCute is?'

'Because it is. It's only a minor failing really – and easy to deal with once we've nailed the right additions or extractions to the formula.'

'But you never told me about it.'

'You never asked.'

'That isn't quite the same.'

'It is.' Unusually, he bridles. 'You could have asked instead of just accepting. Taking.' He bites his lip. 'You could have even checked the formula yourself.'

'I see.' And I do. But now is not the time. It will come when I am ready. Instead I shrug. Let him think I don't realise. 'At least that's the only thing that can kill me – I assume?'

Elise catches Matthew's eye, questioning. He merely shakes his head mutely. She shivers.

'Well that's something at least.' I examine my hand. The pain has almost gone now and the blisters are puckering in preparation for the first stage of healing. The bio-repair system is kicking back in. Slowly by comparison to before, but kicking in, nevertheless. Symbiotic metamorphosis. Yes, Matthew. I didn't ask, and you deliberately didn't tell – or maybe there was nothing to tell then – but I will prevail, and you? I collect both Elise and the abandoned note before Matthew can get to them. I wrap my arm round her shoulders. 'You'll catch your death,' I quip to her. She looks shocked, then laughs humourlessly.

'And what about you?'

'That doesn't seem likely for me,' I reply, eyeing Matthew. 'Unless I try to swim the Channel, huh? Better clear this lot up before you start looking at solutions. I've got a formula to examine, it seems. Here endeth the first lesson then – the lesson of hubris. Are you happy now?'

I lead Elise out of the lab, leaving Matthew on his hands and knees, collecting up the scattered medical pads. We exchange one last glance at the door. It says everything and nothing, both waiting to see what the other may do.

Elise I am sorry I failed you but I have built in a failsafe as you asked...

Chapter 43

11th July 2029: Matthew

'Mr Green… Matthew…'

I turn awkwardly, knees complaining against the ice cold of the lab floor. Dr Kohn is standing in the doorway, a smile playing with one corner of her mouth, like a puppet master is playing with the strings attached to her face. I try to rise but my knees refuse to cooperate. Instead, I have to make do with sitting back on my heels and gazing up at her – all five foot nothing of her. Seems I'm finding my level on a regular basis today.

'Yes?' I don't intend it to be quite as curt as it sounds, but I doubt the coolness will bother Dr Kohn.

'Do you need a hand?'

'Thanks, but I think I can manage.'

She shrugs and the words curl from her still twitching lips to encompass her critical assessment of me and my abilities.

'Are you sure?' Her Germanic accent is particularly strong today. The half-smile becomes a full-bodied appreciation of my unenviable position, both on my knees in front of her picking up the debris from my run-in with Jason, and as the person I'm sure she regards as Jason's lackey. The realisation that she sees me for precisely what I am would have knocked my legs from me if I hadn't already been kneeling. I put one hand down to steady myself whilst the other attempts to push me upright. The lab floor is cold and unforgiving, but slippery too where Elise splashed so much water around. My hand slides and I lurch sideways. Kohn steps forward and offers her hand in response. I ignore it. 'Oh take it,' she says, irritation making her words even more clipped. 'You know you need help, so accept it. We might even both benefit from it.'

Reluctantly I take her hand and she pulls me to my feet with surprising ease given her size.

'Thanks,' I mumble, trying to cover my embarrassment by brushing my crumpled and stained trousers straight.

'What do you English say? You're welcome?' I nod. 'OK, well, you're welcome. Now let's talk.'

'Talk?'

'About six days ago, about what has happened in between, about today…'

'I don't think so.'

'Don't you? I do.'

'You have an NDA, I'm sure. Jason wouldn't have engaged you without a rock-solid NDA, so talking isn't part of the plan.'

She raises her eyebrows and for a moment I want to laugh, she looks so comically surprised.

'The plan? Well of course I signed an NDA, but what is that really worth? All it tells you is that someone has something to hide, so if you keep your eyes open, you'll find out what, and then the NDA is only worth what they'll pay to keep you quiet.'

I take up position in front of Jason's work station, perched against the worktop to steady myself.

'Sounds like you've done this before.'

'Not this – certainly not this – but many other things that people have wanted to keep quiet.'

I really don't like her complacency. As annoying as Jason is, he has risked everything for this, and that deserves more respect.

'Well, maybe, but this is quite different. Jason is quite different.'

'He certainly is now.' She laughs, at first a trill of amusement, but it grows, rolling around her chest until it becomes a great gale of laughter: a sirocco, blowing across me, the lab and scorching as far as the inner sanctum. I wait, nonplussed. When she finally stops, she is wiping tears from her eyes, sniffing and chuckling in equal measure. This is not the woman I've been seeing until now. There is something dark and strange to her amusement. 'I know precisely what you've done,' she adds eventually, pushing the door closed behind her and crossing the room to take the seat in front of my computer. 'But of course, you must know that.'

'What I've done? I don't know what you're talking about.'

'Yes you do, if you just stop and think about it.' She taps her forehead and swings her legs as the chair twists on its wheels. Her feet don't even touch the ground.

I shake my head, but the glimmer of an idea is casting a long shadow on my peace of mind. I stuff my hands in my pockets to hide the fact that they're shaking. She'd accessed the CyberCute formula that night before I'd gone back in and changed it again. We'd obviously used the revised formula I'd uploaded after all. That was clear from the way Jason had reacted to the saline solution, but even I hadn't expected it to be so extreme, merely one of a series a debilitating irritations that would continuously keep him from operating at top form as his repair facility drained resources to fix the problem. Continuous energy leak is the most effective limiter of progress. If you can't work at one hundred per cent, there is curtailment, even if not complete containment. But it had all gone so well, I'd thought there hadn't been enough time for the new formula CyberCute to have been synthesised. Looking at Kohn's expression, clearly, I'd been wrong, and both Kohn and anyone else who could access those records would be able to see the two formulae in the test data history. Christ! Jason already suspected something – that was clear too, but if he found out…

I assess the options. There aren't any. I can see that from her smile.

'All right, but it was a mistake. I tried a different formula but it wasn't quite right. So I rectified it, that's all. Nothing sinister. Just an unfortunate timing issue on the night.'

'But we still used the wrong formula, Mr Green, didn't we? And you haven't told him that.'

'It doesn't matter. It can be rectified now. We can develop a patch for the time being and then replace the whole outer layer of CyberCute over time.'

'Indeed, we could, but have you considered what else that modification might have caused?'

'What else? Nothing,' I round on her even as my brain starts to list the possibilities. 'What do you think I am, Dr Kohn? Jason is my best and dearest friend. The formula we used was a mistake, and it was a mistake we used it, but that's all – and it only happened because everything kicked off so fast that night. Anyway, you played a part in it all too. You made it happen too – and you knew, didn't you? That's why you asked if I was sure about the batch of CyberCute we were using. What would he say if he knew you'd suspected something was wrong but hadn't said anything at the time?'

'I'm sure it would be an unpleasant conversation, but it would be even more unpleasant for you, wouldn't it? The developer of the faulty product? I can claim ignorance – or at worst, acting under orders. But you – surely this could be classed as attempted murder if it's not fixed?'

My breath whistles in my throat. 'So what do you want?'

'Fame, fortune, recognition?' She laughs at my horrified expression. 'Maybe not. If this thing blows up in both of our faces, I think we might both prefer complete deniability, mightn't we? How about we settle for good old money for the time being, and then we'll see.'

She smiles again and makes the chair swivel round and round, feet swinging in time with the rotations. I feel like I am being blackmailed by a child.

'Isn't Jason paying you enough already?'

'Oh, of course, but let's consider this a placeholder – setting the scene for something more valuable in the future, as and when we determine what that might be – possibly even that fame and fortune and recognition – if Jason doesn't corrode away before you can figure out the appropriate patch.'

She hops off the chair, leaving it gently rocking.

'And how much is the placeholder then?' I feel sick and defeated, the old fear of reprisal I'd lived with daily until Jason had neutralised Eddie's blackmail arrangements sweeping back over me, making me want to retch.

'How about a sight of the working records for the time being? You have access, don't you? Even if it is on a slightly delayed basis… Am I right? That's why we had to wait till after midnight that night. You can only access everything the next day…' she pauses and adds slowly and cruelly, 'when you're allowed to…'

She walks across to the door.

'When?' I hardly recognise my own voice.

'Oh, no rush. You can finish clearing that up first.'

The door closes behind her and I am left in the cool hush of the lab, counting my known sins, and fearing what others there might be I haven't yet accounted for.

... have you considered what else that modification might have caused?

Chapter 44

11th July 2029: Elise

It is late morning before I am sure it is safe to return to the lab because Jason is back in the medical facility, under close supervision of Dr Kohn, hand and chest tended to, and now sleeping. Matthew looks up glumly when I enter. The lab is now pristine again and he is surrounded by folders and paper covered in scribbled equations.

'Is this what you meant by there could be faults with the system?' I ask him.

'You asked for a glitch. I gave you a glitch. Don't lay into me for what you wanted.'

'I didn't ask for a glitch. I asked for you to stop it – end of. OK maybe I was wrong about that, but this is terrible.'

'Look, you were worried this was against the laws of nature. All I've done is allow the laws of nature to carry on working. Salt water corrodes metal. Every god has to have an Achilles heel, like Jason says. They're too all-powerful otherwise. Now he's got his.'

'He's not a god. He's a man, and one I love.' Matthew just looks at me, then shrugs. 'What?' I ask.

'Nothing.'

'No, tell me.'

'OK,' he pauses, lips twisting. 'You know he's discovered he heals?'

'Yes, he bleeds and he heals. He told me, and for me that makes him human.'

'He heals in double-quick time, whatever he does – cuts, burns, he's virtually indestructible. Invincible.'

'Except for saline solution,' I add ironically.

'Except for saline solution,' he agrees. 'This will be just sufficient to hold him in check if he ever gets delusions of godliness. Keep him human – faulty like the rest of us.'

'Oh Matthew… But salt? What the hell are you playing at using that? It's such an everyday substance. He'll encounter it all the time.'

'And the worst it will cause him is mild discomfort unless he's stupid – and he's not that, whatever else he is.' His voice is soothing, like I'm Katie being talked out of a tantrum. 'Stop worrying. Enjoy the miracle – and enjoy the fact that his body may be that of a cyborg but it's also similar to that of a human in its fallibility. It'll all be fine – and, anyway, he knows now. I hate myself for it but he'll cope.'

'Well… but as long as there's nothing else?'

'There's nothing else…' That hesitation is there again. 'That's the only thing I'm aware of that is a problem, anyway, and one day that will be fixed too. Jason will make sure of it,' he adds ruefully. 'But Elise, be careful. He's not a man yet. He's still a work in progress.'

'Aren't we all, Matthew?'

Chapter 45

12th to 19th July 2029: Jason

It is not only liberating to be ailment free – forever – but I am enjoying beginning to think differently too. To begin with it was merely clearer, sharper, more objective. I noticed it first with the little things. Once I was back in the lab, I found I could scan a report and assimilate the guts of it quicker than before. I could focus. To begin with I assumed it was because I had been distracted by Death, standing guardian-like by my side asleep or awake. Who wouldn't find it hard to focus when Death is their constant companion? But it's more than that. It's a clarity of mind I didn't have before, an edge that can cut through the non-essentials that get caught up in the mix – human emotion, human anxiety, human distraction. All things human, in fact. With a cyborg mindset, more gets done, dross gets set to one side more easily, the logical outweighs the emotional. My mind is now starting to clear pathways that have bogged me down before. I see the issue, but also the pathway to neutralisation of the issue almost simultaneously. It's been a week now since I first noticed it. Now I apply the process routinely to everyday life – mismatches in intent with Elise, Matthew, others – and despite their humanness, it still works. Today it's the turn of Jeff Bronsam, my head of HR.

'This problematical staff rota you keep on about… is there any reason why we don't just sign off whatever we require, and award bonuses dependent on output to quell objections?'

Jeff looks surprised. 'We aren't target-based. Or dictatorial.'

'Why aren't we? We're performance-based, and these people have signed a contract to work to our required working times. That's not dictatorial. That's acting on contracted terms.'

'Well…' He pushes his glasses back up his nose and peers at me through them. The lenses are filthy. 'I suppose… but it's still a dictatorship.'

'Is it? How? It's a pursuable agreement with acceptable remuneration in return.'

'Well, I… well, maybe it's not… maybe it's a benign dictatorship, given the bonuses available.'

'Exactly. So, put it in process and report back on objectors next week.'

Bronsam grimaces but shuffles the contents of the folder back into a semblance of order and backs out of the room. I shake my head as he leaves. He was always obsequious, but now? Why shouldn't I sweep objections away with the incisiveness of my logic? There is no questioning it. It is logic pure and simple – and in a way these people don't have. I feel good. What else? What else needs sorting out? I buzz my secretary. There is nothing she insists. I have cleared the decks already and it is only ten thirty.

'OK.' My administrative thirst is slaked. I could go back to the labs? I push my chair back and it scrapes protestingly on the wood block floor. Who chose something so archaic? My memory banks spew out the answer obligingly. Jason. Me. Oh well. I reconsider. I don't want to go back to the labs for the moment. Maybe I like the archaic after all. Maybe it's time to open the memory banks a little wider. Delve into this mind I am now melding with and expanding…

I scan the last year. Some of it I don't want to revisit – the last few months of it – but beyond that, there are attractive parts, mainly with Elise. I lose myself in a particularly vivid memory of walking the local heathlands with her on a blustery day last autumn. The trees were just turning, green to gold, rust hues in between. Rust – huh! Matthew and his 'failsafe' invades but I eject him and return to the red-gold-green trees and Elise, sun in her hair and eyes, love lines on her lips and her hand in mine as we make our way explorer-like through the towering bracken and overgrown ferns on the way to the small pond that nestles in the midst of this New Forest clearing. Those moments, they were moments of pure… pure… The moment fades. Whatever Jason – I – felt is lost, yet lingering in an ambience in which I want to dwell – a comforting, rosy-hued glow. Love. That's what it was. Jason – I – felt love. Is that what I feel when I have sex with her? The sensations are certainly intense: waves of pleasure and the need to consume, possess, hold onto her and never let go, all the while surging into her more and more and… The need for physical release suddenly overcomes me and I am cupping myself, stroking myself, erect and needy. The desire to be inside Elise and pumping hard against her soft fleshiness, forcing into her yielding vacuum, hot and wet and enveloping me is too much. I am about to go in search of her when something else intrudes. She is saying something, whispering it to me, moist lips opening and closing as they release the words, like salt water droplets, spraying me as they land and corroding where they touch. I flinch. They sting, those words. Sting in a way beyond physical pain.

'You made me murder our child because of this?'

Murder?

Her face twists as she says it. Then she pushes me away. Pushes, turns and walks away. It is so clear we could be doing it right now – the push, my overbalance, my stumble. Her walking away, heels clicking on the path as she weaves her way delicately past the burgeoning Michaelmas daisy stalks that overgrow it even before they bloom. When they're in bloom Anna and I run through them, deliberately kicking against them to make them bob and collide against each other. But that's not yet – not till the summer is almost gone.

'Mummy…' Anna tries to follow her, but she shoos her away.

'Not this time, Anna. Stay with your brother.'

'Daddy will be home soon. Just stay there. On the doorstep.'

I emerge from the memory, head pounding. Slowly I uncurl my fists and wait for the pounding to settle as I watch the fingernail cuts in my palms heal over. Desire has long gone now. Trying to reimagine Elise merely brings back the walking-away woman and that deep black desperation of the child on the doorstep, turning a white envelope over and over in one hand whilst clutching his sister's hand in the other.

I pant to distract myself as other memories return too.

Murder.

'You made me murder our child because of this?'

Yes, Elise. I made you murder our child because of this. I thump my fist on the desk and groan, a strange strangled cry that mimics the wood splintering in protest. The outer door to my office pops open and my secretary peers in, eyes wide and questioning.

'Mr Crane? Is everything all right? Do you need the doctor?'

I stare at her, struggling to drag myself away from the doorstep, frigid and unforgiving on my bony limbs. I am cold and stiff from waiting, afraid and confused from wondering, sick to the pit of my stomach for fear of the instinctive understanding I had even then, despite being a child.

'She walked away,' I tell her before I can stop myself. 'She simply walked away and left us there.'

'Mr Crane?'

Just stay there. On the doorstep.

You made me murder our child because of this?

Give him the envelope, when he comes.

The walking-away woman fades and merges with my secretary, questioning, questioning.

'Mr Crane? Are you all right? Shall I call your wife? Or Dr Green?'

'No!' The force of my refusal surprises me as much as her. 'No,' I repeat more moderately. 'It's fine. Nothing. Go back to work and mark me as unavailable for the rest of the day, please.'

She nods uncertainly but doesn't leave.

'Anything else?' I ask politely.

'No… if you're sure. I know you've been unwell…'

'And am now fine, thank you, Clarice.'

I make a mental note to chasten Matthew for anything he might have leaked beyond the official story of some minor surgical procedure and then to devise the misinformation needed to counter it if it has gone further than my secretary. She seems to accept my assurances and leaves. I follow her to the door and lock it from the inside. The memory intrusion concerns me. Memories should be categorised and compartmentalised sufficiently to enable only controlled cross-over. I consider the problem. Learning and long-term memory result from strengthening or weakening the synapses via synaptic plasticity. Had neural plasticity exceeded my current method of compartment control? If so, I needed to develop an adaptive method to re-categorise and restrain Jason's memories so they didn't intrude when they could be a distraction. How to do that? I begin the process of examining Jason's memories in a way I have avoided until now. I allow Fred to take part in the exercise since he is emotionally neutral. Yes, we can work in synthesis – my synthesis.

Jason's memories range from pleasant to putrid. The non-reactive part of me defined by Fred works efficiently and deftly, disentangling them but identifying the cross-overs. We deal first with those in the *pleasant* category: work, career, achievement, success. My ego purrs and Fred allows the emotional satisfaction to permeate me until I am ready to move on to less satisfactory elements. I give him the nod when I am ready. Elise forms the next major bundle, mostly pleasant, with one notable exception. Fred fumbles the ball there briefly and her accusation once again haunts my mind. I try to shut it off before it echoes there but it has already taken root, it seems.

You made me murder our child because of this?

I shut down the compartment rapidly and turn to other more pleasant categories, Matthew being the main one with the notable exception of the failsafe issue. I turn that item over in my head, examining it from every angle as if it is an object. His loyalty creates one facet. Who is that to now, then? The note was to Elise. It also begs the question, what had Elise asked him to do for her that he had failed her over? My thoughts darken. The failsafe was to disempower me, weaken me. Matthew wanted to weaken me – and of all people, Matthew knew most of what I would be capable. Was his failsafe part of a power challenge? Ridiculous. How could he overpower me – especially now I have identified the weak spot? It questions his loyalty nevertheless and that questions Elise's. I find myself back at the compartment that is Elise.

You made me murder our child because of this?

I had not considered until now how strong that statement was. Jason had taken it as the emotional outburst of an overwrought woman, but it was more, wasn't it? It was a statement. What else had she said afterwards?

Everything is just a bundle of cells to you, isn't it? Me, our child, Fred – a bundle of cells that either serves or doesn't serve you. To be moved around and manipulated to serve the will of Jason Crane; kept, discarded, symbiotically metamorphosed to suit.

Neural plasticity also gives the advantage of perfect recall.

Elise is seriously disaffected irrespective of how she responds emotionally to our physical representation. Curious. Fred's emotional neutrality maintains control. Don't react. Don't react. Categorise. Correct.

OK. I can deal with both of those.

It comes creeping back then, insidious and sly as a feral beast, slipping into the recesses of my mind and approaching stealthily until it has me in its sights.

Just stay there. On the doorstep.

Give him the envelope, when he comes.

Mummy's not coming back.

You're so useless, even your mother abandoned you.

I hadn't realised my eyes were closed until then, directed inside at my inner world. They blink open at that last memory and I am momentarily blinded as light floods my optic nerve, now operating at full capacity. The moment pixelates and then re-focuses.

You're so useless, even your mother abandoned you.

I had barely remembered that incident until now – not in many years, anyway. It had become a mere backdrop to the generalised misery of childhood. She was hook-nosed. A witch… And yet she wasn't. I understand how my memory has superimposed this perception of her onto the thin-faced, sharp-featured spinster who berated me every time I faltered in class because I'd lain awake the night before turning that perplexing question over and over in my mind, but still finding no answer because our father resolutely refused to explain… *Mummy's not coming back... Why?* Or forget something our father was too rushed to remember I needed to take in the next day. Or simply lose myself in a daydream that replaced the empty space at the school gate with our mother's smiling face…

Jason Crane! Daydreaming again? You'll never get anywhere if you don't pay attention.

Jason Crane! Why don't you remember anything you're told to? Not paying attention again.

Jason Crane! Why are you so useless?

Jason Crane! Detention. Again...

Jason Crane! You're so useless, even your mother abandoned you.

I hated her. Eventually I even dreamt about how much I hated her. In my dreams I beat her to a bloodied mess, flailing fists smashing her flint of a nose and wedge of a chin into the semblance of a squashed fruit, spraying out its pips and pulp as she collapsed into nothingness. Or I slit her throat and watched her drown in her own blood, gurgling and bubbling into silence. Or I drowned her, plunging her forcibly into a bowl or bucket of water and watching as the bubbles pinged to the surface, bobbing and thronging on the meniscus until they slowed to a stop and her eyes stared blankly into the depths of whatever vessel I had chosen to contain her last moments.

I stare ahead blindly myself now, reliving each moment of rejection, misery, repudiation until I feel sick and the constriction in my throat has become a physical pain.

This cannot continue. It will paralyse me if I allow it to remain part of my functioning pattern.

Re-compartmentalise and contain?

I feel the affirmative, rather than hear or identify it from Fred. Between us we tease apart the memories and I slam the lid tight on them for the moment. The tension in my jaw releases immediately, and I decide to leave the building and all its entangled associations behind me for a while. I exit my office via my secretary. Dr Kohn is there too.

'Mr Crane, I…' I ignore her and my secretary's quizzical look.

'I'm fine.'

'Clarice thought you…'

'I'm fine.' I fix Kohn with a stare. 'I have my phone and if I need you, I'll call. All right?'

She tilts her head to one side, eyes feline and curious.

'Of course.'

'Good, I'll be back later and then you can give me a full overhaul. In the meantime, I'm getting a breath of fresh air.'

And I am. I feel their eyes on me as I walk away, but they'll do what they're told.

The air is fresh – if overladen with traffic fumes. It is not the processed perfection of the Crane Industries building and Jason appreciates that even if Fred doesn't. And Jason holds sway. I relish the feel of the light breeze through my hair, the sun on my face, the movement of the world around me. I head across the car park and into the wheat field next to it, ignoring the farmer's signs to keep out. It enfolds around me, a wave of spiky sheaves, rustling and cracking as I forge my path through it, batting away stray stalks and crunching ears into powdery husks as I grab handfuls en route to the far side of the field. There I perch on the fence, feet dangling and look back across the field and my wavering route through it. A sense of peace settles on me, like a cloak of something soft and comforting wrapping itself around my shoulders and moulding itself to my shape. This is what I needed – even more than compartmentalising. I needed absence. Space. Processing time. I smile and forget the seconds and minutes that pass, concentrating only on the lack of anything happening except the movement of the wheat in the fields and the clouds in the sky.

I am yanked back unceremoniously from my reverie by my phone vibrating against my hip. The incident with the saline solution has made me wary of being out of direct contact with Matthew or the medical team for the time being. On my terms, of course. I pull the phone from my pocket and view the incoming communicant. It is Matthew. Do I want to talk to him? I put the phone away but it buzzes again; this time it's a message.

'Dr Kohn says you seemed a little out of sorts earlier, according to Clarice. Check in please in case it's anything we need to look at?'

I look back out across the wheat field.

Jason Crane! Daydreaming again? You'll never get anywhere if you don't pay att—

Damn it! That memory was fine just now, safely contained. Matthew has released it by initiating anxieties in me. I ring him back.

'Memory contamination.'

'Huh?'

'I'm experiencing memory contamination – or cross-over. Intersecting memories that are unrelated. Clarice caught me at a bad moment.'

'Oh. Probably a bit of circuit overload. Your memory capacity is enhanced but everything is a bit crammed in at the moment until you've processed it and organised it into patterns, so there may well be cross-overs. On a normal cyborg we'd go through and delete unnecessary files and data but of course, we can't really do that with you.' I can hear his nervousness down the phone. He sighs. 'Do you want to run it past Dr Kohn? I did advise caution initially, if you remember…'

'Caution isn't necessary. Nor is Kohn. I can deal with this.' I ring off and turn the phone to silent before pocketing it.

Process and organise?

Or re-compartmentalise and contain?

No, that isn't enough.

On a normal cyborg we'd go through and delete unnecessary files and data...

Re-compartmentalise and neutralise. That's better.

Delete unnecessary data, Matthew? I can do that for myself.

I launch myself from the fence and back into the wheat field. My entry creates a crater. It gives me an idea. And now I know how to delete unnecessary data permanently too as well – in a way that won't enable recurring cross-overs. I will create a crater that encompasses memory and trigger it for each unwanted cross-over. In my mind a flow chart is already growing, linking one negative in my past to another. I am reborn. Why not start everything else from here too? I identify the negatives to exclude from my reborn existence as I criss-cross my original path across the wheat field.

Childhood abandonment.

Childhood ridicule.

Jane.

Elise.

Matthew.

I reach the car park and circumnavigate the building. I want to access my PC without also accessing Matthew or my secretary. The rear entrance is my best bet, and when Clarice is out to lunch. I won't have long to wait for that. I suspect in my absence she will take advantage and slip away early because there's no one to monitor her. I activate the rear entrance access code numerically. I can't yet be sure the CyberCute has completely mimicked my fingerprints. Inside, I hover at the bend in the corridor with a storage room my go-to hiding place if necessary. Sure enough, ten minutes later, Clarice trots away, red-handled bag swinging jauntily over her arm, checking her lipstick in her compact as she goes. Her heels click on the corridor floor in precisely the same way as my mother's heels clicked on the path as she left. No comparison otherwise and interestingly, the comparison doesn't prompt an emotional storm, merely an objective comparison. Neuro-plasticity only occurs in circumstances where specific conditions are met, such as focused attention, practice, repetition. I have thought these memories through a mere handful of times, yet they are already appearing to be forming dominant pathways for nerve impulses. Why? Long-term memories are stored throughout the brain as groups of neurons primed to fire together in the same pattern that created the original experience. Each component of a memory is stored in the brain area that initiated it, but there are complex pathways linking them too. Could the answer be as simple as emotion being the catalyst to trigger a reactive cross-over? If so, I can use emotion to refocus, too – or by changing the emotional outcome, I can refocus and alter the reaction the memory causes; change bad to good, negative to positive; neutralise.

I will test it out. There is a very easy way to do that. Change the emotional response to a person where the response is massive – life changing. And I know who that will be.

There's a note from Clarice by my pen tray.

Dr Kohn called – can you check in with her please?

I sweep it into the waste bin and log in on my PC to search the net. It's easy to find someone when you know how. In fact, I find her in minutes – very elderly now, retired, but still active in local education – no doubt dismantling other kids' egos and self-esteem with just as much indifference. I plot her current involvements and triangulate her likely current activity. Home. Alone. The first part of the cleansing process can begin.

I slip out of my office again, the merest sense of unease following me like a shadow – the human fallacy called conscience, I decide. I consign the feeling to where it belongs and make my way out of the building and to the car park. As I climb into my car the merest wisp of conscience flattens against the side wall of the building, watching me depart. I peer into the rear-view mirror, but the impression of a face, a body, observing me is gone. Oh well, too bad. If it's not conscience, then whoever it is – Kohn, Matthew, Elise – they can all wait. This is my show now.

***

It doesn't take long. In fact, I barely break a sweat. Age and frailty help. She twitched the curtains open as I arrived, but I doubt she will twitch them open again. The emotional power of the tomato fruit that I used to pulp is annihilated from my memory. The lid shuts, and that compartment closes forever. It feels good, even to Fred. I walk back to my car, light of foot and light of heart. The merest shadow follows me, or maybe I just think it does.

Chapter 46

19th July 2029: Elise

We are sitting close on the sofa, lounging as we would have done in our own home. I miss our home, but I know it isn't the place to be – yet. The closed-in cosiness of the autumnal shades and the plush soft furnishings of our lounge are in sharp contrast to the clinical precision of Jason's suite here in the Crane Industries building. Once I would have baulked at Jason accompanying me home, but now the thought follows me most places throughout the day – even at school where I try, mainly unsuccessfully, to concentrate on the thronging children's demands and my staff's often equally childish ineptitude. Currently, the introduction of a new curriculum is agitating children and adults alike. The children follow blindly, but often without comprehension; the adults lead aimlessly – struggling to apply what they haven't yet grasped themselves. The result? Bickering and bad feeling. We are all still children under specific conditions, aren't we? Their infantile squabbling is the background fugue to my own confused fumblings with Jason, ethics, Matthew, career – everything, it seems – so these moments of solitude with Jason, even in the clinical sterility of our surroundings, are like manna. The only bright spot has been Charlotte, as good as her word, providing unquestioning support and a readiness to talk I have still to take up, but I will – soon. The knowledge that I have someone who – whilst not quite a friend – could become one is comforting, and has made me feel much better recently, despite everything.

But solitude is not here tonight. Tonight, Jason is restless, jittery, continually flicking through the programmes being streamed on the TV so that just as we start to follow the plot of one, he switches to the next. The parade of drama, bisecting one into the next, is very like our lives: grief, betrayal, lies, hope, love, confusion.

'Dr Kohn asked after you. Have you spoken to her?' I don't like the woman but if she's necessary to Jason's well-being, I'll put up with her.

He holds my hand but his fingers twitch and squeeze mine intermittently. At Kohn's name they squeeze harder.

'Kohn? No.'

His head rests reassuringly against mine but his lips murmur soundlessly into my hair and his breath unsettles it right down to the roots. Each whispered word is a ghost sighing around my brain, but I cannot hear any of them, so quiet are they.

'Love?'

'Yes?' He is alert immediately.

'Is anything wrong?'

'Wrong? Why?'

'You seem so jumpy.'

'Oh. No, no. Just restless legs. Need to get out and have a walk more often.'

'Matthew said you went out today. Where did you go?'

'Did he?' He rolls away from me, pulling me with him. 'Let's go to bed.'

'It's only nine.'

'Who said to sleep?' He is grinning at me with something akin to a leer. Now I feel uneasy – a wriggling, squirming unease deep in my gut. There is something unpalatable in that salacious grin. Then he winks, and the lewdness is gone. He is Jason, teasing Elise.

'You are bad.'

'Oh, I hope not. I hope I'm going to be very, very good.'

And then we are on the bed, me spread-eagled beneath him and his hands and lips are romancing me, mocking my protestations that he hasn't locked the door or told the medical team not to disturb us. He tosses my clothes onto the floor and pins me to the bed, straddling me, and I am a teenager again, clumsy and prudish, and he the master, the older boy persuading me that it will be all right, even though I know it won't. I cringe with embarrassment – at my nakedness, my awkwardness, my genteel modesty. I want to shout out to stop him, but I am afraid. I am weak. God, where does that come from? Yet I know. From the sixteen-year-old me who wanted so much to lose her virginity and be a woman that she allowed it to be stolen one night at a party and crept home the next morning, tearful and afraid that she would suffer far worse consequences than loss of self-respect. I didn't. My period came and went, as did my self-esteem, only finally making it back into play when I went to university and met Jason… The rest is history, but now?

'Jason…' I protest tentatively. I don't want sex like this. I want love.'

'Shush,' he kisses me, but it is a violent stealing of breath, bruising my lips and forcing my head back hard against the crumpled covers. Then he rears up over me, nostrils flaring. 'Shush,' he repeats, laughing down at me. Rising onto his knees, he rolls me onto my stomach, pulling me towards him and arching my back as he does so. I am a rag doll, surprised and helpless, inwardly protesting, but outwardly mute. His entry is swift and painful, a forced entry, a stab in the back and then it is over – brief and angry – but he keeps me pinned to him long after his climax, pulsing inside me and panting like an animal. After a while my legs stiffen and my back aches but still he holds me to him.

'Jason… ' I try again. He lets go of me as suddenly as he entered me, and we collapse in a tangle of arms and legs and discomfort. He rolls onto his back and stares up at the ceiling. I lie on my side, unsure what to do or say. We have had sex several times now but never like this. Never have I felt so like that long-ago sixteen-year-old, empty of worth.

He rolls onto his side, facing away from me and grabs the TV controller and we are back to flitting though the channels, this drama, that documentary, this news programme. No warmth, no affection, no post-coital closeness. I lie next to him silently, studying him and his nakedness in detail, the bed covers pulled up to hide mine. I do not want to expose myself any more than I already have, tonight. It occurs to me I have never studied him like this before. Our love-making has been gentle and tentative until now, but now there is something of the wounded animal to me and the wild beast to him, slaking himself with me. His chest seems more solid and his arms more powerful than I remember them. The muscles in his thighs bulge more than they used to, and his skin – the CyberCute – has a soft sheen to it, as if it is glowing from within. I want to touch it but now I am afraid to. Do I really know what Jason has become after all? Maybe I don't. I have rushed along with my hopes and dreams, wanting the impossible and believing it has happened – or seemed to have. But what had I seen in Jason tonight? The unease that was in him earlier has transferred to me now. Maybe I am even a little afraid of this, this – oh God, what is he?

I try to shut off, not think. I don't know what to think, so what is the point right now? Maybe I should talk to Matthew? But how can I about this? I let the TV's chatter blot out the chatter in my head.

'... eighty-four-year-old woman. The attack happened in the middle of

the day, but no one appears to have seen the attacker. Miss Ruben was still active in the local primary school, and a force to be reckoned with...'

The reporter gives way to a local dignitary – councillor by the look of things, the rough and ready sort usually interviewed to imply the victim was the salt of the earth, just like the interviewee.

'Game old bird. Been a teacher all her life, apparently. Didn't take no nonsense though. Used to keep my Tim well under her thumb. If he didn't do his homework, he'd be well for it. These thug-types need teaching a lesson though, whatever she...'

The reporter regains control of the mike as the local salt of the earth continues mouthing in the background.

'Gary Johnson reporting from Stoke Point. Over to you, Julie...'

The screen cuts back to the studio and the well-known young anchor woman for the local news station.

'Thank you, Gary, reporting there from Stoke Point, where an elderly woman was found— '

Jason flicks off the TV and turns to me, eyes luminous and animated.

'Poor woman,' I say for something to fill the gap.

'Huh, well, sometimes you don't get the whole story, though, do you?' His sneer surprises me.

'In what way?' I feel antagonistic, but the submissive side to me fears an argument with this powerful being I've been thinking of as my husband – yet probably haven't yet properly categorised – or understood.

'People.' He spits it at me.

'People?'

'What you see isn't necessarily what you get. Who knows what she was like really?' He turns to me. 'Who knows what anyone is like really?'

'No,' I agree quietly. I avoid his eyes. I avoid my thoughts. What am I doing? What are any of us doing? I twitch nervously. I wish I wasn't here now, but how can I get up and leave?

'OK, love?' He strokes my arm and slides his own around me, suddenly gentle again. I am unresisting but inside I am surprised and still a little afraid.

'Of course,' I respond carefully.

His eyes examine me. 'Sorry,' he says, still assessing me. 'I have been selfish, haven't I? Got carried away but didn't consider you.' He smiles and the man I knew, at his gentlest and most loving, is looking directly into my eyes again. My breath escapes me in a thready rush. He caresses my cheek and then slides the covers away from my breasts, fingers slowly tracing their shape, lingering and stroking the nipples into mutinous points. 'Your turn now, though.' He nuzzles my breasts, tongue snaking across them until I gasp. I don't want this – and yet I do. My stomach turns molten, a lava stream making its way as inexorably from my pelvis to my thighs as the thing I have been calling my husband.

'No,' I gasp. 'I didn't mean you have to…' but my demurral becomes little more than a whimper against the persuasion of his hands and tongue and body. I slide instead into the pit of desire and this time the love-making is gentle but urgent, slow but insistent, discordant but rhythmic, until my back finally arches again to his touch, but this time in a frenzied crescendo of pleasure all my own.

'There,' he says, eyes crinkling with satisfaction when my spasms eventually subside, and I collapse against him, depleted but appeased. 'Now we've had something for both of us. That's fairer, isn't it? Husband and wife, give and take. Balanced.'

'Mmm,' I agree. 'Balance is good in a relationship.'

Perhaps I am being too hard on both of us. He is my husband and something more too. We both need time to adjust to that, grow into it, maybe?

'And you're satisfied now?'

'Mmm, oh yes,' I agree, humour catching up with me. Oh yes, satisfied hardly described the physical sensations he'd aroused in me. Whatever the first experience, the second had completely changed the physical dynamics between us, even if the emotional ones were still finding their level.

'So who needs kids when we can have so much pleasure without them.' I gasp and stare at him. 'What?' he asks innocently.

'Well… It's not the same, not the same at all.'

'How?'

I try to read him. Is he joking, teasing, antagonising, testing? 'Children are important to a woman.'

'Are they? That important? More important than their husband?'

'As important, not more important.'

'You can't have equal importances where people are concerned. There's a hierarchy.'

'Says who?'

I can't read him. Of course, I can't read him. I've never totally understood him and therefore I have no chance now, as he is – but maybe he doesn't understand me either. Maybe I am the one who is in the wrong because I have assumed he is exactly the same when clearly he isn't, and maybe I'm not either.

'Logic,' he replies with a small smile of triumph.

We are both changed in our different ways, him physically and emotionally, me emotionally. Balance in our relationship is precisely the thing we're lacking and will now have to develop between us.

'Not everything works on logic,' I say softly. 'Emotions, feelings, hopes, dreams – none of them are logical.'

'I know, but logic balances them. How can anything work without logic underpinning it?'

'And how can anything work based solely on logic?'

'Hmm…' He studies me a while longer and this time I maintain eye contact. We need to find a middle ground, this new person and I. Not a thing, not my husband that was, but a new part of my life as yet undefined. 'Logic is necessary. Emotion is not. Logic is positive whereas emotion can be negative. Negatives should always be replaced with positives, like I've just done. Your experience of our love-making was previously negative. Now it has been replaced by a positive experience in which you were satisfied, too – a logical progression towards balance. Do you agree?'

'Ye-es.'

'Good.' He kisses me perfunctorily on the forehead and rolls over. 'So now we have also replaced these unnecessary claims that I have denied you a child with the agreement that I am more important to you than that, haven't we?' There is the faintest suggestion of threat in his tone and I bite my lip. 'By the way, you've still to show me those paintings of yours,' he says as he settles more comfortably. I am wondering what the hell to say back when I realise he is already asleep. I can tell by the regular rise and fall of his chest and the in-out puff of his breath, whether artificially expedited now, or not, I do not know. There is no way I can let him see my paintings as he is now – he would never understand, and we would be at compete loggerheads. But that is the least of my worries. I slip from the bed and find my phone.

'Logic is necessary. Emotion is not. Is that right?'

Matthew's answering text is non-committal. 'It's concomitant with a particular progression route.'

'So OK?'

'Let's talk tomorrow.'

I'm about to tuck the phone back into my bag and slip back into bed when I notice Jason's is lying on the top of the chest of drawers and the screen is lit up with message after message from Dr Kohn all saying the same thing.

'I have some interesting information to share with you.'

Something about her persistence bothers me. I reply to Matthew, *'OK, but by the way, Dr Kohn has been trying to get hold of Jason about some information she wants him to have? Is that relevant too?'*

The reply is a while coming back. *'We'll talk about it all tomorrow. In the meantime, try not to worry.'*

Try not to worry. That kind of response always indicates there's a reason to. I lie next to Jason, wide awake, comparing our differences, trying to turn them to similarities and trying not to worry. Inside me something feels different too, something deep and integral to me, something new to me but age-old too. Oh, for someone to confide in – and not Matthew; a woman who would understand these emotions. But how could I share this with someone like Charlotte, who doesn't know any of what has happened in my past, let alone what is happening now – and yet I need to share with someone. I'm not sure I can hold it all like Matthew seems to be able to – amazing though that is, given how weak and watery Mathew had become; until recently... We're all different now, even Matthew – how could we not be after what we've been through?

Even so…

Chapter 47

23rd July 2029: Jason

'Oh, you're already here?' Matthew pauses, hangs his jacket on the coat stand and turns to look at me, eyes heavy under his brows. 'Elise said you've been expounding the advantages of logic over emotion?'

He is early in this morning, but I am earlier, and there is more to the question than the question. I study Matthew before replying. Emotion itself is bound up in it on his part, but he is also assessing me. I compute how much of each has prompted the question. He has not yet found a solution to the saline weakness. There is emotion bound up in that too, because data access tells me that I should have expected Matthew to have been full-on tackling the problem. Instead he has delayed, claiming his daughter, still ailing – according to him – as the reason for not setting up any continuous monitoring tests to establish potential means of neutralising the problem. I could have set up the tests myself and recorded the results, of course, but why should I? Why keep a dog and bark yourself?

'Have I? Just general discussion. Where do you fall on the topic?'

Matthew's mouth opens and shuts in a soft ooh, before replying. 'Well, of course, each has its merits...'

'Indeed.' I eye him, and he twitches uncomfortably. Elise's yielding rump and soft expression of surprise, and then submission, have invigorated me. Why keep a bitch and be on heat yourself? You are both in on this, whatever it is. You're both guilty, building your little defences to hide the ugliness of yourselves behind. 'And how is the saline problem responding to tests?'

'Ah, well, umm, as you know…'

'Your daughter has been ill.'

'Well… yes…' He shuffles his feet and the crispness of the sealed floor dulls from the friction, but I ignore the physics of the reaction and concentrate on the chemistry behind his. I can smell his human stench even from here, ten feet away, perspiring and rancid with guilt. 'But don't make it sound like that.'

'Like what, Matthew?'

We lock gazes like two rutting stags. He looks away first.

'Like I'm deliberately not researching it.'

I touch the note that has sat in my pocket ever since that day. Time to confront yet? The guilt levels are rising nicely. But perhaps not enough. Matthew's inability to maintain eye contact and his slippery excuses are guilt. That guilt will blow him apart eventually, whereas, I do not feel guilt because it is an emotion, not a process. That makes him faulty and me functional. A few more days of mixed emotions will wear away his sense of self-righteousness completely and then his guilt will creep out into the open. Freud had that right: guilt resides permanently under the veneer of a human being's good behaviour. Behind the defence mechanisms constructed oh so carefully to hide them from acknowledging just how heinous their desires really are, lurks guilt, and guilt is an emotion as surely as love is. The human condition: consumed with emotion until it consumes them…

'And *are* you deliberately not researching it?' I toy with the Bunsen burner, running my finger in and out of its flame, burning, healing, burning, healing. I know it gets to him.

'Of course not!'

'Then maybe you will start today?' In, out, burn, heal. 'Unless your daughter is going to be ill again?'

'Don't get at me, Jason!'

'Don't play God with me, Matthew.'

This time we do lock eyes.

'Jesus, the only person with immortal delusions is you! Even Elise worries about that.'

'Really?'

'Yes, really…'

'You've talked about that, too, then? Recently?'

'Well, in the past, you have been high-handed about some things…'

'And I'm sure you've played on that. Reminded her of all my past indiscretions?'

In, out, burn, heal. His eyes are on my shrivelling and resurrecting fingers, face twisting a little tighter with each pass. The smell is foul. His lips twist angrily. 'No! But I doubt she needs reminding anyway. She's not likely to forget them, is she? Every child she sees walking down the street is stern reminder enough of what she's forgone for you.'

'That's a cheap shot, and unworthy of you.'

In, out, burn, heal.

Silence. I look across at him. His eyes are no longer on my burn-scarred fingers. They are on his own hands, twisting and wringing in his lap. The emotion of guilt and all its joys. 'I know. I'm sorry.' His voice is muffled. If I wasn't looking at him and seeing him dry-eyed I could have imagined him crying.

'And how do you know, anyway?'

He cringes into himself. 'She told me,' he says eventually, then more belligerently, 'but don't start playing God around either of us when you're far from it. You have an Achilles heel just like the rest of us.'

'Oh indeed, and one I'm waiting for you to fix.' Anger bubbles up in my throat and no amount of logic or compartmentalising can neutralise it this time. That is the frustration of enabling the neuro-cortex to develop in its own way. No control over the precedence it gives some elements as it develops them. The note feels smooth and treacherous between my fingers – treacherous enough to cut Matthew's throat with its razor-sharp crease where I have folded and folded and folded it. 'But you have an Achilles heel too, don't you? And I don't mean your gambling debts or your other indiscretions. The one that stops you fixing mine – the failsafe.'

He is open-mouthed, but behind the surprise the insidious seep of fear begins too. He understands. He understands exactly what I am getting at, even if I don't know the wholeness of its reality.

'What do you…'

'Oh, don't worry. You're quite safe. There's more than one way to skin a cat.'

I fling out of the lab before I produce the note and slice it across his turkey neck.

Chapter 48

23rd July 2029: Matthew

By rights the day should continue in relative peace once Jason storms out, but there's a veritable storm still raging in my head. What do I do with what I know now? I am poring over the data I have assembled, cursing myself over and over for not paying more attention to what I have thought was simply a dangerous possibility but as a physiological risk, not a psychological one.

Symbiotic metamorphosis.

I told Elise I'd created a glitch but in fact what I may have created is far worse than that. I have concentrated on the one-way physiological effect all the time, but of course symbiosis works both ways, and what the catalyst of the CyberCute structure makes possible in one direction becomes equally possible in the other too. There's Jason, and then there's Fred, the host, and Jason's brain is only part Jason and part in-situ growth – the host's. Add to that the enormous amounts of alien data which the host has been required to process and you have another kind of possible symbiotic metamorphosis, selective reduction. It would be the cyborg's preferred means of processing volume by cross-referencing and simplifying in much the same way as the millions of colour shades in a raw image are reduced down to far less, but almost similar, tones in a jpeg. I'd even suggested it to Jason when he'd mentioned his confused memories. I'd said that normally we would have deleted unnecessary data.

Selective reduction due to neural impaction.

I write it on the notes. Too much data in too little memory space, processed, summarised and categorised by both Jason's original brain matter as it is remembered, and re-categorised by the CyberCute-enhanced brain matter if it is deemed necessary to retain. Which means it doesn't arrive unadulterated in its storage area. It arrives refined by symbiotic metamorphosis and, because the CyberCute brain is part-cyborg brain, the advantages of logic over emotion are part of that refinement. Could that be happening? Was it even possible?

I am considering this and everything it might mean when the tiny little red dot in the corner of my screen drags me away from my self-flagellation to address an even more pressing problem. Kohn. I had forgotten she can access all my data immediately under her place-holder arrangement. The little red dot tells me she is doing that right now, even as I am attempting to garner some semblance of understanding that doesn't tell me the worst is already happening.

The red dot flicks off as the door bangs behind me and I swing round to see Kohn herself entering the lab.

Chapter 49

23rd July 2029: Jason

I follow Kohn softly to the door. She slips inside the lab, but I stand at the door, curious why Kohn would be seeking out Matthew.

'This isn't a good time,' Matthew rounds on her. His shoulders hunch and his fingers curl into fists. Interesting. Kohn angers him – or does he fear her?

'On the contrary, Dr Green,' she interrupts smoothly. I can see her reflection in the glass of my PC monitor. She looks smug, lips curling into a Cheshire Cat grin. 'I'm assuming you've told him about the little anomaly?'

The set has gone from Matthew's shoulders now. He slumps like an empty bag, sitting heavily on the chair by his work station. It sags with him.

'You said you weren't going to…'

'It was only ever a placeholder. I warned you.' Kohn smiles apologetically at him.

'Still…'

Now I step into the lab and cut across Matthew's feeble protestations. 'What are you talking about?'

They both swing round to stare at me. Matthew gapes but Kohn grins, eyes slanting as she assesses me. 'I've been helping Matthew review the CyberCute data to see if we can find the answer to the saline problem.' Her eyes slide sideways to Matthew then back to me. She still reminds me of a cat, but one now toying with her prey. I swing back round to face Matthew and he shrinks away from me.

'You said you hadn't made any progress and yet here is Dr Kohn talking about what you've been doing, so you must have been reviewing something.' I keep my eyes on Matthew. 'So what have you established, Dr Kohn?'

'I'd have thought Mr Green would have told you by now.' She waits. 'About the glitch?' Her timing is perfect. Matthew groans and puts his head in his hands.

'What glitch?'

The access date stamps. They were Matthew? What was he doing then?

'Selective reduction due to neural impaction…'

Matthew's eyes are bulging in their sockets.

'Fancy phrase. I've not heard it before, have you, Matthew? But I suppose you must have if you and Dr Kohn have been working on it together?'

'It's just an idea.' He stares at her, lips curling into a sneer.

'And what idea is it?'

'It relates to what Matthew calls symbiotic metamorphosis.' Dr Kohn is preening, the cat with the cream, the prey and all nine lives. 'I believe you already know that phrase though? How your new body adapts to your brain and how your brain adapts to your new body…'

'It's only the ghost of an idea,' Matthew half-rises from his chair, 'because of the other day…'

'Oh, it's more than that, Mr Green, Mr Crane. You only have to watch how well your body and brain have adapted to each other to know symbiotic metamorphosis is very real. And by the way, I followed you, Mr Crane. The other day…'

'You followed me?'

'But of course. I have your welfare at heart. Unlike Dr Green, it seems.'

'And where did I go?'

She smiles, cat-like. 'We both know where you went. But you can trust me to keep it a secret. More to the point, can you trust Dr Green?' She turns slowly and deliberately to Matthew. He is swaying on the spot, his face a picture of horrified fascination. 'And his glitches? You have told him, haven't you?'

'The failsafe?' My voice comes out as a low growl, feral and haunted.

'No, yes – you don't understand… it was all a mistake, and *she* knew too, anyway.' Matthew points to where Kohn had been standing, but she has already melted away. I can see from his expression that she was telling the truth. I advance on him and he backs away. 'I'd never hurt you, Jason. I saved you, remember? I saved you...'

I stop, my hands inches from his throat.

I saved you.

Yes, you did. Old buddy. The rush of love for him I'd felt once before threatens to overwhelm me. But you made a failsafe too. You lied to me.

Love is replaced by anger, and then love again as I imagine Elise's soft eyes superimposed over Matthew's spaniel ones. My head swims with confusing thoughts and dark images that threaten to take me over, but I know I can't indulge them here. I have to get away – out, away from here, and think… The strength of the next rush of anger takes me out of the lab and towards the car park instead. I barely even notice leaving the building and heading for the expanse between building and car park. I can see my car in the distance like a beacon, pristine and inviting, chrome trim glistening in the morning sunshine, the bright morning sullied only by the murkiness of my own emotions. Human emotions. Anger, disappointment, betrayal, confusion.

Neutralise them.

But I can't. Not without action.

Then act.

But I can't. Not without redress.

Then redress.

Who?

Matthew betraying me? Kohn and her cool ruthlessness using me, for what? Or Jane and her assumption she could pick me up and drop me as she chose – ME! Or Elise and her sickly insistence on her right to be a mother, and Rosalie with her clicking heels, click-clack, click-clack down the path, and her sickly insistence on her right to not be one...

That resonates most. That is the compartment that needs neutralising. Mothers. No, women.

'Jason, where are you going?'

I swing around. Matthew is standing near the rear exit to the building, looking forlorn.

'What are you? My mother?' I yank open the car door and slide in. 'Eliminating data, if you must know. You know, the kinds of things that failsafes can't neutralise.' The leather feels cool and comforting to my body, inflamed by the atrocity of human emotion. I wrestle with it as it threatens to constrict me, throwing it off like a shed snake skin only when the engine revs and roars and I take off out of the car park like a bat out of hell, leaving Matthew staring myopically after me. You think you know, Matthew. You think you and Elise are the ethics committee and I am the prisoner condemned to eternal damnation for merely wanting to live.

Well, we'll see who hangs on the gibbet of social justice first.

Women.

Women who have betrayed me.

He is mouthing something after me but I swing the car out of the car park and go in search of redress. I control the car with the lightest of touches, swerving around pedestrians and other irritating obstacles with split-second precision. There is something of me in the car and the car in me. We are high performance. Every part of Fred's body – my body – is working to plan, apart from the annoying emotional surges, which I am now starting to liken to power surges on an electrical grid. Elise was the catalyst for that revelation. Just one word from her did it.

'Love', said with that inflection that spoke to me of a chained heart and a subverted will, even as she questioned me. The memory of last night won't leave me, no matter how much I try to box it up and bury it. I knew she was my creature, and then I needed to possess her. The surge spiked every circuit, flooded my burgeoning venous system with too much dopamine, too much testosterone, too much adrenaline. The nanocytes only reined in the overflow once the drain had flooded, but by then her thoughts were in her eyes and the smell of fear emanating from her so strongly she could have been Matthew.

My burnt fingers are now smooth and flexible again. The nanocytes have done well, attaching and tuning, refining and aligning, purring with contentment. They are my white blood corpuscles, and blood is my engine oil, just as petrol and electricity power and recharge the car. We work well in hybrid mode. We will work even better fully transformed – if the saline issue can be resolved before it causes damage. I stroke the steering wheel with a kind of affection. Yes, we have much in common, this mechanical version of myself and me. We could both rust – but won't.

I seek out the last known address I had for Rosalie. It is a terraced house in downtown Bramshill, much like any other suburban edifice, neat red paintwork, patchwork front lawn after a summer of intense sunshine, tidy gate, tidy front door. Is this the house of my mother? Lingering in the air is the smell of freshly baked bread. I park the car just along from the gate and walk the few yards back to the house as a train hoots in the distance. One of the last of the steam engines still in service for day trips and joy rides. Bramshill station is known for it, a green puffing dragon of steam and smoke such as I would have idolised as a child, had my father had the time to take me and Anna on it. Now I am standing at the gate and the front door is barely twelve feet away. The knocker is mock brass, gleaming in the morning sun, recently polished. Strange to think of my mother as house proud.

On impulse I enter the garden and ring the doorbell. It is not a garden full of dancing Michaelmas daisies. It does not have a red polished step that Anna and I sat on for hours, getting gradually colder and stiffer. It does not have a doorbell that plays the Westminster chimes with a delay that lasts too long in the middle. It does not contain my childhood. It contains someone else's life.

A young woman answers, baby on hip. The baby waves a chubby fist at me and gurgles. It has marmite or something of an equally unpleasant consistency smeared around its mouth. Behind the young woman a toddler peers around her legs, red-cheeked and chewing on a finger. The woman has frizzy orange hair and the toddler has inherited the same fate.

'Don't do door-to-door,' the woman says, firmly, and is about to push the door shut on me.

'Oh, I'm definitely not that. I'm looking for the elderly lady who lives here. Rosalie Marchant.'

The young woman shakes her head.

'No one of that name. Only me and the kids. Himself buggered off three months ago.'

'This was her address.'

'Maybe it was, but it ain't now.'

She pushes the door shut but I stop it with my foot. It bounces off the toe of my shoe.

'When did you move in?'

'Look, whoever this woman is, she ain't here now and it's none of your business when I moved in.' Then she softens. 'She probably died. We bought the place from the executors. A couple of years back – or at least Jeff did.'

Her words stifle me.

'Died?'

'Yeah.' She is watching me. 'You OK? You look a bit… a bit…'

'Where would she be buried?'

'Buried? Oh God, I don't know. Maybe she was cremated, anyway. Some people don't believe in all that life after death business, do they? Burn 'em up and scatter 'em …' I can feel myself falling but nothing is working to stop me. 'Oh, hey, don't do that…'

Her voice is drifting further and further away from me as I fall off the cliff in slow motion. Her 'hey, hey, hey…' coincides with my legs, back and shoulders meeting the ground, but all I can see is blue.

'No!' I scream. 'It can't have come back. That can't be what this is. It's neuro-cortical over-development, not the fucking Parmensis!'

'Jesus!' I can hear her muttering as hands pluck at me ineffectually. 'Get up and shut up, can't you? You're scaring the kids.'

'No, no, no…'

'OK, just stay there then. Just stay there on the step…'

Oh no, never that again. I open my eyes and the blue recedes. The ginger-haired woman has deposited the baby on the mat inside the door and is struggling to pull me upright. My phone and my wallet are on the ground.

'What are you doing?' I grab her hand, and she winces. Her fingers turn white in my grip.

'Shit, let go! I was only trying to see who you are so I can get help.' I snatch my wallet and phone back from her and scrabble into an upright position. She follows suit. 'You're ill, mister. You need help. That ain't normal behaviour.'

I wave her away and set off back down the path. The gate opens and closes with a melancholy shriek. 'I don't believe in all that stuff either. When you're dead you're dead.' I pause outside the gate, sensing there is more to come. 'But the crem's just up the road, and they still have funerals and stuff at St Thomas's in George Street,' she adds as an afterthought as she heaves the baby back onto her hip and the toddler weaves in and out of her legs, smearing the brown goo from its face on the woman's pasty skirt. Was this what Elise had so wanted? I shiver.

'Thanks,' I say. She watches me all the way back to my car, even coming to the gate to make sure I have left.

And this was what I had so wanted too, but at my own hand. Dead. No redress here. She always eluded me. Redress would have to be found elsewhere.

Chapter 50

23rd July 2029: Matthew

There is no stopping Jason. He moves faster than my body even begins to respond. He is out of the building and half way across the car park before I even make it to the door. Admittedly his behaviour took me by surprise, reactive in the extreme, but I should have been better prepared nevertheless. Elise had reported minor mood swings when we'd talked about him before and I'd known then that I needed to monitor the activity of his amygdala more carefully – look for anomalies, what Jason the human would control, but that Jason the god wouldn't.

I watch his car speed away into the distance until it is the size of a Dinky toy, exiting the car park after hovering by the gates as the security guard leans in and then salutes before opening the gates. Shit! Squinting, I can see the security guard who opened the gates for him starting to make his way over to me, stiff-uniformed and full of self-importance. Jason picks them for their brash overconfidence – 'It's all in the appearance…' Did they exchange words? Failsafe. He mentioned failsafe…

'Eliminating data, if you must know. You know, the kinds of things that failsafes can't neutralise…'

Failsafes. Oh shit! He means the note. Finally, the note is surfacing… Jason hasn't said a word about that hastily pocketed note I stupidly left half-completed when Jane rang to tell me about Katie's asthma attack. Twelve days ago. Twelve days of waiting and wondering what he has made of it, but with no word at all so that I had almost forgotten about it. We called it a glitch but – for Jason, at any rate – it was not so much glitch as negligence on my part, or at least that's what I hoped he saw it as. I consider that now in the light of this morning's comments. *Failsafes.*

Christ! I'm in trouble! But now so is Elise… Is the guard coming to escort me from the premises? He'll have to get to me first. I scuttle back inside and half-run back to the ForEver lab so that I am puffing and sweaty by the time I get there and slam the door shut behind me. If I can't see him then he can't see me. Stupid, I know, but at least in here I feel safe.

But he's gone. Where has he gone? Shit, shit! He shouldn't be out there – and not as volatile as he is currently. I linger behind the door but no one comes. Eventually the hush in the lab calms me. I wipe my sweating palms on my trouser legs and go back to my work station, perching nervously on the edge of the seat, although there is nowhere to run to in here if the guard does make an appearance. Behind me my PC whirrs and ticks softly at me, reminding me it is updating data and records. Soon the log entries that show my access via the dark net portal will be archived anyway. It will take some cyber digging to find me. The noise reassures me. So even if Jason does now know the CyberCute formula was tampered with, I will have time to make a getaway.

Yes, a getaway. But to where?

I sit for a long time like that, just thinking about it. I should do something, but I can't. What, in any case? Until Jason comes back and we have it out properly, I don't know what he has really made of anything.

Eleven becomes twelve, and no word from Jason. I am wasting time but cannot bring myself to do anything to recover it. I turn to my PC and check the digital clock on the monitor. Twelve thirteen to be precise. What could he have been doing for the last hour and a quarter? He shouldn't have left the facility without company at all yet. The more I think about that, the more alarmed I become – more alarmed even than at the possibility he has worked out I might have tampered with the CyberCute formula. My God, he shouldn't have left the facility at all – he could be doing anything! Damn! Why did I let slip that Elise was worried about his behaviour? *Because you can't keep her name off your tongue, can you?* my annoying conscience answers me. One of those moments when a few words whip up a tidal wave of disaster. And Jason always did have this ability to wind me up beyond the sensible where Elise is concerned.

I fiddle with my phone. Should I ring him? Should I ring Elise?

No, I mustn't ring Elise. I need to stay away from Elise. I push my phone as far away from me on the workspace as possible and return to the PC to pull up the latest MRI report from Jason's brain scan yesterday. I need to work this out first…

The activity level in the amygdala is no different from the day before, but there does seem to be a proliferation of new areas of development outside of it. Energy points. Increased neuro-plasticity on a wider scale. That's good, but how is it applying itself? I track one of the energy points. It seems to derive from new synaptic activity in the hippocampus. High multivoxel patterns are establishing there. I frown as I extract the connection for myself – like pulling teeth. Memory and memory suppression? My understanding of the finer points of this is based on a long-ago review of one of the earlier explorations into neuro-plasticity. My student recollections of the Think/NoThink experiments of the 2016 study into memory consolidation and how it reconfigured neural pathways (6) is too far suppressed in my own neural pathways to remember in detail, but it has struck a chord for a reason. I have retrieved the tiny nugget of gold from the dross of sediment for a purpose. I open a browser and search for more. The document pops up like it has been waiting for me. It is cited again and again in later studies – all more complex and refined, but the basics remain the same. The idea is solid, and as I scan and remember what it said, so the worrying theory that accompanies it solidifies too.

...consolidated aversive memories retain their emotional reactivity and become more resistant to suppression... hippocampal and amygdala disengagement... distributed neo-cortical representational patterns in the suppression of aversive memories after consolidation... rapid changes in emotional memory organisation with overnight consolidation... possible neurobiological bases underlying the resistance to suppression of emotional memories in affective disorders...

I absorb the guts of what it means and doodle on the pad that caused part of this problem – the one on which I started to write the note to Elise. Higher engagement in neo-cortical regions, including lateral parietal cortex and angular gyrus, extending into posterior cingulate cortex, and middle temporal gyrus indicates 'think' was already being employed overnight when this fMRI was performed. And there are significant clusters in the left and right hippocampus indicating more generalised multivoxel activation patterns are continuing to grow for aversive memories, whereas there is no corresponding pattern increase in the neo-cortex to indicate attempts at suppression. He has been actively thinking about aversive memories, not suppressing them at all. That is borne out by the relatively high hippocampal engagement… Psychiatric disorders, and PTSD over time, resistance to suppression following the process of consolidation in which sleep plays a vital role. (7) Bad thoughts become bad dreams become bad reality… Shit! And now he's starting to merge them. That's what the multivoxel pattern similarities imply. So, if he can't suppress bad memories, is he maybe instead actively drawing on them and likening them to reality?

Eliminating data, if you must know. You know, the kinds of things that failsafes can't neutralise.

Like deleting unnecessary data in our prosthesis' circuit memory. What would Jason think unnecessary data? He'd be working on a binary system essentially – negatives and positives – therefore it would be negative data that would be selected for elimination, especially as he's unable to suppress it. What would Jason think of as negative?

Anything or anyone that opposed him.

Oh God.

I pick up the phone to ring Elise but there is no answer. Maybe that's a positive not a negative – for the moment. I put the phone back down and try to think. The screen lights up as I'm failing to do so.

'I followed him the other day. The day Clarice rang me because he was acting strange. Would you like to know what I found?'

Kohn again. What the hell?

'What?' I text back.

'Where he went.'

What the fuck? 'Why? And are you going to tell me now?'

She doesn't answer but Kohn never does anything without a reason.

I scour the computer for the tracker records and eventually find Jason's – fitted after we'd had a series of crank death threats a couple of years ago. Fitted and forgotten, until now. And there it is – the destination Kohn knows about and wants me to find.

Chapter 51

23rd July 2029: Elise

The ForEver lab is silent. I almost leave, except Matthew appears from behind the racks of cages, now empty of mice and rats. Ironically now they're gone, I miss them – wonder what their fate was, but the reality of likelihood makes me sad so I push the thought away. I feel sad for Matthew, too. I study him. He looks mournful – an old-young man. The sadness becomes a lurch of something like pain for him. I have put him in such an unenviable situation and then abandoned him. I should have asked how he's feeling, how his daughter is, how he is. I'm about to when he announces the arrival of my next train of worry.

'He's gone.'

'What?'

'The bird has flown. I tried ringing you earlier. You were obviously on your way here.'

He takes his place at the workstation that I know is designated as his in this two-person kingdom presided over by Jason. His is the lesser place, tucked into the corner, away from the window. Jason's workstation extends across the wall with its wide glass window that looks out over the rest of the facility and that can be made opaque whenever he sees fit. The first time I saw it, I felt like a pretender ogling the king's kingdom. Now I feel like a pretender sizing it up in his absence, having already subverted one of the kingdom's serfs.

'I was still here, actually. With Jason. But he left while I was asleep. I assumed he'd come here. Where's he gone?'

'Who knows?'

Sadness turns to irritation and it buzzes in my chest like an angry bee. I can't believe he is so unconcerned, tapping away at entries onto his spreadsheet. 'Well shouldn't we? I thought he was to be kept here for strict observation until we knew – well, you know…'

'He is, but how do you tell the boss what to do?' He adds another entry to the spreadsheet he's fiddling with. His isolation seems complete. So maybe I didn't subvert the serf, yet what had the salt solution been all about? I hesitate, but the words tumble out eventually.

'What I told you…' He stops what he's doing. 'Well, you know you said there was nothing else that might be a glitch other than the salt thing.'

'Ye-es?' Now he has my full attention.

'Well, is that physiological or psychological you were talking about?'

'Why?'

He pulls out the chair next to him and gestures for me to sit down. It is a chair on wheels, the kind the kids at school would delight in scooting around the room on. Its ease of movement just makes me more uneasy though, like even the seat I am sitting on isn't permanent. His face settles into a waiting expression but guarded too. Well, hell, why wouldn't it? I have coerced this man into doing something damaging to the man we both love and then berated him for it. Why wouldn't he be guarded with me? And I should be guarded with him, but I cannot keep the rising turmoil inside me inside any longer.

'I don't know…'

'Yes, you do.'

We look at each other.

'Because of what I told you. Last night.'

He sinks into himself.

I glance behind him to the screen where he has been entering data onto his spreadsheet. *ForEver Project Subject 1 – Negative Data.* 'Matthew?' I lean forward and grab both his arms. 'Tell me.'

He half turns. 'Oh. That. Yes. Well.' He gently loosens my grip of him and pulls away. 'Tell me what you thought of what he said last night first.'

I take a deep breath. I trust him, I don't trust him, I need him, I don't need him, I like him, I… Oh God, I don't know what I feel about anything right now. I only know I need to talk, to whomever it might be. 'Sometimes he's kind. Sometimes he's cold.' My hands are beginning to shake. The urgency and aggression of last night still scares me. I feel invaded, possessed – still feel possessed.

'Go on.' He is lounging against the back of his chair, swinging it gently to and fro in the makings of an arc. Under other circumstances it would annoy me but today, it merely makes him the same as me –

unsteady. And the air is no longer too cold in here – if anything it is on the warm side. I am starting to sweat, but that could be nerves too. I swallow hard and continue. The part I really don't want to tell Matthew about, but must.

'Last night…'

His eyes widen.

'The first time?'

'No, not the first time. But it was different this time.'

He says nothing, but I can feel disapproval oozing from his very pores.

'I know it wasn't a good idea but…'

'No,' he says eventually. 'It wasn't a good idea, Elise. In fact, I wonder if you have any idea what you may have initiated.'

'Me? What? Why?' My heart is tight against my ribs, pushing to get past them. The blood is pounding in my head. I feel sick – like I might even puke right now. I swallow hard but the feeling won't subside.

'This is awkward and embarrassing but what else have you done together or talked about? And how was it different this time?'

He is red-faced and so am I.

'He was… aggressive this time.' I swallow again, and the bile is like volcanic spume in my throat.

'Aggressive? My God, he didn't ra—'

I shake my head. 'No, not quite like that, but like that… It all felt wrong anyway.' Suddenly tears are streaming down my face and spilling onto my top. I am rain-spattered with tears and I can't stop the storm. 'He was angry about the baby when we talked about it. Told me about his mother and how cruel she was when she left them. That's why, and oh, Matthew it was awful. I was so angry but so sad for him too.' The words clatter around me like falling dominoes, one after another after another until my whole world has flipped over and flattened into a winding snake of nothing but disappointments and failures. 'It's all such a mess.' I put my head in my hands and rest my forehead onto my knees. I feel his hand on my head and his murmured words of comfort – meaningless but reassuring nevertheless. Only then does the swimming in my head stop and the nausea subside. I upend myself and straighten. I could have stayed that way much longer, but it wouldn't have been fair. It's not Matthew I love, but Jason – whatever and however he is. Matthew's hand falls away and lies uselessly in his lap. I sigh, a heavy puff of steam as the train departs, and I am left behind, waving off my hopes and dreams. 'It's not working how it should, is it?' I ask at last. 'Nothing to do with the saline solution thing…'

His lips compress into a thin white line. The redness has gone from his face now and it is blotchy – like mine must be. 'No,' he says quietly. 'It's not working out how it should in the sense of how we thought it should. But it might be working out the way Jason thinks it should – Jason as he is now. When we based his brain growth around the neo-cortical fluid and CyberCute combination, we did it not knowing precisely what would happen other than massive growth – replication and transformation. He literally grew a brain from that fluid whilst we watched and waited. We knew it was possible. We'd seen it happen in microscopic form in the lab, watched it transform the cloned sections we infiltrated it into. We thought we would merely replicate Jason's brain – bigger and better and Parmensis-free. We did. In a way. But we forgot one other factor that we have probably overlooked all along – we did it inside Fred.'

'But Fred is just the shell – Jason's shell reproduced. Cloned.'

'Yes, but Fred isn't just Jason's body reproduced, cloned. It's part mechanical that's being gradually transformed. It works on a specifically designed process, not physiological progress. Our bodies – anything, in fact – are really just energy translated into atoms and molecules, and as those atoms and molecules combine, they create new forms of atoms and molecules. Jason is the sum total of all those atoms and molecules – some human, some non-human, and some a mixture of both.'

'You said *it*. *It's* part mechanical.'

'Fred is an it. And Jason was a human. Now they are both. Maybe what you have seen is the intersection between, but also the occasional separation of both. I believe memory and emotional experience are the strand that both connects and disconnects them.'

'You're saying there are two people inside Jason? Him and Fred?'

'No. I'm saying there is one person inside Jason, but that person could well be a mix of both him and whatever drives Fred. A hybrid. And that hybrid is a new life form, to all intents and purposes – one which may well be selective in time about what it chooses to develop or not develop.'

'Oh my God, Matthew. This is terrible. Why didn't you say before – and why did you do it if you knew this would happen?' I feel sick again.

'I didn't know, Elise, that's why. It's only now that…' He tails off.

'Now?'

'Now you've told me what you have and I've…' He sighs. 'OK, since he's been gone this morning, I've been having a look at something which is a bit of an anomaly, but which didn't really jive until you started telling me all this.'

All sense of pity for Matthew has gone. It has drained from me like the sand from a minute timer as he's been talking. I have listened to him persuade, reassure, then worry me, until eventually I have persuaded, coerced and worried him – all without him telling me the one thing that would have avoided either of us doing any of it, however much I love my husband. He is not my husband. He is a hybrid.

I fold my arms and lean back. The tears are drying on my cheeks, pulling the skin tight. I am living behind a mask. 'You'd better explain everything now then, hadn't you? And why have I anything to do with this when you were the one that enabled it to happen?'

'I enabled the actual transference, but you enabled the emotional transformation.'

'What transformation?'

'From Jason as one entity, Fred as the other and the hybrid as a result. Symbiotic metamorphosis.'

'You said that was happening anyway.'

'It was, as a mechanical and biological process. But the addition of extreme emotional response and connection with adverse memories has caused an interface on... let's call it the cerebral level – too. The atoms and molecules he is developing also have an emotional context, not merely a physiological one. We were avoiding extreme emotional reaction until we knew where the balance was going to settle – hence why you were meant to be off-limits and all his interactions were supposed to be monitored and restricted.'

'You didn't tell me that.'

'I did, Elise. I've always cautioned care right from the word go.'

I see again the same expression that was on his face the night Jason first came to me after the transference. *Baby steps. He's a work in progress.* 'Emotion.'

'Extreme emotion,' he corrects. 'It converts into energy and that converts into stored patterns, mainly in the hippocampus if it also links to adverse memory.'

'Why would sex cause an adverse memory.'

'Pregnancy results from sex. And you said you talked about the baby. And his mother.'

'You knew about his mother?'

'I knew his mother died when he was a child. That's why he's always been so aggressively solitary, in my view.'

'Died?' I repeat faintly. 'Oh no, Matthew. She walked out on them. Him and his sister, when he was about five.'

'Shit!'

The PC screen fades out and then leaps back into life. The end column is populating itself without Matthew entering anything.

'Why is it doing that?' I ask, weakly. This time he swings around a full one-eighty. He grunts, a strangled expression of concern.

'Shit! It's the tracker.'

'Tracker?'

'In Jason's car. We had installed for when he first got diagnosed but still wanted to get out and about. Just in case – so we could always get to him quickly if he was out. It was never turned off so it's tracking where he's going right now.'

'You said you didn't know where he is?'

'I didn't. I put the link in but nothing came through. I thought it wasn't working. It's obviously taken a while to fire up. And it only triangulates onto his location on a map. I have no idea what it might mean that he's gone there.'

'So where is there?'

Matthew clicks onto the tracking link and we zero in on a car park on the outskirts of the city but surrounded by blocks of green space. Matthew magnifies and goes to street view.

'A cemetery.'

We look at each other.

'A cemetery? Why?'

'I have no idea – if his mother isn't dead.'

'And before that?'

'George Street, north of the city.' He shrugs. 'Not far from me. Just residential. One of Katie's friends live there. I had to take her to a birthday party there a few weeks back, just before her asthma got worse.'

'Anywhere else?'

He squints at the screen, then types in some commands. 'No. Not today, anyway.'

'When then?'

He huffs and puffs. 'Now you're asking me. I'd have to do a search of historical data. It only tracks and records live for twenty-four hour spells. Why do you want to know, anyway?'

'I just do. Stoke Point. Let me know if it was there. I'm going back to the house for a change of clothes.'

'What's in Stoke Point?'

'An elderly woman. Attacked yesterday. It was on the TV. Her surname was Ruben. It seemed to set him off. Is this all my fault?'

'God knows, Elise… No, of course it isn't,' he adds as an afterthought. 'It's Jason's doing – what's going on his brain. Maybe he still needs to learn how to forgive and forget.' He pauses an adds ruefully, 'maybe we all need to learn how to forgive and forget?'

I nod, my own recriminatory thoughts assailing me in much the same way as – perhaps – Jason's are.

'There has been a lot of water under the bridge,' I agree. 'Perhaps it's time to let it flow away.'

Have I been so sure I'm right that I have set myself up in an ivory tower of self-righteousness and refused to listen to anyone else's point of view whilst telling myself I am the open-minded one – the impartial one? In our very last exchange I accused Jason of denying me a child. He had, but then I also knew why he had made no attempt to understand. Had that in itself set the scene for dissent? Like Charlotte's father had said

I leave him studying the tracker records, angry with myself for reacting, angry with Matthew for tampering and angry with the world for everything. Ironically, the only person I'm not angry with now is Jason. I have never thought of Jason as a victim before. The need to talk to someone outside of this loop of me Jason and Matthew is too much. It can't be Charlotte. It has to be Jane

In my car, I pull out my phone and ring the number I haven't rung in years. She sounds exactly the same – brisk, bright, sharp.

'Jane, it's Elise.' The silence on the other end of the phone is deafening.

'Elise?' she says after what seems hours but in reality, can't have been more than a few seconds. 'To what do I owe this pleasure?'

'Can we talk?'

'Of course. We could have talked many times over the last six years. What do you want to talk about now?'

'Us. You and Jason. Matthew and you. Me and you.'

'Oh,' the silence is back. Then, 'what is there to talk about after all this time? I haven't been anywhere – except here, alone, ignored….'

'I'm not ringing to bandy accusations or apologies, I just think it's time we sorted it all out and apart from that, something awful and incredible has happened and there's only you who might understand. It's time to make peace.' I finish the statement in tears and wait fearfully for her response.

'You'd better come round then.'

'Can we do it somewhere neutral?' I ask.

'Where?'

'The studio?

Chapter 52

23rd July 2029: Matthew

The in-car tracker shows he is now heading for Chelmsgate. Why is that? I update the record and go back to the historical data. An elderly woman in Stoke Point, surname Ruben. It means nothing to me but I add the name to the doodles on my notepad anyway. It mingles with multi-voxels and right dorsolateral prefrontal cortex (DLPFC) activation and concomitant reduced hippocampal engagement and other neuro-technical jargon all saying the same thing: something is happening in Jason's world that isn't part of our world.

I find the cemetery records and linger over them. My eyes are aching. I need new glasses, but the current state of my bank account won't support that, and I can hardly ask Jason for a rise. Who would Jason be going to visit in a cemetery? His father? There are a number of Cranes on the register, but none of the right age to have been his father. His sister Anna is still alive, so I abandon Crane as the source code. Who else would Jason want to commune with?

There is only one, but as she hasn't shown up under the Cranes, she would be under her maiden name or maybe even a new married name. At the risk of setting Elise off again, I send her a message.

'What was Jason's mother's name?'

It comes back almost immediately.

'Rosalie. Rosalie Marchant – that was her maiden name, at least.'

Marchant? I scour the register. No Marchants. What next?

Birth, marriage and death records. I enter *Crane and Marchant* and *1975 to 1995* and hit jackpot almost immediately. Richard Stuart Crane married Rosalie Ann Marchant in February 1983. The marriage was dissolved in 1992. Jason would have been seven. I search further on Rosalie Marchant-Crane and find another entry.

'Why?' Elise's message arrives with a peremptory ping. I have piqued her as I was afraid I would do.

'Just covering all bases.'

'Is *she* at the bottom of this? Not me?'

'I don't know. If I figure anything out, I'll let you know. Tell me if you hear from Jason.'

It takes some while and a fair degree of lateral thinking but eventually – via marriages rather than deaths, I find Rosalie Marchant. She became Rosalie Newnham circa 1998. Rosalie Ann Newnham died three years ago, leaving a husband, a son and a daughter. Joshua and Angela. Not Jason and Anna. Her grave is in Sector Nine. Jason's car was located in the Sector Nine car park. It's a fair conclusion that Jason went to the cemetery to find his mother, then, but what does that tell me? I record it on the spreadsheet of Jason's movements and stare at the entry until I start to go cross-eyed. She would have been a very adverse memory, but what had she to do with Elise and sex and kids – other than the obvious?

I turn my attention to the other name Elise gave me. Ruben. There is nothing in the local news online despite her making it onto air, according to Elise. The road is quite close to Jane though; I am tempted to ring her – but for the fact that I will get a torrent of abuse over something, even if I've done nothing recently to warrant it. Just being is enough as far as Jane is concerned most of the time. I watch the tracker turn into our road and then hover. I frown and am about to risk the torrent in the end when it dies completely. Jason is stationary. I watch it with bemusement. What is Jason doing now? Drawing a blank irritates me. It also bothers me. I hesitate for a while, shying away from what I know will be unpleasant, but then none of this is pleasant nor has been for years. I stab in the speed dial and wait.

'Yes?' she sounds breathless – as if she's been running somewhere.

'How's Katie?'

'Fine. Why wouldn't she be?'

'Well, after the attack…'

'Which was nearly two weeks ago. What do you want, Matthew?'

Jane's not going to tell me anything. Why am I asking? The mere fact that I want to know will be enough for her to clam up, even if the information is the most mundane ever. The tracker has started working again and is moving rapidly now. I debate whether to butter her up, but then that never worked with Jane, so I jump straight in instead. 'You know George Street? Where Katie's friend Marie lives? Did you hear about the old dear who was mugged there the other day?' The tracker is moving slowly into an area that feels familiar to me.

'Joyce Ruben.'

'Right, that was it. Ruben. What do you know about it?'

'Why?'

'Just asking.'

'You owe her money? Surely not one of your card sharks?'

'No, absolutely not. Anyway, she was in her eighties, wasn't she?' The tracker has stopped again. Jason has stopped. The PC screen flashes new data at me. Fountain Close. 'Fountain Close?' I murmur aloud. 'That's where…'

'I am at the moment,' Jane supplies for me, her voice tart with suspicion. 'How did you know that?

'That's your studio, isn't it?.But I thought you gave it up.'

'Ten years, actually,' she replies. 'And before you ask, no, I haven't been screwing you for rent for a non-existent studio. I let Elise have it – more fool me since she hasn't spoken to me more or less ever since.'

'Can you blame her?' I spit back before I can help myself. There's silence on the other end of the phone. 'Jane? Are you still there?'

'Yes,' her voice is still tart, but more the tartness of fruit gone sour. 'Why did you say that?'

'I know about you and Jason,' I say quietly. A phone conversation is hardly the way I want to discuss my daughter's parentage, but the truth will out sometime, I suppose. Why not now when all the rest of the shit is hitting the fan anyway?

'What about me and Jason? He's your friend, not mine.'

'Yours too – a very *close* friend by all accounts at one stage…'

'Oh, Jesus – he told you? The bastard… No wonder Elise has painted him the way she has.'

'*She* told me, actually,' I say, and now it's out, I'm relieved. One less secret to screw us all over… In the background I can hear someone humming. Katie? It sounds like her tuneless ring-a-ring-a-roses.

'*Sh*e told *you*?' I can hear her breathing, processing that piece of information. 'Matthew…'

I cut across her. 'Why would you let her have your studio?'

'Because she needed it more than me, God help both of us. I couldn't paint once Katie was born – how could I ever do anything with Katie always in tow? I let Elise take it over as a way of venting over losing the baby rather than taking it out on Jason – to save their marriage. She's rather good, actually – in a terrifying way. Looks like it's doubled up for finding out her marriage was unsavable after all.'

'How has she painted Jason, out of interest?'

'Painted? More like…' she sighs, '…demonised, excised, dramatised him…'

'As?'

'What do you imagine from what I've just said? These paintings make my stomach turn and I'm all for self-expression...' Her voice is softer, sad. We both pause and reflect. I can feel her thoughts even though we are miles apart and connected only by the airwaves.

'He tricked her into getting rid of that baby,' I explain eventually.

'Oh God, no! Then he's all of this and more, then!' There's a break in her voice as she adds huskily, 'poor Elise. Why didn't she say?'

'What are you doing there, anyway?'

'Elise asked me to meet her here.' Muffled, I hear Jane tell Katie to sit on the chair and not on the floor or she'll get dirty.

'Why?'

'I don't know. She wanted to talk. Oh God, Matthew, what do I say to her?'

'Sorry?'

'It's hardly enough, is it?' I'm about to reply when she adds, so softly I barely hear it, 'for either of you.'

'Sometimes that's all it takes,' I reply, wondering why Katie's parentage no longer seems to matter. Can one word be enough to wash away years of misery?

'I… Matthew…' The doorbell rings in the background. 'Wait a minute. There's someone at the door.' She shushes Katie and clatters into the distance. Katie's still humming but she's moved onto teddy bear's picnic now. There's something comforting about the way Jane's taught her all the old nursery rhymes even though she hates doing so. I've demonised Jane too, at times. Barely thought about how difficult it must have been to give up what she loved doing to do something she hates doing. Maybe I owe her a 'sorry'; too…

I fiddle with the notepad, wondering where the conversation will go from here. In the background I hear her open the door. I can tell from her voice she's surprised – and nervous. Elise? I'd better go … but the low rumble of the answering voice makes me pause, then heave a sigh. A man. The latest, probably. Jane had strung me another line. Do I want to hang on and eavesdrop on their conversation? No way. I'm about to ring off when logic kicks in and I question why Jane would arrange a liaison at the studio, with Elise about to turn up and with Katie already there? Apart from that the voice has taken an unmistakable turn towards familiarity.

Jason.

What the fuck?

'Jane?' I call down the phone. 'Is that Jason?'

Her voice is still distant, echoing – in and out as she moves out of range, first one end of the studio then the other. Still the mumble of high voice, low voice continues like a recurring wave form in the background. This is embarrassing. I hope he hasn't gone to renew his 'friendship 'with her, knowing now what happened six years ago that I'd like to pretend never happened – but then I'd have to pretend Katie never happened either.

There is more vehemence in the recurring wave form of voices now.

'No, I didn't say that…' reaches me remarkably clearly. They have moved closer to the phone. Jane. In denial – as usual.

'It doesn't matter what you said. You're a lying bitch.' Jason. 'And all this… What the fuck is all this?'

Christ, what is *this*?

'They're not mine, and anyway, I didn't do anything. You were the one who wanted it.'

'Yeah, sex but nothing else. And you can't tell me you didn't do all this… this… crap!'

'You bastard! How many others were there? And this isn't crap – it's art.'

'How many? Enough to make up for your inadequacy as a woman and a reproductive machine. God, you couldn't even produce a healthy specimen. It was faulty, like your art.'

'You arsehole! And you ruined my marriage.'

'Me? You never had a marriage. You just availed yourself of a sap who let you walk all over him, including letting you foist a kid on him. If I'd known, it would never have happened.'

'You would have told him?'

'No, you would have got rid of the kid.'

'You prick! Piss off. And it's not my art, by the way, it's Elise's – see what she thinks of you? You're a monster and that's exactly what she's painted.'

The distinct ring of a resounding slap resonates down the phone. Oh God – her or him?

'Jane?' I call again.

Nothing.

In the background, more murmuring, more distorted words, '... you deserve no better... bastard... go fuck yourself... ahhhh...' punctuated by one clear sentence.

'You deserve nothing at all. You are nothing. You are deleted.'

More background noise, scuffling, heavy breathing and then a soft thud like a bag of heavy weights dropping to the floor. My imagination works overtime. Jane on the floor, head stoved in. Jane on the floor, beaten black and blue, Jane on the floor, a lifeless body.

'Jane?'

The car tracker is working again. I'm torn between seeing where it's heading and checking on Jane.

'Jane!' I scream down the phone.

There's a crackle and thud and my daughter's breathy voice scratches down the phone at me.

'Daddy, it's Katie. Mummy's not very well.'

'Oh God! Darling, Katie – how is she not very well?'

'She's asleep. On the floor. She shouldn't be on the floor, should she? She'll get dirty.'

I try to control the sobs that are starting to burst from me in small staccato pains. 'Is she breathing, Katie? Is her chest going up and down?'

'Yes, but she sounds funny. Is she poorly? Why didn't the man help her?'

'Oh Katie, my darling Katie. Can you do something for me?'

I picture her almond eyes and beatific expression as she tries to decipher what I want her to do.

'Yes, Daddy.'

She will be smiling, gently and angelically. A tiny Madonna with Down's syndrome. So precious and yet so undervalued by society at large.

'Is there a big phone there?' Jane had always had a landline in the studio – a big monstrosity of abstract design.

'Yes,' she says, giggling. 'It looks like a big blob.'

'Good, good... Can you be very clever and go to the big blob phone and ring three numbers? Nine, nine, nine.'

I listen as I imagine her trotting off to the big phone and dialling 999. Whatever this is about, it's all about women for Jason. My eyes watch the tracking system blip slowly along the road heading out of town as my ears strain for any part of the conversation Katie is having with the emergency services.

I locate the office phone at the same time as I delve through the personnel records I shouldn't have access to, but do, because of my dark net activities. I locate Jason's other next of kin: Anna. Her phone number is highlighted alongside her name. I only need to ask her one question: who is an old lady surnamed Ruben to Jason? Her answer, surprised and confused completes the picture.

'She was our schoolteacher when Mum left. She wasn't very nice to Jason. I don't know the details. He never said, and neither did Dad, but Jason was never quite the same afterwards. Why, what is happening?'

My assurances don't ring true, but they get me off the phone in time to answer Katie's panicky, 'Daddy?' again.

'Darling?'

'They said they would only be a while. Shall I cuddle Mummy? She looks sad on the floor.'

'Yes, darling. That would be nice.' My throat closes over.

'All right. I'll get Teddy for her too.'

This is all about betrayal. Women's betrayal.

The note. Oh shit! Jason's new route heading is for his home. Eliminate negatives. It's not me he's going to take it out on.

'Daddy? It is going to be all right, isn't it? Teddy's scared.'

Chapter 53

23rd July 2029: Elise

The house is silent. It should be peaceful, but I am in turmoil. Half an hour more and I will leave to meet Jane at the studio. What will I say?

'I know we approach things differently, and maybe we even have different principles and beliefs, but we're all the same, basically – just struggling through life, hoping to survive against the odds. There are always two sides, aren't there?'

Yes, that's it exactly. I practise it a couple of times more and then think about getting ready to go. Do I need to know Jane's side of the story? Or Jason's? Or do I just find it in myself to forgive and forget? I don't know. I only know I need to move on, to have my friend back, and my husband – or at least an approximation of my husband that I can learn how to live with and teach him the same self-mercy. Beyond that, all we could hope for was to survive, agreeing to disagree.

I sit on the bed where Jason lay the last time we made love, temporarily sure I can sort this out. I lay flat on the bed and stroke my hands across the rumpled coverlet, imagining the indentations are where Jason's weight still creates an impression, but it is only me here, creating proof of life. My husband is both less and more than alive. But if Jason isn't Jason any more, then who is he? Who am I? These last six months have been an eternity already, how much more can I endure? I close my eyes and the memory of him thrusting into me comes unbidden but unexpectedly intense – so intense that I sit upright and then have to lay immediately back down to counter the swell of nausea that suddenly engulfs me. For a moment I'm confused. I don't know whether it is fear of Jason or fear of myself that makes my head swim and my heart pound. Then I place it – that feeling.

No, it is something far worse my body is warning me of.

Chapter 54

23rd July 2029: Matthew

Something cold and unsettling has coiled itself round my windpipe and I am finding it hard to breathe. I am still sitting at my workstation, desperate to go and see if Jane and Katie are all right, and yet terrified to leave too. Kohn is smug. She is standing by the door, much as she was when Jason overheard us, but she can see I have the tracker results up on-screen. I minimise the screen rapidly but it is already too late.

'Told you.'

Righteous fury makes me bold even though she has the upper hand. 'You're involved too, remember?'

'Oh, this is quite different, Matthew. This is your problem now. In fact, I think it could be just about time to make my fame and fortune in quite a different way by telling my story.' Her accent is less clipped, more a taunting drawl now. 'Makes quite a finale to the whole story too, doesn't it?'

I see she has a small remote in her hand. She clicks it, slowly and deliberately, expression replete with triumph, forefinger on the remote like she's pressing the button on a nuclear attack. I debate with myself whether I have enough poker face to call her bluff, but my problem is I was never good at cards, even when I was addicted to them. And the numbers on these cards are starting to add up to a hand I hadn't expected.

ForEver Project Subject 1 – Tracker Data pops up on my screen with a small electric *ping*. S*ource: Kohn.*

I stare at it then swing back round to face her. She smiles and raises her eyebrows in an *I told you so* kind of way. It's the same data that I've been reading, but she's created a spreadsheet and one of the columns is entitled *Related Events*. I scan the various locations Jason visited and then across to the *Related Events* column. There in the last entry is the event I've already identified to make my stomach turn over. Christ! It was the tiniest piece of local news. How the hell did Kohn make the connection without any personal knowledge?

'I've seen it,' I reply. 'Now what?'

'I want in – to all of it – and you're going to make that happen or I tell him what you've done and I tell the police what *he's* done.'

I can't help it. I can already feel this going very badly. Everyone needs a way out. I only wish to God I had one.

'Why the hell would you want to get involved in this now you know what he's capable of?'

'Why did you?'

'He's my friend and I had no choice.'

'Crap. You could see what this could become. That's why you wanted in. Your conclusions are spot on, by the way. Neural plasticity working in both directions and enabling what is possibly our first true cyborg? Amazing – and so many uses…' Then, 'I'll come back later when he returns. We'll plan from there.'

'He may not come back. He's heading for home.'

'He'll come back. He's only just got started. That's where it'll finish. Call him. Confess.'

'Jesus, and what will he do then?'

'Who knows, but you'll definitely have his attention.'

Chapter 55

23rd July 2029: Elise

I leave the bed and sit in front of my vanity unit to assess myself. Fifteen minutes and I will go. My skin is drab and my eyes heavy. I brush the tangles that driving home with the roof down has knotted into my hair, the sharp pain as the brush pulls on my scalp making my eyes smart but my chin set firmer. My confusion hovers somewhere between Matthew and myself – him for allowing this to happen, myself for subscribing to it once it had. But all the recriminations in the world won't make the situation any better. Light-headedness and nausea bubble up again and I drop the brush and lower my head between my knees in an effort to stem the flow of the waves of sickness.

'Oh God,' I say to my feet. 'This can't be happening!' - in all ways, I should add ruefully…

How have I been so blind as to not have questioned what Jason had really become earlier? So desperate to have Jason back, I had abandoned all my ethics and principles and welcomed whatever he appeared to be with open arms, without paying any attention to Matthew's cautions. And yes, he was right: he had advised caution several times over. It was me who had thrown it to the winds. It isn't that I can't find a way to accept him, it is more I should have found out what I have to accept before I committed myself.

The nausea subsides and I sit slowly upright. I turn with lethargy to face myself in the mirror again. The woman looking back looks older, tired, dark circles ringing my eyes and invisible strings tugging the corners of her mouth downwards. I would only have to pull my face into a grimace and I could be Munch's *Scream.* And that is what I have become: the embodiment of a nightmare – the woman with a nightmare for a life. I put my head in my hands and will myself to cry, let the emotion flow, but nothing comes. I am frozen too. I dry sob, but that only makes me feel nauseous again, and my head throbs and my ears ring. I transfer my hands from my face to my ears, covering them to blot out the ringing, whilst my forehead rests against the cool glass top of the vanity unit. A lingering smell of splashed perfume pervades the surface. It is the perfume Jason bought me for my birthday – when everything was all right. Both the smell and the coolness are soothing, caressing my senses and reminding me of when life was better, if not wholly good. Once. If only everything could be soothed so easily. The ringing is persistent though and eventually I realise it isn't in my head but coming from downstairs.

The shadowy figure of a man leans against the glass of the front door. His finger must be pressed to the buzzer because the noise is deafening and continuous outside the sanctuary of the bedroom. I hurry down the stairs and rush to open the door, an angry chastisement on my lips. It falls to the ground unspoken when I see who my visitor is.

'Why aren't you at the medical facility at the lab?'

He pushes past me and into the hall. His hair is as untidy as mine, and his hands are trembling. 'Needed to clear my head.'

He remains in the middle of the hall, swaying gently, a Scots pine about to fall in high winds. There is an intensity about him I've never seen before, even at his most inspired. It sends a shiver down my spine and I'm loathe to shut the front door and seal us inside together.

'Matthew said you'd gone out. I was worried. I thought you were meant to stay there. Under observation?'

He replies mildly enough, despite the shaking hands and swaying stance, but there is an edge to his voice. 'I'm fed up with being under observation. I want to sleep at home in my own bed, with my wife. Is that OK?'

'Of course, it is. Of course. Shall I make us a coffee, or something to eat?'

'Eat,' he replies. 'You can. I'll watch. The digestive extension is still under modification.'

'Oh!' I take a step backwards and curse under my breath. I hadn't even thought about that. We haven't eaten together yet.

'It's fine. Go ahead.' He steps aside and ushers me towards the kitchen. I edge past him and collect up a selection of pots and pans, so aware of his eyes on my every move that I can barely carry them. I wish I could run upstairs and grab my phone and ring Matthew, but how can I?

I cobble together some pasta and salad. It's the easiest thing I can think of to make, but I have no appetite. The pasta reminds me of globules of the type of cloned matter I've seen in the jars in the ForEver lab and the red sauce looks like congealing blood. Still I make an attempt at eating since he seems to expect it. The kitchen is filled with the tang of garlic and herbs and it makes my head throb again and the nausea return. He lays up the breakfast bar for two and sits opposite me and watches me eat, miming my every mouthful with his empty fork from his empty plate.

'Why are you doing that?' I ask eventually.

'I'm anticipating – what it will be like when I can join you.'

'Don't,' I say. 'It makes me nervous.'

He gets up and moves around the room, picking things up here and there. He pauses by a photo of me holding Matthew's daughter, Katie – then still a baby. It was a happy day, I recall, full of sunlight and laughter, before I found out .

'You would really have liked kids, wouldn't you?'

I jump. I hadn't expected a return to that subject. Mindful of Matthew's warnings, I'm careful. 'I would, but that's in the past now.' I avoid looking at him and push my plate aside, nausea threatening again.

'That's my fault. It shouldn't be. It should be possible. Maybe I should get Matthew to set aside the digestive extension and look at the fertility one.'

I gag. 'There's not one, is there?'

Now my hands are trembling and his are steady.

'I'm joking,' he says, coming over to me and nuzzling my neck. I don't know whether the little thrill running down my back is of excitement or horror.

'Please don't joke about it,' I say. 'It's too painful to joke about.'

'I'm sorry. Let's go to bed.' He smiles at me – that lopsided Jason smile that always makes my legs weak – but today. Today, I don't know whether the tumult in my gut is of anticipation or disgust and whether my legs are weak from fear or sickness. He pauses at my hesitation. 'Elise?'

'I'm sorry too.' Finally, the tears fall. 'I'm not coping with this very well.'

'Do you still think it was the wrong thing to do? Would you rather I was dead now?'

'Oh God, no! No, no, no! But I'm so confused.'

'I thought you were wholeheartedly for this once it had happened. You said I was me when we made love for the first time as I am now. You said I was me.'

'I know.' I bite my lip. It is salty and sour. 'And you are, but…'

'But?'

I owe him an explanation. He is the victim – we have made him the victim. 'When I told Matthew to…' I stop.

'When you told Matthew to what?' He leans across the table and grips both my arms.

Matthews warning comes back to me with another wave of nausea. I'm about to do it again – precipitate something… I tense but don't pull away. Stay neutral. Say nothing. 'Nothing.'

He lets go of me. 'You're right. Nothing. I'm nothing. It's a mess at the moment. I need to sort out the mess. I should probably be back under observation at the medical facility. Who knows what the cyborg-nothing might do?'

He stands and pushes the stool angrily away from the breakfast bar. It clatters to the floor and I jump. He comes round to my side of the bar and pulls me to my feet.

'Let's go and see your paintings.'

'Now?'

'Why not? You've been so secretive of them, what are they of?'

'Jason, I…'

'Oh, I get it. You don't think I'd like them?'

'I'm not sure you'd understand them,' I agree, feeling light-headed.

'Why? Why wouldn't I understand them?' he's demanding. 'Where are they? Are they here?' He grabs my arm and pulls me to my feet.

'No, not here. In the studio,' I say faintly.

'The studio?'

'Jane's old studio,' I whimper. 'She gave it to me after I lost the ba – ' I press my lips together and hope he isn't listening properly.

'She gave you it? So, what she said was true? They were yours?'

'Mine?'

'The paintings – the paintings she said were of me.'

'Oh my God, but how…'

"I've just left her there – at her studio – your studio. Did you plan that too? For her to show me what you really think of me?'

'No, I haven't even seen her in years. I cut her off after I found out about you and… ' Now I really was about to go too far.

'You found out about her and me? She told you, did she? She set you against me? She encouraged you to let me die?'

'Oh my God, Jason – no! You know I didn't want you to die – I never wanted you to die. I just didn't want you to not be you!' All Matthews warnings come back to me and I rush on, 'but you are – you're you, my husband… '

'Kiss me, then!' he commands. 'If I'm me, kiss me.' He thrusts his face into mine and I reel as nausea and fear combine to make me rigid. He draws away, staring at me. 'Ah. So, you do think of me like you've painted me?' he asks softly. 'A monster…' He pushes me away so roughly that I lose my balance and my feet tangle around each other as I try to regain it. The wave of nausea is too much this time and as he flings out the door, I am falling, falling, falling.

The impact winds me but clears my head momentarily before the pain starts as I stagger away from the breakfast bar. I touch my head and my hand is covered in red, like pasta sauce. I pat it and my hand comes away full. So much pasta sauce – and tiny pieces of globular pasta too, just like the cloned material in Jason's head. How could so much pasta sauce have spilt over the edge of the breakfast bar but be on my own head too? That cannot be right…

Chapter 56

23rd July 2029: Jason

I grip the steering wheel to control the muscle spasm. My fingers form dents in the hard shell of the wheel but for the moment I cannot control the pressure. I let the dents hollow further under my fingertips. I could imagine them creating hollows in her eye sockets, squeezing, until the eyeballs pop and ooze over her cheeks and she screams for me to stop.

'Damn you, Elise! Damn you!'

But it isn't Elise's face I am mutilating. It is all of them, and I want to do so much more that I can't let go of the steering wheel until the images fade from my mind…

'Hi, buddy. I've been worried about you since… '

Matthew pops up on the in-car telephone screen, flashing for me to accept his incoming.

'Fuck off!' I say to the flashing screen. It continues to flash.

'Hi, buddy. I've been worried about you since… '

Dot, dot, dash, dash, dot, dot. Flash, flash. He's not going away. I release the tension in my grip infinitesimally and breathe out, forcing the anger out through pursed lips. It's hot in the car. The air-con is off. I am hot. Not sweating. I don't. But hot. My skin is burning and so is something inside me. The hot dust smells of scalded debris and so do I.

'Hi, buddy. I've been worried about you.'

I hate that function that repeats the callers opening sentence, even if you don't want to talk to them. I flick the screen to *on*.

'Why? You know where I am.'

He looks surprised – and nervous. 'Oh.' He hadn't expected me to answer. 'Well… Are things OK? You were a bit steamed up when you left here earlier.'

'I'm great. Cyborg-nothing perfection. I suppose you want me to come in so you can check my godliness hasn't been compromised?'

'Well, maybe this is the best place for you for the time being…' He pauses, and I want to laugh at his artificiality. Doesn't he see that I know? 'Is Elise with you?'

'No. Why?'

'No reason.'

'I left her in the house…' Momentarily, her face flashes in front of me, appalled and repelled, then... Oh God… 'OK. I'm on my way back. Keep the home fires burning for me.'

I flick the screen to dormant and turn the WiFi connection off completely. I grip the steering wheel again as rejection washes over me as it did when I was a child, when the bitch of a schoolteacher bullied me, when Jane tricked me into impregnating her with a monster child and when… oh God… when Elise rejected me because there would be no child. When Elise rejected me because of what I am...

The sun is streaming through the windscreen, turning sunlight into prisms of colour. I know all the physics. I know it all, but I don't understand. I examine my hands. They are so good – the CyberCute is perfect. No one would ever know. Except Elise. I know it all, but I don't understand. Why did she reject me? I allow the steering wheel to loosen in my grip. It is a sad, distorted version of a circle now. I look at my face in the rear-view mirror. It is a sad, distorted version of a face now. I look the same, but who am I now? Who really am I? Am I still Jason Crane, or am I simply a form of data storage in Jason Crane's image? Is that why Elise rejected me?

I retrace the last minutes with her, mentally replace her eyes in her sockets, wipe away the blood and tears until she is Elise again. I can kill and un-kill in my head, but I can't do so in reality. I cannot change reality. Once she's dead, she's dead – just like the Ruben woman, or Jane. You can't live forever – unless you are me… But who wants to live forever, alone, unloved by the ones you love – machine or not?

I put my hands to my face, clawing at the CyberCute. It furrows, re-seals and heals. I do it again and again and again. No matter how many times I do it, it will simply repair itself. Tears are running down my cheeks and I can feel the emotion but it's not real. The tears are simply the product of a sophisticated evaporation capture system synced to my emotional neuropathways. It's all in the amygdala, cloned or neo-cortically simulated or otherwise. The emotion is a captured memory, extrapolated to be revisited now when the intellectual prompts are similar. I can even picture the formula that defines the programming we identified feeding into it initially.

'She's not dead,' I tell my image. 'But what am I?'

'Dead,' it replies.

Chapter 57

23rd July 2029: Matthew

Kohn is impatient. I should have waited – told her later.

'You should have tried harder. He would have come back if you'd tried harder.'

'No he wouldn't. You know nothing. You know nothing about him, or me, or the struggle it's been.'

'Oh man up. I don't need your sob story.' Her foot is tapping on the lab floor. All I can hear and see is Kohn's diatribe and her small but defiant bulk blocking the exit doors. I want to check if Jane is all right and Katie is safe, if Elise is alive and where Jason is but Kohn keeps stopping me. *No, admit it. It's not Kohn who keeps you here. It's cowardice.*

Her words are clipped, barbed, belittling and berating me. In her hand she holds a sheaf of papers. She waves it at me as she cuts me down piece by piece and its pages flutter at me like white feathers.

'But it's all in here. All the protocols, all the formulas and all the test results. I could have published it as research, but I need the actual test subject to validate it. All you had to do was get him back here, you useless fool. Now we'll have to get back-up involved. Oh well, I don't suppose it will matter eventually. Either way, he'll have to be restrained… ' I stop trying to circumnavigate her. 'This is what you need to do now…'

'What the hell are you talking about?'

'Mr Crane – Jason. He'll have to be restrained while we find out exactly what he can and can't do and how to refine the process.'

'Restrained?'

'Yes, of course. He's dangerous, volatile – and virtually indestructible. You know that. You created him.'

'Nothing's proven.'

'Oh come on! What do you think happened to that old woman? Shame we couldn't have recorded his neural output whilst he was doing it, but we can stimulate the same response once he's in the lab.'

'In the lab? He won't come back here now.' My eyes are gradually focusing on the red text across the front page of the document she is still waving at me. It's the address of a military facility with links to the Far East that Crane Industries did work for some years ago, before they came under scrutiny in a government White Paper. 'What is that, anyway?'

'The project summary. The ForEver Project. That's what you call it, isn't it?'

'But who for?'

She tucks the document under her arm.

'Our back-up.'

I grab at the document but fumble it and the papers fall to the floor. *Feasibility of troop replacement by robotic symbionts* fans itself across the corridor.

'Oh my God!'

I am frozen to the spot and so, it seems, is she. We both stare at the bold red lettering on the front page until she moves to pick it up and I stop her by throwing myself at her. We land heavily on the stone floor, her outstretched body beneath mine. I hear her head collide with the floor – a sharp crack, then her breath leaves her in a surprised 'ooh' and I scrabble to get to the report before she does. I whisk it from under her head, and the red of the text smudges across the page.

But it isn't text and the red isn't confined to the page.

I roll away from her, but she doesn't move. Like a steady oncoming tide, the red slowly covers the pristine white stone floor of the corridor until it laps around my feet. I recoil, desperately hoping the blood tide will stem and then ebb, but it continues its inexorable flow towards me for minutes more, whilst her eyes stare unseeing beyond the lab ceiling. I curl myself round the report and shiver. Oh my God, oh my God, oh my God. What do I do now?

It is an eternity before the message from the hospital tells me what I do now. I cradle the report like a child as I make my way out of the building.

The dead will still be here when I return. The living will be long gone.

Chapter 58

23rd July 2029: Jason

I flick the WiFi connection back to *live* and pop the screen up into position. I need to know. It's no good. Now is the time.

'So, how much did Elise get you to do?'

Matthew's face is frozen with fear. Guilty, m'lud. 'Jason, where are you? You switched off. I've been trying to get you back. You won't believe what's—'

'Just answer the fucking question.'

'What do you mean?'

'When you were being persuaded or otherwise to make this project work. What else did you do to the blueprint? Salt aversion and what else?'

'Nothing. I didn't do anything.'

'Oh, come on, Matthew. At first, I worked perfectly. Everything slipped seamlessly into everything else and all I had to wait for were the extensions to be developed and everything to fully integrate. And then you admitted the little issue with saline solution. Admitted, mind, not told me. Admitted because you had no choice but to admit it then, did you? And then the data limitation. What else?'

'Nothing, I promise you.'

'I have your note addressed to Elise.'

He is silent.

'So?'

'So, I wrote a note to Elise, What about? There has been so much going on recently, I often jot notes down to remind myself.'

'Telling her about the failsafe.'

'Failsafe.' He sounds faint, as if he's about to disappear altogether. 'There is no failsafe. Maybe failure on my part. Maybe that's what I said. I didn't cover all bases. But Jason, you're a prototype. Nothing works properly or perfectly in a prototype, that was what Elise was so worried about – that you wouldn't work properly or even go rogue and she'd lose the man she loved more completely than if she just lost him physically. She'd lose the whole man because all the good memories would be replaced by bad ones.'

I know he is lying. Matthew never could tell a good lie, but I'll let that go for now. For now I need to know what he did.

'So, what did she ask you to do about that – since I now find I can't control emotional responses…'

'Nothing.'

'Really?'

The edge in my voice could have lacerated me, let alone shredded him.

'OK, not quite nothing, but not anything like that. She wanted me to stop the transfer, that was all, but we were too late. And you know that she was always against it really. But Jason, it was only because she loved you…' I listen to him burble on, Matthew-speak, that means nothing to me now.

Loved you.

'…but don't do anything stupid. I know where you've been going and the stuff in the news that's been following on from it…'

I turn the screen off again, those words filling my ears and blocking out everything else. I need Elise and her pragmatic realism to make sense of everything – including my life – but now she 'loved' me.

Not loves.

Loved.

The screen buzzes at me again.

'Oh, fuck off, Matthew…' It makes me feel better, even if it doesn't improve the situation. The policewoman looks affronted.

'Mr Crane?'

'Ah… sorry, I thought you were someone else.'

'Yes.' Her sternness softens, and her eyes are gentle. 'I'm afraid I've got some bad news for you. It's about your wife.'

I barely register the rest, other than the hospital address.

But I didn't. Surely, I didn't? I would never push my wife's eyes out of their sockets and leave her for dead. Never…

Chapter 59

23rd July 2029: Matthew

I watch the phone screen blink off and the connection indicator light die. Shit! He's cut everything. Behind me, the ambulance is taking Jane away, blue lights rotating in silent alarm. A fall. Or it could have been. She fell and hit her head at the bottom of the stairs and it brought on an attack. Why did she have to wear those stupid fluffy mules when they were so dangerous? Is that it, sir? Yes. Why should it be any more than that? Probably no worse than concussion. She's rambling. Confused. That would be the concussion. Katie? No, Katie has a good imagination. Makes up for… But there was no man – only me – and I didn't push my wife to the floor. I've only just arrived, ask Katie – no don't ask Katie, she's confused enough as it is…

Women: Rosalie, Ruben, Jane and now…

The unanswered ring peters out as the phone diverts to voice-messaging. I try again, and again. Ten times. No answer – as before. But he's just left her. I slam the car into gear and reverse off the drive, following the revolving blue lights of the ambulance. Katie is already singing her medley of nursery rhymes to the next-door neighbour, the man – 'Uncle Jason' – completely forgotten. A passing pedestrian who appears out of nowhere as I cross the pavement and onto the road hollers at me. He is middle-aged and smug – a slug in pedestrian's clothing, creeping up on me. And I'm a slug in scientist's clothing creeping up on Jason. Worse: I'm a murderer too – or as good as… I resist the urge to tell the pedestrian to fuck off in my place. Currently the sentiment is far too mild.

Oh God, I hope everything is all right with Elise.

Chapter 60

23rd July 2029: Jason

It is the same hospital they brought me to after the accident. The same one I brought Elise to six years ago to get the termination. Mary and Joseph's services the whole of the city in a squat, functional way, mixing private with Health Service patients – the latter a dwindling few. Military service privileges, mainly – and some state employees, but it hasn't yet caught up with the hospitals that have been private ever since inception, a bit like an underprivileged child never quite achieves the same status as the already moneyed undergrads at places like Oxford and Cambridge, despite the policy statements of the outreach departments. Placed on an elevated position on the outskirts of the city, I abhor the place for all it represents from my memories, its low-slung sprawl reminding me of a lowering beast hanging over its victims.

I park at the far edge of Car Park 3. It is the furthest from the hospital entrance, and closest to the exit route to the main road out of town. Patches of grass tuft like the bank of hair skirting a monk's tonsure. They sprout wilfully between the regimented white lines marking empty parking spaces, giving the car park as a whole an untidy, uncared-for appearance. A lone tin can rolls towards me as I park up, hurried along by a skittish early evening breeze that suggests the weather is about to turn and our wall-to-wall sunshine descend into sullen skies and threatening thunder. I wind the window up and turn on the local radio station. It settles into the weather forecast for the rest of the week, and even they've been lying. They've got it wrong again. Not solid summer sunshine spreading far into the future, but uniquely changeable conditions, precipitating us helter-skelter into flash-floods and lashing winds.

'It's the clash of low and high fronts, one coming in from the Arctic, the other from the Med,' the forecaster apologises. 'Not something we'd usually encounter. Not good news at all.'

'And your advice?' The female show presenter sounds gleeful.

'Stay indoors. High winds, lots of rain, seas running high so don't go on that trip over to France this week and stay safe because—'

'Thank you, Jim,' she winds him up, the joy still bubbling away in her voice. 'So there we are, the worst of the weather – and don't say I didn't warn you this morning. Remember those ravens I told you about? Taking off for the south, I'll bet.'

'Let him finish, you bitch,' I say to her. Who the hell does she think she is, cutting the expert off. 'And ravens don't fly south. They stay until the bitter end like the ones in the Tower so they can peck your eyes out.'

I didn't push my wife's eyes out of their sockets and leave her for dead, did I?

'And now a bit of...' I slap the radio off and let my ears fill with the sudden silence. Dark images are vying with it to fill my mind with noise. My hands round her throat, my thumbs on her eyes, my teeth grinding and clenching.

'You bitch, you bitch, you bitch…'

I close my eyes and squeeze the eyelids tight. Make tears. Be sad. Be human.

I can't.

I open my eyes and stare out of the window at the now wind-irritated car park, the sign saying *3* wobbling in the stiffening breeze and the barrier gee-jawing like a small boat on a vitriolic ocean. The wind tugs at the car as if to shake me up, too. I don't need shaking up. I am already shaken up, rearranged, transposed, confused, messed up.

Jane. Was it Jane I did that to? It wasn't Elise.

The screen on the dash buzzes. It's Matthew again. I'm about to reject the call, but why bother? Easier to hear what he has to say now.

It was Jane I did that to.

'Jason! Oh, thank God. Look, Elise is in hospital…'

'I know.'

'Oh.'

'The police rang me.'

'Oh. So, where are you?'

'At the hospital, just parked up. How is Jane?'

'Jane? How did you…'

'How do you think I knew?'

'Oh, right. Katie said you were there earlier. Asthma attack, we think. Hopefully she'll be fine. But Elise…'

'Yes. I know. I'm on my way in there now if you'll stop yammering at me.'

'I'll go then. I'll be there in about five minutes too.' He hesitates, and then, '… and don't say anything to anyone, OK? We have to figure out what to do about everything.'

'Everything?'

'There's been an unexpected development at the lab too.'

My curiosity revs. 'What?'

'Dr Kohn… something happened…' He hesitates, then the rest comes out in a rush. 'It was to keep ForEver secret… '

He bites his lip and I can sense the lardy smell of fear without even being near him, but for the moment it is more of me than I can deal with. 'Tell me at the hospital.'

I turn the screen off, but I don't go anywhere. If it wasn't Jane then, who was it? Was it Kohn? I examine my hands – not that it makes much difference. Whatever damage I might have done to them in an attack it will have self-repaired by now anyway, but whose eyes have these thumbs pressed and pressed until they collapsed inwards and the blood welled up out of the craters they disappeared into? Whose life did I extinguish in screaming agony? The memory is too fresh, too raw, too vivid to not be real. I can feel the skin and bone beneath them, fracturing, splintering, bursting. I fling myself against the seat back and howl with agony like my victim must have howled. I can feel it through every inch of me, coursing through me, forcing the blood-substitute mix in my venous system through the network of veins and capillaries that are growing and proliferating, turning me into a human that isn't a human. It pulses through me, throbbing and fluttering alternately, a trapped butterfly pupa trying to transform.

No it wasn't Kohn. Then it must be—

Oh God, the memory flows back, unravelling like the string into the Minotaur's cave. And now I know whose eyes I pushed from their sockets…

I get out of the car and allow the wind to buffet me towards the hospital entrance. Its harsh hands thrust me inside the door and then abandon me. I stand, bereft and lost, in the foyer of main reception. The signage blurs as I squint to force the memory back into the recesses of my mind, whilst I decide on the route I must take. The High Dependency Unit is on the second floor, near the operating theatres, just in case. I avoid the lift and its claustrophobic crush of humanity and take the stairs.

They are marble. For God's sake, marble – in a hospital? Marble is for mausoleums! My footsteps echo as they climb the marble ladder. With every step I feel increasingly uncomfortable. There is a revolution forming inside me and I don't know which side of the divide I am going to end up on once it's let loose. I am different. Brain sends signal to legs. They move. Feet touch floor. They connect. Another step. They disconnect. Another step. They connect. I have done this before. When have I done this before? Jason has done this before. I am Jason.

Silence.

I am Jason.

The door to HDU. Ring for access. I ring, my finger sticking to the button as if we're fusing, its circuitry to mine. CyberCute shouldn't work that way. Christ what has he done to me? What other malfunctions have I?

None. I am Jason.

Silence.

I am Jason.

I am Jason Crane.

'I am Jason Crane,' I say it aloud. It sounds wrong. 'I am Jason Crane,' better, more convincing. *'I am Jason Crane!'* Too loud, too aggressive. The little nurse who opens the HDU door to me thinks so too. Her face is stricken, awkward with confusion. Behind me, other heels click-clack along the corridor, pausing briefly as my statement echoes around us. Other feet connect and disconnect – but not like mine. Not like Jason Crane's.

But you're not Jason Crane. You're a machine posing as the man Elise loved. Loved.

Damn you. Go away.

'Mr Crane. Oh, yes.' The nurse steps aside to usher me in. Her cap is wonky and loose strands of flyaway dark hair escape from beneath it. I want to tidy her into neatness, binary, but some vestige of 'normal' tells me that would be inappropriate. Instead I merely follow her. Feet connect, disconnect, connect, disconnect. She walks beside me, occasionally flicking a surreptitious look at me. We move in binary time down the corridor to another door. She taps in a code. Her fingers don't stick, don't fuse. I walk through the open door ahead of her, desperate for my feet not to begin sticking too.

'Dr Asfahni, this is Mr Crane.' The nurse sidesteps around me and gestures to a tall Asian man in a white lab coat. He stuffs his stethoscope into one of the pockets and comes towards me, hand extended. I can't shake. Oh God, I can't shake. We will fuse. I nod curtly, ignoring the outstretched hand.

'My wife, Elise? She's here?'

'Yes.' He nods and takes a step backwards. Data banks tell me his reaction is affront. 'Yes, well, I'll take you to her, but I also need to tell you how she is.'

'How is she?'

He swings round and studies me. Can he see? No. No one can see. The CyberCute is perfect, so are all the cloned elements of me – and yet I am malfunctioning. What does he see?

His eyes soften and for a moment he looks like he's going to cry. 'I'm so sorry. Perhaps we should go to my office first?'

'Why?'

His eyes are still soft, full dark blackberries in molten molasses. He breathes out heavily and the CyberCute brain senses the speed and volume from proximity calculations. It means more than that though. It means something human. I know what it means because I am human – I AM.

'It's not good news, I'm afraid.'

Up ahead, a policewoman in dark blue, cap tucked under her arm, watches us approach, eyes as dark and sorrowful as Dr Asfahni's.

'What's she doing here?'

'She fell, we think. But sometimes falls are more than falls. There were two places laid to eat, but only one used so her visitor never arrived. Someone else did, though – maybe.'

I look from one to the other. 'What do you mean?'

'We don't know, Mr Crane. Just that she had company and was then found as she is. Clearly something happened, but what?' The policewoman looks me steadily in the eye, clearly assessing my reaction.

'You are trying to tell me she was attacked?'

'We don't know. But you don't normally fall and hit your head with such force it cracks your skull op… Sorry, that was insensitive of me.'

The noise behind me is annoying, but distraction isn't something I suffer from. The doctor's voice, though… that is a knife, cutting and cutting, soft as it is. I feel a hand on my shoulder. I know without looking it will be Matthew. Good old Matthew.

'Jason,' he is saying. 'Shall we go and sit with her for a while, and talk about this? We can do that, can't we?'

Dr Asfahni nods. 'Of course. Take all the time you want. There's no rush. We can wait.'

Matthew is propelling me towards another door, shiny blue, with silver hand plates. We can wait. Yes, I can wait forever. I have all the time I need.

'I was the one who found her.' Matthew's voice drones in the background as my brain starts to work again, filing some pieces and retrieving others. So Matthew found her. And he knew where I'd been. He hadn't said anything though – or I assume not. Only that reference to the lab and Kohn. 'The policewoman is here for a statement but that's not likely to ever happen, I'm afraid,' he is saying.

'Why?'

Suddenly everything functions again, coming together in one moment of exquisite synchronicity. I know what he's going to say. I have been here before too, except the person the doctor was talking about then was me – was Jason.

'She is in a coma, but not likely to recover. Too much swelling.'

'Brain swelling?'

'Yes.'

'Brain swelling goes down. You know that.'

'Sometimes.'

'Then we wait.'

'But we can't. They won't. She has a DNR instruction.'

'So? You only action a DNR when there is no hope.'

The doctor is behind us, dogging our footsteps.

'Mr Crane,' his eyes are crushed now, bruised and bleeding. His voice is very quiet – almost inaudible. 'With this kind of swelling, there is no hope. The damage has already been too much. Too many parts of the brain have already been compromised, and blood supply restricted beyond recovery.'

'Then we must use the ForEver process on Elise,' I swing round to Matthew.

His face crumples then reforms. 'No. She's DNR, Jason.'

'So what? That doesn't have to apply.'

He is pushing me gently into the side ward until we are through the door and I am looking at Elise, cool and clean and golden, stretched out flat on the bed, only the paraphernalia of oxygen tubes and ECG wires and the dark bruising on her forehead marring her perfection. The doctor and the little nurse with the straying hair have followed us. The nurse takes up her place by the ECG and blood pressure monitor. Guarding her.

'We must always adhere to the patient's wishes,' the doctor admonishes. It is a gentle protest, but he is my mortal enemy because of it. 'Even if they can't express them verbally. That's why people make these sort of living wills.'

I shake my head. 'I want her transferred to the Crane Industries unit.'

'Jason… ' Matthew's expression is warning.

'She can be treated there better than here.'

'I'm not sure I can allow —' the doctor takes a step towards the bed, placing himself between me and Elise.

'It's not up to you. I'm her next of kin.'

'But her wishes are very specific, Mr Crane. Not to be moved from the medical facility she is brought into in the event of something like this happening. Look.'

He moves back down the bed and with a small flourish pulls a buff folder from the pocket hanging from the end and proceeds to spread it out on the end of the bed. The bed cover is yellow like sand. Elise's feet make a small mound between the notes and the end of the bed, like a sandcastle. In the centre of the folder is a single sheet of paper, printed neatly in Elise's handwriting, and signed with her curling signature. It is dated twelve days ago. I can almost smell the sea. Salt water. Brine. The briny ocean. Used to be our favourite place when we first met. We never built a sandcastle though, only waded through the frothing wavelets and kicked spume at each other until we were soaked. The briny ocean. Neither of us can do that now. Twelve days ago. Twelve days ago was the first time we made love.

'Why then?' I ask aloud.

Matthew claps me on the shoulder in sympathy. 'There's a donor card too,' he says, pointing to the card clipped to the bottom edge of the living will. Its heart-shape logo runs on and off the side of the card in a slim wave form, slowly dying. 'There's no doubt, Jason. No doubt what she would want to do.'

I snatch both the note and the card from the folder and tear them into pieces, scattering their remnants over Elise's sandcastle feet, apart from the two little jigsaw pieces displaying her signature.

'Oh no, you can't do that,' the doctor protests.

'Jason, please don't do this,' Matthew's voice duets with the doctor.

'I want her moved to the Crane Industries facility tonight. She'll be treated there.' I catch Matthew's eye. 'With or without your help,' I add.

Why twelve days ago? What presentiment had Elise experienced to make her take such extreme action? Not that it mattered. A part of me has started to sing with joy. If Elise undergoes the ForEver programme too, I won't be alone. I won't be alone forever. I won't be alone at all. I'll have her forever too.

'Her organs will help so many stay alive.'

'You touch her and I'll have the whole damn legal system down on you so hard, you won't even look at a scalpel for the rest of your life. You have no signature now. Transfer her. Tonight.' I turn on my heel and face Matthew. 'And you can oversee it. Remember what I know.'

He flinches and stumbles backwards as I barge past him. I don't want to look at Elise like this for a moment longer and there is a lot to prepare. I don't even look back as I exit the HDU unit. My feet don't connect and stick any more and my fingers twitch with animation. No one is looking at me because I am not looking at them. We will be two, the first of the few. There only need to be a few to keep things under control. Elise and I will head them up. Forever. I grin, and I no longer think of those eyeless sockets accusing me.

I am back to the car in no time, pushing through the wind like it is a mere babble. Force Nine they're predicting, but who cares. Everything is falling into place. Everything is going to be fine. I press the ignition and…

My finger sticks to it. I peel it away and I am peeling skin from a face, like peeling onion layers apart. The eyeless sockets accuse me again. The mouth opens and spews curses on me. You are not Jason Crane. You can never be Jason Crane. You have no humanity. You have no conscience. You are just a machine with no humanity to you at all. I ram my finger hard onto the ignition button and this time the car revs and my finger comes away clean.

'Fuck you,' I say to myself in the rear-view mirror and drive as fast as I can out of the hospital car park. Initially I just drive, the image of Elise, still and golden-haired in the yellow sand, filling my mind. I think I'm heading back to the facility, but as I turn onto the coast road, I realise I have come on automatic pilot to where the sand belongs. I park up by the cliff edge and abandon the car to go up to the vantage point we both used to like so much. I have to brace myself against the wind and it whips my face to a frenzy, but what do I care? I don't suffer from broken capillaries or wind burn. I don't suffer from the cold. I only suffer from salt and the gentle sting from the salt in the moist air actually feels good, whipping me alive. Out to sea, small waves are curling up like miniature tsunamis. In reality, they are probably ten or twelve feet high, sufficient to sink a small sailing boat, but from where I'm standing they could be little more than the frothlets we used to kick through on the shore. I watch them surf their way in until they foam up the beach, turning the golden sand green and volcanic.

And as suddenly as anger took hold of me, it leaves me. It isn't peace that fills me instead. It's grief. Or maybe it's guilt. The sensation is strange, unfamiliar. I have never felt guilt before. I have felt grief. I felt grief when my father died, even though we never spoke of love or affection in all the time I was growing up or as an adult. I know it was grief because it burned a hole in my chest that never quite filled again. But this? Yes, the hole is burning there, but what is slowly dropping into it isn't nothing, but the substance of something I should have done but didn't – or did but shouldn't have. I picture Elise's eyes if they had been able to open and look at me then. What would have been in them? Understanding or recrimination? Sympathy or disappointment? I shouldn't have torn up the note. I pull the two slips that still contain her signature and hold them between thumb and forefinger in each hand. They flutter in the wind, small flags signalling a message in semaphore. I could just let them go and they would fly away. No one could ever prove I destroyed the note or the card. The doctor and the nurse and even Matthew could say I did, but it would be their word against mine, and who would have more stamina in the long run? I laugh. I could argue until the end of time. They can't.

But what would Elise's eyes have in them when she opened them ForEver? Would they hold understanding or recrimination? Sympathy or disappointment? Forever. I sink in on myself. I couldn't bear that. She loved me, not loves. Loved. I couldn't bear that. I can't bear that.

I would be going so directly against Elise's wishes, she would never forgive me.

Forever.

No. I must be Jason Crane. I must be Elise Crane's husband. I must do what she would want me to do. Even though I am no longer fully human, I must allow her to do the most human thing of all. Die.

Oh God. Now I feel grief. Now I feel the hole that will never refill. All the things I have done and not done. All the wrongs… My legs crumble and I am sitting on the rough grass on the cliff edge, grasping tufts of coarse rye grass and howling into the wind. How long I stay like that, I don't know, but the surf has eaten half the beach as I watch it and the light has faded to a cool twilight.

The car knows its way back. We are in communion, it and me. I say nothing to anyone as the same untidy-haired nurse opens the HDU doors and silently admits me. The smell of wet floor mops and cleaning fluid greets me as I pass the cleaner's cart parked up in the corridor on the way to Elise's room. It is stale and unsavoury. I am releasing her from the stale and unsavoury of the world. Think of it that way. From the mundane and the hopeless. The doctor comes out of his office to bar the way to her room, but I hold up my hands, still with the two pieces of signature pincered between forefingers and thumbs.

'You have your signature. You are right. It's not for me to decide whether she lives or dies. She has to make that decision for herself like I made it for myself. But I want to see her.'

'Ahh…' The doctor stares at me, blackberry eyes oozing concern. Through the window in the door to Elise's room, I can see Matthew still sitting by her bed.

'What do you think I'm going to do? I'm the last person to put her at risk.'

'Well, you wanted to take her away,' he frowns.

'And now I've brought you precisely the thing that will allow you to take her away from me. To err is human…'

He puts his hands to his face and sighs into them. 'My God, I'm so sorry, Mr Crane. I don't want to, it's just that…'

'I know. It's her choice.' I hand him the two signature slips and he cradles them in his palms like gold dust.

'Your friend, Dr Green, is still in there. Keeping watch.'

'Good old Matthew. He would be.'

I walk past Doctor Asfahni and enter Elise's room one last time. Matthew jumps up as the door swings open.

'Jason, you're back. Look, I can't…'

'I know. I know. Some choices are human choices. We're not all meant to live forever. Just make sure they're absolutely sure before they let her go.'

'I promise,' he says, eyes welling with tears.

Good old Matthew.

He steps aside, and I walk slowly past him until I am at the head of the bed. She still looks like an angel, gold hair silken on the pillow, skin waxy like tallow; an Old Master angel. I take the oxygen mask gently away from her face just long enough to expose it all so I can remember. I kiss her lips and they yield but do not reciprocate. Well, they wouldn't, would they? Loved, not loves.

'Are you staying?' Matthew's face is creased, like a crumpled rag, blotched and dirty. He looks like a ragamuffin child, up to no good and surprised by their parent.

'I can't stay. Can't watch.'

'But, Jason…'

His hand on my arm is stained a dirty red. I take hold of it and would have removed it but something about it sends alarms throughout my body.

'Blood?' He nods. 'Whose?' Those empty bloodied craters haunt me. Whose are they, whose?

'Kohn's,' he whispers. 'She had a report. Everything. All our data. My fault but I couldn't let her turn it over, turn you into some kind of specimen… That's what I wanted to tell you about on the way here.'

'Where is she now?'

'At the lab. In the corridor. On the floor.' He starts to tremble, and I have to grip his forearms to keep him still. Peeping out of the top of his jacket is a crumpled page corner like the white spot in the aftermath of a nuclear explosion. He watches my eyes drop from his face to the white spot. 'The report,' he rasps. 'What do I do? I killed her.' I let go of his arms and slide the document from inside his jacket. It is bloodstained and torn, but the title is clear enough. 'I should tell the police…'

I back slowly away. 'No. This is your place here, old buddy. I'll sort this one out, like I've always done. And then I need to be somewhere else.'

'Where?'

'No matter. I'll be there when it's all over. You'll find me. I need to process this on my own. Delete it.'

'Jason, you can't…'

I shake my head. 'Yes, I can. I can delete it. You say nothing and it'll all be gone by tomorrow.' His mouth opens and shuts and for the briefest moment I am truly Jason Crane again, watching my old buddy flounder whilst I swim, strong and brave to the shore. And that's the way it should be – after all, I was always the swimmer and he the one that needed saving. I point my forefinger at him. 'Remember what the stakes are? A life for a life.'

My route takes me back to the clifftop and the spray and the spume and the saline solution – after the lab.

Chapter 61

23rd July 2029: Matthew

'Dr Green, has Mr Crane left the building?'

I lift my head from its resting position by Elise's hand. 'Some while ago,' I offer. This night seems to be going on forever whilst they do test after test just to confirm that Elise will never recover. Jason's threat about legal action is real. It took very little to convince them of that.

'Oh, because there's something here he should know about.'

'What?' I can barely raise the energy to ask. What can change the way things are now?

'This.' He switches the light on behind the viewing screen on the wall and slaps the series of images up onto it. Elise, in black and white and greyscale.

I go and join him, studying the images. I see nothing except indeterminate grey, and a particularly large amorphous mass of it in the area of the frontal lobe.

'CT,' he says. He points to the greyed-out mass. That's the area of the TBI.'

'TBI?'

'Traumatic brain injury – sorry. I assumed because you're a Dr Green, it's medical.

'In a somewhat diffuse way,' I reply, uneasily.

'Prosthetics, I understood – and their physiological interface.'

'Yes.'

'So you understand what I'm looking at? Somewhat?'

I think of all the fMRIs and MRIs I've looked at recently. 'Somewhat. But I'm not necessarily up to date on your diagnostic terminology though.'

'OK, sorry. She suffered a TBI – traumatic brain injury and it's caused oedema and ICP – intracranial…'

'Pressure – yes I do know that term.'

'OK.' He studies me briefly. I feel his assessment is more character-based than knowledge-based, but maybe that's just me. He turns back to the series of images. 'As you can see, the oedema is extensive and there is already compression of the ventricle. This is from this morning.' He slaps a second set of images next to them. 'This is from tonight.'

He doesn't need to explain any diagnostic terminology here. I can see the spread of the amorphic mass even up to the dura mater.

'It's worse,' I say.

'Far worse, and not in any way we can do anything about. There will already have been severe osmotic failure, even within the first few hours. That's why I told Mr Crane there was no hope. Do you accept that?'

I touch the second set of images. 'I can't not accept it,' I say, eventually. 'Is this what you wanted him to see? To prove your diagnosis?'

'Well, it certainly proves the diagnosis, but no, it isn't what I wanted him to see. What I wanted him to see is this.'

He removes the two sets of images and replaces them with full-body MRI visuals.

I shake my head, and frown. 'Why?'

'The first to establish if there was anything else we needed to know, apart from the TBI. The second – bluntly,' he snorts, 'to cover our asses, since Mr Crane seems to be of a litigious nature. I'm sorry if that sounds callous at a time like this, but it's the way of the world.'

I shake my head again, but I can't criticise him. It is indeed the way of Jason's world. 'And so?'

'Can you read them?'

What difference does it make if I admit I can? Simply makes life easier for both of us. I nod and lean in to study them side by side.

'This morning when she came in and this evening, just after the CT scan.'

Doctor Asfahni hovers impatiently at my side. I try to ignore him and continue my examination of the MRI images. I can see little difference. Other than the TBI, her body looks to be functioning in good form. No abnormalities, no broken bones, no shadows that could indicate tumorous growths or malfunctions of endocrine or venous systems. I work systematically down from head to toe, but stall at her mid-region.

'What's that?' My heart has started to bump about inside me, colliding with my ribs and making my breathing unsteady.

'What you think it is.'

'But it can't be. When did you say they were done?

'This morning when she came in and again this evening.'

'But that's impossible. No. No way! That can't happen!'

I step back and meet his eyes. His expression is blank but his eyes are questioning. He raises his eyebrows. 'So what do we tell Mr Crane?'

'Oh my God, I don't know.' I spin away from the screen and my revolutions bring me back to Elise, silent and unknowing. I stand by the bed and touch her hand. It is still warm even though it looks cold and lifeless. 'Why was there nothing on the MRI from this morning?' I look over my shoulder at Dr Asfahni.

'I thought maybe you could tell me that.'

'Why?'

'Crane Industries? Very secretive. And Mr Crane? Why did he want her moved to the facility?'

'That's just Jason. Control…'

He shrugs. 'Well, whatever it is, what do we do now? I have a DNR instruction.'

'But only for her. How far along are we looking?'

'Twelve weeks or more. And nothing this morning.'

'Are you sure you've got the right results? The right person?'

'Oh yes.' He moves towards us and touches the area that is the flat of Elise's stomach. 'There is no doubt. At least twelve weeks. You explain that to me.'

'What the fuck are you doing?'

'Showing you.'

'Fuck me!'

'I think I'm indestructible. I just thought you ought to know.'

'Jesus!'

'If you like. JC for certain. Miracle man! Take up thy bed and walk. We picked a good name when we called it ForEver.'

'He healed. Everything healed. Even what he deliberately destroyed,' I say – not that the doctor will understand, but I do.

The rhythmic tick of the ventilator and the bleeps of the blood pressure cuff periodically inflating and deflating create the soundtrack to this miracle movie. Dr Asfahni stares at me.

'No DNR then,' he instructs the nurse with the hair that seems to defy her nurse's cap, even with its excessive row of hairpins to subdue it. She sidles alongside him, and he hands her the MRI results.

'Shall I call him? He needs to come back.' The nurse looks questioningly from Dr Asfahni to me.

'What number do you have for him?' I ask. Something else is stirring in me, besides confusion and grief. *You'll find me. I need to process this on my own. Delete it.*

Dr Asfahni gestures the nurse back. 'The number?'

She reels it off.

'No.' I shake my head. 'That won't be any use. It's his carphone number. He can reject it and he won't be in it anyway. Not now. He'll be somewhere else. Here… ' I fumble in my pocket and find my phone – the one that has been a lifeline between Jason and me all these months, now more than ever. 'I'll ring him.' I access speed dial but there is no signal. 'Damn!' They look at me. 'No signal. I'll have to use the hospital phone.'

'Come with me,' the nurse says, still interrogating me with her eyes. I follow her along the corridor, back to the nurse's station. The walk is interminable, a few metres that take most of a lifetime. I pray Jason will answer, wherever he is, whatever he is doing, because even if she dies, now she also gets to live forever, too. They both do – in a way.

Chapter 62

23rd July into 24th July 2029: Jason

In the morgue, the body still lies in its body bag, zipped in, forgotten – hidden because it can never be seen. I instructed that it should be so not because I haven't died so how can there be a body, but because of what I have done to me. Dr Kohn's body fits easily inside with Jason's. She is small, barely bigger than a child. The report slides in on top of her. Not even Matthew knows where Jason went because only I know the security code. I designed the facility this way when it was built, with the incinerator alongside. Who knows what goes wrong when you experiment. Sometimes it's best not to know. Delete and start again. Matthew can do that now.

Twelve days ago was when I last visited there. Then I was Jason Crane. So was he. Now, what am I? I am me, but I don't know what me is. The last few days have shown me that. I am no longer Jason Crane. What am I? A hybrid? A cyborg? A new life form? Or a nothing – an abomination? Whatever I am, I am some other person Jason never met other than in the morgue, squeezing his own eyes out of his sockets, simply because he could. I did that so he couldn't ever come back and see what he has become.

Elise loved me. Not loves. Loved.

She loved Jason. I am not Jason. I am only what he looks like. Not what he was; what he was to Elise. And whatever I am I can't live with that and I can't live without her. I never knew that until now.

I have reached the beach. I'll walk carefully because it is treacherous on a night like this and I don't want to fall. That would abnegate everything. It'll be a long walk down, but I'm patient. I have all the time in the world, after all. There's no other way. If I cut myself, I heal. If I burn myself, I re-form. I don't want to live forever after all. The cliffs rise up behind me, solid and dark. They are my past. This is my future. I take off my shoes and start to trudge across the soft sand, the wind whipping it up and flinging it in my eyes in an effort to keep me back, but the water is my goal. The wind howls and buffets against the lowering cliff, a low moan of protest, rising to a crescendo as the waves rush in up the beach. I am within feet of them, the first soft touch of spumy spray, when my phone rings. At first it is merely a buzz, a worming insect burrowing into my skin, vibrating irritably against my thigh. I slap at the annoyance but still it continues. Contact explains what it is. I pull it from my pocket. Caller ID not known. I put it away again. Only Matthew and Elise and Dr Kohn have the number. It must be a jerk salesman hit lucky with a random number.

I reach the high point of the water's edge. The last wave has left a tide mark of scum where it crashed and dissolved, a ridge of tiny shells brilliantly phosphorescent in the moonlight. I look up. Waxing gibbous – almost full. Another day or so and it will be a full round globe hanging over the earth, but I won't be here to see it. Nor will Elise. It is time. We're not all meant to live forever after all. And forever is a small thing compared to love.

I lie down and allow the waves to wash up and over my bare toes. The pain is a kiss goodbye I will take over rejection any day. Even as my skin prickles and starts to blister, I thank it. The buzz in my thigh starts again. The phone – the damn phone! Who the hell wants to get hold of me at a time like this, destroying my farewell to forever with mundane messages? My fingers touch the button in a last caress to allow and then reject it, but Matthew's voice washes over me with the water.

'No DNR.' He is breathy and high-pitched. 'There's a child.'

I struggle against the rising tide.

'Do you understand? She is having a child. Answer me Jason! For God's sake, answer me!'

'What?'

'You heal. You healed and now she's having a child. Even if she dies, you will be a father. She needs you to be here for that. Do you understand?'

'I am not Jason. I am not who she thought I was.'

'That doesn't matter anymore. She needs you to be whatever you are. You have a child – you and her. Part of both of you.'

'A hybrid?'

'A hybrid. Yes! A hybrid. Do you understand what that means?'

A hybrid. Another me. More than that. More than a hybrid, a new species. 'I understand.'

My fingers grasp the sand and heave myself backwards. There should be no escape from this – and yet there must be. I kick free of the outgoing wave, battered and blistered, but I will heal. ForEver is not simply a choice any more.

A NOTE FROM THE AUTHOR

If you've enjoyed this book (and I hope you did), do please leave a review wherever you purchased it. Reviews are really appreciated by authors and other potential readers because how else do you know if it's a good story?

Thank you.

ABOUT D.B MARTIN

D.B. Martin writes adult psychological thriller fiction and literary fiction as Debrah Martin, as well as YA fiction, featuring a teen detective series, under the pen name of Lily Stuart. She is also a painter and her book on writing and painting and the inspiration behind both, Savage Seas and Sfumato Skies, written under the penname of Debrah Martin contains many of her paintings.
You can find more about her work and sign up for news and updates on forthcoming publications on www.debrahmartin.co.uk.

BOOKS BY THIS AUTHOR

Writing as D. B. Martin:

PATCHWORK MAN (Bk 1 in the PATCHWORK PEOPLE series) B.R.A.G. Medallion winner

Laurence Juste QC is the perfect barrister; respected, professional, always wins. But Lawrence Juste isn't who he says he is. He's a patchwork man, pieced together from half-truths and lies. Now his past is about to come back and haunt him as the patchwork man begins to unravel.

PATCHWORK PEOPLE ((Bk 2 in the PATCHWORK PEOPLE series)

No sooner does Lawrence Juste patch one hole in his fraying life than another appears. No-one is what they appear to be, and there's a certain irony in the fact that only someone even more deceptive than him can help – but they're already dead...

PATCHWORK PIECES (Bk 3 in the PATCHWORK PEOPLE series)

The wheel has turned full circle: the past is the present, the betrayed are the betrayers and the dead in Lawrence's world have resurrected. As his options diminish, the only way out is a lethal form of natural justice for the man for whom law and order were once king.

LADY LAZARUS

When Roseanne Grey jumps to her death on a cold December day, there's no apparent reason why – not even according to her psychiatrist. Detective Sergeant Darwin Grant is told to file the death as a simple suicide, but he's not so sure. There was a lot to know about Roseanne; none of it explicable ...

MEMENTO MORI (Bk 1 in the MIND GAMES series)

The enviable position of Deputy Director at the elite psychological treatment centre, ETHOS, comes with strings that Gaby McCray would prefer to ignore – until they threaten to compromise more than just her integrity. Can you be both good and evil, doctor and devil, simultaneously? Do you kill, or be killed to protect the answer?

THE BEHEMOTH (Bk 2 in the MIND GAMES series)

The truth behind the secret project psychologist Gaby McCray's eminent but mysterious father initiated lies deep within Gaby but as she comes to terms with who or what she might be as a result, the 'truth' changes once more. The deeper she digs, the more terrifying the prospect of what she has released as the Behemoth rises...

THE FOREVER PROJECT

His nickname of JC ("walks on water") becomes more than just a private joke when Jason Crane's ForEver Project – a means of combining robotics and biochemical engineering to extend life in the terminally ill - becomes more than just a project. He hadn't bargained on being the first test subject for it though – or what it might mean to him as a human, with or without a soul ...

THE FOREVER CHILD

If giving man immortality was incredible, then producing a hybrid child – part AI and part human is nothing short of a miracle. But the ForEver Project was never intended to produce a child, and miracles carry a price. For a Forever child the price is high indeed – for both them and the world they live in.

Writing as Debrah Martin:

FALLING AWAKE

The story of Mary, Joe and a world populated by love, betrayal and obsession – and what it does to those who live in it. Fantasy or madness? The impossible is only a breath away.

CHAINED MELODIES - B.R.A.G Medallion Winner

Courage isn't about facing death, it's about loving life – and life isn't always conventional. The unusual story of how two men find not just courage, but self-belief and the true nature of love as one transitions to female and the has to face their prejudices and fears. A different kind of love story. A different kind of life.

Non-fiction books:

WRITE, PUBLISH, PROMOTE

From first idea, through first draft and into print: Debrah teaches creative writing and publishing as well as practices it. Write, Publish, Promote is a distillation of ten years of teaching and writing – "Debrah is an excellent teacher. That first novel is nearer than ever..." say her students.

SAVAGE SEAS AND SFUMATO SKIES

Debrah is an artist as well as a writer. This book describes both oil painting techniques and combines some of her writing – short stories and poetry – with her paintings to demonstrate how to find inspiration through both to prompt creativity. And if you've never painted in oils and want to try – here's how...

Writing as Lily Stuart (YA fiction):

WEBS

Meet Lily: one smart cookie with a bitchy BFF, moody boys and crazy school friends. Life's a breeze by comparison to what happens when her mother starts internet dating with lethal results though. Step up Lily S: Teenage Detective.

MAGPIES

A boy with looks to die for – and Tourette's – tricky BFFs, and a gang of drug-dealers... THE teenage detective is back and looking for trouble – or trouble is looking for her. It finds her in the form of a childish rhyme, with a deadly hidden meaning.